Praise for the novels of Susan Wiggs

"Wiggs writes with an even hand, thus adding another excellent title to her already outstanding body of work."
—*Booklist* on *Table for Five*

"Wiggs excels at portraying the delicate dynamics among lovers, friends and family members, and her keen awareness of sensory detail ensures that the scents and sounds of Rosa's kitchen are just as palpable as heady attraction between the protagonists."
—*Publishers Weekly* on *Summer by the Sea*

Rave Reviews from *Publishers Weekly*

starred review

"Wiggs's characterizations are strong, jumping off the page with a winning blend of realism and warmth. A richly textured story…this book will polish Wiggs's already glowing reputation."
—on *Passing Through Paradise*

starred review

"Wiggs richly evokes her multi-faceted setting while depicting equally complex human relationships… the story's theme—the all-encompassing power of love—is timeless, and it is this theme, along with the author's polished prose and well-rounded characters, that make Wiggs's story so satisfying."
—on *A Summer Affair*

starred review

"With its lively prose, well-developed conflict and passionate characters, this enjoyable, poignant tale is certain to enchant."
—on *Halfway to Heaven*

SUSAN WIGGS

Table *for* Five

MIRA

ISBN 0-7783-2286-6

TABLE FOR FIVE

www.MIRABooks.com

Printed in U.S.A.

To Jay

part one

Some things are so unexpected that no one is prepared
for them.

—Leo Rosten

chapter 1

"Hey, Miss Robinson, want to know how to figure out your porn-star name?" asked Russell Clark, bouncing on the balls of his feet toward the school bus.

"I think I'll make it through the day without that." Lily Robinson put a hand on the boy's shoulder to keep him from bouncing off the covered sidewalk and into the driving rain.

"Aw, come on, it's easy. You just say the name of your street and—"

"No, thank you, Russell," Lily said in her "enough's enough" tone. She hoped he didn't really know what a porn star was. "That's inappropriate, and you're supposed to be line leader this afternoon."

"Oops." Reminded of the privilege, Russell stiffened his spine and marched in a straight line, dutifully leading twenty-three third-graders to the area under the awning by the parking lot. "I'm going to Echo Ridge today," he said, heading for Bus Number Four. "I have a golf lesson."

"In this rain?"

"It'll clear up, I bet. See you, Miss Robinson." Russell went bounding toward the bus, hopscotching around puddles in the parking lot.

Lily doled out goodbyes and have-a-good-days to the rest of her students, watching them scatter like a flock of startled ducklings to buses and carpools. Charlie Holloway and her best friend, Lindsey Davenport, were last in line, holding hands and chattering together while they waited for Mrs. Davenport's car to pull forward.

When Charlie caught Lily's eye, she ducked her head and looked away. Lily felt a beat of sympathy for the little girl, who was painfully aware that her parents were coming in for a conference after school. The child looked small and fragile, trying to disappear into her yellow rain slicker. Lily wanted to reassure her, to tell her not to worry.

Charlie didn't give her a chance. "There's your mom," she said, giving Lindsey's hand a tug. "'Bye, have a good weekend," she called to Lily, and the girls dashed for the blue Volvo station wagon.

Lily smiled and waved, making an effort not to appear troubled, but seeing them like that, best friends skipping off together, reminded her of her own childhood best friend— Charlie's mother, Crystal. This was not going to be an easy conference.

"Hey, what's the matter?" asked Greg Duncan, the PE teacher. After school, he coached the high school golf team, though he was known to be a full-time flirt.

"You're not supposed to notice that anything's the matter," Lily told him.

He grinned and loped to her side, a big, friendly Saint Bernard of a guy, all velvet brown eyes, giant paws, a silver whistle on a lanyard around his neck. "I know exactly what's wrong," he said. "You don't have a date tonight."

Here we go again, thought Lily. She liked Greg a lot, she really did, but he exhausted her with his need for attention. He was too much guy, the way a Saint Bernard is too much dog. Twice divorced, he had dated most of the women she knew and had recently set his sights on her. "Wrong," she said, grinning back. "I've got plans."

"Liar. You're just trying to spare my feelings."

Guilty as charged, Lily thought.

"Is he hitting on you again?" Edna Klein, the school principal, joined them under the awning. In her sixties, with waist-length silver hair and intense blue eyes, Edna resembled a Woodstock grandmother. She wore Birkenstocks with socks and turquoise-and-silver jewelry, and she lived at a commune called Cloud Mountain. Yet no one failed to take her seriously. Along with her earth-mother looks, she possessed a Ph.D. from Berkeley, three ex-husbands, four grown children and ten years of sobriety in AA. When it came to running a school, she was a consummate professional, supportive of teachers, encouraging to students, inspiring confidence in parents.

"Harassment in the workplace," Lily stated. "I'm thinking of filing a complaint."

"I'm the one with the complaint," Greg said. "I've been hitting on this woman since Valentine's Day, and all I get from her is a movie once a month."

"At least I let you pick the movie. *Hell on Earth* was a real high point for me."

"You're a heartless wench, Lily Robinson," he said, heading for the gym. "Have a nice weekend, ladies."

"He's barking up the wrong tree," Lily said to Edna.

"Are you this negative about all men or just Coach Duncan?"

Lily laughed. "What is it about turning thirty? Suddenly my love life is everyone's business."

"Of course it is, hon. Because we all want you to have one."

People were always asking Lily if she was seeing anyone special or if she intended to have children. Everyone seemed to want to know when she was going to settle down. They didn't understand. She *was* settled. Her life was exactly the way she wanted it. Relationships were scary things to Lily. Getting into an emotional relationship was like getting into a car with a drunk driver. You were in for a wild ride, and it was bound to end with someone getting hurt.

"I'm meddling, aren't I?" Edna admitted.

"Definitely."

"I can't help myself. I'd love to see you with someone special, Lily."

Lily took off her glasses and polished the lenses on a corner of her sweater. The world turned to a smear of rain-soaked gray and green, the principal palette of an Oregon spring. "Why won't anyone believe that I'm satisfied with things just the way they are?"

"Satisfaction and happiness are two different matters."

Lily put her glasses on and the world came back into focus. "Feeling satisfied makes me happy."

"One of these days, my friend, you'll find yourself wanting more," said Edna.

"Not today," Lily said, thinking of the upcoming conference.

A group of students clustered around to tell her goodbye. Edna took the time to speak to each child personally, and each turned away with a big smile on his or her face.

Lily felt a small nudge of discontent. *Satisfaction and happiness are two different matters.* It was hard enough to make herself happy, let alone another person, she thought. Yet when she looked around, she had to admit that she saw people do it every day. A mother coaxed laughter from her baby, a man brought flowers to his wife, a child opened a school lunch box to find a love note from home.

But the happiness never lasted. Lily knew that.

She lingered for a few minutes more while the children were set free for the weekend. They ran to their mothers, getting hugs, showing off papers or artwork, their happy chatter earning fond smiles. Watching them, Lily felt like a tourist observing a different culture. These people weren't like her. They knew what it was like to be connected. By contrast, Lily felt curiously distant and unencumbered, so light she could float away.

While waiting for the Holloways to arrive, Lily checked the conference table, low and round and gleaming, surrounded by pint-size chairs.

The desks were aligned in neat rows, the chairs put up so the night crew could vacuum. The smells of chalk dust, cleaning fluid and the dry aroma of oft-used books mingled with the ineffable burnt-sugar smell of small children.

She set out two things on the table—a manila folder, thick with samples of Charlie's work, and the requisite box of tissues, Puffs with lotion, which Lily bought by the case at Costco. A roomful of eight- and nine-year-olds tended to go through them fast.

She moved along the bank of windows, adjusting the shades so they were all even at half mast. The glass panes were decorated with the children's cutout ducks in galoshes, each bearing the day's penmanship practice: "April showers bring May flowers." Outside, a jagged bolt of lightning raked across the sky, punctuating the old adage.

With a grimace, she turned to the calendar display on the bulletin board and silently counted down the column of Fridays. Nine weeks left until the end of school. Nine weeks to go, and then it would be sunshine and blue skies and the trip she'd been planning for months. Going to Europe had always seemed such a lofty, barely reasonable goal for a school-teacher in a small Oregon town, but maybe that was what made it so appealing. Each year, Lily saved her money and headed off to a new land, and this would be her most ambitious trip yet.

She tugged her mind away from thoughts of summer and concentrated instead on preparing for a difficult meeting. She inspected the classroom as she always did before conferences. Lily believed it was important for people to see that their children spent the day in a neat, organized, attractive environment.

At the center of the front of the room was a dark slate blackboard. She'd been offered a whiteboard but declined. She preferred the crisp, controlled quality of her Palmer-method script on the smooth, timeless surface. She liked the coolness of the slate against her hand when she touched it, and the way her fingertips left a moist impression, before evaporating into nothingness. The sound of chalk on an old-fashioned blackboard always reminded her of the one place she had always felt safe as a child—in a schoolroom.

This was her world, the place she best belonged. She couldn't imagine another life for herself.

Glancing at the clock, she went to the door and opened it. Her nameplate read "Ms. Robinson—Room 105" and was surrounded by each child's name, neatly printed with a photo on a yellow tagboard star.

Lily adored children—other people's children. For one special year of their lives, they were hers to care for and nurture, and she put all of her heart into it. Thanks to her job, she was able to tell people she did have children, twenty-four of them. And in the fall, she would get twenty-four different ones. They gave her everything she could ever want from a family of her own—joy and laughter, pathos and tears, triumph and pride. Sometimes they broke her heart, but most of the time, they gave her a reason for living.

She loved her students from September to June, and when school ended, she sent them out the door, giving them back to their families, pounds heavier, inches taller, drilled in their multiplication and division tables, reading at grade level or better. In the fall, she shifted her attention to the next crop of students. And so it went, year after year. It was the most satisfying feeling in the world, and best of all, it was safe.

Having children of your own—now, that was not so safe. Kids were part of you forever, subjecting you to crazed heights of joy and bitter depths of sorrow. Some people were cut out for that, others weren't. A good number weren't cut out for it but fell in love and had kids, anyway. Then they usually fell out of love and everyone within shouting distance got hurt. Charlie Holloway's parents were a case in point, Lily reflected.

"My Favorite Things" had been today's creative writing lesson. The children had three minutes to write down as many of their favorite things as possible. Lily always did the exercises right alongside her students, and she always took them seriously. The kids stayed more interested and involved that way. Her list, written hastily but neatly on a large flip chart, included:

Japanese satsumas
snow days
science projects
the sound of kids singing
TV miniseries
mystery novels

first day of school
take-out restaurants
sightseeing
stories that end happily ever after

She ripped down the chart and crumpled it into a ball. It was a little too revealing. Not that her list would surprise Crystal Holloway. They'd known each other since Lily was Charlie's age, maybe younger, and Crystal had been a gum-popping preteen babysitter.

What a long way we've come together, thought Lily. This was a new one for them both, though. Telling parents their child was failing third grade was hard enough. The fact that Lily and Crystal were best friends only made it worse. In doing what was best for Charlie, Lily was going to have to say some difficult things to her dearest friend. And on top of that, the divorced Holloways couldn't stand each other.

Ordinarily, the idea of teaching Crystal's kids was uniquely gratifying. Lily was like their special aunt, and when each one was born—first Cameron, then Charlie and finally Ashley— Lily had wept for joy right alongside Crystal.

Cameron was bright, eager to please and as quick to grasp academics as he was to pick up tips on his golf swing from his pro-golfer father. Now fifteen, Cameron was the best player on the high school golf team.

Charlie, however, was a different story. From the first day of school, she'd struggled and balked at basic concepts. Lily had met with Derek and Crystal separately throughout the year. They'd engaged a tutor and claimed to be working hard on Charlie's reading outside of school. Despite everyone's efforts, though, Charlie had shown no improvement. She seemed caught in a mysterious block that could not be attributed to learning disabilities or detectable disorders. She was simply…stuck.

Lily looked again at the clock and smoothed her lilac cotton sweater over her hips. The Holloways were due any minute.

"How about some bottled water for your conference?" asked Edna, poking her head inside Lily's classroom.

"Thanks. I think they might be delayed because of this weather."

Edna glanced at the windows, gave an exaggerated little shudder and pulled her hand-knit Cowichan shawl tighter around her. She set a six-pack of bottled water on the table.

"To tell you the truth," Lily said, "I'm not looking forward to this one."

Edna studied Charlie's school photograph at the center of her yellow star. She looked like Pippi Longstocking, complete with strawberry-blond pigtails, freckles and a missing front tooth. "I take it she's not handling the divorce well?"

"It's been pretty chaotic. Derek and Crystal have only been divorced a year, and the breakup caught everyone by surprise. Although of course," she added, remembering her own family, "an unhappy marriage is never much of a surprise to the children."

Looking at her ghostly reflection in the classroom windows, Lily remembered the day Crystal had come to her with the news of the separation nearly three years ago. Her stomach had been big with her third pregnancy, and her cheeks were glowing. Up to that point, Lily had believed Crystal led a charmed life. She was a former Miss Oregon USA who became a devoted wife and mother with beautiful children and a hugely successful husband. Her life looked like a dream, so Lily was shocked when she announced that her marriage was over.

"They handled the split as well as can be expected, under the circumstances," she added, cautioning herself to be fair to both parents. Crystal had wanted custody, but Derek took her to court over the matter, forcing her to settle for joint custody. Since the parenting plan had been finalized last year, the kids were required to spend alternating weeks with each parent. The summer would be split up between them, five weeks with Crystal, then five with Derek.

Edna hesitated, studying Lily. "This is going to be hard for you, isn't it?"

"You know my opinion of Derek as a husband. He makes a much better ex, but I've always thought he was a good father. I promise you, I'll keep the focus on Charlie."

"If you'd like me to stay for the conference, I'm happy to do so," Edna offered.

Now, that was tempting. Calm, centered and mature, Edna always brought balance and wisdom to the table. They had worked together since Lily had graduated from college, and they'd built a strong mutual trust. However, Edna's indisputable authority could also be a liability, overshadowing the classroom teacher's role.

"Thank you. For this meeting, I think I'm better off dealing with the parents on my own." Lily squared her shoulders.

"All right. I need to check something. There's a car in the parking lot with its lights left on. After that, I'll be in my office. Let me know if you need me."

Lightning slashed from the sky, causing the lights to blink, and thunder crashed, reverberating through the building.

Alone in her classroom, Lily massaged her throat, but the ache there wouldn't go away. She felt torn between her loyalty to a friend and the needs of a student. In all her life, she had only had one true friend—Crystal. They were closer than sisters. Crystal was the reason Lily came to live in the town of Comfort in the first place. She guarded her heart from everyone else.

$$chapter\ 2$$

Friday
3:15 p.m.

Derek Holloway was the first to arrive, a whirlwind in a dark raincoat and broad-brimmed waxed cotton hat. "Sorry I'm late," he said, removing his dripping hat.

"I'll take that. Your coat, too." Holding them away from her, Lily carried the sopping garments to the cloakroom and hung them over the boot tray. The jacket was made of Gore-Tex, according to the label, size large/tall. The company logo—Legends Golf Clubs—was stitched on the front breast. Probably one of his sponsors, she thought.

His body warmth and the intriguing woodsy scent of after-shave lingered in the lining of the coat, and she chided herself for even noticing. Biology at work, she insisted to herself. Derek Holloway was a scoundrel, a man who had cheated on his pregnant wife. The fact that he was a hunk with a dazzling smile who smelled good was no compensation for that, although some women believed it was a reason for forgiveness.

"Sorry about your floor." He tugged several brown paper towels from the dispenser over the sink and laid them along the wet trail.

"Not a problem." She welcomed him with a smile she hoped didn't look forced. Might as well start on a friendly note. She couldn't think about the fact that not so long ago, Crystal had nearly collapsed from weeping thanks to the terms Derek forced her to agree to in the divorce decree. Hostility, Lily told herself, would not be in Charlie's best interest.

"Can I get you something to drink?" she offered. "I've got water, and there's coffee and soft drinks in the faculty lounge."

"Nothing, thanks."

The scale of the furniture in the room made him seem even larger than he was, which was plenty large. He was impeccably dressed in creased wool slacks and a V-neck sweater of fine-gauge cashmere. He appeared little different than he had when Lily was in the Holloways' wedding sixteen years before. His looks had grown more mature and refined over the years, his personal style more sophisticated. And of course, his sense of entitlement had risen along with his success as a professional golfer. One of the top players in the PGA, he seemed to have no doubt that he deserved everything that came his way, and that included the women who threw themselves at him on tour.

"Here's some of Charlie's artwork." She indicated a molded plastic tote tray with "Charlene" neatly printed on it. "You can have a look while we wait for Crystal." She hadn't seen him since the last meeting about Charlie. At that conference, he and Crystal had agreed to engage a tutor—which they had—and put their daughter's difficulties at the top of their priority lists—which they had not.

He glanced at his watch, a Rolex that was probably another freebie from a sponsor. "She's always late."

What did he think, that Lily was going to agree with him? "The weather's horrible," she pointed out. "I'm sure she'll be here soon." Though she was careful not to show it, Lily was a tad irritated, too. This meeting was about their daughter. Lily had not summoned them lightly. The least Crystal could do was show up on time.

"That's a sweet one," she said as Derek studied a crayon drawing of a koala, its baby clinging to its back. "She drew that after our field trip to the Portland Zoo. Charlie has a real eye for detail. When her curiosity is piqued, she doesn't miss a thing."

He nodded and looked at the next one. It showed a ladder running up the long side of the paper, a tiny plank with a figure perched on the edge, about to jump into an even tinier bucket of water. "And this?"

"Vocabulary work. The word of the day was *dare*, I believe." The other children had written *dare* on their drawings, but not Charlie. She avoided writing or reading anything at all. "She's very clever," Lily said. "She has an inventive mind and uses some sophisticated thought patterns."

He came to a picture of a house surrounded by spiky green grass and blooming flowers, blue sky and sunshine in the background. The house had four windows lined up in a row. All the windows were filled with black scribbles.

When Lily had asked Charlie why she'd scribbled the windows black, the little girl had shrugged. "So you can't see what's inside." She always tried to give a minimal response.

Derek didn't ask about the drawing but moved on to the next, a remarkably vivid study of a small brown-and-white dog with a black patch around one eye. "And this?"

"Vocabulary again. The word was *wish*."

"She's been bugging me for a dog," he said. "Maybe this summer."

Just don't tell her maybe unless you mean yes, Lily thought. Charlie had enough uncertainty in her life.

Finally, Crystal arrived in a swirl of haste and apologies.

"My God, I am so sorry," she said, talking rapidly as Lily took her coat, hat and umbrella. "The roads are a nightmare. I nearly got killed on Highway 6, trying to make it on time."

When Lily emerged from the cloakroom, Crystal offered her trademark beauty-queen smile. Despite the weather, her makeup looked freshly applied. Knowing Crystal, Lily guessed that she'd taken time in the car to fix her hair and face.

"Hello, Derek." Wafting the scent of Gucci Rush, Crystal sailed in front of her ex-husband and sat down, a silk Hermès scarf fluttering around her shoulders, her shapely legs crossed at the ankles and angled demurely despite the awkwardness of the low chair. Crystal had always known how to use the power of her beauty.

Together, she and Derek resembled a toothpaste commercial. But looking like the all-American success story hadn't saved their marriage.

Lily put on her glasses. Even though they were Fiorelli, with handmade barrister-style frames, she knew they made her look like a dork. She ought to quit wasting her money on trendy glasses, because once she put them on, they tended to look like any discount brand. There was something about her earnest face that could transform designer frames into blue-light specials. She'd tried contact lenses, but had an allergic reaction every time she put them in.

Tamping the manila file folder on the table, she took a deep breath and looked from Crystal to Derek, who sat as uncomfortably as she did in the undersize chairs. Lily caught Crystal in an unguarded moment, and the expression on her face was startling. She was eyeing Derek with raw, undisguised yearning, her lovely face registering a wounded animal's un-comprehending pain.

Lily ached for her friend, yet at the same time she felt a faint nudge of exasperation. Today was about Charlie, not about Crystal and Derek and what they'd let love do to them.

With controlled, precise movements, Lily handed them each a copy of the ORAT printout. "This chart shows the re-sults of the Oregon Reading Abilities Test," she explained. "It's given to every third-grader in the state, every March." With the eraser end of her pencil, she traced the gray line on the chart. "This is the average score for the whole state. This red line above it is the average for Laurelhurst students." As a private, selective school, Laurelhurst always showed test re-sults well above the norm.

Lily cleared her throat. "The blue line shows Charlie's performance on the test." The line crawled miserably amid the lowest percentile rankings, at intervals even flirting with zero. She watched the Holloways' faces, seeing the expected sur-prise and disappointment. She'd been disappointed, too—but not surprised. As Charlie's third-grade teacher, she had seen the child's struggles from day one. She'd tried to prepare the Holloways in previous conferences, but the reality simply hadn't sunk in. Maybe today, it would.

Crystal gazed at Lily, her eyes filled with bewilderment. She seemed fragile, as though everything hurt her these days. Derek merely looked angry, defensive perhaps. Both were classic reactions of loving parents. No one wanted to see that their child was having trouble, and once they did, the child's failure not only hurt, but attacked the character of the parents themselves.

"As you know," Lily said, "I'm not a fan of standardized testing. This was state-mandated. So this test doesn't really tell us any more than we already know about Charlie."

"She still can't read." Derek's voice was almost accusatory. His large hands, tanned from a recent golf round in Scottsdale, pressed down on the surface of the table. "You know, I'm getting pretty damned sick and tired of hearing this. I pay that tutor what, a hundred dollars an hour? And we're still not seeing results. What kind of teacher are you?"

"Derek." Crystal reached out a hand as though to touch his sleeve, but then seemed to think better of it. She folded her hands tightly together, her flawless manicure gleaming.

"I don't blame you for being frustrated," Lily said. "I think we all are, Charlie included. Believe me, I know how hard everyone's been working on this all year." She was careful with her choice of words. It was true that, in addition to engaging the tutor, the Holloways had subjected Charlie to seemingly endless testing, from a pediatric checkup to psychological evaluations to a battery of tests by a reading specialist in Portland. The results were inconclusive. There was no scientific name for the sort of block Charlie seemed to be experiencing. Lily wished she could believe the homework she sent for Charlie to do with each parent was done with diligence. She knew better, though. Crystal and Derek loved their daughter, but given the state of their lives, they hadn't made her schoolwork a priority.

"I know we all hoped to see more progress," she added. "However, that's not the case. Given that it's nine weeks from the end of school, we need to talk about Charlie's options for summer, and for the coming year."

Crystal nodded and blinked away tears. "I think we should hold her back."

"Oh, now we're talking about flunking her. That's just great," said Derek.

Lily bit her tongue and kept her face immobile. Derek clearly had issues with failure. But this was about Charlie, not

him. It was not even about Crystal, whose heart was breaking right before Lily's eyes. Urging retention was often the
panicked, knee-jerk reaction of a parent. Lacking a complete
knowledge of all the options, some parents tended to favor re-
peating a grade, unaware of how the extreme solution could
traumatize a child. "In this case, I don't think retention is the
answer."

"So you're just going to promote her like they've done
since first grade?" Crystal's tears evaporated on the heat of
anger. "That's been a huge help, let me tell you. A huge help."

Lily swallowed hard, feeling her friend's anguish. A parent-teacher conference was such a theater of the soul. Everyone involved was stripped bare, their emotions stark and
honest. So much of a parent's identity was wrapped up in the
child: love, pride, self-worth, validation. It was an unfair burden on a small human being, but every child bore it, the lofty,
seemingly unreachable expectations of her parents.

"I've mapped out several options for Charlie," Lily told
them, handing each a packet. "You can go over these at home.
For now, let's assume we see some progress this summer and
she goes on to fourth grade here at Laurelhurst."

"In other words," Derek said stiffly, "you might not want
her back here."

Behind Lily's left eye, a tiny headache flared to life like a
struck match. Laurelhurst was a nationally recognized inde-
pendent school; the waiting list for admissions was years long.
A man like Derek—successful, accomplished, privileged—regarded any other school as subpar. "This is about what's best for
Charlie, not about what I want. What we should really focus on
is the summer. I'm hoping that intensive training at the Chall
Reading Institute in Portland will initiate some real progress for
Charlie." The program was a huge commitment of time and
money for the whole family, but its success rate was unparalleled.

"This is ten weeks long," Crystal said, studying the brochure. She regarded Lily with dismay and flipped open a well-worn leather Day-Timer. "We're booked on a Disney cruise for ten days in June. In July, she's got riding camp. And August—"

"The kids are with me in August," Derek said. "We've got a rental booked on Molokai."

Lily had trained herself to hold back and choose her words carefully during a conference. It was particularly hard in this case to assert the child's needs. How easy it would be to simply say, "Sounds great! Have a wonderful summer." And then next year, Charlie would be some other teacher's problem.

However, Charlie was Lily's main concern, no matter what she felt for Crystal. The outcome of today's meeting could very well test their lifelong friendship. But a child's future hung in the balance, and Lily was determined to save her at any cost.

"I'm hoping to stay focused on Charlie's needs throughout the summer," she said.

"Weren't you listening? It's a *Disney* Cruise," Crystal said, an edge in her voice. "It's all about kids and fun. I've been promising them all year. And camp, that's totally about Charlie. You wouldn't believe the strings I had to pull just to get her in. It's at Sundance, for heaven's sake. She probably had to edge out Demi Moore's kids just to get a spot there this summer."

"How much is this riding camp going to cost?" Derek asked.

"Probably less than your damned house on Molokai," Crystal snapped.

"I'm still paying off your Christmas trip to Sun Valley."

"I know where you rank in the PGA. Unfortunately for you, I can find that out on ESPN. You can afford Sun Valley."

"Not the way you spend. You've given a whole new meaning to 'spousal maintenance.'"

Lily sat impassively, biting her tongue until it hurt. When a couple argued about money, it was never about money. It was about power and self-worth and judgment; that much Lily had learned from her own parents as she lay awake at night in the dark like a shipwreck victim adrift in a storm at sea, with the tempest raging around her.

In the eight years she'd been a teacher, she'd held a number of conferences. She had weathered many spats, and she found that it was best to allow them to play out and lose their intensity. It was like allowing a pressure cooker to let off some steam, making room inside for something else—in this case, Lily's input about Charlie.

Her headache deepened, the pain turning arrow-sharp and burrowing into a tender spot behind her eye. Neither Crystal nor Derek seemed to notice. Lily had sat too many times in the presence of a couple sniping at each other in the age-old tug-of-war over the most fragile prize of all—a child.

Sometimes it took all of Lily's self-control to keep in the righteous anger, to stop herself from blurting, Will you listen to yourselves? How is this helping your child? And she hadn't even told them everything about Charlie yet. A tiny devil of impulse tempted her to hold back, to keep Charlie's secret for her, but Lily couldn't do that. The little girl had issued a cry for help.

"Could we get back to Charlie?" she asked. "Please?" Taking advantage of a pause in the argument, she said, "There is something else to discuss."

Crystal and Derek glared at each other, visibly shelving the argument. Derek clenched his jaw and folded his arms across his chest as he swiveled to face Lily. Crystal pursed her lips and closed her Day-Timer, also turning her attention to Lily. Whatever their differences, they still had their love for their children in common and were trying to put aside their own agendas for the sake of Charlie.

Lily did her best to ignore the splitting headache an regarded them both. "We've talked a lot about Charlie's academic challenges," she said. "Lately, I've seen some behavioral changes in her, as well."

"What do you mean, behavioral changes?" Derek remained defensive, no surprise to Lily.

She didn't want to sugarcoat anything. "In the past couple of weeks, she's been stealing."

The room filled with silence. Shocked, disbelieving silence. Both faces lost the ability to register expressions. Finally, Lily had their attention.

She took advantage of the silence. "First off, I need to tell you that stealing is very common in kids this age. A lot of them go through it. And second, in most cases, definitely in Charlie's, stealing is not about the objects stolen."

"Whoa," said Derek. "Just a damned minute. Stealing? You say she's stealing. What the hell are you talking about?"

"We've always given Charlie everything she's ever needed or wanted," Crystal swore, and Lily could tell she genuinely believed it.

"Of course you have," she agreed, though her tone conveyed an unspoken *however.* "As I mentioned, it's a fairly specific behavior. With a basically honest child like Charlie, its significance is not what it seems to be on the surface." She wondered how technical to get at this juncture. The syndrome was deep, complex and far-reaching. Yet it was also a problem that was solvable if dealt with appropriately. For now, she thought, she needed to stick to the facts and let Charlie's parents work through their shock and denial.

In a gentle voice, she said, "Let me tell you what I've observed and what I think is going on with Charlie."

"Please do," said Crystal, her voice faint. For a moment she looked so utterly lost and sad that Lily flashed on Crystal as a teenager, Lily's idol and role model. They had needed each other from the start, and now their roles were reversing. Crystal was the needy one. Lily was desperate to help her.

She felt a peculiar malevolence emanating from Derek. It would not be the first time a parent regarded her with suspicion and distrust. Hazard of the profession, Edna always assured her.

Trying to project calm competence, she said, "At the beginning of the week—it was Monday after PE—a student reported to me that a harmonica he'd brought for show-and-tell was missing from his tote tray." She gestured. "That's the plastic tub each child gets for storing his things. I assumed he'd misplaced it, but even when I helped him look around, we couldn't find the thing."

"A freaking harmonica," Derek said.

"Hush, let her finish," Crystal told him.

"Then on Tuesday after music, three different children were missing things. At that point, I questioned the whole class collectively. No one spoke up, but I noticed that Charlie seemed agitated." Lily had questioned both the PE and music teachers, and both seemed to recall that Charlie had asked to use the restroom during class. "As I said before, she's a very honest child. Being deceptive is foreign to her nature."

Crystal took a tissue from the box on the table and idly shredded it. "She's never been good at hiding things."

"I agree," Lily said. "At recess, I spoke with her privately, asking her again if she knew anything about the missing objects. She wouldn't meet my eye, and when I asked if she'd show me what was in her desk and tote tray, she got upset. I told her it would be a lot less trouble if the items were found sooner rather than later. One of the girls claimed her charm bracelet was a family heirloom, so I was anxious to find it by the end of the day." She didn't reveal that the theft victim was

Mary Lou Mattson, the class drama queen, who had sworn her father, a prominent lawyer, would sue the school for millions. "Charlie was very cooperative. She went straight to her book bag, opened a zippered compartment and handed over the missing items."

"Oh, dear God," Crystal said, practically whispering. "A harmonica? A charm bracelet? Doesn't she know I'd buy those things for her if she would only ask?"

"Maybe that's the trouble," snapped Derek. "You're always giving her everything she wants. She's spoiled."

"Actually," Lily intervened, "I believe this behavior is more about wanting something else."

"What else could she want?" asked Crystal. "What could she possibly want?"

Lily had a list. "We should discuss that. Let me just finish going through the week with you. I talked the situation over with Ms. Klein and the school counselor. Together we agreed to take a low-key approach. Often when a child steals, the correct response is to require her to give the items back and apologize. In Charlie's case, we told her I would return the objects and no more would be said. That way, she could save face and the kids would get their belongings back. All I wanted was her assurance that this wouldn't happen again, and her promise that we would talk about why she did it. On Wednesday there were no incidents, but yesterday I discovered something of mine missing."

"Great," said Derek. "You let her get away with it, so she tried it again."

"It's more complicated than that." Don't get defensive, she reminded herself. Just work the problem. "To make a long story short, I questioned Charlie and she handed it over." She picked up the snow globe paperweight Charlie had taken from her desk. It had been a gift from the Holloways' firstborn,

Cameron, seven years before, when he'd been in Lily's class. The figure inside the globe was an angel in winter, wrapped in a swirling white robe. "After she gave it back, I called both of you rather than waiting for conference week to go over the test scores."

"It was the right thing to do," Crystal said loyally. "We need to get to the bottom of this immediately."

"We are at the bottom," Derek said. "How much worse can things get with this kid? She can't read, and now she's turned to a life of crime."

"Maybe she's troubled by your hostility," Crystal said.

"Maybe she's troubled because you baby her so much she doesn't know right from wrong," he replied.

Lily tried to reel them back in. "Have there been any recent changes in Charlie's life or routine? I think this behavior could be a response to change."

"She was six years old when we separated, seven when we divorced," Derek said. "She's had plenty of time to adjust."

Lily wondered if he understood what a tough adjustment divorce was for a kid—at any age. The emotional rug had been pulled out from under Charlie, and she was still trying to find her balance.

"She could be having trouble adjusting to your girl-friend," Crystal said, clipping off each word with a razor precision.

"Charlie's known Jane for three years," Derek said.

"Ever since you had an affair with her." Crystal sent him a look of disdain and turned to Lily. "They say someone always falls for your ex-husband. I should have stayed married to him as a favor to womankind."

Lily cleared her throat. This would be an excellent time to bring the conversation back to Charlie. "Actually, Charlie has been telling the class a lot about her uncle Sean. She seems to like him a great deal. He recently moved back from overseas, didn't he?"

"Everybody likes my younger brother," said Derek.

"Everybody but the Pan-Asian Golf Association," Crystal said, still clipping her words. She angled herself toward Lily. "His brother spent the last ten years playing in Asia. Then he cheated in a tournament and was disqualified—"

"He was set up," Derek said quickly.

"—and eventually he was banned from the tour."

"It was all political," Derek said.

"He's a commitment-phobe," Crystal said to Lily. "He's always walked away from any situation that challenges him. I suppose that's why you haven't met him yet. He's been too busy walking away."

Lily had only a vague memory of Sean…his name wasn't Holloway because he and Derek were half brothers with different fathers. Maguire, that was it. Sean Maguire. She'd met him sixteen years ago when she was fifteen and he a cocky eighteen-year-old. They'd both been in the Holloways' wedding. Lily had felt nervous and self-important in her lavender bridesmaid's gown and dyed-to-match shoes. When she saw him on the dance floor at the reception, she felt sure he had learned his moves from *Dirty Dancing,* which had been her favorite film that year. Sean kept sneaking beers from behind the bar and hitting on every girl in the room with a sweet, slow smile and husky voice: *Want to make out?* But he didn't say that to Lily, of course. No one hit on Lily, except to make fun of her glasses and the braces on her teeth.

"So I take it he's living in Comfort for good?" she asked, eager to get back to Charlie.

"I don't think Sean does anything for good," Crystal said. "Maybe Charlie learned stealing from him."

"Maybe she learned it from your wacko mother," Derek said.

At that, Crystal burst into tears. "I can't believe you said that." She crushed the tissue in her fist and dabbed at her eyes. "What Derek so rudely brought up reminds me, there has been another change in Charlie's life. I...finally had to move my mother to a higher-level nursing home in Portland. I knew this was coming, that it was inevitable, but I had no idea it would be so hard." She stared down at her tightly fisted hand.

Before Lily could even react, Derek was out of his chair and down on one knee in front of his ex-wife. He rested a hand on the edge of the table and the other on the back of the chair, an embrace that didn't quite touch her. "Jesus, Crys, I can't believe I said that. I can't freaking believe it. Please, please forgive me."

His soft, sincere apology made even Lily want to cry. That was the Derek Holloway charm and charisma, his ability to melt away resentment and anger with a few choice words, a soft-toned voice. Even Crystal, despite all the rage of the past two years, didn't seem immune to it.

"I've always thought the world of your mother," he added. "I hate that this is happening to her."

"I know," Crystal whispered, brushing away the last of her tears. "I know."

Lily shut her eyes briefly, feeling an echo of that sorrow. She loved Dorothy Baird, too, a woman she'd known since she was Charlie's age. Growing up, Lily had sometimes escaped her grim home life by stepping into Crystal's world, a household undimmed by tragedy, where people knew how to forgive one another. It was terrible to know a massive stroke had stripped Dorothy away from everyone, even herself.

The emotional moment marked the end of the meeting, Lily could tell. She could feel them withdrawing and leaving the problem with Charlie suspended in midair. The conversation was far from over, but she knew they needed time to mull over what she had told them. "There's a lot more to discuss regarding Charlie," she said, not quite sure they were listening. "For now, I hope you'll each speak with her calmly and in private about the stealing. Let her know it has to stop and try to get her to talk about what's behind it. We can discuss it again on Monday."

"I'm out of town on Monday," Derek said. "Got a tournament."

"I'm coordinating a Special Olympics sponsors' meeting that afternoon," Crystal said. "I was going to have Mrs. Foster stay late to watch the girls."

And that, Lily knew with bleak resignation, was exactly why Charlie was in trouble.

chapter 3

Friday
3:45 p.m.

"They want to do the right thing," Lily told Edna in the teachers' lounge after the conference. "The trouble is, they're so wrapped up in other issues that they're not seeing Charlie."

Edna took a sip of herbal tea. While most of the faculty consumed coffee by the gallon, Edna favored homeopathic and herbal concoctions, all designed to bring about inner peace. Lily eschewed coffee, too, and only drank organically-grown herbals, but that didn't bring her inner peace. A better sleep cycle, maybe.

She and Edna were the last two left at the school. Laurelhurst had a relatively small faculty. On a stormy Friday like this, everyone was eager to get home to loved ones, or to get ready for the weekend. It was an unspoken fact that Lily and Edna were the only unattached people on the faculty.

Lily was slightly in awe of Edna, but she also felt a bit sorry for her. Edna's most marked quality was her willingness to plunge into relationships and to risk her heart. She'd been smashed into the dirt time and time again, but she always dusted herself off and plunged right back into the next doomed relationship. Lily didn't get it. Why set yourself up for hurt?

"Well, the fact that they adore her means they'll work with you," Edna said. She added a small dab of fireweed honey to her tea.

"I hope so," Lily said, idly perusing the faculty bulletin board. "Available for summer house-sitting," read one notice. "Prefer beach or river house." This time of year, teachers were all about summer, and Lily was no exception. She had plans. Big, grand plans. This was something she loved about her job—a teacher had an entire summer to recover from the emotions of loving, educating and cultivating a group of children.

Parents never get that chance, she reflected, thinking of the Holloways. There's no downtime when you're a parent.

"It's going to be a long haul with Charlie," she told Edna. "We didn't even finish discussing the reading institute. They didn't seem to want to hear about it, except to say it would directly interfere with Mom's plans for a Disney cruise and horse camp, and Dad's month in Hawaii."

"Now *I* want to be their kid," Edna said.

"I think they already have as many as they can handle," Lily told her.

"Maybe the reading institute isn't the right choice for this family," Edna said. "They might need more flexibility." She took a sip of her tea, then regarded Lily thoughtfully. "You could be her tutor."

Against her better judgment, Lily felt drawn to the idea. Like everyone else, she adored Charlie and felt that teaching her one-on-one could lead to the breakthrough Charlie needed. Unfortunately, the situation was complicated.

"I could never do that," she said. "You know my policy. I need a life separate from school. And I believe in treating all children equally."

"They don't all need you equally," Edna pointed out.

"Not possible," Lily said. "With this family, it would be extremely tricky."

"I should think it would be extra easy since you and Charlene's mother practically grew up together."

"Her ex can't stand me," Lily said. "He thinks I'm a lousy teacher."

Edna shook her head. "Just like he's a lousy golfer."

"Not quite," Lily said. "A professional golfer loses a game, maybe a bunch of money or even his PGA card. Big deal. When a teacher screws up, it affects a child."

"True, but that's not what I see happening with the Holloway girl. You're doing a good job, even though at present, her progress doesn't reflect that."

"I've been working on this all year. I don't have enough time to get Charlie on track." She could read Edna's thoughts. *So give her more time.*

A part of Lily yearned to do just that, to gather the little girl close. But that—well, that would just be dangerous. Life had not equipped Lily for this: quite the opposite. At an early age, she had learned to protect her heart, even from a child like Charlie. Perhaps *especially* from a child like Charlie.

Outside, lightning flashed and thunder cracked so close that the windowpanes rattled. Rain washed down the glass, smearing the view of the nearly empty parking lot outside. Lily made out two red squiggles of brake lights as a vehicle left the lot. Judging by the size, that was probably Derek's SUV.

"I'll be glad when this year is over," she said, and cinched the belt of her raincoat snugly around her. Summer meant renewal and refuge from troubles she couldn't solve. She needed that, needed time to recover from the emotional roller coaster of the school term.

"It's too bad about that family." Edna sighed, rinsing her mug at the sink. "I've known the Holloways since they enrolled Cameron here ten years ago. I sure as heck didn't see the divorce coming."

No one, Lily thought, not even the most perfectly matched couple, seemed to make it anymore. They could be blissful one day and in divorce court the next.

Crystal often urged Lily to settle down, marry and have a family, and Lily had no idea why. After all she'd been through, Crystal was still a true believer. Not Lily, though. She was a pragmatist, a planner. It was easy to do when there was no one to plan for but her.

Lily's life was arranged exactly the way she wanted it. She had children to love and time for herself. This was her own personal formula for contentment, and she guarded it from anything that might upset the balance, never letting herself question the reason.

chapter 4

Friday
3:45 p.m.

Crystal Baird Holloway jabbed the key into the ignition of her station wagon. She forced herself to take a deep breath, close her eyes and count to ten. She needed to get a grip. In this weather, driving angry was a truly bad idea.

She opened her eyes and deliberately reached around for her seat belt. Torrents of rain glazed the windshield with dull silver streaks, distorting her view of Derek. He appeared ghostlike and indistinct under his black-and-white Ping umbrella as he splashed across the asphalt parking lot to his Chevy Tahoe. A crow with ruffled feathers scurried in front of him and then took wing. Watching him get into the late-model, luxurious SUV and drive into a shroud of fog, she felt a twinge of resentment. He got a new car every year from a sponsor.

There were several things she definitely missed about being married to him, though she would never admit it.

All right, she thought, noticing how quickly the windows had fogged. Don't freak, as Cameron would say. Charlie's going to be all right. How can she not be all right with Lily as her teacher? Okay, so it's been a shitty day, but the worst is over.

Giving a firm nod, like a genie magically transforming chaos to order with a blink, she turned the key in the ignition.

Click.

It took just that one dry, dead-sounding *click* for her to know she was screwed. However, she tried turning the key several times for good measure. *Click. Click. Click.* Nothing but a weak flutter, like the rhythm of a failing heart on a monitor.

Great. What the heck was wrong now?

Oh, Crystal, she thought. You didn't. Her fingers trembled as she reached for the headlamp knob, and her stomach sank. It had been left in the on position.

"Could you be any more stupid?" she muttered.

Even though she knew it wouldn't work, she checked to see if the dome light would come on. No such luck. The car was deader than...a stale marriage.

Damn this weather. Where else but in Rain City, Oregon, did you have to use your headlights in the daytime, ensuring that one day you'd be upset or in a hurry and you'd dash out of the car, forgetting to turn off the lights?

This was all Derek's fault. Every trouble in the world could be traced to smiling, sexy, talented, charming, renowned Derek Charles Holloway. If not for him, she never would have moved out here to the rainiest spot on the planet. If not for him, she'd be fine right now, just fine.

But Derek took up a lot of space in a woman's world. He was larger than life in every department: athletic prowess, looks, spending habits. Oh, and his appetite for women. Let's not forget that, Crystal thought. He was definitely larger than life in that department.

It was because of all his appetites, his greed, his careless-ness in matters of the heart that she found herself sitting in a dead car with the rain beating down, crying her eyes out.

I'll hate you forever, Derek Charles Holloway, she thought, digging around in her purse for a Kleenex. She came across everything but a tissue: her prescription slip (yet another er-rand she needed to run before picking up the kids), an ancient Binky dusted with bottom-of-the-purse lint (Ashley had sur-rendered her Binky six months ago), a couple of stray ball markers and tees with Derek's initials on them (Was her purse really that old?), a tiny three-pack of Virginia Slims samples given out at a tournament (Yes. It really was that old.), a pack of matches from Bandon Dunes Golf Course. And she still hadn't found a Kleenex.

By now the windows of the car were so steamed up, pas-sersby might think there was some hanky-panky going on. Ha. Hanky-panky was a thing of the past for Crystal. Hanky-panky was what got her here in the first place. And the sec-ond. And the third.

God, what happened to my life? she wondered. Derek. Derek Holloway happened.

She'd been a student at the University of Portland, with ev-erything going for her. She was a freaking beauty queen, for Pete's sake. She had stood upon the mountaintop as Miss Or-egon U.S.A. of 1989, heavily favored to win the national title. Then along came Derek. Three months later, she'd cheerfully handed her crown over to her first runner-up, a dull-witted, laser-toothed blonde from Clackamas County.

Crystal had been so stupid in love that she hadn't even cried, giving up her crown. She was pregnant—on purpose, though Derek never knew that—and about to marry a man who, by the age of twenty-two, had already been on the cover of *Sports Il-lustrated* three times. Really, what was there to cry about?

She snorted into the wet sleeve of her microfiber raincoat, making up for lost time. Her sleeve made a lousy Kleenex, so she simply gave up crying.

"Enough is enough," she said. And again: "Get a grip." Somehow she managed to compose herself. She sat for a moment in the pall of silence. It was a dead car, for Lord's sake, not a cancer diagnosis. She had weathered childbirth, heartbreak, infidelity, divorce, single parenthood, financial ruin, and the world hadn't come to an end. Surely a dead battery was not going to finish her off.

Will it matter in five years? Her therapist's favorite question popped into Crystal's mind. For once, the answer was no. No, this stupid dead car she was forced to drive because her stupid attorney hadn't milked enough spousal maintenance out of Derek would be nothing more than a bitter memory five years from now. She glanced at the crumpled pink receipt from the medical lab test on the console. Snatching it up, she stuffed it under the visor. Now, *that* was something that would matter in five years. It would matter forever.

She wished it wasn't raining. If the sun was out, she'd abandon this piece-of-shit car, stride with her pageant runway walk over to Rain Shadow Lexus and slide right into the cushy leather interior of a brand-new car, one that shut its own lights off if the driver forgot. She'd sweet-talk the dealer into easy terms and drive off into the sunset.

Driving. She and Derek used to drive all over together. After they'd moved here to Comfort, a short distance from the magnificent Pacific Coast, they used to drive out to the edge of everything and explore the twisting, cliff-draped coastal highway to their hearts' content. Sometimes they'd even pull off at a scenic vista and make love in the back of their minivan.

It was raining harder than ever now. She briefly considered prevailing on Lily for help, but dismissed the idea. She knew

Lily would drop everything to help her. She'd wade through a flood if Crystal asked her to. Crystal didn't want to ask. Lily had already been such a good friend to her, helping her out of one jam after another. It was high time Crystal started rescuing herself. And frankly, Crystal was tired of feeling like an idiot.

As she took out her cell phone, she held her breath. If this battery was dead, too, she'd shoot herself. She pictured herself slogging back into the school, a two-time loser, needing to use a phone.

"Work, please work," she said, flipping it open.

The display leapt to glowing blue life, playing its happy little "Turn Me On" ditty. Finally, one thing went right today. Not only that, Crystal had, like the soul of competence and organization, clipped her auto club card to the visor. How smart of her.

She entered the toll-free number, then followed the prompts, submitting her membership number.

"We're sorry," said a soothing female voice. "That number is no longer valid. Please call our customer service department between 9:00 a.m. and 6:00 p.m. eastern time to renew your membership."

"Screw you," Crystal muttered, pressing End. The phone's clock told her it was well past 6:00 p.m. on the stupid East Coast.

Like everything else in their marriage, Derek had let the auto club membership expire and hadn't bothered to tell her.

Swearing under her breath, she took out the sample package of Virginia Slims and the book of hotel matches. She put one of the ancient cigarettes between her lips and lit up. She gagged on the smoke, being an intermittent smoker at best, but lighting up was an act of defiance, a reaction to all the frustrations building inside her. For one moment, she could do something reckless, senseless, dangerous, and the only one to suffer the consequences would be her.

Calmed by the cigarette, Crystal pressed the button of her seat belt. It retracted with a snaky slither and she felt suddenly unburdened. Free.

Finally, she knew exactly what she was going to do. She was going to kill him. She smiled, took another puff on the cigarette and flipped open her phone again. Her fingers remembered his number and dialed it by touch alone. She didn't even have to look.

He answered on the first ring because she had programmed him to respond quickly. With three kids, you never knew what emergency might be going on.

"My car's dead," she said without preamble. "I need you to come back to the school and give me a jump."

"Call the auto club," he said easily. "I'm busy."

She could hear his car radio playing a Talking Heads song in the background. "You let the auto club membership expire," she said.

"No, you failed to renew it," he said.

"I would have done so if you'd told me it expired."

"Call a tow truck, then."

"Fine. That'll cost a hundred and fifty bucks. I'll send you the bill."

"Oh, no you—"

"And since I'm going to be sitting here for hours, you'll have to pick up the kids, even though it's my turn to take them. I'm sure you don't have any plans for this evening."

"Come on, Crys. Get somebody from the school to help you. Lily. Get your buddy the schoolteacher to help. Maybe she can help you more than she has Charlie."

"Oh, don't start." Crystal acknowledged to herself that this wasn't really about getting a jump for her car. This was about getting Derek to jump for her. "Quit trying to hand off your problem to someone else."

"There's got to be a maintenance worker at the school, or—"

"Derek. In the time it takes to have this argument, you could drive back here and give me a jump. Then you'll be a free man."

"You're pissing me off, Crys. You are really pissing me off."

She smiled. "See you soon."

The phone went dead. Crystal took it away from her ear and looked at the screen. It said Call Ended, not Signal Lost. The bastard had hung up on her.

She thought about what to do next. In a raging storm, with darkness falling all around, in a dead car, no one could hear you scream.

She opened the door and threw out the stale cigarette. Then, through the rain-blurred windshield, she saw a pair of headlights approaching. Friend or foe? she wondered. The day seemed darker than ever. The headlamps blazed, blinding her in a blue-white flash of lightning. The vehicle approached fast, coming straight toward her. Crystal was too surprised to scream. She clutched the steering wheel and braced herself for impact.

The vehicle stopped mere inches from her front bumper. She blinked at the strong stream of light stabbing right at her. And saw a flash of cobalt blue.

Derek. Bless him, the bastard had come back for her.

chapter 5

The bitch just sat there like a queen, barely acknowledging his presence. Derek had the high beams on intentionally, and left them on, glaring straight at her. Take that.

He offered her a steady stream of opinion in terms so foul it would curl her ears if she could hear him. But she couldn't, of course, which made him wonder why he bothered.

He stuffed his arms into the sleeves of his Gore-Tex jacket and shrugged the hood up over his head. He reached down and popped the hood of the truck. Without acknowledging Crystal or even glancing in her direction, he went to the back of the Chevy and got out the cables.

He felt her watching him and knew damned well what she was thinking. This was a power play. They both knew it. And by getting him to come back for her, she'd won the first round. But the fight wasn't over. They both acknowledged that, too.

Propping open the hood, he felt the first cold trickles of rain pouring into his shoe. He looked down to see that the water was ankle deep.

"Fuck," he said, wishing she could hear, because she hated that word so much. "Fuck, fuck, fuck."

He clipped the cable to the corresponding battery terminals, hoping like hell he got it right. Then he turned his attention to Crystal's car. Correction, *his* car. The one she'd stolen from him, along with the house and everything else in the divorce settlement.

At least she was smart enough to pop the hood release without being told. He found the battery terminals caked with corrosion and had to chip the flakes off with his pocketknife. Then he connected the jumper cables and stepped out from under the hood. With a flick of his wrist, he signaled for her to try the ignition. It was raining so hard he couldn't hear the engine engage.

She opened her door and shouted, "It's not working."

"Try it again."

She shot him a look and turned the key. With the door open, he could see her do it. Nothing happened—no panel, no dome light, no nothing. Complete failure.

"Try again," he yelled.

She shook her head. "Still not working."

Out of patience, Derek motioned for her to move. She had to clamber over the console, and he was treated briefly to a flash of beauty queen leg. Even standing in a puddle in the midst of a storm, even knowing all the reasons he had divorced her, Derek felt a jolt of such irrational sexual hunger that he groaned aloud.

This of course was Crystal's great power. This was why he'd stayed with her fifteen years instead of fifteen minutes. She was the sexiest woman he'd ever known.

And now she sat next to him, silent and ungrateful, smelling of designer perfume and… He glared at her questioningly. "Smoking, Crys?"

She offered him a skinny, flat package of cigarettes that had seen better days. "Join me?"

"Those things will kill you."

"We all have to die of something."

Derek shook his head in disgust while he confirmed what he'd known since he saw the condition of her battery. "It's dead," he said.

Rainwater dripped from his hooded jacket to the cloth upholstery.

She said nothing. She didn't have to. Her tight-lipped, pale-faced, narrow-eyed expression said it all.

"Fuck," he said, banging the steering wheel with the heel of his hand. "Fuck, fuck, fuck."

She used to wince when he talked that way. That was, actually, his primary reason for talking that way. Now that she had no reaction, he shut up. Then he took a deep, cleansing breath to clear his head, filling his lungs from the top down the way his breathing coach had taught him.

Yes, he had a freaking breathing coach. He had coaches and trainers for every possible angle, physical or mental. If he didn't watch out, one of these days he'd find himself with a coach for taking a piss.

The car was littered with carelessly strewn effluvia. A clump of sodden Kleenex told him she felt as lousy about the teacher conference as he did. A pair of earrings he didn't recognize lay in the ashtray. Crystal had a way of littering herself throughout the car, stamping it with her presence. It was littered with memories, too. This had been a brand-new car the day they'd driven Charlie to school for the first day of kindergarten. She'd sobbed miserably while big brother Cameron looked on in disgust.

Then, realizing the nest was truly empty, they'd driven to Lovers Lane, a private cliffside parking spot off the coastal highway. It was a place Derek remembered from high school, an outcropping so lofty and sheer that an ordinary car felt like the cockpit of a spaceship. That day, with both their children in school for the first time, he'd made love to her in the back of the station wagon on the scratchy gray carpet littered with golf tees, scorecards, plastic Happy Meal toys and lost pennies. He could've taken her home that day, to their own bed, but at home, phone calls and work awaited him.

Back then, she'd wrapped her strong bare legs around him and sighed with satisfaction. Now she handed him her cell phone. "Call your auto club."

He snatched it from her, got the number from his wallet and made the call. The rain came down harder. The dispatcher said the first available assistance would arrive in three to four hours. When Derek told Crystal this, she said, "I'm not waiting here."

"Go inside the school and wait."

"That's ridiculous. Cameron needs to be picked up in an hour and a half. And then Charlie after that. She's playing at her friend Lindsey's house. I don't know how long you told the sitter to keep Ashley."

The baby wasn't with her usual sitter, but Derek wasn't about to disclose that until he had to. Crystal was pissed enough at him.

"Tell you what," he said, "get Lily to give you a ride home. I'll pick up the kids and bring them to your place."

"No. I'm not imposing on Lily."

"She's your freaking best friend," he said, yelling now. "She'll bail you out, no problem."

"Yes, she would, if I asked her to. But I won't. Our children are not Lily's responsibility." She regarded him with those beautiful, cool blue eyes, and it was a look of such obstinacy that Derek felt himself conceding the battle without even saying a word.

Having a family had always seemed like a reasonable prospect to Derek. A wife and kids. What could be simpler or more pleasant?

Where Crystal was involved, nothing was simple and very little was pleasant. And who knew what a circus act it actually was to juggle three kids? The laundry, the phone calls, the homework, the carpools, the scheduling of sports and music lessons. Hell, you needed an air traffic controller to manage everything.

No wonder Charlie was in trouble. Someone had dropped the ball with her, and she was failing in school. A hard knot of guilt formed in Derek's stomach. *Charlie.* His little chip shot.

He checked his watch. They still had an hour and a half to kill before it was time to pick up the kids. He drew on the hood of his jacket, shouldered opened the door and went back out into the roaring storm. He disconnected the cables, closed both engine hoods, then went around to Crystal's door and yanked it open.

"Get in the truck," he yelled.

"But why—"

"Get in the damned truck." He turned away, got in the driver's seat, put on his seat belt and watched her. Even in the teeth of the storm, she moved with the unhurried grace of a queen, opening her red umbrella and then stepping out of the car. She got into the truck, then folded the umbrella and slid it under the seat.

"Did you leave your keys in the car?" he asked.

"Of course. I'm not stupid, Derek."

"No," he said, putting the truck in reverse. "You're not." Things would be easier if she was.

He headed west on the river road, the wipers thumping rapidly across the windshield.

"Where are you going?"

"We've got an hour to talk," he said, ignoring her question. "So talk."

He could feel her glare as she clicked her seat belt in place. "Charlie's in trouble. Fighting about it for an hour isn't going to solve anything."

He glanced over at her and saw no trace of sarcasm in her expression.

"Then let's not fight." He wondered if she heard the weariness in his voice. It was exhausting, trying to figure out what to do with a love gone wrong, especially when kids were involved.

With sullen reluctance, the rain let up and finally stopped altogether. Derek turned off the river road and drove up the ramp to the highway. Here at the coast road, the sun was trying to peek through the broody, black-bellied clouds over the churning sea.

The view was spectacular no matter how many times he saw it. He and Sean had grown up in Comfort, and on the weekends they liked to come out to the coast to hang out on the beach or play a round of golf at the seaside links course. As they grew older and went up to Portland for college, they continued to come out here. The highway department's scenic vista pullout was the perfect place to bring girls for make-out sessions.

The first time he'd dated Crystal, he'd brought her here. It was no accident that he'd chosen the spot today.

He maneuvered the truck along the winding road, finding it deserted except for the occasional darting squirrel or deer heading pointlessly from one side of the road to another. The economic recession had hit the county hard, and its budget troubles showed in the condition of the road. Potholes were patched here and there, guardrails were down or missing altogether. The shoulder of the road was collapsing in places from mudslides. The macadam surface was slick and he could feel the tires of the truck trying to hydroplane. In the burgeoning sunlight, wisps of steam rose from the wet pavement.

Derek tried to think of something to say that wouldn't lead to a fight. An impossible task with Crystal these days. She was as fragile and brittle as her name implied, and the slightest upset could cause her to shatter. However, with Charlie in trouble, they had a difficult conversation ahead of them.

"So," he said at last, "what do you make of our conference with your friend?"

"Lily was speaking to us in her capacity as Charlie's teacher," she said, "not as my friend. And to be honest, I'm actually glad to have Charlie's problems out in the open. It's time to stop fooling ourselves. From our first meeting with Lily last September, it's been clear that Charlie's way behind the curve. Now we need to figure out what to do."

"Charlie never had any problems until Lily's class." Derek gritted his teeth. That was going to piss Crystal off. Too bad. This was about Charlie. His daughter, his heart.

"Oh, so you think Lily is the cause of Charlie stealing and being behind in school? Lily is the best teacher our kids have ever had."

He pulled off at the scenic vista. For a moment, he flashed on a vivid memory of the first time he'd brought Crystal here. She was his beauty queen from Beaverton, he was a hot stick striving for his PGA card and they were in love. She gave up her crown for him and he'd vowed to leave his party-animal ways behind. Their future was golden.

That golden future had been tarnished by the patina of

time, of betrayal, of all the myriad strains of trying to stay on his game.

"I'm saying you might want to consider the idea that Lily could actually be part of the problem."

"That would be so much easier than considering the idea that *you* might be part of the problem." She caught his glare and amended, "All right, maybe we're both part of it. I trust Lily implicitly. When she taught Cameron seven years ago, you had no complaints about her. He flourished in her class."

"Cameron is a no-brainer. A monkey could have educated him. He was the perfect kid." Derek wondered if his son knew he thought that. Only this morning, they'd had their usual fight over the usual topic—golf.

"What's that face?" Crystal asked. She could still read him like a rule book.

"Cam's pissed at me again," Derek confessed. "He doesn't want to play in the tournament this weekend. I don't get it. He's a brilliant golfer." He thumped his hand on the steering wheel. "Maybe he was just trying to get a rise out of me. In fact, now that the rain's stopped, he's probably hitting a bucket of balls for practice. Kid can't stay away from the game."

"Which shows how much you know about your son," Crystal said.

"Now you're telling me he doesn't like golf."

"He likes you. He thinks he has to play golf so you'll give him the time of day."

"That's shit." Derek thought about the strained conversation he'd had with Cameron that morning. The strain had flared into out-and-out hostility from both sides. Somehow, battling his son brought out the worst in him. "I can't believe he's fighting me over golf. When I offered to talk to Coach Duncan about it, Cam freaked on me, completely freaked."

"Don't talk to Greg Duncan," Crystal said quickly, sharply.

Derek frowned.

She said, "Let me talk to Cameron—later." She unhooked her seat belt and got out to pace in front of the truck. He had no choice but to join her. The air was still chilly and smelled of damp asphalt, cedar and madrona. Far below, waves breaking on the rocks threw up rainbows of light. This place used to hold such magic for them. Even the abandoned lighthouse way out on Tillamook Rock, miles offshore, had been part of the spell. It was a famous columbarium where old bones and ashes were put to rest. They used to swear they wanted to be placed there when they died, after growing old together.

"We need to focus on Charlie right now," Crystal said. "Not Cameron. And not Lily."

"She's part of Charlie's troubles," Derek pointed out.

"She's my best friend," Crystal said.

"Maybe that's clouding your judgment."

"Damn it, Derek. Look at the facts. Charlie isn't reading and she's been stealing. Lily didn't cause that. She's trying to fix it. We need to rethink our plans for the summer."

"Meaning?"

"Meaning Lily wants us to do what's best for Charlie, not what's good for your career."

"Oh, so you're just going to cancel your plans and stay home, carting the kid to Portland every day to study."

"I think we should consider it. Sorry if that interferes with your plans."

He barked out a short laugh. "It doesn't interfere, honey. It negates them completely. You know I won't do anything this summer without Charlie."

"What a shame you and Joan will have to miss out on Hawaii."

"It's Jane," he said automatically, but of course she knew that. "And it's not so much that missing Hawaii is a problem.

I need to play in the majors. How the hell do you think we're going to pay for things like a private clinic in Portland, along with everything else you claim you need?"

"Maybe if you managed your money better, you wouldn't have to worry about that."

"What the hell's that supposed to mean?"

"You earn huge amounts, Derek, but you spend even more. How many are on your payroll now, a dozen? Twenty? Do you really need to travel with your own personal massage therapist?"

"As a matter of fact, yes. My people are the engine that keeps this train on track. You know that, Crystal. You know." He aimed a meaningful look at her designer shoes and the diamond pendant glittering at her throat. "Maybe you should lay off the shopping. Ever think of that?"

She glared at him, then glanced at her watch. "We should go. It's time to pick up the baby at Mrs. Foster's and Cameron at the country club." She got back in the truck and put on her seat belt. She was utterly self-possessed, expecting the world to wait on her.

He got in and started up the truck. Steam still rolled off the hood and the asphalt. It was no longer raining, but fog hung thick in the ditches and vales surrounding the road.

"Cameron doesn't mind hanging around the club," Derek said, hoping to deflect her attention from who was watching the baby. "Now that Sean works there, they sometimes get in a round together." He slammed the truck into reverse and peeled out, rear end fishtailing on the slick surface of the road.

"I think Cameron's been spending too much time with your brother."

"For God's sake, Crystal. The kids have a right to get to know their uncle. Cameron likes him. Sean's good for his golf game."

"Giving him pointers, like teaching him how to cheat?"

Derek took the next curve a little too fast, swinging onto

the shoulder, veering into the gravel along the shoulder. "That was a low blow. Sean's no cheater."

"No? Then he was banned from the Asian Tour for...what? Having a bad hair day?"

"For getting mixed up with the wrong woman," he said. Then a devil inside him made him add, "God knows, I can relate to that."

"You bastard, you—" She broke off, looking at the road. "You just missed the turnoff into town."

"I'm taking Echo Ridge."

"Then you'll have to go through town to get to the sitter's," she pointed out.

All right, thought Derek. He might as well go for broke. "Ashley isn't there. She's with Jane."

She sucked in an audible breath. "Well, that's just peachy. The thought of my baby in the hands of your jailbait girlfriend makes my day."

"Jane Coombs is twenty-four and already has her Ph.D."

"You love reminding me of that. I don't give a shit about her academic credentials."

Derek knew she did. Crystal joked about getting out of college with only her "MRS" degree, but the fact that she had never finished her education was a sore spot, something probably only Derek knew.

"Jane loves Ashley," he said. Then he took a deep breath. "And you might as well know she's moving in with me."

"Ah, living in sin. You're such a perfect role model for our children."

"We won't be living in sin." His hands were suddenly drenched in sweat, slick upon the steering wheel. "Crystal, we're getting married. We plan to tell the kids next weekend."

"You bastard," she said, her voice eerily quiet. "You damned, fucking bastard."

He glanced over at her and had the strangest sensation of déjà vu. And then he laughed. He *was* a bastard. His stepfather used to remind him of that all the time. And the fucking part? Well, that was certainly true. He fucked anything that twitched a tush at him, and on a pro golf tour, there was a lot of twitching.

"You think this is funny?" Crystal demanded.

"I think it's hilarious. We're hilarious. God, look at us, Crystal. Look at the mess we made, me with my pecker and you with your purse." He chuckled, feeling giddy and lightheaded as though he'd just slammed down a shot of tequila. He looked over and caught her staring at him with her heart in her eyes.

"Damn it, Crystal," he said, "I was so damned in love with you, but you made it so damned hard to stay that way."

Her eyes misted and for just a moment he saw the girl she had been, the dream lover he thought he wanted for the rest of his life. She had worshiped him with a fervor that was a turn-on. Where had that gone?

"God, Derek," she said, "it's so much easier than you— look out!"

He yanked his gaze back to the road in time to see a doe and her spotted fawn gambol down the fogged-in bank, stepping directly into the roadway right in front of him.

Derek had grown up in this place. He knew every curve of the road and every outcrop, every sheer cliff, and every thick-girthed cedar and Douglas fir that bordered the wild highway. He even knew that the Huffelmanns owned property for the next mile along the road and had posted it No Trespassing. Old man Huffelmann would not even give the highway department permission to put a guardrail alongside the steep incline, so there was no barrier to keep him on the road.

The tires screamed on the wet pavement and he dialed the

steering wheel frantically in the opposite direction of the skid. Crystal stayed completely silent, though she threw her hands in front of her and braced them on the dashboard. Somehow, Derek wrestled the car back into its lane.

Crystal glowered at him. "You drive like a maniac."

"You used to like that about me."

"I used to like a lot of things about you."

"Hey, at least I didn't cream Bambi and his mom." He could tell she was in no mood. Fine, he thought. He might as well get on that last nerve of hers right now and get it over with. "I suppose this is as good a time as any to tell you I have to miss Ashley's birthday party."

"Derek, come on."

"I'm sorry, but I have to be in Vegas for a big tournament, so I need you to change the party date."

"I'm not changing a thing."

"She's only two. She'll never know. She's just a baby. It's no big deal." A pair of madronas, the bark peeled off to reveal bloodred branches, grew beside the sharp curve in the road ahead. He ignored the yellow-and-black caution sign and accelerated.

"No big deal," she echoed, her voice soft with restrained fury. "Well then, I suppose that now would be as good a time as any to tell you the baby isn't yours."

part two

The beauty of a strong, lasting commitment is often best understood by men incapable of it.

—Murray Kempton

chapter 6

And here's the challenger, Sean Maguire, aiming for the green and a possible eagle putt. No one in the crowd is breathing as the challenger selects a Titleist forged-iron pitching wedge, assuming his famous stance. An easy, athletic swing, a flawless follow-through and…he's on, ladies and gentlemen. He's on the green and rolling twenty, fifteen, ten! He's just ten feet from the hole, and that's one putt away from a historic win. Not only will he take home one million dollars and the championship trophy, but he'll also be having sex with identical blond twins who magically turn into beer and pizza at midnight. Ladies and gentlemen, you can hear a pin drop as the challenger steps up to address the ball. All that stands between him and victory is ten feet of putting green. This should be no trouble for the legendary Maguire. He adjusts his stance, glides into his famous backswing, preparing to make history. Smoothly the club head descends toward the ball, flawlessly aimed, and—

"Hey, mister."

Sean's arm jerked and the head of the putter missed. The golf ball bobbled away from the hole. Gritting his teeth in frustration, he straightened up and scowled at the kid, who stood at the edge of the practice screen.

"Yeah?" Sean immediately regretted the annoyance in his tone. The wide-eyed kid was probably a fan, asking for the autograph of the legendary Sean Maguire. "What can I do for you?"

"You got change for a dollar?"

Great. He scrounged the change from his pocket. He had only thirty-five cents. The coins felt light and insubstantial in his hand.

He leaned down and grabbed the ball from the rain-soaked green. His four o'clock lesson hadn't shown, probably due to the weather, so he'd passed the time practicing his own game. To what end, he had no idea.

"What do you need, kid?"

"Change for the Coke machine." He shuffled his feet and, probably prodded by some latent lesson from Mom, added, "Please, mister."

"You can call me Sean."

"Really?"

"I just said you could. I can make change in the clubhouse." He jerked his head toward the long, low building. His place of employment. He'd capped off his stellar career as a professional golfer right where he'd started, here at Echo Ridge.

As the kid fell in step with him, Sean asked, "What's your name?"

"Russell Clark."

They shook hands and kept walking.

"Hey, want to know how to figure out your porn-star name?"

"My what?"

"You know, your porn-star name. Porn stars never use their own names."

The kid was ten years old if he was a day. What did he know about porn stars? "Is this something you ask all strangers, or just me?"

Russell shrugged, so Sean said, "Okay, sure. Sure. I'm dying to know."

"Tell me the name of the street you live on."

"Ridgetop Avenue." In yet another nondescript apartment. He'd never lived in a place he actually cared about.

"Now tell me the name of the first pet you ever had."

"When I was about your age, I had a shepherd mutt named Duke."

The kid roared with laughter. "Then your porn-star name's Duke Ridgetop."

Oh, that's brilliant, thought Sean. Just brilliant. "Maybe he'll pay my bills for me."

"Guess what mine is. Betcha can't guess."

"You're right. I can't. What is it?"

"Pepper McRedmond. Cool, huh?" Russell laughed and slapped his thigh.

"Whatever tees you up, kid."

Inside the clubhouse, Sean made change and then Russell scurried off to the Coke machine. Kids belonged to an alien nation, Sean thought. He'd never understand them. Shaking his head, he noticed his weekly paycheck in his in-box. He stuffed it in his jacket pocket without even looking at the amount. He knew he ought to be grateful for steady money, but hell, he used to tip his caddie more than that amount after just one round. Used to.

Sean checked the time. He was finished here for the day,

but in three hours he'd be back in the bar upstairs, fixing Manhattans and cosmopolitans for local lawyers and leather-skinned retirees. It was hardly worth going home in between. Maura, his girlfriend, was at the hospital until late, and early in the morning, she had to drive to Portland for a seminar. Sean was surprised to feel a twinge of sentiment; he would miss her, he thought. These days, he didn't trust his own judgment about women.

With this current rotation, she tended to crawl into bed and sleep when she wasn't working, anyway. They didn't exactly live together, but lately they'd slept at his place every single night, and item by item, her things were migrating over to his apartment. Two days ago, she'd brought her CD collection and a picture of her family. This was as close to a permanent arrangement as Sean had ever had with a woman. Well, almost.

He looked around the clubhouse, where a few groups of golfers milled around, comparing scores and tallying up debts. Due to the storm, there weren't many of them. Only the die-hards were out in weather like they'd had this afternoon. Sean listened to them laughing and talking, and it made him remember that golf was supposed to be fun. A game. He missed those days.

In the locker room, he changed out of his chinos and club-logo windbreaker—Echo Ridge didn't permit jeans—and slipped on his favorite Levi's.

His cell phone rang, and when he recognized the number of the incoming call, his pulse sped up. "Yeah?" he said.

"Hello to you, too, pretty boy." The voice of Harlan "Red" Corliss, Derek's agent, was broad and smooth with a smile.

"You sound happy with yourself." Cocking his head to hold the phone, Sean transferred the things from the pockets of his work pants to his jeans.

"What are you doing next Saturday, Maguire?" Red asked.

Sean dropped his keys and clutched the phone hard. "You got me in the Redwing tournament."

"That I did. I have a few sponsors' exemptions and I used one just for you, kid."

Tournament play. It used to be what Sean lived for, what defined him. He used to be a rising star, a hero of the game. Now here he was, shadowed by disgrace, nobody's hero. No matter what he did, he could still feel the sick sense of shame and guilt that had shrouded him like a pall.

"Hello?" Red asked when the pause drew out too long. "You're not worried about your game, are you?"

Sean prowled back and forth in the clubhouse. "The talent's intact."

"Forget talent. You have a talent that's almost freakish. So big deal. Forget you know how to hit a ball at all and work your ass off." Red was quiet for a moment. "It's not that, is it?"

"You know it's not, Red."

"Look, you can't worry about that. You didn't cheat. You were set up. It'll be ancient history before you know it. Hell, it's already ancient history."

Sean leaned his forehead against the locker door. It didn't matter that he'd been set up. He was guilty of stupidity. He deserved to be back where he started, climbing his way out of a hole of his own making.

"Got it, Red. Ancient history." He stood up straight, turned and looked out the window. Freshened by the rain and bordered by majestic ancient cedars, the golf course looked green and bright enough to hurt the eyes. And in that moment, it hit him. This was a chance to get back in the game.

"Damn, Red." Throwing off his doubts, Sean grinned until his face ached. Finally. Sure, Maura would tell him it wasn't practical to go chasing after a game, and Derek would warn him he wasn't ready, but Sean didn't care. This was the break he'd been waiting and hoping for. Another chance at the sport he loved. He'd arrived in the States too late to compete in Q School, in which golfers earned—or requalified for—their PGA card, and he'd resigned himself to waiting another year to go through the process. But Red was one of the best in the business, and he was putting Sean on the fast track.

"Damn is right. I'm having Gail messenger the contracts over, and I'll call you tomorrow with all the details."

Sean was still grinning when the clubhouse door opened and shut.

"What's funny?" asked Greg Duncan, the high school golf coach.

"Did you know there's a way to make up your porn-star name?" Sean didn't want to say anything to Duncan about his news. It would seem too much like gloating. Greg Duncan was a damned fine golfer who wanted his PGA card with a hunger that was palpable. He'd competed in Q School a few times but never advanced past sectional competitions. The guy needed a break, but that was golf for you. A heartless game, like Red always said.

"Uncle Sean?" Stomping his muddy shoes on the bristled mat, his nephew, Cameron, called to him from the doorway. "Hey, Coach."

"Hey, Cameron." Greg Duncan dropped his spikes in his locker and slammed it shut. "I'm out of here. See you Sunday, okay?" Without waiting for a reply, he headed for the parking lot.

Cameron Holloway bore an almost eerie resemblance to Derek. He had the same sandy-colored hair and intense eyes, the same lanky frame that moved with surprising grace, the same startling talent at swinging a club. He was the best thing that had happened to the local golf team in years. And from the looks of him—cheeks reddened by the wind, hair damp, shoes muddy—he'd been out practicing.

"What's up?" he asked.

"Um, my mom was supposed to pick me up a half hour ago, but I guess she forgot." He looked sullen as he said it. "She forgets everything lately."

Sean bore no love for his former sister-in-law, who had taken Derek to the cleaners and back in the divorce, but it didn't seem right to let Cameron badmouth her. "She probably got delayed in the rain," he suggested. There were a lot of things Sean envied about Derek, but he sure as hell didn't envy his brother's crazy-ass ex-wife. Crystal was enough to drive anyone bonkers.

"Naw, she just forgot, and she's not answering her cell phone. Neither is my Dad."

Sean dug in his pocket for his keys. "I'll give you a lift."

"Thanks."

"Meet me in the parking lot." Sean told Duffy, the greens-keeper, that he was taking off and went out to his truck. Cameron was loading in his clubs, a set of Callaways with graphite shafts, which were better quality clubs than some of the well-heeled doctors at Echo Ridge played. The clubs were hand-me-downs from Derek, who got a new set every year from his sponsor.

Sean reminded himself that his brother had earned his success, stroke by stroke, tournament by tournament. He deserved every perk that came his way. And Sean...well, he got what he deserved, too.

As they pulled out of the parking lot and headed down the steep, winding road, he said, "Why don't you call your mom, tell her you got a ride home with me so she doesn't come looking for you."

Cameron took out his phone and thumbed in the number. "She still won't answer."

"Just tell her voice mail."

There was a silence, then Cameron said, "It's me. You were late picking me up, so Uncle Sean is giving me a ride home. See you."

Sean glanced sideways at him. "That tone was borderline rude."

"It's over-the-border rude to leave me stranded."

"I'm sure there's an explanation."

"There's always an explanation."

"You shouldn't be rude to your mother."

"What do you care?"

Sean ignored the question and turned on the radio. Nickel Creek was playing "Angels Everywhere." He tried to remember if, at fifteen, he'd been so angry all the time. He was pretty sure he hadn't. Then again, he'd had nothing to be angry about. He'd been a happy-go-lucky kid, obsessed with golf and girls, in that order. All these years later, a hell of a lot had changed. Maybe he ought to be angry right along with his nephew. But he still had golf and girls on his mind.

"Did you play a round this afternoon?" he asked by way of making conversation.

"Nope. I hit three buckets of balls and practiced chip shots. There's a tournament this weekend against Portland Prep."

"So how's your game?"

"Fine."

"Just fine?"

"Good enough to win this weekend." He spoke with confidence, not vanity.

"That's good, then."

"I guess."

Sean wondered why the boy didn't show a little more enthusiasm, but he figured it wasn't his business to ask.

As he turned into the tree-shaded, manicured subdivision

where Crystal lived, it occurred to him that he'd never been to the house on Candlewood Street. While he was married, Derek had lived here for years, but Sean had never visited the house his brother had shared with his beauty-queen wife. Sean had been overseas, playing on the Asian Tour, and hadn't come back to the States until circumstances forced him to.

He knew the house, though. It was the biggest and oldest in Saddlebrook Acres, an area of large, elegant houses built in the era of the timber barons. When he and Derek were kids, they used to ride their bikes past this very house, admiring the vast lawn and the gleaming white cupola, the wrap-around porch.

"Someday I'm going to live there" became the boyhood vow. Yet oddly, the vow had come from Sean, not Derek. It was a place of permanence and splendor, the sort of place a person could imagine spending a whole life. But somewhere along the way, he'd set that dream aside, finding a far different sort of life as a professional golfer. And somehow, Derek had appropriated the dream Sean had come to see as an impossibility.

For a long time, Sean's half brother made it all come together—the career, the family, the house, everything. From Sean's perspective, it all seemed to work like a charm. He couldn't believe Derek had managed to blow it. You'd think, with all of this at stake, Derek could have kept his pecker in his pants at that tournament in Monte Carlo. But, Sean supposed, that was Derek's business. Judging by the way she'd cleaned him out in the divorce settlement, Crystal Baird Holloway was no picnic to live with. Still…

Sean flicked a sideways glance at Cameron. He was a good enough kid even as he navigated the rocky shoals of his parents' split. Sure, he had an attitude these days, but who wouldn't, being shuffled back and forth between houses on alternate weeks. It was the one issue in the divorce agreement on which Derek would not budge. He wanted his kids fifty percent of the time, and his lawyer, whose fees made even Derek shudder, secured joint custody.

"So how's school?" he asked Cameron, trying to shorten the gap of silence between them.

"Okay, I guess."

Sean grinned over the arch of the steering wheel. "Bad question. I ought to know better than to ask how school's going."

"I don't mind it."

Communication in the form of meaningful conversation had never been a forte in the family, Sean reflected. Apparently Cameron was carrying on the tradition.

Sean pulled into the smooth asphalt drive of the house on Candlewood Street. He had every intention of dropping Cameron off and heading home for a quick shower and a bite to eat before going back to work. But some indefinable impulse made him shut off the engine and get out.

"I'll grab your clubs," he offered, opening the tailgate of the truck.

"Thanks." Cameron shouldered his backpack and went to unlock the side door.

Sean followed him inside, leaning the clubs against the wall of a small mudroom crowded with shoes in varying sizes, a fold-up baby stroller, a selection of umbrellas and hats, and a basket filled with gloves and mittens. From somewhere in the house, a distant beeping sound pierced the silence.

"Answering machine," Cameron said. "I'd better go check it."

They stepped into the kitchen, and Sean took it all in with a glance. This was the house of his boyhood dreams, but he'd never been inside it. Now here he was, and the whole place seemed to enfold him. The cluttered kitchen had a wooden floor and glass-front cabinets filled with Martha Stewart–style green glassware. A refrigerator was plastered with a calendar, various lists and kids' artwork. As he followed Cameron to the front entranceway, he noticed wood paneling, an imposing staircase, framed pictures of the kids everywhere.

Cameron hit Play on the machine. The first message was from someone who identified herself as Lily. "Hello, Crystal, I was just calling to see how you're doing. I hope you think the meeting went all right, so call me."

"Charlie's teacher," Cameron explained.

She did sound sort of prim and proper, Sean thought, picturing a blue-haired woman with bifocals. "You don't want to tangle with a woman like that," he said, nudging Cameron.

Next: "Crystal, this is Jane Coombs…" In the background, fussy baby noises punctuated the message. "I was expecting Derek to pick Ashley up this afternoon, but he seems to be running late. Anyway, I have a class to teach tonight, so I'd appreciate it if you'd come and get Ashley as soon as you get this message."

"Oh, Mom's going to love that," Cameron said.

The third message was from someone RSVPing for Ashley's birthday party. It seemed strange, like planning a party in a war zone. Sean's younger niece had been born into the turmoil of an exploding marriage, but of the three kids, she was the least affected, too young to understand what she'd lost.

Then Charlie had called the machine. "Pick me up," said a petulant voice. "I'm at Lindsey's house and you said you'd pick me up and you're still not here. Pick me up, you're late."

The final message was nearly unintelligible, but Sean could tell it was from a girl who was more articulate at giggling than at speaking. Clearly, she wanted to talk to Cameron. Just as clearly, he was mortified that she'd called for him. Sean could see the heat of embarrassment in Cameron's red ears, his averted gaze, his hands pushing into the pockets of his jeans.

"End of messages," said the mechanical voice in the machine.

Sean felt a weird tightening of his gut. "Call your mother again."

Cameron shrugged and dialed the phone. "No answer," he said.

"Now your dad."

As he held the phone to his ear a second time, Cameron showed the first sign of worry—a small tick in his jaw. "No answer," he said again. "I've already left them messages."

"Any idea where they might be?"

"Nope."

It figured. Kids tended not to keep tabs on their parents. Now what? Sean wondered.

The phone rang, startling them both. Cameron snatched it up.

"Hello?" His face flashed momentarily with hope, then fell. "Oh, hi, Jane. No, my mom's not here. You can drop Ashley off with me, I guess, since I'm home." A pause. "You're welcome." He hung up. "I have a ton of homework, but I won't get anything done now," Cameron said. "Ashley's a pain in the neck to babysit."

Sean's tiny niece was so cute you'd have to be made of stone not to like her. Babysitting her, though, was another issue entirely. The prospect of looking after a barely verbal toddler was terrifying to Sean. "I bet your mother will be home any minute," he said.

Cameron shrugged again.

"What about Charlie?" Sean asked.

"Sounds like she wants to come home."

"Any idea who Lindsey is? Where she lives?"

"Nope." Cameron looked at the small screen on the phone. "The number's on caller ID."

"I'd better give them a call." Sean punched in the number. A woman's voice answered, and for a moment he blanked, then said, "Ma'am, this is Charlie Holloway's uncle, Sean Maguire. I'm calling about my niece."

"Oh! I'm Nancy Davenport. Would you like to speak with Charlie?"

"Actually, I was just calling to let you know…I'm afraid her mother might not be there to pick her up. She's been…delayed. Charlie's brother is here with me, so I'll come and get her."

"That's no problem," the woman said. "I'll run her home. I haven't started dinner yet."

Sean thanked her and hung up. He looked at Cameron.

"No clue," the boy said, but his gaze shifted to the door and then to the floor, a little too quickly. "My mom's always got something going on. She probably forgot to tell anybody."

Sean wandered into the kitchen. He studied the calendar clipped with magnets to the refrigerator. The current date had a notation. "Conf. w/Lily & D., 3:15 p.m."

"What do you make of this?" he asked Cameron.

"Lily—the teacher on the answering machine. Miss Robinson. She was my third-grade teacher and now Charlie's in her class. Maybe there was a conference with her. Charlie's been doing lousy in school all year." Cameron rolled his eyes. "How does a kid flunk third grade, that's what I'd like to know."

They waited. Talked golf a little, just to fill the silence and maybe distract themselves. "So you have a tournament coming up this weekend," Sean observed, noting the team calendar stuck to the refrigerator with magnets.

Cameron turned away.

"Don't bowl me over with your enthusiasm, okay?" Sean said.

The kid hunched his shoulders even more. "My coach is a dick, okay?"

"Greg Duncan? He seems all right to me."

"Yeah, whatever."

Sean dug in his pocket and took out an Indian head penny. "This was my good luck charm. I've used it as a ball marker since I was younger than you."

Cameron turned, took the penny and examined it. "That's cool."

"You want to borrow it?"

"You just said it's your good luck charm."

"Was. I said 'was.' It kind of deserted me."

Cameron nodded. He knew about the fiasco that had brought Sean home. "Did you like playing over there, in Japan and Indonesia and stuff?"

"Sure, while it lasted." Sean tried to imagine what he'd be doing in his old life as a tour professional in Asia. Once he'd started seeing Asmida, he used to play in Malaysia every chance he got. After a round, there would be far too much drinking and plenty of mindless, gratifying sex in opulent hotel rooms or in expensive cars. It didn't last, of course. How could something like that last? Especially, he remembered with a twinge of pain, with the daughter of a yakuza mobster? No one could ever accuse him of having good judgment, that was for sure. Derek often ragged on him about mapping out a career plan. Of course, in order to do that, Sean needed a career.

Cameron pocketed the token. They called both Derek and Crystal again and got no answer. Cameron drank a slug of milk straight from the carton, then offered some to Sean, who declined.

He didn't like the unfamiliar feeling in his gut. It was a cold, hard squeeze, brief and intense, like a fist of ice. He said nothing to Cameron. No point in worrying the kid.

He took a stroll through the downstairs, checking out the house. This had been Derek's world for more than a decade. It seemed strange that Sean had never been here. He'd been too busy chasing prize money and easy women half a world away, and hadn't bothered to come back even for a visit. There was a big living room and a long hallway where, Sean imagined, Derek had obsessively practiced his putts. The dining room had a table and chairs and a tall glass cabinet that was practically empty, probably because it had once held Derek's favorite trophies. Sean shook his head, thinking about his brother, feeling love and admiration and envy all in the same heavy wave.

"You don't have to stay," Cameron told him. "I can handle the girls."

"That makes one of us, then," Sean said. "I'll stick around until we figure out where your mother went."

Darkness crept down and shadows crowded into the corners of the large, empty rooms. Sean switched on a couple of lamps. The tense quiet in the house was broken when Cameron turned on the radio, tuning it to a hip-hop station.

A few minutes later, a car pulled up, headlights swishing across the living room walls. Sean's gut turned watery with relief. Crystal might not be thrilled to see him, but that was too damned bad. He had a few choice words for her.

His relief evaporated when he saw that the visitor was Jane Coombs, lugging a red-faced Ashley and an overstuffed diaper bag. Sean liked Derek's girlfriend well enough, he supposed, though he barely knew her. At the moment she wasn't looking to be liked. She had that tight-lipped don't-mess-with-me expression people wore when their last nerve was about to snap.

"Oh, hi, Sean," she said, clearly surprised to see him. "I can't believe Crystal stood up her own kid like this. Anyway, here you go." She dumped the baby into his arms. The two-year-old regarded him with apprehension.

"Have you heard from Derek?" Sean asked, shifting the baby awkwardly.

"Not a word. We must've all got our signals crossed. Listen, I'm grotesquely late," Jane continued, "so I need to hurry." Spying Cameron, she said, "Come and get the car seat, will you? God, thanks, you're a lifesaver."

When Ashley saw her brother, she squealed with delight and reached for him. "Cam! Cam!"

"Yeah, I'll be right back," he said, and followed Jane out to her car.

When the baby realized he was walking away, she arched her back and let out a wail that penetrated like an armor piercing bullet.

"Hey, now," said Sean, his chest filling up with panic. "It'll be all right. He's coming back."

She thrashed her head from side to side and cried harder. Her tiny fists alternately clutched Sean's shirt and pummeled him. He was reminded of the creature in *Alien* popping from the stomach of an unsuspecting man. What the hell was it with babies? he wondered feverishly. They were like another life form to him, a dangerous and sinister one at that. She was loud and smelled funky, too. He suspected Jane, in all her self-important rush, had not bothered to check the kid's diaper.

It felt like an eternity before Cameron returned with the car seat. The second Ashley spotted him, she quit yelling and lurched toward him, nearly leaping out of Sean's arms. He clutched the writhing little body to keep her from falling, then quickly handed her over. "I don't think she likes me."

"Naw, she's just cranky. Probably tired and hungry, aren't you, sugar bear?" Cameron jiggled her on his hip. "I'll go get her something to eat."

"'Nana. Want a 'nana," Ashley chortled good-naturedly as he set her down and led her into the kitchen. In a heartbeat, she'd turned from the Tasmanian Devil into an angel. How did she do that so quickly?

A moment later, Charlie came barreling in through the front door, a towheaded dynamo.

"Uncle Sean!"

He caught her up in his arms. Her wiry limbs felt surprisingly strong, and something—her hair or skin—had a bubblegum smell. This was more his speed, a niece who actually liked him. "Hey, short stuff. How you doing?"

"I'm starving to death," she said, clutching her stomach and reeling in his arms. "Where's Mom?"

He set her down carefully, keeping his hands on her shoulders. "I'm going to be staying with you until your mom gets back."

She gave him a look of skepticism, narrowing her eyes and twirling one pigtail with her finger. "Really?"

"Yeah. You got a problem with that?"

"Maybe I do." She yelled with delight as he chased her to the kitchen.

There, the baby was happily cramming a chunk of banana into her mouth. Charlie helped herself to one. "Did you know monkeys peel bananas like this, from the bottom up?" She demonstrated.

"I guess that makes you a monkey."

"I wish I *was* a monkey," Charlie said.

"You look like one," Cameron said.

Charlie stuck her tongue out at him.

"Monkey," Ashley echoed around a mouthful of banana.

"Why do you wish you were a monkey?" asked Sean.

"Then I wouldn't have to go to yucky, sucky school."

"Sucky," Ashley said.

Sean looked at Cameron. "Is she allowed to say that?"

"Probably not."

Sean turned to Charlie. "Don't say sucky."

"Okay." Charlie bit into her banana.

"Sucky," Ashley said again.

"I'll be right back." Sean hurried out of the kitchen and went to the phone in the front hall. He picked up the handset and glared at it. What the hell was going on? This was starting to be truly…sucky. He wondered how long he should wait before getting seriously worried.

With a scowl, he dialed Derek's cell phone. Derek always answered his phone, always checked his messages. When the voice mail clicked on, Sean said, "Hey, bro, it's me. I'm here with your kids at Crystal's house, and she's not home. What's going on? Call me." He found Crystal's number by the phone, got her voice mail and left a similar message. He wished, just briefly, that he knew her better. He wished he knew if she was the sort of woman who would temporarily forget her kids.

Now what? he wondered. He tried Maura. He didn't know why. His girlfriend barely knew Derek and had never met Crystal and the kids. The people in his life didn't know one another. His connections with family were disparate and shallow, something that had never occurred to him until now.

"Dr. Riley," she answered with crisp efficiency. A fourth-year medical student, she was working at Portland's Legacy West Hospital this year.

"Hey, Doc, it's me."

"Sean!" A smile brightened her voice. "What's up?"

"I'm not sure. I'm with my brother Derek's kids. There was some mix-up and their parents are MIA."

"So call them and—"

"I can't get hold of either one of them."

"Well, then…look, I'm in the middle of rounds. And I'm staying in the city for a seminar, did I tell you that? Can I call you in a few?"

"Sure, whenever. Bye." He had no idea what he expected

her to do. She didn't even know these kids. This sure as hell wasn't her problem.

Ashley was yelling and banging something in the kitchen. Cameron had turned the radio up loud again.

Sean hit the caller ID button on the phone and looked at the display. The first came up Private, the second was "Coombs, Jane." The next one was "Robinson, Lily."

The schoolmarm, he thought. There was something vaguely familiar about the name. Maybe he'd met her before, though he doubted it. He tended not to hang out with school-marms, but maybe that was about to change.

"Help me out here, Miss Robinson," he muttered as he dialed the number.

chapter 7

Friday
7:30 p.m.

Lily sighed with contentment and snuggled down into her favorite overstuffed chair. There was a large bowl of popcorn and a glass of red wine on the table beside her. On the coffee table in front of her, a map of Italy lay spread out with the sinuous route of the Sorrentine Peninsula highlighted in yellow. The names of the towns, which she'd circled in red, came from story and legend—Positano, Amalfi, Ravello, Vietri Sul Mare.

Two more months, she thought. Then summer would be here and she'd go jetting off on an adventure she'd been dreaming about for half a year. She'd be all by herself, gloriously, blissfully alone.

Her colleagues at school thought it odd that she loved to travel solo, but for Lily, making her own way and answering to no one were her favorite parts of the adventure. Her annual summer trip was hugely important to her. It always had been.

Travel gave her balance and perspective and made her feel like a different person. It occurred to her to wonder why she would want to be a different person, but she didn't think too hard about that.

She loved seeing new places and making new friends. Crystal always asked her what was wrong with the old ones. Nothing, Lily thought, except that sometimes they made you do exhausting emotional work. Lily was good at a lot of things, but not at nurturing the deep, sometimes painful bonds of true intimacy. Life simply hadn't prepared her for that. She could understand the heart of a child, could find ways to inspire and teach, but she'd never been capable of taking a headlong plunge into lifelong commitment. Some people, she had long ago decided, were not cut out for the dizzying, dangerous adventure of loving someone until it hurt.

That didn't mean she was immune to the occasional pang of yearning. Maybe she'd even have a romantic fling this summer. A flirtation, free of complications and commitments. It was supposed to be easy to do in Italy. At the end of summer, she would return to Comfort refreshed and ready to greet a new crop of students.

This, the cycle of school year and summer, was the rhythm of her life, and it made perfect sense to her. She had only to look at her own family to know she was right. Following a tragedy that was both shrouded in mystery and publicly recorded, her parents had spent their entire marriage making each other miserable. They were still at it to this day.

Lily had taken the lesson to heart and plotted out her life carefully. Her younger sister, Violet, had taken the opposite route, opting for an early marriage and two kids, a husband who earned too little money and a large rental house in Tigard they couldn't afford.

By comparison, Lily had a job she loved, a small but comfortable place of her own and the freedom to do as she pleased. She meant to keep her life this way, quiet and safe.

You're all alone, said an inner voice.

She ignored the voice, which sounded remarkably like Crystal, and sipped her wine as she read an article about a ceramics shop in Ravello where Hillary Clinton and Dustin Hoffman ordered their dishes. After a while, she set aside the map and glanced at the clock. Her usual Friday night routine was a movie at the Echo Ridge Pavilion, but the rain had started up again, and she didn't feel like going out.

A guilty pleasure video, then, she thought, perusing her DVD collection. That was another advantage to being a free agent. If she had a man in her life, she probably wouldn't be choosing something like *Steel Magnolias* or *Two Moon Junction.* To her knowledge, no man in history had ever willingly sat through *Sense and Sensibility.*

She narrowed her choices down to *Under the Tuscan Sun,* which would get her in the mood for Italy, and *Bull Durham,* about a sexually liberated schoolteacher getting it on with Kevin Costner in his prime. She thought about his famous speech about kisses that last for three weeks, and the decision was made.

As she was watching the opening credits, the phone rang. "Great timing," she muttered, but stopped the disc and went to get the phone. Crystal, probably, calling to talk about Charlie.

Just the thought brought a heaviness to Lily's heart. Ordinarily, school and personal matters were kept strictly separate, but in this case, they intersected. Her best friend, and her best friend's precious daughter.

It seemed to amuse Charlie that she knew her teacher outside of school. The little girl usually got a secret smile on her face when she called Lily "Miss Robinson," but she never took advantage of her intimate knowledge of her teacher's personal life. In school, Charlie tried not to draw attention to herself at all. Which was why this current habit of stealing was so alarming.

"Hello?"

"Uh, yeah. Is this Miss Robinson?" The male voice was deep and strong, completely unfamiliar.

"I'm afraid I don't accept solicitation calls," she said crisply, and started to put down the phone.

"I'm not—wait. This is about Crystal Holloway."

Lily frowned and cradled the receiver against her cheek. Was Crystal seeing someone? Last time they talked about it, Crystal said she was swearing off men once and for all. "I blame men for all my troubles," she'd said dramatically, not long ago.

"Don't you mean one man specifically?" Lily had asked.

"No, actually." Crystal hadn't elaborated.

"Who is this?" Lily asked the caller.

"Sean Maguire. I'm Charlie's uncle."

Ah, yes, Lily thought. The fabled Uncle Sean, one of Charlie's favorite topics for show-and-tell. Since he'd moved back to town, Charlie had related several overly long stories about him, but the main point always got lost in translation. Hero worship was usually the topic.

According to Crystal, Sean was cut from the same cloth as Derek, "only younger."

Lily had the vaguest memories of him from the Holloways' wedding. He had reminded her of Brad Pitt in his first movie, but that only made her dislike him more. "Never trust a pretty man," Crystal had once told her.

"Hello?" His smooth, somewhat disturbing voice intruded on her thoughts.

"Mr. Maguire," Lily said. "What can I do for you?"

"I'm not exactly sure." There was a muffled sound, as though he was intimately cupping his hand around the mouthpiece. "I'm here at Crystal's house, watching her kids. She's not home yet."

"I see." What a loser, she thought. Couldn't look after his own flesh and blood without calling for help. "And how can I help you?" she asked.

"I figured you might know where she is." Tension crackled in his voice.

"Well, I don't," Lily said. "You should call her cell phone. I can give you her number, or you can get it from the kids—"

"I've been trying her cell phone all evening," he broke in. "She doesn't answer. Derek doesn't answer his, either."

Lily's grip tightened on the receiver. She frowned, causing her glasses to inch down her nose. "That's not like either of them." With three kids and two households, both Crystal and Derek were vigilant about making sure they could be reached at all times. They had tormented each other through separation and divorce, but to their credit, they'd tried to shield the kids from the worst of it.

"I agree," said the stranger.

"When was the last time you were in touch with them?"

"As near as I can tell, you were the last one to speak with them," he said, and Lily wondered if she detected a hint of accusation in his voice. "Crystal forgot to pick up Cameron from the golf course and Charlie from her friend's house. Do you have any idea what's going on?"

Now the phone felt damp and slick in Lily's hand. "No. I'm afraid I don't."

"I see. Well, then." He made an impatient sound, clearly about to hang up. "Thanks, I guess."

Lily flashed on the notion of hanging up and going back to her movie. Finishing her wine and reading up on the Amalfi Coast. Now, however, that was no longer a possibility. She would simply worry about Crystal and the kids all night.

"Why did you call me, Mr. Maguire?" she asked.

"I heard your message on the answering machine, so I figured you might know something."

She wondered what Crystal would think of her ex-brother-in-law, in her home, listening to her messages. "Well, I don't know where she is. Sorry."

"All right. Just thought I'd ask. I have a night job, and I figured—never mind. I'll call in and let them know I can't make it."

"Mr. Maguire—" Lily broke off when she realized he'd hung up. "Nice," she muttered, setting down the phone. She paced back and forth, trying to decide what to do. A few minutes ago, this was her living room, her refuge, a cozy place filled with books and one shelf of framed photographs. A favorite shot of her and Crystal, laughing on the beach in front of Haystack Rock, caught her eye. Something was the matter, Lily knew it in her heart.

As she grabbed her purse and rummaged for her keys, she glanced in the hall tree mirror. "Nice," she said again with an even more sarcastic inflection.

She was dressed for DVD night in heather-gray yoga pants and an oversize hockey jersey, which was the only thing of value left behind by Trent Atkins of the Portland Trailblazers. He hadn't been a serious boyfriend, just someone she'd gone out with a few times. She couldn't remember why a basketball player was in possession of a hockey jersey and decided she didn't care.

She wore no makeup and her brown hair was caught back in a scrunchy. So what? she thought, pushing her feet into a pair of red rubber gardening clogs and donning a rain hat, thus completing the look. "Early frump" might be a good term for it.

Like that mattered, she thought, grabbing her raincoat and dashing out the door.

chapter 8

Friday
7:40 p.m.

Sean Maguire wasn't pretty anymore, Lily observed the moment she opened the door. He was utterly, undeservedly, unjustly devastating. He was what the girls at school liked to call the whole package, in perfectly faded jeans that hugged his body, a golf shirt with the Echo Ridge logo, a lock of hair falling negligently over his brow and contrasting with the piercing blue of his eyes, a five o'clock shadow outlining the strong lines of his facial structure. He had a mouth that made her think about Kevin Costner's *Bull Durham* speech, but at the moment, Maguire wasn't smiling.

"I was hoping you'd be Crystal," he said, holding open the door.

How gracious of him.

"Lily Robinson," she said in her most prim tone. She always sounded insufferably prim when she felt defensive, and she always felt defensive around devastating men. She definitely felt that way now, as she stood dripping on the door-mat. Her Totes rain hat was functional though hardly attractive, with its deep brim currently serving as a rain gutter. A steady drip trickled down, right between her eyes, splashing on the mat.

She took off the hat and hung it on a hook behind the door, admonishing herself not to feel self-conscious as she surrendered her coat. He towered over her, even taller than his older brother. Against her will, Lily felt a brief, subtle spasm of reaction to his nearness. He was just a guy, she reminded herself. If not for the kids, they'd have nothing to do with each other.

"Where are the kids?" she asked, removing her fogged-up glasses.

"Upstairs. I told them there's probably some mix-up in the plans. The girls are watching a video and Cameron's watching them."

Or more likely, thought Lily, he was watching instant messages on the Internet. Clearly this man knew nothing about children.

"Any word from Crystal or Derek?" She finished polishing her glasses and put them back on.

"None." He shot a glance at the stairs. "Let's go in the kitchen."

That was all. No "thanks for coming." He was worried, she conceded. So was she.

As Lily followed him, she couldn't help but notice the absolute perfection of his butt. Crystal had mentioned his golf career was on the skids. With that butt, he could always turn into a Levi's model.

A moment later, she realized he'd turned around and caught her staring. Mortified, she shifted her gaze to a stack of three pizza boxes on the cluttered table.

"Want some?" he asked.

For a moment she felt disoriented and a bit flustered. "No, no thanks."

"So here's a rundown," he said, hooking his thumbs into his rear pockets and pacing. "Derek's fiancée, Jane, has no idea where he is."

"She's his fiancée?" Lily felt her stomach lurch. Crystal didn't know that. If she did, Lily would have been the first to hear of it. Actually, the whole town probably would have heard the screams.

"I guess. As of last weekend, they made it official."

"When was he planning to tell Crystal?" Lily sat down on a stool at the breakfast bar. She eyed the pizza boxes again, but felt too nervous to eat. Especially pizza. She hadn't eaten pizza in ages. It was a nutritional nightmare, and stuffing herself with carbs and fats wouldn't help anything.

Over the years, she'd spent countless hours in this kitchen, sipping herbal tea with organic honey and a slice of orange, savoring the company of her best friend. It felt weird being here with a stranger, speculating.

"Oh, God," she said. "I bet he told her today. Maybe that's why they didn't come home."

"Why would they disappear with their cell phones turned off?"

"They probably drove somewhere out of range."

He turned and looked at her, one eyebrow lowered in skepticism. How did he do that with just one? she wondered.

"I don't get it," he said.

He wouldn't.

"Think about it. If Derek remarries, these kids' lives are going to change drastically. Crystal and Derek have got a lot to talk about." She didn't elaborate. Maybe Maguire knew more about the situation, maybe he didn't. Lily didn't see it as her place to enlighten him.

"I can't believe they'd just take off without checking in with the kids," he said quietly, as though talking to himself.

She drummed her fingers on the counter. An unexplained disappearance wasn't impossible. In the final years of their marriage, Derek and Crystal had been known as the Scott and Zelda Fitzgerald of the PGA, with a reputation for partying, passion and public rows. They had a way of focusing on each other with total absorption, letting the world fall away as they went at each other. It wasn't too much of a stretch to imagine them so caught up that they temporarily forgot the kids.

Love did strange things to people, Lily reflected, then shivered with the next thought. Had they harmed each other?

She forced herself to ask the hardest question of the night. "Have you called the police?"

He winced. "Yes. I told them the make and model of both cars. There hasn't been any report of an accident from the highway patrol."

A small measure of relief seeped through her. "I'm glad to hear that. So are they out searching?"

He shook his head. "No. Once they established that Derek and Crystal are adults with no medical conditions, they put me off. Twenty-four hours seems to be the magic number."

"This is not going to take twenty-four hours," Lily said, pushing her hand into her pocket to keep from biting her nail.

"So now what?" Sean asked.

Before she could reply, a crash sounded upstairs, followed by a loud, angry cry from Ashley.

Both Sean and Lily ran to the stairs. He took them two at a time and she followed close behind.

Crystal had remodeled the upstairs some years ago, creating a common playroom for the kids' toys, plus a nook for a TV and their own computer. Now Lily found Ashley sitting beside a broken bean-pot lamp and howling while Charlie looked on with a tight-lipped disapproval that eerily resembled Crystal. At the computer, Cameron ignored them both as colorful instant-messaging boxes cluttered the screen. They didn't completely manage to mask the browser window with the ominous title, "Porn Ponies."

Lily took this all in with a glance. She reached down and scooped Ashley into her arms. She'd always felt proprietary toward Crystal's children. "Hiya, sweetie," she said in a soothing whisper. "Are you all right?"

The child's sobbing subsided. Then she looked at Sean and howled again. "Don't like you," she wailed.

He turned his hands palms up. "I never did a thing to her," he said.

"I like you, Uncle Sean," Charlie said, climbing him like a tree. "Hello, Lily." Outside of school, she was allowed to call her teacher Lily. She hung upside down on Sean's arm and offered a gap-toothed grin.

"How's my big girl?" Lily patted the baby's back.

"We're waiting for Mom," Charlie said.

"I know." Lily sidled over to Cameron. "Lose the Porn Ponies," she murmured. "Now."

"Porn Ponies?" Sean scowled. "You were looking at porn on the Internet?"

"He always looks at porn," Charlie said, dropping to the floor.

"Do not," Cameron said.

"Do so." She stuck out her tongue at him. "You look at it so much, I bet your pornograph machine's going to break."

"Moron." He clicked the mouse and the screen went black. Ashley stopped crying and stuck her thumb in her mouth.

Note to self, thought Lily. Check parental controls on the computer.

"What are you doing here, Lily?" Charlie asked. "If you came to see my mom, she's not home yet."

"Tell you what," Lily said. "You and Cameron get that lamp cleaned up. Your uncle will help you. I'm going to get our little friend here ready for bed."

Ashley's mouth made a popping sound as she removed her thumb. "No bed," she said, and put her thumb back.

"You're right. You need a bath first, you smelly little thing."

As she carried the baby to the bathroom, Lily buried her concern behind a smile. She chattered cheerfully away as she ran a shallow bath and peeled off Ashley's clothes and diaper. The bathroom was cluttered with brightly colored plastic toys and bottles of shampoo and bubble bath, combs and toothbrushes, barrettes and mismatched towels.

Crystal always made this look so easy, Lily reflected, trying to keep hold of the squirming child while opening a bottle of baby shampoo. Lily couldn't abide the thought of letting go of Ashley or looking away for a single second, so she opened the cap with her teeth. The taste of baby shampoo filled her mouth.

"Ptooey," she said, wiping her mouth on her shoulder.

Ashley laughed at her and splashed her hands on the surface of the water.

And to think the evening had started out with Italy, wine and Kevin Costner in his prime, thought Lily. Now, with every moment that passed, her conviction that her best friend was missing tightened in her chest.

Missing. There could be no other explanation. Something was terribly wrong.

chapter 9

Friday
9:00 p.m.

Sean stood in the kitchen and contemplated the empty pizza boxes. Nearly empty. He picked up the last piece of hamburger-black olive and stuffed it in his mouth. Whoever heard of hamburger-black olive? That had been Charlie's suggestion. It wasn't half bad, he thought, wiping his hand on his pants.

Upstairs, it was quiet at last. Lily Robinson had taken charge. The baby was asleep, and Lily and Charlie were reading a book together in Charlie's bed.

Miss Lily Robinson to the rescue. She was not the heavy-set, blue-haired schoolmarm he'd expected. She just had the personality of one. Still, Sean was grateful that she'd come to help out.

Cameron was back on the Internet, probably surfing for porn even though Sean had warned him not to. Sean had come downstairs to dispose of the broken lamp and clean up the kitchen.

Pizza boxes had been designed, he decided, by someone who had never taken out the trash. There was no way to fit one into a receptacle. He set it on the floor, stepped on it and then folded it in half once, twice, then crammed the cardboard into the kitchen trash can, shoving it down with his foot. He repeated the process for the second box, then the third.

When Lily walked into the kitchen, Sean had one foot in the trash can and his mouth full of pizza. She eyed him as though he were one of the kids in her schoolroom, not with dislike or disapproval, but with a kind of bemused tolerance that made him want to misbehave.

This was the gift of a schoolmarm, he thought. With one look, she could make a grown man feel an inch tall.

He managed to swallow the last of the pizza and extract his foot with a tug, hopping backward and grabbing a chair to keep from falling.

"Hey," he said, acting casual, crossing his foot at the ankle. "The kids in bed?"

"The girls are. Charlie just fell asleep. Cameron's doing homework."

"I'm calling the police again," Sean said.

"I think you should." Her face was pale, and she kept worrying a silver-and-turquoise ring around her finger.

She wasn't bad-looking behind those thick glasses, Sean reflected as he picked up the phone. For a marm.

He hit Redial and got the now-familiar recorded menu of options, pressing three before the falsely soothing canned voice finished the instructions.

"This is Officer Brad Henley."

"I'm calling for Officer…" Sean consulted the name he'd jotted down. Unable to find a piece of paper, he'd written it in ballpoint pen on the palm of his hand. Lily said nothing but frowned at the hand.

"Nordquist," Sean said.

"Gone for the day," Henley said in a bored voice.

Great, they'd changed shifts.

"This is in regard to a matter I called about earlier," Sean said. "My name is Sean Maguire."

"Uh-huh. What can I do for you?"

"I called about my brother, Derek Holloway, and his ex-wife, Crystal." Sean listened to the silence for a few seconds.

"Yeah, okay. I see it in the call log here. What can I do for you, Mr. Maguire?"

Find them, he wanted to scream into the phone. Find them and bring them home so I can get back to my life. My sorry-ass life. Which, if things go okay at the tournament next week, I might just have a shot at getting back on track.

"I still don't know where they are. There's been no word of them." Sean glanced over at Lily, who watched him with a furrow of worry on her brow. The conversation felt slightly surreal as he said, "My brother's missing and so is his ex. You ought to be out searching for them."

Another pause. Sean could hear the tap of a keyboard. "Do either of them have any type of medical problem or impairment that—"

"I answered all this before," Sean said, fighting to keep his voice down. "They're both in perfect health, sound of mind and body. Which is why it's completely unlike them to disappear."

"Sir, at this time, it's not an emergent situation and we can't give it airtime or attempt to locate missing adults."

"Why not?"

"Because they're never missing," the cop said wryly. "I'll put the info out on the city channel for now."

"What's that?"

"Dispatchers' network."

"There are three children involved," Sean reminded him. "Do you have that in your notes?"

"Are they in any danger?" the cop asked.

"No. Absolutely not."

"Then I can't—" There was a pause on the line. "Is your brother Derek Holloway, the golfer?"

Celebrity had its perks, Sean thought. "The very same."

"Well, we can't do an attempt-to-locate at this time, but I'll send someone out," said Henley. "What's the address?"

Sean looked up at Lily. "Address?" he mouthed.

She handed him an envelope from the pile of mail on the table.

Good thinking. At least one of them could still think. He read the address into the phone.

"Someone will be right out," he reported to Lily after he hung up.

"When?"

"He said right away. I assume that means immediately."

"What if it doesn't?"

Sean felt a tic leap in his jaw. "Look, right away means right away. Like now."

"You don't have to snap at me."

"I didn't snap at you."

"Yes, you did. And you're still doing it."

"Hey, I don't need a scolding here."

"I wasn't scolding." She sniffed. "I just don't like being snapped at."

"I didn't—" Sean forced himself to stop. It was idiotic, bickering with this woman while Derek was God-knows-where. "Okay," he said, getting up to pace some more. "All right, I'm sorry. I didn't mean to snap."

She turned to the sink and started rinsing the dishes. "I'm every bit as worried as you are, Mr. Maguire."

"Sean. Call me Sean."

She opened the dishwasher and rolled out the rack. "Why should I do that?"

"Because I'm sure as hell not going to call you Miss Robinson, *Lily.*"

She pivoted away sharply and began to load the dishwasher. He checked messages on his cell phone, finding nothing new there. Lily lined up the plates in the rack and separated the silverware into baskets according to category—all the forks in one, the spoons in another. She was stymied by a spatula until she laid it carefully in the top rack. Then she put in the glasses, upending each one according to height. Finally she picked up the box of soap powder and appeared to be reading the directions.

"You need some help with that?" he asked, putting away his phone.

"No. It's just that I've never used this brand before. It says 'super concentrated' so I think I might need less. Ah, here we go. Two ounces for the normal cycle." She opened a drawer and rummaged around inside it. "Now, two ounces. I believe that's the equivalent of two level tablespoons…."

Sean couldn't help it. He snatched the box of detergent from her, dumped some of it into the trap until it overflowed, then snapped the thing shut. Finally, he closed the dishwasher and gave the knob a twist until he heard the shudder of running water.

When he straightened up, he saw her staring at him as though he'd crossed some line with her. Hell, maybe he had.

He spied a stray coffee mug on the counter. Its rim bore a half moon of lipstick. Without taking his eyes off her, he opened the dishwasher and stuck it in haphazardly, then shut the machine again, pushing the door with his hip.

"There," he said. "That's done."

"Thank you," she said faintly.

"I guess I could take out the trash," he said, gesturing at the overflowing receptacle.

"I believe the cans are in the garage. You'll want to make sure the lid's on tight to discourage raccoons."

"Yes, ma'am," he said with exaggerated courtesy. He picked up the kitchen garbage and headed out the back door. When he turned to close it, he saw Lily Robinson open the dishwasher and carefully put the coffee mug in its proper place.

chapter 10

Friday
9:25 p.m.

In a way, thought Lily, Sean Maguire was a blessing. He was so incredibly obnoxious that he distracted her from worrying herself to the point of despair. So she supposed he was good for something.

When he came in from taking out the trash, she didn't acknowledge him. She was busy clearing off the countertops in order to give them a good cleaning.

It wasn't like this was a social situation, anyway, she thought, feeling unaccountably defensive. They wouldn't have a thing to do with each other if not for the bizarre situation they found themselves in.

"I'm going to go check on Cameron," he said.

"That's probably a good idea." She set down the bottle of Windex. "So how worried is he?"

"Plenty. It's completely unlike Derek to just take off without explanation."

"Crystal would never do that, either."

"Oh, no?" He lifted one eyebrow. "She left them overnight at Derek's two weeks ago."

"That's different. She missed a flight and she was completely in touch by phone the whole time. Listen, Crystal's my best friend. I've known her since I was Charlie's age. She's a good mother, and I'm sure there's an explanation for whatever's going on."

He studied her hard, with a blue-eyed gaze that probed almost insultingly. "Have we met before?"

She went back to cleaning the countertops. "Why do you ask?"

"You seem familiar to me."

She finished the counter and moved on to the range top. She found plenty of spattered grease to attack there. Crystal had never been the world's greatest housekeeper. When she was married to Derek, it hadn't mattered because they employed full-time help. Now Crystal was on her own.

"We were both in their wedding," she told Sean.

"Oh." He looked blank.

"Sixteen years ago," she reminded him. "I was just a kid," she added. "You wouldn't remember me."

He snapped his fingers. "As a matter of fact, I do. I made fun of your glasses and braces. 'When do train tracks have four eyes?' Remember? I thought that was so hilarious."

She scrubbed furiously around a knob. "You were a real charmer."

"I was a punk," he said easily. "You should have told me to get lost."

"I believe I did just that." Agitated, she moved on to the cabinet faces, spritzing the entire row above the counter. When she came to the end of the row, Maguire stood in the way, leaning back against the counter. He didn't move, so she spritzed him, too.

"Oops," she said. "Sorry."

He caught hold of her wrist and gently took the Windex bottle away from her. "Tell you what, Lily," he said. "Let's both go talk to Cameron."

His touch drew a quick, shocked gasp from Lily. She pulled away and cradled her wrist in her other hand.

"All right," she said, ducking her head. To her dismay, a hot blush crept up into her cheeks. How stupid was that? He'd barely touched her, and she was acting like a complete Sabine.

She told herself to get a grip, but the fact was, good-looking men intimidated her. She was always convinced they were making fun of her. It was ridiculous, at her age, to feel that way, but she couldn't seem to stop herself. No wonder she preferred third-graders.

The phone rang. Sean snatched it up, spoke briefly to the caller and then hung up. "They found Crystal's car. Dead in the school parking lot. What do you make of that?"

"It means they're probably together."

"At least we have something to tell Cameron."

They found Cameron with a biology book open on the desk in front of him, but he was staring at the clock rather than studying.

"Hey, sport." Sean went over to the desk and leaned against the edge of it.

Lily had to admit he seemed relaxed and natural around Cameron. Like her, he was being careful not to appear frantic.

"Got a minute?" Sean asked his nephew.

"Who was on the phone? What's going on?"

"Well, for one thing, your mom's car has a dead battery and

she left it in the parking lot of Charlie's school. So now we're guessing your dad gave her a ride."

"A ride to where? Chicago? They've been gone for hours."

"We don't know where they are yet, but we're going to find out. The police are going to drop by and get some more information from us."

"When? When are the police coming?"

"They said they'd send someone right away," Lily said.

"What's that mean, right away?"

Sean looked over at Lily. "I swear, you two…soon, okay? And I'm sure they're going to want to talk to you."

"I can't tell them anything," Cameron said, closing the textbook with an angry thud. "All I know is my loser mother didn't show—"

"Cameron," Lily broke in. "Watch what you say about your mother." She bit her tongue to keep from taking the thought further. She was thinking of how guilty he'd feel if he found out something terrible had happened.

"I can say what I want," he retorted.

"Don't snap at her," Sean warned.

"I wasn't snapping."

"Yes, you were. And you're still doing it."

The doorbell rang and the three of them froze. Then, as one, they broke for the stairs and hurried to answer the door.

chapter 11

Friday
10:00 p.m.

This sucks hind tit, thought Cameron, eyeing the cops sitting at the kitchen table. Having two parents missing was actually worse than having them both in your face.

There was a guy and a woman. The guy looked young and kind of geeky, taking notes on some sort of Blackberry device. The woman was older, with a calm demeanor and the no-nonsense air of a math teacher.

Uncle Sean was jumpy but gave them straightforward answers to their questions. Unfortunately, he was clueless. He'd known Cameron's dad longer than anybody, but didn't have the first idea of where he might have gone. Lily was trying to act brave, but Cameron could tell she was freaking. Behind her thick-lensed glasses, her eyes seemed too bright, as though she had a fever. She'd bitten off the fingernails of one hand and would probably start on the other when no one was looking.

As for Cameron, he was pretty ticked off by the whole situation. It was probably nothing, just a stupid mix-up. It wouldn't be the first time his parents caused some big idiotic mess, getting everyone all freaked for nothing. They'd been doing it for years. Just because they were divorced didn't mean they'd stop.

"So they left the school at three-forty-five," said Officer Vessey, the guy with the Blackberry.

Lily nodded, her brown ponytail bouncing like a cheerleader's. "Yes. I went to the faculty lounge to talk with my school principal, and I looked at the clock that hangs over the coffeemaker. It was three-forty-five."

"Do either Mr. Holloway or his ex-wife suffer from any incapacitating medical condition?"

Everyone looked blank. Officer Franklin said, "Sometimes that accounts for a disappearance."

"They're both fine," Cameron said, and it came out sounding belligerent. Too bad, he thought.

Sean said, "You already have that information."

"Miss Robinson, did you see them leave together?" asked Officer Franklin, unfazed.

Lily took a sip of her herbal tea. Mom always kept a box of assorted weird tea on hand for her. Lily was a health nut, and chamomile tea was probably the strongest thing she ever put into her body. No wonder she bit off all her fingernails.

"They left my classroom together," Lily said. "They walked out of the building at the same time. I didn't actually see them get into Derek's car together."

"Would it have surprised you, seeing them drive off together?"

Lily didn't like the question. Cameron could tell by the way she shifted in her seat.

"I suppose. But maybe not. They both take very laudable interest in their children. Now that we know Crystal's car had a dead battery, we know why they drove off in the SUV. It makes perfect sense."

"And what was their state of mind? Can you describe that to us?"

Lily flicked a quick glance at Cameron. He put on a bored expression, like he didn't give a crap.

"Well, as I said before, it wasn't a happy meeting. Their daughter Charlene has been struggling in school."

Like that was a surprise, thought Cameron.

"Were they contentious at the meeting?"

Lily lifted her hand to chew on her nail, then seemed to think better of it and tucked it under her leg. "I wouldn't say 'contentious.' Strained, maybe. Listen, if you're trying to figure out if they were apt to harm each other—physically—the answer is no. Absolutely not."

"You're sure of that."

It was creepy as hell, Cameron thought, the way these cops assumed the worst of his parents. It must be such a drag, being a cop. You had to deal with people at the worst moments of their lives, and you never got to see their good side.

"As sure as I can be," Lily said. "I told you, I've known Crystal since she was thirteen and I was eight. We're as close as sisters, maybe closer. I'm her children's godmother and she is a gentle, loving, reasonable person."

Cameron sensed his uncle's skepticism. He didn't exactly roll his eyes but shifted in his chair and let out a restless sigh. He tried as hard as he could to feel absolutely nothing, just a cool sense of wait-and-see. It was getting tougher by the minute, though. He was starting to wish he hadn't eaten so much pizza earlier. The way his stomach felt, it was threatening to make an encore appearance.

The cops stayed focused on Lily, like maybe she was holding something back. "Miss Robinson, how long have you known Derek Holloway?"

"Since they got engaged about seventeen years ago. I can't say I was ever close to him, and since the divorce, I've only seen him in my role as Charlie's teacher."

"What was your opinion of him?"

Go ahead and say it, Cameron thought. You hated his guts.

"He adores his children," Lily said. "I don't believe he would ever harm Crystal."

"And you have no idea where they might be right now."

"None," said Lily. "It's completely unlike Crystal to fail to come home to her kids." There was a hitch in Lily's voice, and the sound of it stabbed into Cameron.

He felt defensive, prodded to speak up. "It wouldn't be the first time," he said.

Everyone swung to face him. You could hear the *shush* of the dishwasher in the stillness. Cameron felt his ears turning red. "She blew us off last month when her flight from Denver was delayed."

"She called to say she would be late," Lily stated in her know-it-all teacher voice.

"Yeah, but only after she was like four hours late, and Dad had already left town, too, for a tournament." Cameron bristled with resentment. "I had to give the girls their supper and put them to bed." He couldn't help it. He glanced at the clock over the stove. Way more than four hours had passed. He wondered if he should say anything more. As the one person who had witnessed his parents' marriage from a front-row seat, he knew things no one else possibly could.

"That's completely different." Uncle Sean spoke up, sounding more calm and reasonable than any of them. "Someone knew where they both were."

Then it was his turn to be interviewed. "Mr. Maguire, can you characterize your relationship with your brother?"

Cameron ground his teeth in frustration. Here they were reviewing the history of his wacko family when they should be out searching for his parents. But where? Where?

Sean's jaw developed a tic and Cameron sensed his impatience, too. He took a deep breath. "We're half brothers. We have the same mother. His father passed away in the sixties and our mother married my father. We both grew up right here in Comfort. Both played golf, both went pro. I joined the Asian Tour and Derek kept his PGA card. I moved back here and I'm working at the country club."

Cameron knew there was a lot more to that story. A whole lot more. Like the fact that Dad's father had never been married to his mother and was broke when he died. And the fact that Grandma had married Patrick Maguire just six months later. And Uncle Sean was born just a few months after that. But that was all ancient history. It probably wouldn't help them figure out where his parents had gone.

Something not so ancient burned inside him like a bleeding ulcer. He was never meant to know about Ashley, but he'd found out and now the weight of that crushed him. It wasn't his to tell, he reminded himself, especially to a room full of strangers.

"When was the last time you saw your brother?" the cop asked Sean.

"Last night. He came into the clubhouse for a drink, and we talked."

"Did you get any sense that there was a problem?" asked Officer Franklin. "Any issues between your brother and his ex-wife?"

Just that they hated each other, Cameron thought bitterly. Just that they kept secrets from each other.

"None at all," said Sean. "Crystal is the mother of his children, and he's always been good to her."

It was on the tip of Cameron's tongue to address that statement, but he said nothing. He couldn't do it. He simply couldn't imagine talking to strangers about stuff he barely let himself think about. Besides, he could be wrong.

Now it was Lily's turn to get skeptical. She didn't exactly roll her eyes, but she pursed her lips as if thinking, "Uh-huh. I'm so sure."

The kitchen phone shrilled suddenly. Cameron's heart leaped. Everybody around the table jumped at the handset. Cameron grabbed it first. He was the one who lived here, after all.

"Hello."

"Cameron, it's Jane."

Great, he thought. He looked at the four expectant faces around the table. "Jane," he said.

"Derek's girlfriend," Uncle Sean explained to the cops.

"Do you know where my dad is?" Cameron asked her.

"Actually," she said, "I was calling you with the same question."

Cameron felt his hopes deflate like a pricked balloon. "I think you should probably come over," he told her in a dull voice. "He and my mom haven't come home and the police are here asking questions."

There was a brief, fragile silence, and then she made a terrible sound, like there was something caught in her throat.

"Jane?" Cameron asked.

"I—um, I'll come right over."

"Girlfriend?" asked Officer Franklin.

"They're very close," Uncle Sean explained. He glanced at Cameron.

"You can talk about it in front of me. It's not like I didn't know," Cameron said, trying to regain his equilibrium after the phone call. He preferred bored impatience to sick dread any day. "She was going to move in with him."

"Does your mother know this?" asked Lily in an edgy voice.

Cameron shrugged. "I didn't tell her. I guess Dad was going to eventually."

A short while later, Jane burst in without knocking. She had really short blond hair and sharp features, and at the moment she smelled faintly of cigarette smoke. She never smoked around Cameron and the girls.

Cameron knew his mother smoked sometimes, too. Last fall, as they were finalizing the divorce, he found her on the back steps late one night, smoking a Marlboro and flicking a lighter on and off, watching the flame.

She'd turned to him with the saddest smile he'd ever seen. "Don't ever smoke, baby," she'd said to him in a tired, husky voice. "It just tells people when you're unhappy."

"Got it, Mom. Never let on when you're unhappy. Check."

He remembered realizing the sting of his sarcasm hit home. Though it was dark outside, he could see her wince as if in pain.

"I talked to him just before 3:00 p.m.," Jane was saying. "He was very clear. He would pick Ashley up by four-thirty this afternoon and take her to her mother's house. I had a class to teach tonight, so I brought the baby here myself."

Dumping her like a sack of old mail, Cameron added silently. The truth was, he didn't really mind Jane, but at the moment he was looking for someone to be pissed at.

They briefly filled in Jane on what they knew so far. The two of them had left Charlie's school together, presumably because his mom's car wouldn't start. Neither responded to repeated calls on their cell phones. There had been no reports of accidents despite the inclement weather. The cops explained that some cell phones had a GPS device and could be tracked down, but apparently his parents' phones didn't have this feature.

Unexpectedly, giving him no chance to think about his answers, Officer Franklin started questioning Cameron.

"Did you talk with your father before school this morning?"

"Yes, ma'am." Fought with him would be more accurate, but no one needed to know that.

"Did you talk about anything in particular?"

"Not really. We have to change houses every Friday. That's in the parenting plan. I said I was going to the golf course after school and I'd see him in a week." What he'd actually said was, I hate you, you son of a bitch. I hope I never see you again.

His father had responded in kind. Go ahead and hate me, you little shit. Just make sure you don't screw up in the tournament this weekend.

It's not like you'll even be there to see me screw up, Cameron had concluded.

"After that," he said, "I got my things and caught the bus to school."

"Did you see your mother today?"

"No. She was supposed to pick me up at the golf course and she didn't show." He went to the window and stared at it, seeing only his own ghostly reflection. It weirded him out to imagine what was going on in the cops' heads about his parents. They were probably thinking of people messing around in a sleazy motel or getting drunk and screaming at each other. "Look, can't you just go find them? You're not going to learn anything more here."

"At this time, we can't do an attempt-to-locate," said Officer Franklin. "When two adults in good health are involved, they eventually show up. This has already been put up on the city channel where the dispatchers chat among themselves, but until there's a true emergent situation, we can't do a broadcast."

Which was her way of saying they were shit out of luck. Nobody was being protected and served here, Cameron thought. He wondered if he should point that out.

"For the time being," Officer Franklin went on, "you can call the state patrol and area hospitals. I appreciate your alarm, but I'm sure they'll show up with an explanation."

Uncle Sean stood up, his lips tight with unexpressed anger. "I need to put gas in my car before the station closes. Then I'm going to start looking."

Cameron stood up, too. "I'll go with you."

"We need for you to stay right here," Officer Franklin said.

Although she barked it like an order, Cameron sensed the compassion beneath the words. It would be a mistake for him to go out looking for his missing parents.

He might not like what he found.

chapter 12

"**W**hat exactly is an APB, anyway?" Jane Coombs asked Lily. She spoke without looking up from the screen of her cell phone. She'd been staring at it as though willing Derek to call.

"It stands for all points bulletin," Lily said. "It means each law enforcement agency within a prescribed radius receives a broadcast of the alert."

"And they're not going to do that for us," Jane said, a quaver in her voice.

"Not until they've been missing twenty-four hours. That seems to be the magic number." She felt like quavering, too. She hated the icy knot of worry in her gut.

Other than the sound of the shower running upstairs for Cameron, the house was eerily, uncomfortably quiet. Soon after Jane's arrival, the police had left, promising that if Crystal and Derek didn't return by four o'clock tomorrow, they would initiate the mysterious business of conducting a missing-persons search. Until then, there was nothing to do but wait. And worry.

Sean had been like a caged lion, prowling through the house. Finally, he'd emptied the coffeepot into a thermos and gone off on his own to search.

"I can think better when I'm driving around," he'd said. Then he left her with his cell phone number and took off.

He hadn't asked Lily if she was willing to stay and look after the kids. She was, of course, but it would have been decent of him to check with her. Tonight, however, she perfectly understood his preoccupation. She wasn't herself, either. Peculiar and possibly terrible things were happening. People couldn't be expected to behave in normal ways.

Sullen with ill-concealed anxiety, Cameron had announced that he was going to have a shower. The water had been running for twenty-five minutes.

And Lily found herself strangely alone with Derek Holloway's girlfriend. She tried to hold in her resentment. Jane hardly looked like the human wrecking ball Crystal had described. According to Crystal, Lily ought to be wearing a rope of garlic around her neck when Jane was anywhere in the vicinity.

She didn't resemble a typical "other woman," if there even was such a thing. Certainly she was no golf bimbo, all legs and no brains. In fact, this woman had a Ph.D. She was young and seemed oddly fragile, undone by Derek's disappearance. But that didn't mean Lily had to like her.

"I'm going to make more tea," Lily said. "Would you like some?"

"I'm a coffee drinker," Jane replied. "I'll take coffee, please."

It took Lily a moment to realize the wrecking ball was

watching her expectantly. She turned around, feeling the edge of the counter pressing into the small of her back. "Just so you know," she said quietly, "I'm on my last nerve."

Jane's eyes widened. "I'm the one suffering here. My fiancé is missing with his ex-wife."

The word *fiancé* drilled into Lily. She glanced at the doorway to the kitchen, hoping Cameron hadn't overheard. Reassuringly, the shower was still running.

"Crystal didn't know Derek was planning to marry you." Lily felt ill. "When was he going to tell her?"

"Today, as a matter of fact. Derek and I are going to tell the kids together next Friday. We have a nice dinner planned at the country club."

Lily had the urge to slam the teakettle on the burner. She set it down with exaggerated care and turned the fire up high. She stared at the flames, seeing the translucent blue of Sean Maguire's eyes. Then she scolded herself. What was she doing, thinking about Sean Maguire? Crystal was in for the shock of her life. Her ex-husband and the father of her children, once the grand passion of her life, had chosen another wife.

Ah, Crystal, thought Lily. I'm so sorry. I'm so, so sorry.

She had the urge to turn on Jane, unleashing a barrage of bitter thoughts. Did Jane expect congratulations from Crystal's best friend? She'd be waiting a long time. Lily shut her eyes for a moment.

You're marrying Derek? she wanted to ask. Brave of you. Don't you know he fools around? Oh, but of course you know that. He was cheating with you when he was married to Crystal. Once he's married to you, who will he fool around with?

It would be best, she decided, to let go of the subject. Apparently Jane thought so, too. She checked her cell phone for messages and helped herself to a cup of herbal tea from the pot Lily fixed.

"According to the label on the box," Lily said, "we're supposed to feel gently soothed and relaxed."

"Yeah?" Jane took a sip and grimaced. "It's not working. I wonder if there's any Diet Coke."

"I doubt it. Crystal drinks Tab."

"I didn't even know they made Tab anymore." Jane opened the fridge and found a bright pink can, popping it open. "This is driving me out of my mind," she said. "I should have gone out looking with Sean."

"Do you really think he's looking or just out driving around?"

"Not sure." Jane took a swig of her soda.

For some reason, watching her drink Crystal's Tab was deeply offensive to Lily. Cradling her mug between her hands, she sat down at the table and tried to concentrate on her breathing. She'd been studying yoga for years. She was supposed to know this. But all the lessons had flown out of her head.

"What do you think of Sean, anyway?" Jane asked.

"I don't have any opinion of him," Lily said. "I don't know him."

"He's drop-dead gorgeous," Jane said. "Even better-looking than Derek."

"Then maybe you're engaged to the wrong brother."

"I'm *so* not his type."

Apparently proper grammar and a Ph.D. were not mutually inclusive, thought Lily.

"Why not?" she asked, mainly just to keep from sustaining the conversation herself.

"Sean is eye candy. I'll bet he's fun in bed, but I don't think there's much more to him than that."

"Like I said, I don't know him."

"Know who?" His hair slicked back and wearing his golf team warm-ups, Cameron returned to the kitchen.

Lily set down her mug. She had an overwhelming urge to grab Cameron and hug him the way she used to when he was tiny. He was practically grown, she thought, noting his large hands and feet, the freshly razored square jaw and piercing blue eyes. Yet despite his grown-up appearance, she still detected shadows of the child he'd been. She could still see his face shining with joy on his birthday or when Crystal brought a baby sister home from the hospital. She could still remember the little-boy smell of him, like freshly turned earth, and she could still hear his choirboy voice, singing along with Disney soundtracks.

Lily had celebrated birthdays with Cameron; she'd admired his lost teeth and perfect report cards. She'd helped him mourn and bury goldfish and pet mice, had taught him phonics, cursive writing and long division. She'd attended scouting ceremonies, soccer games and golf tournaments.

And now Jane Coombs was going to have all that. Lily tried not to feel resentful, but it was hard. She adored this boy and wanted only good things for him. Was Jane a good thing? She couldn't imagine.

"Your uncle Sean," she said in response to his question. "I don't know him at all. What's he like?"

"He's okay." Cameron went to the fridge and took out a gallon jug of milk. Before either Lily or Jane could suggest getting a glass, he'd upended it, impressively drinking without spilling a drop. When he lowered the jug, he looked at them both, his face stiff with worry. "I know what you're trying to do. You want to distract me so I quit thinking about all the bad stuff that might have happened to my parents."

"They had a lot to talk about," Lily said carefully. "The time probably just got away from them."

"Until one in the morning?" He put the cap on the milk carton and shoved it back into the fridge. "They didn't even talk that much when they were married."

Jane snatched up her raincoat. It was one of those stylish designer ones from Canada. According to Crystal, Jane's fashion sense had improved dramatically since she'd started spending Derek's money.

"You know what?" she said. "Sean is right. Sitting around here waiting for the phone to ring is nuts. I'm going home to check my answering machine."

"All right," said Lily, trying not to sound too eager to get rid of her.

"You have my home number and my cell." Jane pulled on her coat and adjusted the Hermès scarf under the collar. "Call me the second you hear anything."

"Of course."

"I'll do the same, tell you the minute he calls." A peculiar brightness hovered in her eyes, the sparkle of tears.

All right, so maybe she did love Derek, Lily conceded, and offered a quick smile. "Drive carefully. The roads are still wet."

Jane tugged her Louis Vuitton satchel over her shoulder and went out the front door. Lily stood on the porch for a moment. The night air was chilly and damp from the day's rain, though now the sky was clear. Against perfect blackness, the stars stood out like shattered glass flung up in the air.

With a shiver, she stepped back inside and shut the door. Only then did it occur to her that the whole time she was here, Jane had never once asked about the girls. And upon leaving, she hadn't even said goodbye to Cameron or offered him a word of comfort.

And this woman was going to be their new stepmother? The air pressure felt different after she left. Lily shivered again, then composed her face before turning to Cameron. "How are you doing?"

"How am I supposed to be doing?" His voice was edged by annoyance.

"You think I have the answer to that?" Then she caught herself. "Look, I'm sorry. The last thing we need is to fuss at each other."

"Nobody says 'fuss' anymore."

"I do. I'm a third-grade teacher, remember? I fuss at people all day."

He almost smiled. Then he flung himself on the living room sofa, draping it with loose limbs. "This sucks," he said.

She sat down next to him. "Yes," she said, "it does suck."

"It sucks hind tit," he added.

"Yes, it sucks…what you said." She bopped him on the head with a pillow.

He gave a small, desperate chuckle. "You'd never make a golfer. You're too uncomfortable with the language."

He picked up the remote and switched on Conan O'Brien. "I'm going to kill them as soon as they get home."

"Good plan," said Lily.

chapter 13

Saturday
4:45 a.m.

Sean was thinking up ways to commit fratricide as he drove along the deserted, unlit roads of western Oregon. And ex-in-law-icide, too, whether or not it had a name. What were they thinking, ditching their kids like this?

They weren't thinking of the kids, that was for sure. They were thinking of themselves. That was Derek's specialty.

And it usually worked for him. By looking out for Number One, he had kept himself at the top of his game. He had never been a beloved player. He was no John Daly, no Craig Stadler. But he was definitely respected and admired. Respected for his ability to focus on winning and getting ahead, and admired for his sheer athletic talent.

Sean was one of the few who knew where that talent came from, and it wasn't exactly a gift from heaven. It came from hitting a thousand balls in a single practice session. Or from putting until your kidneys ached from bending. Or practicing chip shots and pitches until the club face wore out. Like the most successful players in the game, he knew better than to rely on luck and talent.

Ah, but those could take you far, Sean thought, reflecting on his own checkered career. He'd milked both luck and talent for all they were worth, but ultimately he'd walked away from the hard work involved. Now, of course, he was paying the price. But at least he hadn't been taken to the cleaners in some screwed-up divorce.

Sean eased up on the gas pedal as he took a curve in the road. The headlights pierced through wisps of fog shrouding the low spots in the landscape. The phone call from Red about the upcoming tournament didn't even seem real anymore. If it was real, Sean would be home asleep right now. He'd get up early and practice, thinking of nothing but his game. Now the opportunity was as far from his mind as an unremembered dream.

He picked up the thermos and lifted it to his lips. There was only one swallow of coffee left, and it was cold. The clock in the dashboard read 4:58. He blinked, and the rectangular blue-green numbers blurred, then came back into focus, changing to 4:59.

In the headlights, a huge shape flashed, inches from the front bumper.

Sean swerved, the truck nearly clipping the guardrail. The tires whined sideways on the wet pavement as he dialed the steering wheel with both hands. The motion spun him in a complete one-eighty-degree turn, and he didn't stop. Like a carnival bumper car, the truck spun out, careening toward the rail again, slinging him close enough to see its rotted-out posts. Below the edge of the roadway, the rocky cliff formed a sheer drop into the sea.

He braced himself against the dash, his feet now pumping

the brakes. He heard the sound of breaking glass and gritted his teeth, expecting a bone-crushing impact. Seconds later, he realized it was the thermos being flung to the floor with hurricane force, the glass lining shattering on impact.

The truck groaned to a stop, shuddering like an exhausted animal.

Very slowly, he turned his head and looked out the side window, half expecting to find himself hanging off a cliff.

He wasn't hanging. The left side of the truck hugged the guardrail.

In the rearview mirror, bathed in the red glow of brake lights, a full-grown buck paused, then loped up the bank beside the road and disappeared.

"Damn," Sean said, breathing hard. He was bathed in sweat, yet his skin felt cold. The clock in the console read five o'clock.

Since he was already stopped, he decided to check in with Maura.

She answered in a sleepy voice. "I'm not on call."

"I'm not the hospital."

"Sean." A rustle of bedclothes. "Where are you?"

"Derek still hasn't shown up so I've been driving around looking for him and trying to figure out where he is."

"You are not your brother's keeper."

"No. I got stuck with his kids, though."

"You left them alone?"

"Lily's with them."

"Lily."

"The schoolmarm. Charlie's teacher."

"Nobody says schoolmarm anymore."

"You would if you saw Lily." Sean wiped his brow with his sleeve. "This has me pretty damned worried."

"He's a grown man, Sean." A yawn elongated her words.

"He took off with his ex-wife yesterday afternoon and they haven't been seen since."

"Of course they haven't. They're sneaking around and don't want to be seen. Come home, Sean. I have to go to Portland for a seminar, and I want to see you before I leave."

He pictured the rumpled bed, her sleep-warm body in her favorite oversize surgical scrubs, her soft hair in disarray.

"I can't say when I'll be back," he said.

"Oh, well. You do what you have to do, I guess." Another yawn. "Sorry. I had a hellacious shift. Two MIs and an MVA."

He was quiet, trying to work out the abbreviations. She was in the midst of an emergency-ward rotation and often spoke in jargon.

"Two heart attacks and a multiple-vehicle accident," she translated for him.

He winced, thinking of Derek. "I better go. I just thought…I'd check in."

"Wish you were here." She sighed into the phone.

He thought about the way her hair smelled. "Yeah, me, too. Anyway, I guess I'm going to head over to Crystal's again. Maybe they're back."

"Come home."

"No. Meet me there."

"I'm not going to show up at your ex-sister-in-law's house. I have to go to Portland. I can't get out of it. Listen, keep me posted, okay?"

"You got it." He set down the phone and rubbed his damp palms on his thighs. So that had accomplished next to nothing, except to interrupt the sleep of his already sleep-deprived girlfriend.

Funny how she had turned into his girlfriend, literally overnight. When they'd first met in a Portland club, he'd been looking to avoid one more lonely night. It was only the next morning, facing the glare of a rare spring sunrise through the unadorned windows of his apartment, that he'd discovered he wanted more from her.

She was beautiful and smart, a fourth-year medical student with lonely eyes and a low-key, undemanding charm.

He told her so right away, while making her breakfast that morning. He'd felt different around her. She brought out his serious side. For a guy who had once referred to his girlfriend as the nineteenth hole, this was a leap of maturity. "I wish I'd had better manners around you before we slept together," he'd told her.

He'd set a plate of eggs in front of her, leaning down to place a soft, sincere kiss on her lips. People thought he was lucky with women. Hell, *he* thought he was lucky with women, but the fact was, he'd never gotten past the lust and excitement to see what lay on the other side. Every once in a while, he wondered about that. "Now that we've gotten to know each other," he'd said to Maura that first morning, "we should do it again."

He tried to smile at the memory, but he was too tired and worried. And, uninvited, an image of Lily Robinson, thin-lipped and scowling, pushed into his mind. He'd ditched her with the kids and Jane, and she hadn't even complained. She seemed like an interesting person. Yes, that was the word for her. Interesting, with a lot of unspoken thoughts behind brown eyes made bigger by thick eyeglass lenses. Her compassion for the kids was unmistakable, but that wasn't what made her so interesting. She was uptight and judgmental, yet he sensed something in her, a peculiar heat she kept trying to snuff out.

Slowly, he pulled back onto the empty road. The headlights illuminated a set of skid marks snaking across both lanes. That was the closest he'd ever come to hitting something, except for the time in college when Derek had driven him out to the coast to hit drives off the scenic overlook. Sean recalled that darkness had fallen on the way home and a raccoon had crossed their path. Derek had creamed it. He'd pulled over and wept.

With that thought, Sean felt his hands turn wet again. What was up with that?

He hadn't thought about the coast road in years, hadn't been out here since moving back to the States. But maybe...

Sean drove west. He didn't question the terrible feeling that sent him there. He didn't even trust that he could find the spot once again. It had been years since he and Derek used to bring girls here, hoping they'd get lucky.

He had no idea why Derek would bring Crystal to the overlook. Maybe it was like Maura had said on the phone. Maybe Derek and his ex-wife really were sneaking around together.

That was, after all, his brother's specialty.

Sean veered away from the thought. He was in no position to judge Derek.

He tried not to think the worst when he turned onto the coast road and noticed tire marks around the sharp hairpin turns. Everybody had trouble navigating this road, he told himself.

Derek drove the latest model with all the latest features. A major sponsor had just given him the SUV and he knew better than to wreck it.

The adulation, gifts and money heaped upon Derek boggled the mind. And Derek, of course, worked hard for those things, which made him such a good prospect for sponsors. Sean often lay awake at night, battling a poisonous envy. He often had to remind himself that Derek had earned everything that had come his way.

He and Derek had both had the same shot at the moon. In fact, there was a time when Sean had been strongly favored over his brother for a stellar career in the PGA. He'd been the one with the early career high, the revved-up sports agent, the sponsors clamoring, the ranking on the PGA money list.

It hadn't lasted, of course. Sean didn't know how to make things last.

The truck fishtailed a little around a sharp, steeply downward bend in the road. The headlights streamed over the outside edge of the curve, and the guardrail disappeared. It was just starting to get light outside. Sean looked around. He vaguely remembered some sort of property-and-easement dispute that ended right there, at a sharp curve in the road, where the angry black slash of tire tracks arrowed straight at a pair of broken madrona trees.

Sean killed the truck's ignition. For a moment, perhaps the space of three heartbeats, he sat in utter silence. Then he switched off everything else—all the feelings of fear and panic—as he entered the numbers of Derek's cell phone, pushing the buttons one by one with special care.

When it started to ring, he stepped down from the truck, slammed the door and stood in the predawn quiet, hearing nothing but the shush of the waves far below and…the distant ringing of a cell phone.

He was like an automaton, crossing the road to the opposite shoulder. His footsteps sounded like a robot's, perfectly even, brisk but unhurried as they crunched in the roadside gravel. When Derek's voice mail kicked on, Sean ended the call, paused and redialed. The ringing started again, louder now, closer.

He was a machine. Nothing could penetrate his iron shell. He had a flashlight in his hands. He knew he'd need it.

He felt nothing. He couldn't let himself. Because even before he climbed down the steep, sheared-off bank, toward the sound of the ringing phone, he knew what he would find.

He stumbled, fell, held on to thorny vines snaking down the slope, cursed and eventually made his way down through the wild blackberries and red-boned madrona trees growing out of the side of the cliff. He paused again to redial, then followed the sound of the ringing. A thorny branch raked like talons across his face. He felt something trickle down his cheek and swiped at it. His hand came away dark with blood.

He was breathing hard, wheezing as he slipped and slid his way down. Early daylight crept over him. Dawn was breaking, though the deepest of shadows still haunted the primordial folds of the ravine. The flashlight's beam flickered off something that didn't belong there—the dull, intestinal undercarriage of the upside-down SUV.

A chink opened in Sean's self-imposed armor and a white-hot arrow of pain shot in, startling him with its intensity.

No. The roar of denial erupted through him, but he made no sound as he approached the vehicle. The flashlight shook uncontrollably as he shone it toward Derek's truck.

No. He wrestled the flashlight into submission and forced himself to hold it steady. What kind of chickenshit brother was he, shaking like a girl when he knew damned well his brother was—

No. He plunged to his knees beside the window. It had broken into a zillion shatterproof pieces, and then had somehow been ripped out of the windshield. It took him a moment to realize the truck was teetering, and there was still plenty of distance yet to fall.

Jesus. Oh, Jesus. Someone had once taught him how to pray, but that had been a long time ago. It was too late for that, anyhow. He knew it in his bones.

The beam of light was steady and unwavering as Sean forced himself to ignore the precarious creak of the teetering truck. From deep within the vehicle, a cell phone beeped, signaling a message waiting. He found a gap where the window had been and shone the light inside.

Live, goddamn it. Be alive, please.

He found Crystal. Though she lay at an impossible angle, her beauty queen face was a perfect mask. She looked like a statue of a renaissance angel. Even her eyes were a statue's eyes, open, unblinking and blank. There was no expression on her face. He forced himself to say her name, to gently touch her, to check for breathing and a pulse. Nothing. Judging by the eerie chill of her smooth skin, she had been gone for a while.

Sean had seen his mother dead, but this was different. Painful as it had been, his mother was supposed to be dead. After suffering for a year with her illness, everyone had expected it, and she'd been laid out for viewing, a decent Irish Catholic to the end. There was nothing remotely decent about this, he realized, his thoughts tumbling over one another.

Derek. Where was Derek?

A lash of panic whipped through Sean. He called his brother's name, his voice echoing through the ravine, into the dawn silence. It seemed weird and horrible to be yelling while Crystal lay there, but he called again, startling a pair of birds skyward. Maybe Derek had been thrown from the truck, or maybe he'd survived and gone to look for help.

But maybe not.

Sean squatted down and peeled away the remains of the windshield. Something sliced into his hand but he kept working. The truck teetered some more but he didn't stop.

Everything in the SUV had landed in the wrong place. There were stray golf clubs stabbing into upholstery, a lost shoe on the crushed dashboard. The DVD player, of which Derek was so proud, was mangled and smashed. He came across Crystal's purse and it was virtually empty, as though someone had turned it inside out.

Sean became desperate, half crawling into the truck, searching for his brother. He brushed past Crystal's bony limbs. Something slick coated the heaved-up dashboard. A terrible odor infested the cab.

Then he realized where Derek was.

Sean paused to gather his thoughts. It couldn't be done. It was impossible to think. Slowly, gingerly, he got out of the car, slipping in blood. His hand shook so bad he couldn't hold his phone still enough to dial. He finally sank to his knees, putting the phone on the ground to keep it steady while he stabbed at the numbers: 9-1-1. *Send.*

chapter 14

Saturday
6:30 a.m.

Lily was startled from sleep. She should not have been sleeping at all, she thought, leaping up from the sofa, pacing the living room as soon as her feet touched the floor. She hadn't meant to fall asleep. She had no right to relax her vigilance until she made sure Crystal was all right.

She checked the wall clock—6:30 a.m. Outside, the world was a monochromatic gray. She grabbed the handset of the phone and quickly checked the caller ID to make sure she hadn't missed a call. She had not. Still, she felt guilty for having dozed off.

Maybe she should have had coffee with Sean Maguire. No, she thought. Coffee was bad for you, even in an emergency. She shuddered herself fully awake with the thought. Get a grip, Lily.

The TV, which she'd muted hours ago, flickered with the

hyperrealistic colors of a paid-programming broadcast. She picked up the remote to click it off. Then a terrible thought seized her and she switched to a local station and turned up the volume. A talking-head anchorwoman, looking impossibly perky at this hour of the morning, offered a farm-and-ranch report.

Lily muted the sound again but left the station on the local news. She punched in the number of Sean's mobile phone. Funny how she'd memorized it instantly, the moment he gave it to her. She got a recording and hung up without saying anything. He was probably out of range. Then she tried Crystal's number, praying with every cell of her body that her friend would pick up, laugh and explain that she'd been swept away and ended up at a roadside motel with her ex-husband.

No such luck.

With a sigh, Lily tiptoed upstairs to check on her friend's children. Crystal's house was cluttered but beautiful, vintage furniture giving it a special air of permanence. It felt strangely intimate, almost invasive, to watch Crystal's children sleep.

Cameron lay facedown and spread-eagled, the covers in a tangle around his gangly limbs. Dim light through the window washed over the clutter of his room—schoolbooks, laundry, golf paraphernalia. There was a peculiar smell of gym shoes and grass in here, and the trash can overflowed with empty food wrappers. Crystal said he ate like a tapeworm host.

Lily backed out of the room and closed the door, then went to check on the girls. Charlie slept amid a litter of stuffed animals. The glow of a SpongeBob night-light gave the toys a glassy-eyed, strangely sinister look, though Charlie seemed content enough.

Across the room, Ashley had thrown off all her covers. She stirred and snuffled as Lily bent over the side of the crib and pulled a blanket up over her. As she tucked it around Ashley,

Lily felt a peculiar warm contentment, stirred by the simple act of checking on the sleeping baby. The girls were so little, totally dependent. For someone not cut out to have kids, Lily was occasionally a victim of biological impulse, attacked by untimely tugs of a yearning she didn't know how to assuage.

A peculiar weight pressed down on her. She was going to kill Crystal for being such a flake and disappearing like this.

She tiptoed out of the baby's room and went downstairs to put the kettle on. She caught a glimpse of herself in the hall mirror and grimaced. Her hair was frizzed, her cheek imprinted with the texture of the sofa's upholstery. How charming.

She ducked into the bathroom to rinse her mouth, splash water on her face and drag a comb through her hair. Then she pressed her hands down flat on the countertop and tried to make them stop trembling.

It didn't work. Nothing worked. Only seeing Crystal walk through the door, blowing kisses and waving excuses around like a lace handkerchief, would help now.

Worry felt like a live, loathsome thing, twisting and writhing in Lily's gut. This, she thought, feeling nauseous and light-headed, this was what loving someone did to you. The moment you started to care about someone, they made you frantic with worry. As soon as you let yourself love someone, you were doomed.

She rinsed her face again and glanced into the mirror. This was how she would look forty years from now, her face scored by lines of concern, eyes troubled and haunted by factors beyond her control. Old and afraid—that was how she looked.

Crystal liked to tease her about her habit of avoiding matters of the heart. "You're like someone who's afraid of water," she once said.

"I *am* afraid of water," Lily had reminded her.

"And it's totally irrational."

"No, giving yourself heart and soul to someone else and expecting to be taken care of, now, that's irrational. Why would I do that?"

Crystal had offered a smile that, after the end of her marriage, had been wistful and sad with hard-earned wisdom. "Because that's when life finally makes sense."

My life makes perfect sense right now, Lily thought as she left the bathroom. Or rather, it had until last night, when she'd rushed over here to a missing-persons situation.

She put the phone handset into the charger and went to fix a cup of herbal tea.

Ginseng this morning, to sharpen her mind. The coffee smelled almost unbearably delicious, but she didn't go near the glossy blue sack of imported Lavazza. When you were already insane with worry, she thought, why would you consume something that irritates your nerves?

She paced the kitchen, waiting for the water to boil. Crystal called her kitchen Mission Control, but it usually looked like Mission Out-of-Control. Letters, bills and junk mail littered the built-in desk. The fridge was plastered with schoolwork old and new, recipes and diet tips, expired grocery coupons and school forms and permission slips, most of them out of date.

Lily put away the clean dishes. In the process, she came across a mug that still bore a smudge of lipstick in Crystal's favorite shade. She moved to wash it off, then hesitated and set the mug on the sill above the sink. Then she nervously tried organizing the spice rack. She listened intently to the water in the kettle and took it off the heat before the whistle blew, then set the tea to steep.

She tried to spend her nervous energy on tidying the cupboards. They were so disorganized that the kitchen was barely functional. Crystal was a creative person, but not an orderly one.

Lily was standing in the middle of the kitchen, trying to decide where to stash a Pyrex measuring cup, when the sound of an engine crescendoed and then stopped. She heard the heartbeat thud of a car door opening and closing.

Thank God, Lily thought, rushing to the back door. She's finally home.

It was Sean Maguire's truck, she saw, her stomach dropping. He was alone. And walking slowly toward her.

The rising sun painted everything with precise strokes in roseate hues. Each blade of grass, every brick of the driveway, the texture of the tree bark, the shapes of budding leaves—all had been picked out in excruciating, exquisite detail by the glowing light. The colors of the sunrise lay upon Sean Maguire's broad shoulders, his unkempt hair. His imposing silhouette stood out starkly as the new sun lit him from behind.

Lily stood on the threshold of the kitchen, her heart knowing the truth before her mind did. She couldn't make out the expression on his face as he came toward her but, of course she didn't have to. The terrible truth was in the aching stiffness of his gait as he approached.

There was a moment—a split second, really—in which she allowed herself to hope. But that quickly died when he stepped into the slant of light from the kitchen and she saw his face.

Lily decided to speak up first. At least that would buy a few more seconds. A few more seconds to believe the world was normal. A few more seconds to believe nothing had changed.

"The children are asleep." It came out as a whisper.

He nodded. His throat worked up and down as he swallowed. Lily kept focusing on details—the way the beard stubble shadowed the shape of his jaw, the luxurious thickness of his eyelashes. She noticed a thin, fresh cut across the ridge of his cheek, held together by two small white butterfly bandages. The fact that he looked immeasurably older than when he'd left the house last night.

Lily thought about screaming. Maybe if she screamed, it would drown out the words he would inevitably say to her. She didn't, of course. No amount of screaming would make the truth go away.

Stop. She made herself stop. This was absurd. "Where's Crystal?" she finally asked. Oh, no, she thought, changing her mind, don't say it, please don't say it. A thickness of tears gathered in her throat.

"It was an accident," Sean said.

It was what he didn't say that roared loudest in her head. He didn't say Crystal was all right. He didn't say they were working on her, that she'd make a full recovery. He said nothing of the sort.

"Both of them?" she heard herself ask.

He nodded, his eyes tortured.

Lily had forgotten she was holding the Pyrex cup until she heard a thud and realized that she had dropped it. The cup hit the threshold and rolled onto the concrete walkway and, quite unexpectedly and bizarrely, stayed intact.

Both Lily and Sean ignored it.

She felt herself falling in slow motion, and the only way to stop was to fall against him, against his chest, and let the stranger's arms come up around her.

She felt the strength of him but found no comfort there. Crystal was already gone, and the truth of that tore a gaping hole in the world.

And then it hit Lily that the man holding her had lost his brother. He shouldn't be propping her up when he had grieving of his own to do.

She pulled away from him. There were screams of shock and horror that needed to erupt from her, but she wouldn't let them. She would do at least that much for Crystal. She would not let the children find her a sobbing, incoherent mess.

Later, she told herself, stepping back from Sean Maguire. I'll cry later.

chapter 15

"**W**here?" Lily asked, her whole body aching as though she'd been in an accident, too.

"The coastal highway, a few miles south of the Seal Bay exit."

She wondered what they'd been doing way out there. "What happened?"

"The car went off the road. He might have been swerving to keep from hitting something. The pavement was slick, and they went over an embankment."

"When did the highway patrol find them?" The idea of Crystal trapped in a car, injured and terrified, haunted Lily. She saw Sean's face change, stiffening with inner pain. "Oh, God," she said. "You found them, didn't you?" Recoiling, she closed her eyes to shut out the look that flashed across his features.

"It was a couple of hours ago." His voice was low and husky with grief and lack of sleep.

"I'm sorry," she said, feeling the urge to take his hand but deciding it wouldn't help. "That must have been so terrible for you." She kept imagining what it was like. She wondered if they'd suffered, if they'd struggled to stay alive, but she couldn't bring herself to ask. For herself, she wanted to believe Crystal had gone suddenly, never knowing what had hit her.

"Now what?" she asked Sean, holding on to sanity by a slender thread.

"The highway patrol is sending someone," he said, his voice toneless with shock. "I told them to let me go ahead, you know. I didn't want the kids waking up to a bunch of patrol cars and strangers all over the place."

"That's…that's the right thing to do. I guess." *Like this is something I would know.* Lily's mouth felt completely dry. She could not believe how hard it was to speak or even to move. "This is bad," she muttered, forcing herself into action. She went into the kitchen and looked at the half-organized cupboard. "I'm losing it, and that's bad. I need to hold myself together for the children."

He crossed the kitchen and gripped her shoulders firmly, then looked down into her eyes. His hands felt unexpected, discomfiting, a stranger's touch. "Yes," he said firmly, "you do. And you will. We both will."

How was it that staring into his eyes just for a moment helped her reel her unraveling sanity back in? She had no answer, but his stare—it was more like a glare, actually—worked, maybe because deep within his gaze she detected a powerful hurt. She forced herself to stand up to the truth. Crystal was dead. Derek was dead. The children were alive, and they needed her.

"Yes, okay," she said, clearing her throat. "All right. The kids. They're absolutely our top priority. The way we tell them right now is going to affect how they handle it."

"Yeah." He let go of her shoulders. "I agree. The highway patrol is also sending over someone from Child Protective Services to check on the kids."

"Child Protective Services?" Lily was baffled.

"They said it's standard in cases like this, when…when both parents are gone." He paused and seemed to have trouble taking the next breath.

Lily thought again about reaching out, as he had to her, but her hands stayed at her sides, crushed into fists. "I imagine it's their job to make sure someone's looking after the children," she said faintly.

"I told them the kids were safe and sound, but by law they have to check." He reached up and absently massaged his neck. "They wanted to send someone right away, but I said I thought I should be the one to tell them first."

Lily felt a jolt of apprehension. "You hardly know these children," she said, picturing their sweet, unsuspecting faces.

He glared at her. "I'm all they've got."

In terms of actual family, he was nearly correct, Lily reflected. Crystal was an only child. Her father had died before Ashley was born and her mother was in a nursing home. On her best day, Dorothy Baird remembered her own name and nothing more. The most recent stroke had left her barely able to speak at all. Now her diminished capacity was a blessing, because she wouldn't understand that her daughter was gone.

Derek had a stepfather who lived in Palm Desert and that was about it. That, and Sean Maguire.

"She's my—" Lily stopped, took a breath, steadied herself. "She was my best friend." There. She'd said it. She had spoken of Crystal in the past tense. "These children are like my own." The strength of her own conviction surprised Lily. She had never quite articulated the children's hold on her heart like that before. She was shaken by an alien sensation, the fierce protectiveness of a mother eagle swooping in to defend her own. The notion frightened her with its power, and she realized the children didn't need her as a friend or teacher. They needed her in a way that could alter her life for good; they needed things she wasn't sure she possessed.

Sean headed toward the living room. "We'll tell them together."

"They might not get up for a while," she said. "It's not a schoolday, so—"

A cry sounded upstairs.

No, thought Lily. Not yet, please, not yet. Let them sleep awhile longer, let them have just a few more moments of blissful ignorance.

The cry sounded again, more insistent this time. Lily and Sean exchanged a glance. "I'll go," she said, heading for the stairs.

"I'll go, too."

They found Ashley standing up in the crib, fists clutching the rail, face screwed up in preparation for another wail. She stopped when she saw Lily, smiled and reached out, hands opening and closing as if to grab the air. In the bed across the room, Charlie stirred but didn't awaken.

Lily tried a soothing *shh* as she lifted Ashley from the crib. The toddler's diaper had a leaden, claylike feel. Lily noticed Sean standing uncertainly in the doorway, and reality poked through the fog of shock. This child was utterly helpless, and now she was an orphan in the care of an uncle who seemed more like a big kid and a woman who had sworn never to have children.

"I've got this," she told him, though her voice sounded wobbly with uncertainty.

"I'll go make coffee," he said, heading for the stairs.

Lily was on her own. "That's helpful," she murmured, carrying Ashley into the bathroom. "Just what we need."

"Okeydokey," said Ashley.

Lily found that by focusing on the baby's face, she could hold herself together, but it wasn't the baby's face that needed attention. Lily's inexperience showed as she fumbled through the diaper change, though Ashley submitted with a curious patience.

The stretchy, fitted jumpsuit was awkward to remove, though the diaper peeled off easily enough. Then Lily stood there with the balled-up dirty diaper in one hand, her other on the baby to make sure she didn't roll off the table.

"I can't just leave you here while I go put this in the trash," she explained to the baby.

Ashley babbled and smacked her lips. "Want juice," she said. "Want cookie."

"In a minute. Let's get you dressed." She opted for putting the diaper on the counter to dispose of later. Where was the trash can? she wondered, exasperated. Crystal had never been the most organized person, but you'd think she would put both the trash can and clean diapers within reach.

"Lily sad," Ashley observed. "Got tears."

Lily realized her cheeks were drenched. "You're right," she whispered, using a baby wipe on her face. "I'm all right," she assured Ashley, though she felt herself unraveling like a runaway spool of thread. She didn't belong to herself now. Her best friend was dead and Lily could not break down and cry for her. "I'll be fine." She pasted on a bright smile. "Okay?"

"'Kay."

She fumbled around, managing the diaper, a shirt and pull-on pants. As she lifted Ashley up and set her on the floor, Lily caught a glimpse of herself in a round wall mirror framed by pink fairies.

She looked the way she'd expect to look after the sort of night she'd had. Inside, everything was different. A terrible darkness bloomed there, obscuring everything else. As she hurried after the baby scampering toward the stairs, she knew with irrevocable certainty that her life would never be the same. She felt like a different person, a stranger in her skin.

Ashley held on to her finger as they went downstairs with excruciating slowness, each step of the descent drumming home the reality of what had happened. Sean waited at the bottom, the expression on his face inscrutable. When they were halfway down, Lily sensed a presence behind her and turned.

"Charlie."

"Mom," said Charlie in a sleepy voice. "Where's Mom?"

"Mom!" echoed Ashley in her cherub's voice.

Lily and Sean exchanged a terrible look. The sight of Charlie's face, soft with sleep, nearly undid Lily again. How? she thought wildly. How would they break this to her?

"Good morning, kiddo," she said, stroking the little girl's tousled hair.

"Hi, Lily. Hi, Uncle Sean. What happened to your face?"

"Hey, short stuff," Sean said. "Why don't you go see if Cameron's up?"

"He never gets up early on Saturday," Charlie pointed out. Somber-faced, she looked from Sean to Lily. And in her eyes was a deep comprehension that caused a chill to creep up Lily's spine.

"All right," she said with quiet resignation. "I'll go get him."

"She knows something's wrong," said Sean.

Lily picked up the baby, brought her to the kitchen and settled her into a high chair. "She's known that since yesterday."

He grabbed a box of Peek Freans and handed one to Ashley, watching her as though she were a time bomb. She gazed at him for a moment of eloquent silence, then took the biscuit from him. "'Kyou," she said.

She seemed to like Sean better this morning.

Lily picked up the cup of tea she'd brewed earlier and tried to take a sip, but the brew was lukewarm and bitter now. She remembered setting it to steep before Sean got home. That had been eons ago, it had happened in a different era, before she had to face the fact that her best friend and Derek had walked out of her classroom yesterday and had driven over a cliff.

"What's going on?" asked Cameron in a grumpy, just-awakened voice.

Charlie scurried in and went straight to Sean. "I made him get up and he's all mad at me."

Lily filled a sippy cup with juice and gave it to the baby. Cameron stood, stolid and wary, straddling the threshold as though about to flee.

Lily felt Sean's eyes on her. Now? he seemed to be asking.

These poor kids, Lily thought, clamping her teeth together to keep in a sob. We're as lost as they are.

Sean cleared his throat. He kept hold of Charlie's hand and looked into Cameron's eyes. "There was a car accident yesterday…"

Charlie's face crumpled and her shoulders drew inward and trembled. Sean put his arm around her. Lily moved toward Cameron, her hand outstretched. He ignored the gesture and right before her eyes, he seemed to turn as cold as stone, although his expression didn't change.

"Your mom and dad were driving together, and the weather made it dangerous," Sean continued, a subtle note of disbelief in his voice, "and their car went, uh, it went down a bank."

While Lily listened, she watched Sean's face grow whiter. Cameron's expression vanished to nothing.

A thin sheen of sweat glistened on Sean's brow and upper lip. Lily thought about what this night had been like for him while the rest of them slept. She considered the scratches on his face and hands, his torn sweatshirt, the muddy boots parked outside the door. He'd been the one to find his brother and Crystal. What had those haunted eyes seen? Had he touched them? Had he cried?

She wondered all these things as if she should be concerned, but to her mild surprise, she felt a numbness. She could register facts, but God help her, she couldn't match them to any tangible feeling.

There were too many things to feel, to talk about. Too many inexplicable things to explain. Lily slowly lowered her hand, touching Cameron's. "We don't know what to say," she whispered.

"You don't need to say anything." He glared at her.

"Yes, we do, but no one knows where to start."

"So what are you looking at me for?" Cameron wrenched his hand away from hers. His face registered shock and pain for a fleeting second before the uncomprehending expression of a wounded animal masked his features.

Seeing his agony, feeling it pierce through the numbness— that was when Lily discovered something worse than her own grief.

chapter 16

Saturday
7:05 a.m.

Sean struggled to find the words to speak the unspeakable. His mouth was dry as dust.

"So where are they?" Cameron demanded.

"Mommy," Charlie said in a tiny whisper.

"Emergency workers got them out." Sean could still see the flash and glare of the generator-powered spotlights, the shower of sparks gushing from the cutting tool they used to make an incision through the crushed cab, the undisguised disappointment on the geared-up rescue workers' faces. They were trained to save people. Recovering corpses was the last thing they wanted to do.

One of them, carrying a toolbox and a tank of oxygen, had paused to check on Sean. "How about you?" he'd asked. "You okay?"

"I'm not hurt," Sean had told him, dry-mouthed. He'd felt

a strange, numbing gauze enfolding him, softening the edges of his vision, muffling sound, insulating the distance between him and the world.

"Hold still," the guy said. "I'll clean up those cuts for you."

"You don't have to—"

"It's my job." He flung a blanket around Sean's shoulders and set down the toolbox, which doubled as a stool. It contained an array of masks, shears, forceps, tubing and bandaging, instruments Sean couldn't identify. Then he switched on his headlamp and a penlight.

Sean winced at the glare as the penlight stabbed at his pupils. "It's just a couple of scratches."

"Then this won't take long." The rescue worker cracked open a styptic pencil, disinfectant pad and wound-closure strips, and with surprising delicacy cleaned the cuts on Sean's face and hands.

When Sean tried to protest one more time, the worker glowered. "Hey, buddy, you look like shit, okay? I don't think you ought to go see these folks' family looking like this."

He had a point, but Sean shook so much a second rescuer had to come and hold him still. Their gloved hands felt warm and rubbery against his skin. One of them was chewing spearmint gum, the scent distinct and strong but not quite masking the reek of motor oil and blood. The guy with the bandages positioned himself between Sean and the wrecked car, probably deliberately so Sean wouldn't see the grim business of extracting the bodies. Beyond the worker's shoulder, he watched the dawn breaking over the landscape, the ruined bank, the steep slope, the No Trespassing signs.

"They have other family in the area?" the worker asked, turning the gum over and over between his front teeth.

"Three kids," Sean said.

"Man, that's tough."

In the kitchen, now bathed in golden morning light, Sean still flinched from the echo of those words. "Your mom and dad didn't make it," he told the children. "The rescue workers said they died…right away. They didn't feel any pain and they weren't scared."

He felt Charlie in his lap, trembling like a baby bird that had fallen from the nest. He tightened his arms around her and lowered his head, resting his chin on her soft hair. He wanted to circle her completely, engulf her, form his body into a hard protective shell around hers. "I'm so sorry," he said. "I'm so sorry." Never had those words seemed more inadequate.

"Now will you tell us what happened to your face?" asked Charlie in a fearful whisper.

"A few scratches, that's all," he whispered back. "From some branches."

"Does it hurt?"

"I'll be all right."

"Who's going to take care of us?"

"I will, honey." The patrolmen at the scene had verified that he was the next of kin and that the children were being cared for. Later, a case worker would evaluate the situation, making certain there were adequate arrangements for the kids. Sean had barely had time to ponder the ramifications of that, but there was no way in hell he could look Charlie in the eye and give her anything less than his full commitment.

"We both will," Lily said. Tears streamed down her face, but her voice was steady.

Cameron still hadn't moved from the doorway. He looked painfully tense, keeping his emotions coiled inside. Probably better than anyone present, he clearly understood his world had broken away like an iceberg in the night, and he'd never get it back to the same place again. Life as he knew it was over; his childhood lay behind him.

Lily took his hand again, even though he'd rebuffed her a moment ago. "Cameron, I'm so sorry."

Once again, he shook her off and backed away. "Now what?" he asked, his voice sharp with anger.

Lily looked over at Sean, her eyes swimming with sadness. She seemed to be just inches from losing it, but she didn't. Their gazes held for a long moment. He hardly knew this woman, yet he recognized the pain he saw in her eyes. Then she blinked and the moment passed. They were just two strangers again.

"Cameron," she said, "we're not sure. We have to take this one step at a time."

"More," said Ashley, rattling her sippy cup.

Sean, Lily and Cameron moved to help her at once. They were all desperate to do something normal—give the baby some juice, wipe a crumb from her mouth, answer the phone.

Sean couldn't believe someone was calling at this hour of the morning. Maybe it was Maura. Maybe it was the highway patrol, saying there had been a mistake, that was some other accident Sean had come across. He set Charlie aside and snatched the receiver from the wall phone. "Hello?"

"This is Melanie Larkin from KBUZ News. I'm calling for details of the Highway 101 tragedy—"

"Piss off," said Sean, slamming down the receiver.

"S'off!" said the baby, slamming down her sippy cup.

Charlie regarded him with saucer eyes.

Sean felt his neck redden. "Sorry for my language. That was some news reporter wanting to ask about what happened."

"How do they know to call here?" Cameron asked.

"They monitor all the police and emergency frequencies on the radio," Sean said. "No idea how they got this number—"

The phone rang again.

"Check the caller ID," Lily said.

Cameron looked at the small screen. "Says Wireless. I don't recognize the number."

"We'll let it ring, then," Lily said.

"Better yet, we'll unplug the God—the darned thing." Sean tugged the phone jack from the wall.

Elsewhere in the house, another extension continued ringing, then stopped as the answering machine picked up. The sound of Crystal's recorded voice was a soft ghost moving through each of them.

Charlie tilted her head to one side, listening. "Mommy," she whispered.

In the ensuing silence, Sean suddenly felt every nanosecond of his sleepless night. "Let's sit back down," he said.

Charlie slid into his lap again, and he found the warmth and weight of her, the cotton-candy smell of her hair oddly comforting. And instantly, he felt guilty for taking comfort in this terrified, hurting child.

Lily poured Cheerios into a plastic bowl and gave them to Ashley. "'Kyou," said the baby.

"You're welcome."

Cameron was still wary, on edge. He perched on his chair as though poised to flee.

The phone rang again.

"Why are so many people calling?" Charlie wailed.

"I'm afraid a lot of people are going to be calling," Lily said.

"Because of Dad," Cameron said. "Because he's famous."

"Because both your parents have a lot of people who love them and are concerned about you. We'll ignore the phone and only talk to people we want to talk to, okay?" Lily said.

"Somebody from the highway department is going to be here any minute," Sean said.

"Why?" asked Cameron. "Are they giving Dad a ticket?" His anger was firming up like epoxy, growing harder by the minute.

"They're probably going to be asking some questions. It's standard." He didn't finish the thought. Standard procedure in a fatality accident, they told him at the scene. "And they're sending a social worker to make sure everyone's cared for. Anyway," he continued, "we need to call Jane."

"She might have heard already," Lily pointed out.

"We still need to call her. And I'll call my father in California." He felt light-headed again. How the hell was that done? How did you pick up the phone and say the words *Derek is dead.* "What about Crystal's family?"

"Her father's gone, mother's in a nursing home," Lily said. "She doesn't have anyone else."

"Grandma Dot is sick," Charlie informed him. "She doesn't know who anybody is."

"She had a series of strokes, and the last one was severe," Lily explained.

Sean suspected she didn't want to go into more detail in front of the children.

Charlie's weight, slight though it was, started to feel heavy to Sean. Her bony little frame pressed into him.

"You should call Jane, then, I suppose," said Lily.

Something about the directive irritated him. He glanced at the clock and nodded. The morning news might report the accident. He had a thought of Maura. While driving away from the wreck, he'd called her but got no answer. Sean had left a message: Call me the second you get this. It's important.

She hadn't called yet.

Lily looked pale and shaken. He could see a brittleness around her, as thin and fragile as a coating of ice around a twig. It wouldn't take much for her to break. He suspected the kids alone were the reason she held herself together.

He patted Charlie on the head. "I'd better do that."

She clambered off his lap and Lily opened her arms. "Climb aboard."

Solemn-faced, Charlie did so, leaning her cheek against Lily's chest. The kid was crying, not making a sound. Sean found a box of Kleenex and set it on the table by Charlie.

"Me, too," said Ashley, opening and closing her hands. Sean looked at Cameron. Derek's boy was lost somewhere, staring out the window.

"Cameron, keep an eye on Ashley while I make this call," Sean said.

Cameron nodded and put more juice in the baby's cup.

Sean picked up a slip of paper with Jane's number and used his cell phone to make the call. How do I do this? he wondered, noticing the shaking of his hand. He forced himself to hold it steady. While it rang, he wandered out onto the patio. He had no idea what to say to this woman, how to break the news to her. He wanted to do this right but he barely knew his brother's girlfriend. He'd always thought he and Derek would grow closer now that he was back from overseas. He'd thought they had all the time in the world.

"Jane," he said when her voice mail picked up. "Call me right away, the second you get this message." He left his number, then took a deep breath as he walked through the patio gate. The world looked exactly the same, as though nothing were amiss. The urge to keep walking was strong. He'd walked away from things before, refusing to make someone else's problem his own.

Then, as he reached the end of the driveway, a flashbulb went off in his face, momentarily blinding him. "Get the hell off this property," he said, unable to see through the fog of red residue from a flash.

chapter 17

Saturday
11:15 a.m.

"Thank you for your time," said Lily, holding open the back door for the highway department officer and the social worker.

"Call me anytime, night or day," said Susie Shea, the caseworker who had jumped into the situation with both feet. She had been at the house for hours, helping them get through the day and explaining what would happen, step by step. Though compassionate, she didn't sugarcoat the situation. The Holloway children were now, at least temporarily, wards of the state, subject to close supervision and regular reports.

Lily shut the door behind them and paused, leaning her forehead on the doorjamb. She had never felt quite so exhausted in her life. It was as if she'd been uncapped and drained dry, and there was nothing left but an overwhelming ache of grief. She turned from the door and noticed a stack of library books on the hall table—*Cruising the Caribbean,*

Genetics for Dummies, The Nursing Home Survival Book, Horton Hears a Who. According to the stamped pocket on the back, they were all overdue. Next to the books were a dry-cleaning slip and a receipt for film processing. Reality came into sharp focus. This was a life interrupted, everyday errands that would never get done, and the prospect of sorting everything out crushed down on the already unbearable weight of grief.

Crystal's children were orphans now. Lily could scarcely get her mind around the idea. They were completely alone in the world. For the time being, the foster care system would place them in the care of Sean Maguire, and they would live with him here. Lily tried not to be taken aback by this, telling herself it was the logical arrangement—in the eyes of the child welfare system, anyway. Their closest blood relative, Dorothy Baird, was not medically competent to step in, so Sean was next in line for the time being, at least until they learned whether or not there was a legally designated guardian. When Ms. Shea had explained as much to him, he'd looked shell-shocked and said, "Yeah, all right, I guess."

Lily wasn't certain he'd understood. He might have given the same response if she'd asked, "Do you want fries with that?"

All three children would start immediately with a grief counselor. Charlie and Cameron were high risks for trauma over abandonment issues. Ashley's risk was lower. She might not suffer at all; it was too early to tell.

As Lily carefully stacked the library books by the door, she tried to make herself accept the situation. The unthinkable had happened, the thing people never actually believe would come to pass. She only hoped Crystal and Derek had prepared for this. For the short term, Sean Maguire was in charge. *Sean Maguire.*

"Lucky them," she muttered under her breath.

"Lucky who?"

Startled by the masculine voice, she turned and nervously wiped her hands on her thighs. Maguire unsettled her, or maybe it wasn't him. Maybe it was this whole surreal situation.

"Where are the kids?"

"Upstairs. Ashley's napping, Charlie's watching a video and Cam's...staring out the window. Lucky who?" he asked again.

"Nothing. Just thinking aloud." She set down the books and glanced at the envelope in his hand. It was the paperwork outlining the arrangements for the children's care. "Are you sure you're willing to take this on?" she asked.

"Willingness has nothing to do with it. They're my brother's kids. I'm all they've got."

"Crystal wanted me to take care of her children," she told him bluntly.

"How the hell do you know that? Did she leave you a note or something?"

Lily took a deep breath, forcing herself to ignore his tone. "I'm their godmother. And we talked about it after she had Ashley and her mother had her first massive stroke. She told me she was revising her will, and if anything ever happened to her and Derek, I would be in charge of the kids." Lily and Crystal had joked about it. "You with your vow never to have children," Crystal had teased. "Someday, you could wind up with three." They'd laughed together, imagining Lily's orderly world disrupted by the chaos of family life. Of course they had laughed. The very idea was ludicrous.

Despite barely sleeping at all last night, she paced in agitation. "You know, it was one of those conversations about something that'll never happen."

He nodded. "I understand. Ms. Shea said most couples don't bother with making wills, but I'm pretty sure Derek and Crystal have them. Still, designating someone to take your kids…" He shook his head. "Most people think, why? It's like buying flight insurance."

"I always buy flight insurance," Lily said quietly. She was beginning to feel punchy, perhaps slightly ill. "I told Crystal fine, of course I'll look after your kids. I was supposed to sign something prepared by her lawyer, but the subject never came up again. Why would it? Things like this just don't happen."

He was a man of disconcerting stillness, Sean Maguire. In silence he took her measure with a look she couldn't read, then asked, "Is that what Derek wanted?"

She felt an ugly little tug of resentment. "I don't know what he wanted." Except a divorce. He'd wanted that, and he'd gotten it on his terms, which included joint custody of the children.

She refrained from saying anything. This man had lost a brother. Her opinion of Derek wouldn't ease his shock and grief or her own.

All right, she told herself, get a grip. Every time she tried to think straight, a huge, overwhelming thought detonated in her head. Crystal was gone.

How could that be? she wondered, looking around the kitchen. The mug with Crystal's lipstick on it still sat on the windowsill. She wasn't supposed to be gone; there were errands to be done, engagements marked on her calendar in her loopy scrawl. She was supposed to come back here to her house, her children, her life. It seemed impossible that she wouldn't.

Lily squeezed her eyes shut and imagined a series of clear freeze frames, like a slide show of beloved snapshots—Crystal as a coltish teenager, laughing as she taught Lily how to do a cartwheel. And later as a young woman, flush with victory at winning one of a dozen beauty pageants. Crystal as a bride, looking like something out of a fairy tale, and then as a mother, bathed in sweat and triumph moments after giving birth to her children. Only yesterday, she'd sat in Lily's classroom, shredding a Kleenex and holding in tears as she discussed her troubled daughter. She'd been so vibrant, so overwhelmingly *alive.* How will I hold on to all the memories? Lily wondered. How will I help the children hold on to them?

The thought rattled aimlessly around inside Lily. Her heart had held a cherished friend. And now…nothing but a terrible bright void where Crystal had been.

Lily opened her eyes and raised them to Sean. "So did you and Derek…ever talk about it?"

"No. Never. It's like you said. Your mind doesn't go there. No one's does."

"These children need answers now. They need to know what's going to happen to them, not just for the next week but for the next year, for the rest of their lives."

"I know."

Susie Shea had told them to come up with a temporary plan for the children to make sure they were cared for in the short term.

"I suppose we'll find out more later in the week," Lily said. "You know, when the wills are read."

An awkward silence stretched out between them. The faint sound of the TV drifted through the house.

"What about Jane Coombs?" asked Lily. "I thought she'd come right over as soon as she heard."

"You'd think."

"But…?"

"She got hysterical on me when I told her. She offered to come right over but I told her to wait until she pulled herself together. Didn't think it would do the kids any good to see her like that."

"She was about to become their stepmother," Lily said. "How could she stay away?" She got up, looking for something to straighten or clean. She grabbed the mug with the lip-stick, started to wash it, stopped herself. She put it away on a high shelf, lipstick and all. She turned to find Sean watching her without expression.

She refused to explain herself, saying, "So now what? The children need answers, Sean. They need to know who's going to fix their breakfast in the morning and get them off to school. They need to know who they'll celebrate Christmas with and who's going to sign their permission slips and take them to the doctor when they're sick. That's what they need. And they need it right now, not after the funeral or the reading of the will."

"Whoa, slow down. One step at a time." He steepled his fingers together and frowned. "Let's figure out a plan."

She felt a small beat of panic even as she nodded. I'm not ready, she thought. I can't do this. Then she reminded herself that these were Crystal's children. It didn't matter how ill equipped she felt for the disaster. "I can stay through the weekend," she said slowly. "I'll take next week off from work to be with the children." She studied his face, his troubled eyes. "Are you all right with that?"

"I…yeah, thanks. For now, we'll go with that plan." He glanced toward the stairway. "Sleeping arrangements?"

"I'll take the guest room," she said swiftly. She couldn't possibly sleep in Crystal's bed.

He looked at the stack of publications the social worker had left for them to go through—*Growing Strong, Grief Counseling for Children, Adjusting to Foster Care, Tips for Transitions.* They were the sort of things Lily saw in the faculty lounge or professional library at school, and until now, they'd always seemed remote and theoretical. Now the very titles frightened her.

"I wonder, um…" Sean paused and swallowed. "Maybe you could help me with her room."

Lily knew exactly what he was asking. "Let's change the sheets and clear out a space in the closet. I know where she keeps everything."

His expression softened with gratitude. Lily went through the motions like a robot, getting fresh sheets from the linen closet and making up the bed. There was a curious, discomfiting domesticity to the situation and she hurried through the motions. Then she filled a big tapestry suitcase with dresses and scarves, skirts and blazers and shoes. She worked swiftly, trying not to think about what she was actually doing—putting these things away because Crystal was dead. As she zipped it up, she noticed the luggage tag, Handle With Care.

"Just put it up on the shelf for now," she told Sean. "It's much too early to—" She cleared her throat. "We're not getting rid of anything for a while."

"Fine with me." His phone rang and he stepped aside to answer it.

Lily finished up in the closet, surrounded by the familiar scent of Crystal's perfume. The packed suitcase made it easy to imagine that Crystal wasn't dead, but merely away on a trip.

She picked up a book from the bedside table. *Sins of the Father* by Gail Goodman. The page was marked with a business card with the Laurelhurst School logo. It was a card for Greg Duncan, the PE teacher and golf coach. Lily flipped the book open. Crystal had been right in the middle of the novel. She'd never know how it ended.

Sean flipped his phone shut. "Derek's agent is coming in. He caught a plane from L.A. as soon as I called him," Sean said. "He takes care of all of Derek's business."

Will he take care of his kids? Lily knew she didn't need to ask that.

"His name is Red Corliss," Sean continued. "He, uh, he scheduled a press conference."

"A press conference?" Lily was incredulous. "Tell me you're joking."

"I don't like the idea, either," Sean said, "but Red knows what he's doing. He says that way we can control the information, and if we're lucky, get the press to keep their distance."

She shuddered at the very idea of announcing Crystal's death as though she'd won another pageant. Turning to Sean, she searched his face, feeling a curious and unexpected intimacy with this stranger. They'd known each other less than twenty-four hours, yet there was a terrible connection between them, forged of the unthinkable.

"Do you know how much I hate this?" she asked.

"Yeah," he said. "I do."

chapter 18

Saturday
3:20 p.m.

Red Corliss steamed into town like a freight train, shouting into a cell phone while issuing orders as he cut a swath through everything in his path. When Sean was younger and a client of Red's, he'd been a little in awe of the sports agent's aggressiveness and his brusque manner. Now, a dozen years later, he saw Red for what he was, an ambitious, confident professional whose attitude masked an unexpectedly tender heart.

Within a short while, Red had somehow managed to round up the key players and assemble them at Echo Ridge, Derek's home course. An hour later, Red arrived at Crystal's house.

"How'd it go?" Sean asked, holding the door for him.

"It went. I gave them the facts, released the statement we drew up, told them to respect the family's privacy, yada yada yada. They'll make of it what they will. If they know what's good for them, they'll report the facts, not the gossip."

Overnight, rumors had inevitably swirled up. What was an

estranged couple doing together on a remote coastal highway? Was it really an accident or was foul play involved? Red made it his mission to tell the world that this was a tragic accident in every sense of the word, and to suggest otherwise was a vicious insult to the victims' families.

"Red!" Charlie ran into the living room, her arms flung out in greeting.

"There you are, Princess Carlotta." Red set down his briefcase and scooped her up in his arms.

"Every time I think about my mom and dad, I cry," she said. "And I think about them all the time."

"Sure you do, sweetheart." Red's gruff exterior melted. "They loved you with all their hearts."

"That does no good at all if they're not here with me," she said.

"I know, princess. I know. Where are your brother and sister?"

"Ashley's in the kitchen with Lily."

"Who's Lily?"

"My teacher."

"She's Crystal's friend," Sean said. "She's been with the kids ever since this all started."

"Cameron is in his room," Charlie told Red, "listening to his stupid music."

"I'll go round him up," Sean said, and headed upstairs. He found Cameron lying on his bed, staring up at the ceiling, lost. He wore headphones, the tiny iPod balanced on his chest like a pacemaker. The expression on his face was surprisingly contented. Music couldn't save you, Sean thought, but occasionally, just for a time, it could fill the empty spaces inside a person. The headphones emitted a faint tinny sound and Cameron took his time removing them when he noticed Sean.

"How you doing?" Sean asked.

"Just swell."

"Red's here. He needs to talk to us all."

"What about?"

"A lot of things." It was hard to figure out where to begin again. "Funeral arrangements. Some other stuff, too. We need to meet with Logan, Schwab and Fuller to go over what your parents wanted for you."

"That's easy," said Cameron, utterly serious, hard-eyed. "They wanted— Never mind."

"What were you going to say?"

"Never mind." Cameron tossed the player onto the bed. "Let's go see Red."

Sean checked his phone for messages. No response from Maura, he noticed. Out of town at her seminar, she couldn't know what was going on with him, but she sure as hell ought to return her damned calls.

He swallowed his irritation because he had to. This wasn't about him and his grief. It was about figuring out what was best for Derek's kids. If he started letting himself feel his loss in the depths of his soul, he might get sucked so far down into a dark hole that he'd never find his way out. And that would make him useless to these children.

God, Derek, he thought. *How the hell am I supposed to do this?*

He and Cameron went into the living room, where Red, Lily and the girls were waiting. He stood there in the door-way for a second and looked at Lily. She'd been here for the past twenty-four hours, taking care of the kids as best she could. She hadn't changed her clothes, though she'd found time to duck into the shower, and when he'd passed by the bathroom door, he'd heard her crying in there. He'd paused, picturing her with her face in the spray, sobbing. Now she sat with Ashley on her lap and Charlie snuggled up against her side, and her face was ashen with shock, taut with unexpressed grief. Yet when she looked at Sean, he detected a subtle hostility. She felt proprietary when it came to these kids. Well, hell, so did he.

Red shook Cameron's hand, treating him with a kind of dignity that didn't seem forced. So there were allies. There were small gleanings of grace here and there.

Sean nodded to Red and took a seat in a leather chair. He picked up a thick folder of forms and brochures.

"There's going to be a funeral service for your mom and dad," he said. "Red and Lily and I will make sure it all gets organized."

He sent Lily a questioning look and she offered a barely perceptible nod. "We don't want you to worry about anything except adjusting to your new situation," she said.

"I don't want to adjust," Charlie said. "I never want to."

"Honey, we don't have a choice," Lily said. "I sure wish we did, but we don't. The funeral is to celebrate their lives. Lots of their friends will come. We have to know if there's anything special you want at the service, some certain music or a particular reading."

"What kind of music? What kind of reading?" asked Charlie with fear in her eyes.

"Something short, maybe from the Bible or from a book you've read, to comfort you. Maybe a special song, too," Lily said.

"I don't like to read," said Charlie.

"Usually someone else does the reading."

"I like *Trumpet of the Swan*," Charlie suggested.

Cameron snorted. "Not that sort of reading."

Lily put her hand on his sleeve to shut him up. It worked. Cameron stared out the window. Charlie studied her pink sneakers.

"You don't have to think up something right away," Sean said. "Tell us later if you think of anything, okay?"

All three kids were eerily subdued, chastened. Even the baby was quiet and watchful, understanding nothing but sensitive to everyone's mood. Sean did his best to explain what was going to happen, then said that he and Red had to go out and meet with the people who were going to plan the funeral. It was surreal, the idea of going to a funeral parlor and figuring out how to bury his brother. The urge to run was strong.

"When will you be back?" asked Charlie.

For once in his life, he wasn't free to run away. He tamped down the urge. "Later tonight, after you're asleep. Lily's staying with you tonight."

"Lily," said the baby, pointing with authority.

"I'll be staying here all week," Lily said. "The class will have a substitute teacher, and you and Cameron can stay home from school." She glanced at Cameron. "That is, if you want to."

"I don't mind skipping a week of school," he said.

Carrying the baby, Lily went to the door with Red and Sean.

"You call me if you need anything," Sean said.

"I will."

Red handed her his card. "Same here. And listen, is there anything you think Crystal would have wanted? You know, for the service."

Lily bit her lip. "She loves flowers. All kinds. And pink. Pink's her favorite color. I'll let you know about the music later."

"We'll do our best," said Sean.

As he walked away from the quiet house, Sean wished he could have stayed. He wished he could've done anything but the grim business of seeing to the funeral of these kids' parents. He glanced back to see Lily standing at the door, both arms around the baby like a shield. She had a determined set to her chin, and the breeze plucked at her hair. Sean lifted his hand in a halfhearted wave. She didn't wave back, but turned and went inside, closing the door firmly behind her.

"I remember meeting her a time or two, back when Crystal and Derek were married," Red said, noticing Sean's look. "Don't know her well, but I bet that pruny uptight attitude isn't her. She's hurting. Bad."

"Yeah, well, she's not the only one. She's the least of my worries."

Red got in the rental car, which already smelled like his favorite cigars. "Think again, kid. Either get her on your side or prepare yourself for a fight."

"What the hell's that supposed to mean?"

"Maybe nothing. Now, about the Redwing tournament—"

"It's out."

"I know it's out. Everything's out until we get through this."

Sean hated the thought that flashed through his head. Leave it to Derek to screw up my shot.

chapter 19

Saturday
7:05 p.m.

When Sean and Red finished their meeting with the funeral director, he came home and there was a changing of the guard. Lily promised she'd return shortly, then stepped out into the cool, damp night. For the first time in hours, she took a deep, unencumbered breath. She couldn't believe how physically exhausted she felt. What had she done all day but pace and worry?

As she drove home, a feeling of escape pervaded her senses. She was on her own once again, in charge of her own life. If she chose, she could drive right past the turnoff to her street and head to the next town, to Portland, to the airport.

The fantasy flared like a brief fire, then was quickly doused by reality. Escape was not an option. She didn't belong to herself anymore. She belonged to three orphaned children who were even more lost than she was.

She let herself into the quiet, empty house. Everything

was as she'd left it, *Bull Durham* in the DVD player, a map of Italy spread out on the coffee table, a glass of wine sitting nearby. Slowly and deliberately she folded the map shut.

While she was throwing a few things in a bag, she was startled by the sound of the door opening and shutting. "Hello?" called a voice.

"Mom." Brushing her hands off on her pants, Lily met her mother in the living room. "What are you doing here?"

Sharon Cutler Robinson offered a thin smile. "I came as soon as I heard."

Lily studied her for a moment. Her mother was an infrequent visitor, as distant and cool as the moon. At one time, she had been pretty, perhaps even beautiful; Lily knew from looking at old photographs. Over the years, her mother's looks had taken on a brittle edge, hardened by unhappiness and a fierce dedication to her job as a product safety manager. Yet her eyes held sympathy, and Lily hugged her briefly, breathing in the familiar scent of Elizabeth Arden cologne.

"Thanks for coming. Can I get you a cup of tea?"

"Nothing, thank you. Your father sends his love, by the way. He's in Saigon." Terence Robinson was an executive with Nike who spent half his life overseas. Sharon removed her raincoat and hung it by the door. She wore a cloud-soft white angora sweater that should have looked too young on her, but didn't. "I wanted to find out if you're all right, and what's happening with Crystal's family."

Lily's chest ached as she recounted the past twenty-four hours, yet she spoke in a strangely dispassionate voice. When she was around her mother, she always felt silly being emotional. *What's the point of crying?* Mom used to say when she was a kid. *It doesn't change anything.*

What Lily had discovered then was just as true now. It hurt more to keep it in.

"It's terrible," Sharon said when Lily described Sean's early-morning discovery. "What were they doing all the way out at the coast? What were they thinking?"

"We'll never know."

"Something drove them out there and made them reckless," Mom said. "I wonder what it was."

Troubling news about their daughter, thought Lily, unable to help herself. "I need to finish packing," she said, and headed toward the bedroom. The guilt slithered through her chest. She couldn't stop wondering if things would have turned out differently if she'd broken the news about Charlie with more compassion, or not at all. I want that hour back, she thought, breaking apart inside. I just want that hour back.

"Where are you going?"

"To Crystal's house."

"I thought you said their uncle was in charge over there."

"He is, but he's a single guy, Mom. He just moved back from the Philippines or Malaysia, somewhere like that. I want to make sure I'm there for the kids." She felt her mother watching as she folded jeans and socks, tucked in a bag of toiletries. "What?" she asked finally.

"Be careful you don't get too attached."

Lily stopped in the midst of zipping her suitcase. "What are you talking about?"

"They belong to their uncle. It's inevitable."

Lily resumed the zipping, but it snagged on a bit of fabric inside and refused to budge. "No one knows what will happen. They're wards of the state. Temporarily, anyway. Crystal asked me to sign an affidavit agreeing to be the kids' guardian if anything happened to both her and Derek. I never did sign anything because…well, why would we be in a rush? Now, if Derek's will contains something that contradicts that—"

"You'd better hope it does. Don't fight their uncle on this,

Lily. You can't take on three kids. It wouldn't be fair to anyone involved." Her mother stepped forward. "Here, let me get that unstuck for you." She pushed Lily's hand aside and backed the zipper up, then pulled it smoothly back on track. "You have to regard the Holloways as you would other children you teach. They're yours for a time and then you let them go."

"This is different. She's—she was my best friend, Mom, my only close friend. I made a promise to her. That's not something I can let go of." Lily put a hand on the bedpost to steady herself, praying she wouldn't lose it in front of her mother. "Did you know…all day long at odd moments, I've thought of Evan." She instantly regretted saying the name of her brother, so many years gone and unremembered by Lily and her sister. Taking her mother's hand, she said, "I'm sorry. I shouldn't have brought him up. It's just that a loss so terrible…my mind is trying to draw comparisons."

Her mother took her hand back. "Aren't things bad enough?" She pivoted away, turning her attention to the closet. Unlike the rest of the room, it was cluttered with shoes and bags, clothes crammed together on mismatched hangers. For some reason, Lily could never seem to keep her closet organized.

Stupid of her to mention Evan, to remind her mother that she'd once had three children. Born two years after Lily and a year after Violet, Evan was the youngest child. He had died, an event they never spoke of but one that had defined her entire family for all the years that followed.

"People don't wear black so much anymore," Sharon said, inspecting Lily's clothes, none of which were black. "I think any color is fine so long as it's respectful."

Cameron sat in his mom's station wagon, which was parked in its usual spot in the driveway, as though his mom was inside talking on the phone and filing her nails. The car had just been delivered to the house, the battery recharged, all ready to be driven again. His mother had golf team driving duty this week. There was a tournament in Hood River, and she'd signed up to drive both ways. Of course. She always did, ever since he was in eighth grade.

Hell, now he could quit the team altogether. It was what he'd been wanting to do, anyway—to quit, walk away, forget that whole part of his life. Yet even now that they were gone, he felt the weight of their expectations. Cameron's golf was important to each of his parents, each for wildly different reasons.

He wished both his parents hadn't been so important to him. That's what pissed him off, more than anything.

The car smelled very faintly of stale cigarette smoke—his mom's secret vice. In the ashtray was a half-smoked Virginia Slims, stubbed out and broken. The console was littered with spare change, rubber bands and a pad of Post-it notes with a shopping list in his mother's slanty handwriting. It was weird, seeing something in her writing, and the list seemed so ordinary—Kleenex, baking soda, Tab, paper towels, spaghetti sauce.

Where the hell was the Mennen deodorant? he wondered in annoyance. He'd told her he was out and needed more. What the hell was wrong with her?

Maybe she'd left her cigarettes behind. He leaned over and looked in the glove box, but found only the insurance card and registration, maps and other junk. He checked under the visor, finding a pair of sunglasses, a book of matches and a crumpled pink receipt. He started to put it back when the heading caught his eye—Riverside Medical Laboratories. It was a verification of Ashley's blood type.

Cameron's gut turned as cold and hard as a block of ice. Sean was appointed guardian because it was assumed he was their closest blood relative. What would happen to her if the truth came out, that he wasn't related to Ashley at all? Cameron crumpled the report in his fist and stuffed it in his jacket pocket. Then he changed his mind and took it out again. He opened the car door and used a match to light the paper on fire, letting it drift to the ground and burn to a brown autumn leaf. For good measure, he ground it out with the heel of his shoe.

Scowling, he extracted his wallet from the rear pocket of his jeans. He took out the learner's permit he'd earned only days after turning fifteen and a half, and got back in the car. He was due to get his license in just a few weeks and wasn't supposed to drive unsupervised until then, but what the hell. It's not like his parents would worry themselves to death if he drove away.

What were they doing, disappearing like that? Why? Didn't they give a shit that people needed them? What could be so bad between them that they'd drive off together and wreck the car?

He knew what. He knew. He wasn't supposed to know but he did.

"Screw it," he said, putting his hand on the key in the ignition. But before he turned the key, something weird happened. His right hand froze like a block of ice, and needles of pain pulsed in his fingertips. His heart tried to hammer its way out of his chest and suddenly his face was bathed in sweat. His underarms, too, and since he was out of Mennen, there was no stopping it. He tried to breathe but couldn't inhale deep enough to feed air to his lungs.

A heart attack. He was having a freaking heart attack. He was going to die right here at the wheel of a car, thus carrying on the newest Holloway family tradition.

He scrambled out of the car, desperate to escape. His jacket snagged on the emergency brake lever, holding him fast. He yanked at it, hearing the cloth tear as he pulled free. He staggered onto the driveway and moved away from the car.

Gradually, the heart attack subsided.

"Jeez," he muttered, wiping his brow with a sleeve. How stupid was that, to be afraid of a car like it was something out of a Stephen King novel.

Chagrined, he told his uncle he was going over to a friend's for a bit. To his relief, Sean seemed to understand he needed to get the hell out of the house for a while.

"I know what'll get your mind off things," Jason Schaefer said later that evening.

"A lobotomy?" Cameron had coasted to his friend's house on his skateboard and was dribbling a basketball in Jason's driveway. The Schaefers had heard the news, and Jason seemed kind of wary around him, like losing your parents off a cliff was somehow contagious. Jason seemed desperate to avoid all thought of the accident, like that could happen.

"Ha-ha," Jason replied. "Mailbox baseball."

Cameron kept dribbling the ball. "That's lame."

"It rocks. You'll see. We can take the Jeep." Jason already had his license and wanted any excuse to drive. "Let's pick up some of the other guys and go to that new subdivision out on Ranger Road. There's a whole row of them—*pow!*" He pantomimed the swinging of a bat.

Maybe he was right, thought Cameron. Maybe he needed to do some damage.

At 10:20 p.m., Lily fell apart. She was sitting on the bed of the guest room in Crystal's house, listening to the silence. At her insistence, Sean was using Crystal's room, which was too filled with reminders for Lily to face. It was quiet in there and no light showed under the door, and she envied him for sleeping. She had taken another shower and was wearing a borrowed terry-cloth robe with sleeves that were way too long. She felt warm and clean, and when she reached into the pocket of the robe, she found a crumpled Kleenex and a note scribbled with 503-555-2412. The number was surrounded by the little bubbles and swirls of Crystal's doodling, and for a moment, just a split second, she thought about going downstairs and having a cup of tea with Crystal and handing her the slip of paper.

The finality of the loss hit her—no more cups of tea, no more long phone calls or shopping excursions. Nothing. Yesterday she'd had a best friend. Today, just like that, she didn't.

A terrible howl of pain and grief welled up inside her. All day long, it had been building and swelling, clamoring to erupt. Around the children, she'd held in the consuming wildness of her grief through sheer force of will.

Now her control slipped away and she fell back on the bed, hugged a pillow against her face and let go. The sobs came like a great, unstoppable storm, lashing through her. Her anguished voice was muffled by the pillow, but in her head it sounded as loud as a scream.

Crystal was gone. The reality consumed Lily. Without warning and with irrevocable finality, her best friend, the sister of her heart, was gone. Lily wept for all the laughter and conversation they would never again share, for all the time they'd never have together. She wept for the children who would grow up without a mother and for the horrible injustice of their pain, which they'd done nothing to deserve. She wept until she felt emptied out, weak and raw and scraped hollow with a grief that seemed to have a peculiar energy of its own.

"Lily?" A small voice intruded.

She sat up, already scrubbing her face with her sleeve. Charlie stood in the doorway, looking uncertain and frightened as she clutched a stuffed toy in her hands. "I saw you crying."

"Oh, Charlie," Lily said. "I'm sad about your mom. I'll be all right, but I needed to cry for a bit."

"I woke up and started feeling sad all over again," Charlie said. "I can't sleep."

Lily got up, feeling as though she'd run a marathon. "Come on, sweet thing. Let's go eat some ice cream."

"I'm not hungry. I'm not...anything."

"Then how about I sit with you for a while." She took the little girl by the hand, walked her back to her room. They stopped to check on Ashley in her crib, tucking a blanket around her. Then they sat together in the window seat, moving aside the stuffed toys and pulling back the curtain to reveal a misty moon. Lily brought Charlie against her, stroking her silky hair. "We have to whisper so we don't wake Ashley."

"She sleeps through anything," Charlie said. She was silent for a few minutes, her small, spare body fitting itself against Lily's. "I know how to figure out your porn-star name," she said.

"Have you been talking to Russell Clark?"

"Yep."

"Do you even know what a porn star is?"

"I asked Uncle Sean. He said it's someone who uses a phony name made out of the name of your first pet and your street. At the school carnival last year I won a goldfish and named her Zippy, so mine's Zippy Candlewood."

"That's very...clever."

"So what's yours, Lily?"

"I never had a pet."

"Never? Not even a goldfish or a baby bird you rescued?"

"Not even a pet rock." Lily's parents had been adamant about pets. "They never outlive you," her mother had reasoned. "They cost a fortune and then break your heart."

Charlie shifted against her chest. "I wish I had a dog. Mom

and Dad never let us have a dog even though I want one worse than anything."

A pained silence spun out. Lily thought Charlie might have fallen back to sleep, but then she stirred again. "Lily?" she asked in a small voice.

"Mmm?"

"I'm afraid."

"I know, sweetie. But you're safe."

"Not like that." She shifted back to gaze up at Lily. In the shadowy light, her eyes looked enormous. "I'm afraid…I think I made them mad. I think they were mad at me because I'm so dumb in school and because I stole stuff. Maybe that's why they—"

"Oh, my God." Lily didn't let her finish. She cupped Charlie's face between her hands. "That is absolutely, completely wrong. Your parents loved you with every inch of their hearts."

"They were mad at me for stealing."

"Never. They weren't mad and neither was I. Your mom and dad would never, ever want you to think that. We had a conference because we love you and care about you. Promise me you'll believe that because it's the absolute truth."

She nodded. "All right."

Lily lifted her up and carried her over to the bed. She tucked her in, then arranged her two favorite toys—a well-worn lamb and a one-eyed monkey—on either side of her. "You should sleep."

"I will. But Lily?"

"Yes?"

"I thought of a song."

"A song."

"For the funeral."

Lily took a deep breath, held it in. Hang on, she told herself, letting the breath out by inches. Hang on. "What song is that?"

"I want 'Rainbow Connection.'" The third grade class had been learning the song in school and Charlie clearly loved it, particularly the original version sung by Kermit the Frog.

She bent down and carefully kissed Charlie's forehead. "I think that can be arranged."

part three

For what is it to die,
But to stand in the sun and melt into the wind?
—Kahlil Gibran

chapter 20

In the early hours of the morning before the funeral of his brother, Sean Maguire played a round of golf. If it seemed irreverent or disrespectful in any way, he didn't give a shit. This was the golf course where he and Derek had spent the days of their boyhood. Together, they'd played each hole innumerable times. They knew every blade of grass, every rise of a bunker, every dimple on a green. They had laughed and taunted and competed with each other in the golden summers of their youth, neither of them imagining that anything bad could ever happen to them.

And for a good long time, nothing did. They played golf through high school and college, laying ribbons and trophies at Patrick Maguire's feet like sacred offerings. Each had earned his PGA card the first time through Q School. Derek, the elder, was the hard worker, the consistent player. Sean, with more talent but less dedication, always seemed to be in his shadow, but no one was forcing him to stand there. The fact was, Sean had been comfortable flying under the radar. People had no expectations of him, so he rarely disappointed them. And sometimes, like that one amazing year at Augusta, he surprised them.

With Derek gone, there was no shadow to fall over him, and Sean wasn't certain he could stand the glare of attention. Red had done his best to keep the media at bay, though when a beautiful young couple in their prime are killed in a mysterious accident, there was no avoiding speculation. The reporters and cameramen circled. *How do you feel about losing your brother?* The shouted questions made Sean's blood boil.

How did he feel about losing his brother? Were they kidding? Did they think he had an answer for that?

He was doing his level best to play the stoic, to act like the man of the family now, even though he was a wreck inside. A nightmare haunted him. The highway patrol investigators had not detected skid marks on the road where Derek's car had gone down the bank. Sean kept imagining Derek and Crystal airborne, Tillamook Rock in the distance, regarding each other with shock and disbelief, because they were flying.

Not knowing how to grieve or say goodbye had brought him out early this morning, to the lonely quiet of the empty course. Standing at the first tee, he took a deep breath of evergreen-scented air, taking in the hushed beauty of the landscape and feeling the dig of a piercing pain. Damn it, Derek. I miss you, he thought. They'd had their rivalries and their troubles, but they'd never lost their love and respect for each other.

Now Sean played alone, dedicating the round to his brother. This was the week he was supposed to play in his first major in the States, battling his way back onto the tour. Instead, he was making a final private farewell to Derek, and he knew from the second he stepped up to the tee that it was the right way to say goodbye.

He took his first swing, a movement as clean and sharp as an executioner's sword. The ball flew straight down the middle of the fairway. He could hear its gentle thud as it landed exactly where he'd intended, giving him a perfect shot at the green. The entire round went the same way, as fine a game as he had ever played. There were birdies and even an eagle, dead-on chip shots and putts that were drawn to the hole as if by a magnet. His focus and concentration had a Zen-like intensity, allowing no room for doubts or mistakes. He honored his brother with every shot, recorded scores most golfers could never imagine.

For you, Derek, he thought as he finished the last hole by sinking a thirty-foot putt.

Red was waiting for him when he walked off the course. The agent held out his hand for the scorecard, studied it briefly and said, "If you could do that in competition play, you'd be back in the game in no time."

"Uh-huh." They walked to the clubhouse together and Sean put away his golf bag. "I'm not thinking about the tour."

"Not today, but…soon. I mean it, Sean. What the hell else are you going to do?"

Sean had no answer for that. Maybe Red was right. He'd never held down a normal job. The game was in his blood and bone, and it felt unnatural when he wasn't playing. He didn't know who he was if he wasn't a golfer.

"I can't be touring if I'm in charge of Derek's kids."

"I say it can work out. Face it, Sean, a racehorse has to run." Red sent him a meaningful look. "I'll see you at the church."

Sean drove home slowly through a town he remembered like the tune of an old song. Comfort hadn't changed much, and this morning the familiarity was painful. Derek was everywhere in this town, or so it seemed. Every single place Sean passed, from the Comfort Food Bar & Grill to the vacant lot adjacent to the hardware store, reminded him of his brother and filled him with regrets that he hadn't stayed closer, known Derek better at the end of his life. Like everyone else, he had thought they had all the time in the world. He wondered why people always thought that way.

He found Maura working at the computer. In an elegant black dress and high heels, she looked beautiful and very serious. He hadn't seen much of her this week, since he'd been staying with Derek's kids. Lily had finally shooed him out of the house this morning, telling him she'd look after the kids and meet him at the church later.

"Hey," Maura said, "are you all right?"

He bent down and kissed her cheek, catching a sharp whiff of perfume. "I need a shower and shave."

"I'm ready to go when you are."

He hurried through the shower and put on a dark suit he'd bought in Malaysia. Actually, Asmida had bought it, back when they thought they were in love. They probably had been in love. Sean's trouble was that he didn't know how to stay that way.

Maura was waiting in the foyer when he came down. The sight of her made him smile a little, at least. She was attractive in an athletic, fiercely intelligent way that she claimed most men found intimidating. Not Sean, though. He thought she was sexy and she thought she was good for him.

Her work ethic sure as hell was. When he'd moved back to the States he'd been adrift, gravitating toward more stupid mistakes like getting back on the tour. She and Derek had set him straight. He needed steadiness, a regular job, time to get back on his feet.

"You look wonderful," she said with a warm smile.

He nodded distractedly and took out his keys. "I hate this."

"Everybody hates this," she assured him, then touched his cheek. The scratches had nearly healed. "I wish I'd known your brother better."

"So do I." As they drove to the church, Sean wondered why the two most important people in his life barely knew each other. He could always blame Maura's work hours and Derek's own busy career. Now it was too late and there was no one at all to blame.

"Is it weird, living at that house with that woman?"

Yes. "She just stayed the week. The kids need us both."

"You're speeding," Maura pointed out as he headed up the state road toward the old part of town.

He eased his foot off the pedal and forced himself to relax his grip on the steering wheel. Maura rested her hand lightly on his shoulder until the pager on her cell phone went off. As she checked it and made a call, Sean felt his jaw going tight. She had done her best to get the day off, but with a job like hers, she could never be completely free.

When he turned into the church parking lot, he knew the day was rapidly getting worse. Red had warned him that the media would be here in force. There were, of course, the inevitable rumors circulating. What was a supposedly estranged couple doing out together, driving the coast road? Was foul play a factor? And what about reports that despite his success at golf, Derek Holloway had financial troubles?

News vans were already parked along the street and in the church lot, thick black cable snaking across the pavement. Sean drove directly to the rear door, surrendered his car to a waiting attendant; then he and Maura ducked inside to a small reception room behind the sanctuary.

He had no idea how to behave, how to be in charge of this. He shook hands with the minister and accepted his condolences; he went over last-minute details with the funeral director. He thought, with a weird sense of unreality, that the caskets he and Red had picked out were handsome and so shiny that the hard-polished surfaces reflected the framed photos and hundreds of flowers covering them. The caskets were closed, a small mercy, he supposed. At least Derek's kids didn't have to look at their parents' empty faces.

Nothing felt concrete or had any substance. Sean had a peculiar sensation that he was about to drift away and disappear like the soft, nasal strains of organ music that haunted the church, along with the smell of gardenias and chrysanthemums. The grief counselor working with the family had warned him to expect feelings of detachment. Apparently this was a common sensation in people experiencing loss. There was nothing anchoring him to earth.

"Sean?" Maura's soft voiced tugged at him.

"What's that?"

"You're a million miles away."

"I'm right here." He was still floating, but he didn't tell her that. Derek wasn't in the casket. He couldn't be. His presence was too palpable. Sean could still hear the sound of his voice and was convinced that all he had to do was phone him, tell him the jig was up, this isn't funny anymore and wasn't in the first place.

"The doors are about to open. We're supposed to wait with the director until five minutes before the ceremony. Are you sure you're all right?"

The question came to him as though through a long, hollow tube. *Are you sure you're all right?* Hell, no, he wasn't sure. He had no idea how to do this, how to bury his brother and take care of three kids, but he heard himself tell Maura he was fine.

He paced the reception room, occasionally glancing at a video monitor showing the sanctuary. The doors were opened and people poured in. *Mourners.* One moment they were Derek's friends; now they were mourners. There were hundreds of them, it seemed.

Sean pulled his gaze away and looked out the window. A gleaming limo pulled up and a driver with white gloves opened the door.

"That's the teacher?" Maura asked. In the chaos of the past few days, she hadn't met Lily and the children.

"Yes," he said, and felt himself settling back to earth, grounded again. "That's Lily. Come on out and meet everyone." He strode toward the car.

Cameron emerged first, followed by Charlie, who looked taut-faced and terrified. "Uncle Sean," she said, flinging her arms around him.

"Hey, you."

"I'm scared," she said, her voice muffled against his coat.

"Me, too." He had discovered very quickly that it did no good to lie to Charlie. She saw right through him, every time. "Let me help Lily with the baby and then I want you to meet somebody special."

"I'm Maura Riley," he heard Maura say as he bent to unbuckle Ashley from her car seat. The baby crowed and said, "Hi!" with a big smile. He lifted her out and set her on the ground, and Lily took her by the hand.

Sean straightened up and introduced Maura to everyone. She had the awkward manner of someone unaccustomed to children, though her smile was genuine. Charlie regarded her warily, Cameron dismissively. Ashley hid in Lily's skirts. "Did you know my mom and dad?" Cameron asked.

Maura shifted her bag from one hand to the other. "No, but I know they were both terrific. I wanted to be here for your uncle Sean because I care for him a lot. I hope you'll tell me all about your parents."

"You bet," said Cameron. "Love to." He headed for the reception room.

His sarcasm took Maura off guard, but at the moment,

Sean had no chance to make his nephew apologize. He felt stupid for expecting something to happen, some magical *poof* of chemistry and they'd all be one big happy family.

"Time to go inside," he said quietly.

Jane Coombs was late, which seemed to be a pattern with her. She came rushing in and swooped down on the kids, weeping and needy, the way she'd been all week. Sean bit his tongue, wanting to tell her to chill out, that her crying was upsetting Charlie and Ashley. But who was he to criticize the woman? Maybe she couldn't help it.

Three people he didn't recognize arrived, even later than Jane. "My parents and sister," Lily explained. "Excuse me for a moment."

She went over and greeted them. Her parents were a handsome couple, impeccably dressed and treating Lily with a curious reserve. For God's sake, give her a hug, he found himself thinking. Can't you see she needs it?

Fortunately, the sister seemed to, grabbing Lily and reeling her in, holding on tight until Lily's hat fell backward off her head.

"Sean Maguire," he said, retrieving the hat and then shaking hands with each of them—Terence, Sharon and Violet. "Thank you for coming."

"Grandpa, you made it," Charlie said, her face lighting up as she rushed toward the door.

"Hello, gorgeous, of course I made it." Sean's father, Patrick Maguire, had arrived the night before. He greeted Lily and the others, then shook hands with Sean. "You holding up all right?"

For a second, Sean had a wicked urge to say no. As in, No, Dad, I'm in big trouble here. How about you give me a hand? He would never say that; he knew better, because he knew the answer he'd get. His father would hem and haw, enumerating all the reasons he couldn't possibly help with Derek's kids. "Yes," Sean assured his father, "all things considered."

"Sorry I couldn't get away sooner," said Patrick. "I had some things to finish up."

Of course he did, thought Sean. "No problem," he said to his father. What he really wanted to do was to grab him, shake him, demand to know had happened to their family. Like that mattered now. He disengaged his hand and rested it on Charlie's shoulder. "We need to get started."

As everyone assembled to proceed into the sanctuary, Sean paused to have a look at them all. The children appeared scrubbed and apprehensive in their best clothes. At the same time, there was a heartbreaking air of dignity about them. Cameron looked like a junior version of Derek in a new suit and shoes hastily bought for the funeral. Charlie wore a dark green dress with a black ribbon and Ashley had on a miniature version of the same outfit. Lily was in dark blue, with low-heeled shoes, a purse clutched in one hand and a small stack of neatly printed index cards in the other. She wore a hat and no makeup, and looked nervous and earnest, determined to deliver a proper eulogy for her friend.

The funeral director had them all escorted to their seats in the front pews. The principal of Charlie's school was right behind them on the end, ready to whisk Ashley away if she got too loud. The honey-oak caskets, draped in flowers, gleamed in the sunlight filtering through a window with a Holy Spirit design. And Sean was floating again in a high arc overhead, unable to keep himself anchored to the earth.

chapter 21

The funeral was a brutal spectacle that was part media circus, part solemn ceremony. Lily felt battered and sore on the inside, exhausted to the point of numbness. The service went by in a blur of tears and music and heartfelt eulogies. Everyone present tried to express the inexpressible—grief for a shocking loss and, perhaps worse, the sadness and quiet terror of three children who would grow up without their parents.

Lily was surprised and moved when her family showed up. They hadn't known Crystal well, but they knew how important she was to Lily. When it was her turn to speak up, she sent a panicked glance toward her mother, receiving a calm nod of encouragement: *You can do this.*

Lily stood and made her way to the podium. Somehow, for the sake of the children, she managed to speak in a clear, steady voice, telling the packed church that Crystal had been the best friend, mother and person anyone could imagine.

"Best friend and loving mother" had seemed like the proper words when she'd written them late last night. Yet uttered over the PA system to a packed church, they sounded hollow and impersonal. Lily set aside her note cards, shut her eyes briefly and made a picture of Crystal in her mind.

"I was eight years old when I met my best friend," she said, then opened her eyes again. "She was thirteen and had no intention of being my best friend or anything but my babysitter. That came later—the friendship. And it's lasted a lifetime—" Lily paused, taking a breath and trying to keep her voice from wavering. "When I was small, I thought she knew everything. Twenty-two years later, I know it's finally true. Thanks to her beautiful children, she knows the joys and triumph of living a life filled with love. And that's all anyone ever needs to know, isn't it?" Lily was surprised by the words coming out of her. This wasn't in her notes. Her notes contained a résumé of Crystal's accomplishments, a loving salute to her character. It was too late to backtrack now, and because of all the other tributes, she'd promised to keep hers short. She paused again and focused on the children. Edna had taken Ashley away when she started fussing. Charlie sat unmoving, staring straight ahead. Next to her, Sean wore a curiously similar expression. Cameron seemed angry, almost defiant as he shifted restlessly in his seat.

Lily had been gratified to see students and teachers from the high school, but they looked ill at ease, shifting and whispering in the back rows, clearly wishing they could be somewhere else. She hadn't spotted Greg Duncan and found that disappointing. As Cameron's golf coach, he should have been there, but that was Greg for you.

"I can't find any meaning in the way my friend died," she said. "Maybe I'm supposed to, perhaps one day I will. For me the meaning is in her life, not in her death. I loved Crystal Baird Holloway. For the rest of my life, I will live to celebrate that friendship." She cleared her throat, the knot of pain nearly stopping her breath. "Goodbye, Crystal. You live in the hearts of those who loved you."

Dr. Sachs, the grief counselor, had told Lily that medication was available if she felt she needed it. As she stepped down from the podium, she found herself wishing she had taken advantage of the offer.

As she left the podium, Charlie's requested song was played. Kermit the Frog singing "Rainbow Connection" might have seemed ludicrous under the circumstances, but for some reason, the song's subtlety, wistfulness and simple message struck the perfect note.

Lily put on a brave smile for Charlie and Cameron, although inside, she was a broken wreck. Sean Maguire offered his hand to help her into the pew. Hers was ice cold and damp with sweat. How pleasant for him, she thought fleetingly.

His girlfriend, Maura, seemed distressed by the whole situation. In her smooth black dress and wrap, she also looked beautiful, like a Victoria's Secret model. Next to her, Lily felt dismally ordinary.

Under the circumstances, she should not feel anything of the sort, but there it was. Her best friend was dead and Lily was having petty thoughts. She was a terrible person.

For Derek, there was a graceless but moving tribute from his caddie, who sobbed through the whole thing. Travis Jacobs had been with Derek for fifteen years and knew him in ways no one else would or could. Given what Lily knew about him, the eulogy was generous, sometimes funny and utterly sincere. When Travis concluded his reading, the sound of Louis Armstrong singing "What a Wonderful World" drifted from the speakers, and Lily's heart was seized by melancholy.

She kept an eye on Jane Coombs, who sat beside her lawyer across the aisle. Judging by her devastated expression, she was in shock and grieving deeply. Jane hadn't had much to say over the past few days. She behaved as though she didn't know the children at all and was as lost as they were.

Lily tried not to think ill of the woman who had stolen her best friend's husband, but it wasn't easy. She distinctly remembered Crystal's shell-shocked expression when she had come over to Lily's house one night and said, "Derek has someone else. And I'm pregnant." All in the same breath. Either one would have rocked her world. Together, they changed her life.

Lily tried not to think about that time. She tried not to think about all the hurt and humiliation Crystal had suffered. As she said in her tribute, Crystal had experienced soaring joys and profound blessings. That was what Lily told herself to dwell on. Not the other things, the failed marriage and the money troubles, or the fact that, right before she died, Crystal's best friend had told her Charlie was failing third grade.

Crystal's pain and confusion that day followed Lily to bed each night and haunted her dreams when she slept. She had no idea how to get rid of it. She glanced around the church and tried to take comfort from those gathered here—friends and associates, people from work and school.

Somehow they made it through the rest of the service, which included prayers she felt all the way down to her soul and songs that bore a hole in her heart. There was only one reason she managed to stay standing, and that was the fact that Crystal's children were depending on her.

This was an issue, she expected, that would be addressed at the reading of the wills.

Charlie tugged on her hand. "When are we going to the seminary?" she whispered.

"Cemetery," Lily whispered back. "In a little while. After 'Over the Rainbow,'" she added, remembering that she had requested the version sung by the late Hawaiian artist, Iz. She thought it might remind Cameron of the time he and Crystal had taken ukelele lessons together. He hadn't wanted any input into the service and in general was disconcertingly quiet about the loss of his parents.

She leaned closer and said into Charlie's ear, "Why do you ask?"

"I need to know when to really say goodbye," Charlie said.

Lily slipped her arm around the little girl's shoulders. "Oh, honey," she said in an aching whisper, "you don't ever have to say goodbye."

chapter 22

Lily had no idea what to wear to the meeting. What in the world did a person wear to the reading of a will?

Her choices were limited. Although she had been at Crystal's place for nearly a week, she hadn't brought much with her. It occurred to her that her school wardrobe didn't seem quite right. A sweater embroidered with teddy bears might look fine in the classroom, but not at a serious meeting.

Her one and only business suit would suffice, she supposed. There would be lawyers present, finance would be discussed. She owed it to Crystal to appear professional.

She felt a keen sense of mission as she put on a white blouse and tied it in a crisp bow at the throat. Then she pulled on a dark A-line skirt and blazer with brass buttons. Great, she thought, stepping into low-heeled pumps. I look like Sergeant Pepper.

She pulled her hair in place with a pair of barrettes, then frowned at her image in the mirror. How did women pull this off? she wondered. Was there some trick to looking professional she didn't know about?

The superficial questions made her feel guilty, so she quickly applied a single layer of tinted lip gloss and declared herself ready.

All three kids were in the kitchen at breakfast when she came down. Charlie was glued to the Cartoon Network, as usual, and Ashley was eating applesauce from a plastic bowl. Cameron was bent over a physics textbook, holding his head in his hand while glowering at the page. Sean had gone to see Red Corliss before the meeting.

"Hi!" Ashley banged her spoon, then held it out to Lily. "Taste."

Lily pretended to have a bite. "Mmm, delicious." She reached over and turned down the volume of the blaring cartoons. Once things settled down, she was going to have to curb all the TV watching. Living in a house full of children was like visiting a third world country, a place filled with color, noise and strange smells. She had been doing her best to bring order to chaos, but things kept getting away from her.

"I'm off to my meeting," she announced. "I'll be gone for a couple of hours, I imagine. Cameron, you're in charge."

"Got it," he said in a bored voice.

"Got it," Ashley echoed. "Out." She squirmed in her seat.

"Cameron will take care of you," Lily said, placing a kiss on the child's head on her way toward the door.

As Lily drove to the downtown law offices, she had the strange feeling that this was not her life anymore. She was living someone else's life, with children and a host of responsibilities so numerous she couldn't even begin to address each one adequately.

An offhand promise to a friend—I'll look after your kids, no problem—had turned into a commitment she was completely unequipped to make. She had taken the entire week off school, but come Monday, she had to go back to her own house, to her job. Life had to go forward for all of them, and that would be one of the topics of today's meeting.

The law offices of Logan, Schwab and Fuller were plush and quiet. She was ushered into a conference room where everyone was assembled—Sean Maguire and Red Corliss, Sean's father, Patrick, and Derek's girlfriend, Jane Coombs, and her own lawyer. Frances Jamison, Crystal's divorce attorney, was present as well, Lily saw with a small eddy of relief. Everyone else was here for Derek.

Not quite, she observed as Susie Shea entered the room. The social worker was there as the children's advocate.

Peter Logan, looking like an elder statesman in his couture suit, opened the meeting by welcoming everyone and consulting a voluminous folder of papers.

"Thank you for being here, ladies and gentlemen," he said. "I'd like to express my heartfelt condolences to the family and friends of Derek and Crystal Holloway. I know their loss is deeply felt."

Lily sneaked a glance at Sean. It had been the strangest of weeks, living with this man. He obviously cared about the children, but when it came to parenting them, he was as lost as Lily. He looked haggard but paid close attention as Logan read down a list of declarations. Next to Sean, his father, Patrick, appeared well rested and full of vitality. He was an immensely handsome man, tall and lean, with abundant salt-and-pepper hair. As Derek's stepfather, he was the only grandparent the children had, utterly charming, with smooth manners and a winning smile. It was funny, though. When Lily looked into his eyes, she didn't see much.

People perked up as Logan reached the meat of the reading—the disposition of Derek's estate. There were bequests to Red Corliss, Travis Jacobs, Patrick Maguire and several other associates of Derek. He left his brother all of his clubs. Sean looked neither pleased nor disappointed. Lily couldn't read his expression.

"The remainder of my estate, such state consisting of—" Logan passed copies of a list around "—shall be equally divided among my beloved children, Cameron Craig Holloway, Charlene Louise Holloway and Ashley Baird Holloway. If they are of minor age at the time of my death, the inheritance is to be held in trust by Crystal Baird Holloway, or in the event that she is not available, my brother, Sean Michael Maguire, until such time as they gain their majority."

The final disposition fell into a silence so profound that Lily could hear the man next to her—Jane's lawyer—breathing. So Jane had been stiffed, thought Lily. Well, well, well.

The reading went on, answering the question of who the children's designated guardian would be. First named was his ex-wife, Crystal Baird Holloway, of course. Next in line was Sean Michael Maguire. A judge of the probate court would issue an order after the noticed hearing had taken place.

More silence hung over the conference room while people digested this. Derek had not designated Jane, who claimed she had every intention of marrying him. He hadn't chosen Patrick, either; Patrick didn't even bother hiding his relief. No, Derek had picked Sean Maguire, his half brother, a man who had barely been a presence in the children's lives.

The social worker quickly jotted down the information as Mr. Logan prepared to turn the reading over to Frances Jamison, Crystal's lawyer.

Jane pushed back from the table. "I've heard enough," she said quietly, then left with her lawyer.

"Not a happy camper," Frances murmured under her breath.

Lily tried to focus on the pages Frances held before her. The document was dated five years ago, when Crystal and

Derek had drawn them up together. There were bequests to Dorothy and to Lily, who had expected nothing: "To my best friend, Lily Elaine Robinson, I leave the sum of $10,000 along with my wardrobe. Lily, you were never much for fashion, but maybe you've changed."

Lily was struck by her friend's sentiment and by the echo of Crystal's own authentic voice. She groped for a Kleenex in her purse, but found she'd used them all up. Without a word, Sean turned to the credenza behind him and grabbed a box, pushing it across the table to her.

Crystal's disposition to her children was identical to Derek's except that, in the event that the children were minors, the estate was to be administered by Crystal's mother, Dorothy Mansfield Baird. Dorothy was also named guardian of the children.

Frances tapped the stack of papers on the hard leather surface of the table. "Ladies and gentlemen, this part is problematic, which is why I've asked Miss Robinson to attend today. Dorothy Baird has succumbed to a massive stroke. At present, she is bedridden and shows no recognition of friends and family. Her prognosis is poor, so she won't be able to undertake any of the responsibilities noted herein. As a matter of fact, I had a meeting scheduled with Crystal to address just this issue. She wanted to change her will, designating Miss Robinson the children's guardian in the event that her ex-husband could not undertake that duty."

"That contradicts Mr. Holloway's document, which, unlike his ex-wife's, is dated, signed and properly filed," said Mr. Logan. "The designated guardian is supposed to be agreed upon by both parents, and since that didn't happen, we expect the court to rule for the father's wishes."

Lily knew the devastation was still stark in her eyes as she lifted them to look around the table. No one even seemed to notice that she was there except Sean Maguire. He was watching her with an intensity that made her shiver.

She ignored him and tried to focus during the rest of the proceedings. Ms. Fuller delivered a preliminary financial disclosure that seemed to take everyone but Red by surprise. Sorting through the rhetoric and studying the columns of numbers, Lily realized Derek was up to his eyeballs in debt. Crystal was in nearly as deep. With the extravagant lifestyle they'd enjoyed both before and after the divorce, they had managed to spend even more than Derek's considerable earnings. No one said it aloud, but everyone knew that in layman's terms, this meant they were close to broke.

Red looked around the table. "Professional golf is a heartless game. You can make a million dollars one year and the next year get zilch."

There was a long explanation of the provisions of Derek's insurance policy and how the bequests would work in the absence of actual cash, but Lily didn't listen. She had other things on her mind, and when the meeting ended, she went straight to Susie Shea. "I should be taking care of the children, not Maguire," she stated without preamble. Just like that. The decision had come to her swiftly, not really a decision so much as a compulsion. She had made a conscious choice to be alone all her life. Now she was choosing to end that isolation.

"Maybe Maguire has an opinion about that," he stated, his tone hostile. "Maybe Maguire's opinion is that you should butt out."

"For the time being," said Ms. Shea, "Mr. Maguire is the designated guardian. However, Mr. Maguire, I hope you understand that Miss Robinson means a great deal to the Holloway children."

"I'm not going to run her off, if that's what you're asking, but someone needs to be in charge, and that's me."

Ms. Shea nodded and stepped aside to consult with the lawyers.

Lily bristled as she faced Sean. She wanted to understand what drove this man, but the two of them were worlds apart, united only by their compassion for the children. "I don't think you're considering the long term. This is a huge commitment."

"You think I don't know that?"

"They're in a post-trauma situation and just getting them through that is going to take an enormous effort," she said. "While they're dealing with that, life doesn't simply stop and wait for them. There are school issues, potty training and tantrums, illness, puberty, and you never get time off for good behavior. This is a life sentence."

"Gee, you make it sound like a real picnic."

"This is not about having fun."

He chuckled, but his eyes were flinty with anger. "Oh, that's classic. 'This is not about having fun.'" He did a wicked imitation of Lily.

She stifled a gasp of outrage. "I'm just trying to make clear to you—"

"That fun is out of the question?"

"That our priority is the children."

"Let's see. Which of us is better for them? You, because you'll make sure they go to bed on time every night, or me, because I'm not afraid to let them learn that life can be fun again? Let's ask Dr. Sachs." He took out his cell phone.

She didn't know what possessed her to touch him. She put her hand on his arm. "They need us both."

He looked at her hand, then at her. Self-conscious, she moved away.

"Tell me why you're so fired up to step in and raise these kids," he said.

"Because it's what Crystal wanted. Because I'd do a good

job." She spoke with unthinking swiftness and vehemence. "I made a promise."

He folded his arms across his chest. "I'm not hearing you say you *want* this," he pointed out.

"I want what's best for these children." Suddenly the life she thought she had, the future she'd planned for herself, looked completely different. Her palms were sweating, though she resisted the urge to wipe them on her skirt. "I'm sure you want that, too, Sean. I know you care about them, but that doesn't mean you have to sacrifice everything—"

"It wouldn't be a sacrifice. It would be...living. Doing what people do all over the world, raising a family and getting through the day. It's common sense that the kids need stability and consistency, and since Derek's will is clear on the point of guardianship, that means they're staying with me."

"I should raise them." Even as she said the words, her blood froze in trepidation. Say yes, she thought, and then, please say no. Lily drew herself up. She'd been knocked out of the way by Derek's will, which left his unsuitable brother as guardian. It wasn't right. "I'm serious," she said. "And you know I'm right."

"My brother had another opinion."

"Just because he chose you doesn't mean you're the most suited."

"Just because you've known them longer and have a frigging degree in education doesn't mean you are," he shot back. "Besides, I've got something else, Lily."

"And what's that?"

"I'm not afraid. And you are."

Even as a denial leaped to her lips, she felt something cold and dark reverberate inside her like iron struck with a mallet. How had he known? Could he smell fear like a predator?

Lily turned away and went over to the water cooler, trying

to compose herself as she filled a cone-shaped paper cup and took a sip. He'd nailed the truth; she *was* afraid. She had built her life up around her like a wall, barricading her heart against hurt. She had never, ever planned to have a family. It was a conscious choice. She wanted her life to be her own, wanted to be free to go where she pleased and do what she wished, answering to no one. Taking on three children would change that irrevocably.

Ah, but look what it could give you, whispered Crystal's voice in her ear. Some things are more important than being afraid.

"We're wasting time arguing about this," Sean said. "I need to get home. The kids deserve to know what's going on. They love you, Lily, and if you show them that you have any doubts about this situation, they'll know. Is that what you want?"

They love you, Lily. The words shuddered through her. "I want them to feel safe and secure."

"My brother trusted me with these kids. Whatever you and Crystal might have thought of him, he was a caring father. I'm not going to let him down."

She crumpled the paper cup in her hand and dropped it into the wastebasket. "There's no money. You understand that, right?"

"Hey, I'm a dumb jock, but I can add and subtract." He loosened his tie and glared at her. "You're starting to piss me off. No, I take that back. You've already pissed me off a number of times today."

She glared up at him. "You've made me angry today, too."

"Pissed, Lily. The word is *pissed.*" He spoke so loudly that heads turned in their direction.

Her cheeks burned. "How mature of you. That will probably go into the report to the probate judge."

"What, that you have a way of pissing people off?" He offered a disarming smile despite his words. "Let's end this discussion and go see the kids."

"This discussion is not over."

"Yeah, it is. You're off the hook. You can go home now. I'm not going to walk away from this."

"You've walked away from everything else in your life," Lily pointed out. "Crystal told me so. She said you walked away from your career."

"We're talking about kids here, not a career. You don't walk away from kids. I won't be perfect at this but I'll put everything I've got into it."

She drew herself up, already thinking of a counterargument. Then his words sank in and her shoulders relaxed a little. "Good answer."

chapter 23

"Lily and I have news," Sean announced to Cameron and Charlie when they arrived home. He tried to sound positive and upbeat. That was what the social worker and the counselor advised him to do. Sound positive and upbeat without denying the tragedy. Reassure the children that life would go on and things would get better.

Like they could get any worse. What was worse than being a kid and losing both parents on the same day?

Sean had been an adult when his mother died five years ago, and he still bled from that wound. One of the last things she'd said to Sean had always puzzled him. She told him to fall in love, settle down, make a family. "It's what you were made for, more than any of us." Over the past five years, he'd done his best to ignore that advice. Now, looking at his nieces and nephew, he thought of her. She'd always had a great sense of humor.

"Hi, Lily," said Ashley, playing with a plastic spatula on the floor by her feet.

"So what's the news?" Cameron asked, his arms tightly folded across his middle.

"We had a meeting with your mom's and your dad's lawyers today to read their wills. They both left you pretty much everything they possessed."

"Everything?" Charlie's eyes goggled.

"Almost. Your dad left me his golf clubs, and there were bequests to Red, Travis, Grandpa and some others. And your mom remembered her mother and Lily, here." Good old Lily, he thought. He was still ticked off by the things she'd said to him, challenging his fitness to take care of this family. It was like she wanted to undermine his confidence.

She offered a hard-won smile. "Your mother wanted me to have her clothes. She was always after me to dress more fashionably, you know."

"And that's all?" Charlie asked. "That's absolutely all? There wasn't anyone else who gets something?"

"Not that I recall." Sean looked at Lily. "You?"

"I think that covers it."

"Phew." Charlie slumped back against the sofa cushion.

"Is there someone else who should have been mentioned?" Sean asked.

"Nope, not at all, no way," Charlie said immediately.

She was a funny little thing, Sean reflected. In a lot of ways, his niece was hard to know. Cameron glared at her and mouthed something Sean couldn't discern. She stuck her tongue out at him.

"So are we getting placed in foster homes or what?" Cameron asked.

"Of course not," said Sean.

"Why would you think such a thing?" asked Lily.

"We're in the foster-care system. I was wondering if we'd be farmed out to foster parents."

Charlie's chin trembled. "I don't want to be in foster care."

"Your brother's full of sh—crap," Sean said. He tried to be patient with Cameron's attitude, but it was hard. "Nobody's going to farm you out anywhere. You're going to live with me. Or actually, it would be more accurate to say, I'm going to live with you. Right here in this house."

It felt surreal to be saying it. Sean had gone from having no one but himself to having a house in the suburbs and three kids. He couldn't quite get his mind around that. Like Lily said, this was a life sentence.

"Is Lily still going to sleep in the guest room?" Charlie asked.

"She's not staying, genius," said Cameron.

"You're not?" Pigtails flying, Charlie whipped her head around to face Lily.

"I can't, sweetheart," Lily said. "But I promise I'll be here for you. I'll see you at school every day, and I'll come on the nights when your uncle is working."

Sean let out the breath he'd been holding. They'd gone over something called a preliminary parenting plan with the social worker. Sean could tell Lily wasn't happy with the arrangement, but she didn't let the kids know how she felt. That was the thing about Lily. She definitely put the kids first. He knew she was furious about the terms of the will, yet for the sake of these kids, she was keeping her disapproval to herself.

"Who'll take care of us when we go to Dad's?" asked Charlie.

"We're not going to Dad's, moron," said Cameron. "He's not there. Don't you get it?"

"Hey," Sean told him. "That's enough."

Charlie hung her head.

"Look, we're going to make this work," Sean said, but no one was listening because Ashley chose that moment to flip the waist-level switch of the garbage disposal. The buzz of the machine startled her into wide-eyed silence. Then her face crumpled like a wadded-up Kleenex and she let out one of those armor-piercing howls.

Everyone in the room went for her—Sean, Lily, Cameron and even Charlie—all desperate to console her. Sean reached her first, scooping her against him. Around midweek, she'd decided he was all right and now let him hold her whenever he wanted. She clung to him and eventually the fearful sobs shuddered into silence. Then she pushed her fists against his chest and looked him in the eye.

"Da," she said.

An eerie sensation crept over him. "Uncle Sean. That's my name. Can you say it? Un-cle Sean."

"Da," she said again, and stuck her thumb in her mouth.

Charlie came into Cameron's room late that night, looking scruffy and a little lost in their mother's nightgown, her eyes wide in an expression he would have laughed at if he hadn't recognized the terrible fear she was feeling.

"What's the matter?" he asked. "What are you doing up?"

"It's about Ashley," Charlie said in a small, frightened voice.

Oh, man. Not Charlie, too. Who else knew about this?

Cameron felt sorry for her so he put his arm around her and hugged her close. She felt warm and solid against him and her hair smelled of baby shampoo.

"What about her?" he made himself ask, even though he knew. God, he knew and he was getting just as scared as Charlie.

"Mom said dad isn't Ashley's father. She said Ashley has another father."

Cameron took a deep breath. What was he supposed to do, tell the kid their mother was a liar or let her know she'd slept around?

"When did she say that?"

"After spring break. She was all mad that dad took us to California."

A cold fist squeezed Cameron's gut. "Did she say that to Dad?"

"No. Just me. She, um, she was sad and mad and there was nobody else to talk to."

She'd probably had a bottle of wine that night, like the night she'd told Cameron. Anger at his mother burned like acid in his stomach. It did no good at all to feel pissed at his parents anymore, but sometimes he couldn't help himself.

"There's probably some mistake," Cameron said. "You heard it wrong. She didn't mean anything."

"She told me," Charlie said. "People think I'm stupid but I'm not. She said Ashley has another daddy and I'm scared he's going to come and take her away."

Cameron was afraid of that, too. "The most important thing is to keep quiet. It's just a story and you'll only cause trouble if you say something."

"I won't tell," she whispered.

"You don't need to. Nobody's going to take her away," he vowed, putting his other arm around her. Saying so made him feel the way he always felt—he didn't even know whether or not he was telling the truth.

Charlie sobbed so hard that she choked, so he hugged her again. "Hey," he said, rubbing her back through the silky, too-big nightgown that still had their mother's scent. "Hey, try to calm down, okay?"

"I try that all the time, but I *want* them, Cam. I have to talk to them and hug them. I miss them so much." She seemed to be having trouble breathing between sobs.

"I miss them, too." He stroked her hair. In a way, Charlie was luckier than he was. Her feelings for their parents were simple and clear. She adored and worshipped them. Even the fact that she knew something was up with Ashley didn't tinge her adoration. When she remembered them, she would think only of their perfection, not their flaws.

Cameron, on the other hand, was old enough to know his parents were human and very flawed. Still, he found himself wishing he hadn't had that stupid fight with his father on what turned out to be their last morning together. He wished he'd been more sympathetic to his mother when she broke down and told him about Ashley.

"I need them, Cam," Charlie whispered against his chest. "I need them to come back."

"Yeah," he said, his voice gravelly, his eyes stinging. "Me, too."

chapter 24

Sean regarded the splat of Gerber oatmeal on the kitchen wall, then glared at his younger niece. "Everybody's a critic," he said.

She glared right back. "It's yuck."

"Eat the damned oatmeal," he snapped.

She gasped audibly, as though he'd struck her, then burst into tears. "It's yuck," she sobbed. "It's yuck."

"Aw, come on, Ashley," he said pleadingly. "I didn't mean to yell at you." But she was lost to him, lost in a world of misery. "Damn it," he muttered.

"Damn it," she howled. Before he could stop her, she flung another spoonful of oatmeal. This time it hit him smack in the face, the lukewarm cereal sliding down his cheek.

Ashley went silent, her teary eyes wide with apprehension. She was only two, but she knew what naughty was.

Sean felt himself losing it. He'd gotten up extra early today and dressed in a good shirt and tie, because he had to take Charlie and Cameron to school. Slowly, the oatmeal dripped down into the corner of his mouth. He could tell the baby was winding up for another howl.

"Oh, man," he said, getting a taste of the cereal. "It *is* yuck." He made a terrible face and clutched at his throat.

Ashley couldn't resist that, and she giggled until she got the hiccups. Sean made a big production of cleaning the oatmeal off his face and out of his shirt collar, which made her laugh even more. Relieved, he talked her into eating a piece of banana bread, one of the dozens of things brought by concerned friends and neighbors. He was running out of space in the freezer for all the stuff people were bringing. At this rate, Sean reckoned, he wouldn't have to learn to cook for a year. He sure as hell intended to cross oatmeal off his list.

Charlie wore a foul expression as she marched into the kitchen and dropped her backpack on the floor.

"Next crisis?" he said.

"Cameron's taking forever in the bathroom and I didn't even get to do my hair."

"Do what to your hair?" Sean handed her a hunk of banana bread and poured her a glass of milk.

Charlie's chin trembled. "Mom always did my hair, except when I was at Dad's."

Sean knew he had to do something fast or she'd start crying. When she cried, Ashley always joined in, and then he'd be back to square one. "Did your dad do your hair?"

She scowled at him. "No way."

"I bet I can do it," Sean said.

"Uh-uh."

"Uh-huh." He opened a utility drawer, where he'd spied a jumble of hairbrushes and shiny hair clips and ponytail holders. "Have a seat, madam."

Shooting him a look of suspicion, Charlie sat on a counter stool. Ashley watched, rapt with fascination. Sean wondered what he'd gotten himself into. His niece had bright, silky curls that looked just fine to him, but she insisted she wanted braids and barrettes. It had a kind of softness he'd never felt before. He didn't know how to braid hair but he figured out what a barrette was. "This is the best braid ever," he assured her, twisting two ropes of hair together. He picked the shiniest, gaudiest barrettes and ponytail holders, and when he was finished, she didn't look half bad.

"Done," he said. "You look like Cher."

"Who's Cher?"

"One of the best-looking women ever," he said. "Eat your banana bread."

"I don't want to go to school," Charlie said, picking at her breakfast.

Cameron ambled into the kitchen, his hair still damp from the shower. "Me, neither."

"Fine. You can stay home and clean this place up." Sean gestured around the kitchen. Lily had left only yesterday, yet somehow the dishes in the sink had multiplied and clutter had gathered on every available surface. "Your choice," he said.

Charlie eyed the smear of oatmeal on the wall. "School," she said sulkily.

"Whatever," said Cameron.

"I wish I was going to Italy," Charlie said.

"Why Italy?"

"'Cause it's not here. Lily's going to Italy for the whole summer."

Good for Lily, he thought with a spike of envy.

Lily watched Sean striding down the corridor to her classroom, with Charlie in tow. He held her hand but walked so fast she practically had to run to keep up. They both looked grim, and Lily's bright smile of greeting failed to impress them. "Go on in, sweetie," she said, "your friends are waiting for you."

Lindsey Davenport, bless her, grabbed Charlie by the hand and pulled her inside.

"It's not working," Sean said when she was out of earshot.

"What's not working?" she asked in an undertone. She kept her eye on Charlie, watching the little girl put up her backpack. The other kids came to welcome her back, exclaiming about her hair and treating her with the sort of fragile tenderness children instinctively showed when one of their own had been wounded.

"Everything. This whole arrangement. It's chaos at the house, getting everyone up, dealing with the baby, getting out the door on time. It's insane."

"Women do it every day of their lives," she couldn't help saying.

"And that's supposed to help?" He rubbed at a spot of something on his shirt. His expression changed to a smile as Charlie approached him.

"See you, Uncle Sean."

He touched her head awkwardly but with affection. "You have a good day, sugar."

"Okay." Charlie was now surrounded by a few of her friends who had come to check out her uncle. In chinos and a shirt and tie, he had a sort of flustered, rumpled charm. Children seemed drawn to him, as though they recognized a kindred spirit.

"Let me know how it goes today," he murmured to Lily.

And honestly, she decided as the day moved forward, it seemed to go well enough. She couldn't deny her relief at being back in the classroom, her safe world, in control once again. Here, she was her best self, confident and caring with the students she loved. After the chaotic, emotional week at Crystal's, this felt normal.

So why did she find herself missing the chaos of that house?

Lily pushed aside the thought and kept an eye on Charlie, who was subdued throughout the day, and near the end, Lily felt hopeful. Traditionally, she set aside the final twenty minutes for reading circle.

"Boys and girls," Lily said, settling on the floor pillows and motioning everyone to gather around. "We're going to start a new read-aloud book today. *Charlotte's Web* by E. B. White."

"I saw the cartoon on TV," said Eden.

"The book's always better, isn't it, Miss Robinson?" said Sarah.

Lily nodded, then paused to wait for everyone to be quiet. She opened the book to the familiar first page. It was a risky choice under the circumstances, but she trusted her instincts. This was, bar none, a flawless novel and one of the best ever penned for children. Or for adults, for that matter. She hoped the story of a friendship so powerful that it transcends death would have special meaning for Charlie.

Lily took a deep breath and started reading. " ' "Where's Papa going with that ax?" said Fern to her mother as they were setting the table for breakfast…' "

There were probably worse things than coming back to school after your parents drove off a cliff, but at the moment, Cameron couldn't think of any. This was it, right here. As his uncle pulled to the front of Comfort High School, he felt as if he'd been knocked into a dark hole, the way he'd felt the morning Sean had come home with the news.

Ignoring his babbling baby sister, he slammed the car door shut and stood in front of the school, which at this hour swarmed with students. The booster club members were stringing a banner up between two big sycamore trees, promoting something or other. Mr. Atherton, the vice principal, led a chain gang of morning detention students on garbage patrol.

Cameron turned away and hunched up one shoulder, hoping he wouldn't be recognized. He didn't think he could handle Atherton's jovial "Gee-kid-tough-break" greeting just yet. Or ever, for that matter. But it would be wishful thinking to expect people to treat him as though nothing had happened.

It was one of those blustery April days that held out the hope of a power outage and school cancellation. Ordinarily, he'd like that, but nothing was ordinary anymore. He didn't want to be at home, and he didn't want to be at school. He didn't want to be anywhere.

He shifted his backpack from one shoulder to the other and headed up the walk. The wind plucked at his jacket and hair.

"Cameron?"

He kept walking, though he knew that voice.

"Cameron, I just want to say, I'm so sorry for what happened," said Becky Pilchuk, hurrying to fall in step with him.

Becky Pilchuk. Just his luck. He glanced around to see if anyone noticed him walking with her. On the chalkboard in the boys' locker room, where he and his friends rated the girls in their class according to relative hotness, she was in the bottom ten percent. It was a game the guys played, and it would be incredibly insulting to the girls if they knew about it.

"I tried to see you after the funeral service, but I couldn't find you," Becky said.

"I didn't feel like being found," he said. He'd felt like breaking something. In fact, he'd done so. Right there at the church, he'd wandered outside to the parking lot. They were loading his parents into the hearses and it was completely gross. His father had Travis, Sean and a bunch of golfers as pallbearers. His mother had the husbands of her friends from the Special Olympics committee and the garden club and whatever the hell else his mother was into. It was too much, thinking of them sealed up inside those gleaming boxes, so Cameron had ducked away when no one was looking. He ran until his breath came in strangled sobs and wound up at the rear of the church, looking at the colored windows framed in soaring arches. At the top of the arch was a roundel. He knew it was called that because they'd studied Gothic architecture in World History. The roundel depicted a dove hovering over a flame—the Holy Spirit.

Cameron had picked up a smooth, rounded stone. He wound up and threw it as hard as he could, and the stone smashed through the window with a satisfying clatter. He wasn't worried that the noise would alert anyone, because the recessional music blared from speakers and everyone had left to go to the stupid cemetery to bury his parents in the ground. In no hurry, he'd sauntered away to rejoin the others in the stretch limo with air freshener that smelled like overripe bananas.

He tried not to look at Becky, but couldn't help himself. She held a sort of weird fascination for him and had ever since she'd moved here last fall. She had all the components of the uber-geek—the brains, the eyeglasses, the complete cluelessness about the way she dressed—yet he had this really strange reaction to her. His heart sped up and he felt all nervous. And when she mentioned his parents, his throat and eyes hurt, like he was going to start bawling at the drop of a hat.

"Well," she said, her voice wavering uncertainly, "if you ever feel like talking about it, I—I'm willing to listen."

For a wild moment, he had the urge to tell her about the church window and about the fact that ruining things had a curious way of beckoning to him. He wasn't sure why that was. Breaking something or messing it up didn't help a thing. It was pretty lame, because all it meant was that somebody had to fix whatever he broke. Big deal. If he told Becky, then she'd know he was wacko for sure. "I doubt I'll want to talk about anything. It completely sucks. That's all I have to say."

"Okay, sorry," she said. "Anyway, I'd better go. I have a paper I need to turn in before first bell." A tinsel-wrapped smile flickered and disappeared. "So I'll see you around, okay?"

He didn't answer, but watched her go, plucking a crisp white report from her notebook as she soldiered toward the front door of the school. When she had nearly reached the building, a gust of wind snatched the paper and blew it high overhead.

She gave chase, but the paper wafted a few yards away, where a group of jocks were pushing and shoving. One of them spotted the paper and slammed his foot down on it. Becky rushed in, grabbing it. She pulled too hard and the page tore.

The jocks laughed, giving each other high fives while Becky clutched the paper, red-faced, and scurried away. As she crossed in front of Cameron, her eyes met his briefly, and in that moment, he could tell she knew he'd seen the whole thing. He instantly felt guilty for not stepping in to help, and then he got mad, because he hated feeling guilty.

And somehow, his anger turned on her. The dweeb. She ought to know the last thing he'd want to talk about was his parents, and the last person he felt like talking to was Becky Pilchuk.

He rushed to his homeroom and tried to slide invisibly into his seat in the back. No such luck. Shannon Crane spotted him and yelled, "Cameron's back. Oh, Cam, we missed you."

He tried to act all normal as his friends gathered around. A few of them had been at the funeral, but he hadn't really talked to them. He'd been too busy trying to avoid cameras from ESPN and the local news station that kept getting in his face. Now he stood in the midst of his friends, and he felt more alone than ever.

They chatted away, filling him in on school gossip—Maris

Brodsky broke up with Chad Gresham, the girls' volleyball coach had been written up for foul language and the theme of the senior prom was Sailing Away, like he gave a rat's ass about that. Cameron didn't move, but he felt distant from these people, a visitor from another planet. He was a stranger in his own skin. He didn't know how to act anymore. When was it okay to joke around with his friends again? When was it okay to think about something other than the giant void inside him? When was it okay to care again?

He had no answers, only questions rushing in to fill the void. Pretty soon his friends turned their attention away from him and he sat alone at the one-armed desk, staring at the glossy fake-wood surface. From the pocket of his backpack, he took out his compass. It was a precision instrument, his geometry teacher had lectured when he'd passed them out to everyone. Keep the cap on the sharp point so you don't gouge anything by accident.

Cameron didn't gouge the desk by accident. He did it on purpose, etching the word *FUCK* in the shiny surface, then *EVERYT*— He didn't get a chance to finish. The bell rang and everyone surged up and out of their seats. He stabbed the compass into the surface of the desk, slung his backpack over one shoulder and left with everyone else.

Throughout the day, there were moments that made him regret coming back to school in the first place. When his English teacher, Mr. Goldman, put his hand on Cameron's shoulder and said, "How are you doing?" Cameron almost lost it.

"Just swell," he said. "Absolutely super."

"Would you like to talk to someone about it?"

That was pretty much all he did these days. He talked to social workers, to counselors, to Lily and Sean. He was sick of talking.

"No," he said.

The day was only going to get worse from here.

part four

The child endures all things.

—Maria Montessori

chapter 25

"All right," said Greg Duncan, helping supervise the bus circle on Friday afternoon, "what's your excuse this time?"

Lily bade goodbye to the last of her students and then turned to him. "Excuse?"

"For not going out with me tonight."

She paused and tapped her foot. "Um, you haven't asked me yet?"

"So I'm asking."

"And I'm saying no thanks." She tried to summon a smile, but felt the corners of her mouth trembling. "I'm not very good company." She wished he was the sort of friend she could unload on, wished she could tell him how physically and emotionally drained she felt from grieving. He wasn't, of course. Come to think of it, most of their conversations revolved around his golf game and his gripes about paying child support for kids he never saw. She felt guilty for the thought and said, "Thanks, though. I appreciate it, Greg."

"Tell you what," he said, rocking back on his heels. "How about you call me when you feel like doing something."

She nodded and managed to come up with a smile that was a little more genuine. "I will. That's a promise."

He went to join a group of other teachers standing around while the last of the buses pulled out. The easygoing conversation and occasional burst of laughter sounded so…so normal. Lily couldn't find that anymore, couldn't figure out what was normal. She went back to her classroom. She studied the calendar. Seven weeks left to the school year. Then it would be summer, her time for adventure and renewal.

She thought about the trip she'd planned so carefully. She imagined herself sitting at a lido café in Positano, all by herself, sipping a limoncello and watching the fishing fleet in their colorful boats. She knew exactly what would be going through her mind—Crystal's children.

She grabbed her tote bag and headed out. It didn't matter what Derek's will dictated and the probate court decreed. She felt an obligation to that family that wasn't written in any document.

Instead of driving home, she drove to Crystal's house. She'd made a promise to Charlie that she would visit often, every day if Charlie needed her to, and she meant to keep that promise.

"Lily!" Charlie whipped open the door before she even rang the bell and leaped into her arms. "Come on in. We're just having a snack."

Sean came to greet her. Ashley yelled something, spraying crumbs from her mouth. "You hungry?" he asked Lily, gesturing at the coffee table. It was spread with squirt cheese and crackers, cans of soda and Crystal's good highball and martini glasses.

"We're having happy hour," Charlie said. "I'll make you one."

Sean cleared a space on the sofa and Lily sat down. "Happy hour?" she asked.

"I'm never actually happy anymore," Charlie said, "but Uncle Sean says we have to eat."

"That's true." She turned to Sean and their gazes held fast for a strange, electric moment. There was something between them, the painful bond shared by shipwreck survivors. She looked away quickly with the odd feeling that he'd seen something he shouldn't.

"Here you go." Charlie offered her a Ritz with a tower of cheese.

It looked like a heart attack on a cracker. "That looks...delicious." To avoid putting it in her mouth, she indicated a box on the coffee table. "Your Brownie badges?" she asked.

"Yep. I'm supposed to sew them on a sash to wear with my uniform." She picked one up, looking completely lost. "Mom was going to help me do that."

Lily tried to say something, but she couldn't find her voice. This happened so many times a day to Charlie, to the whole family. It was the unbearable cruelty of untimely death. Things were left undone, interrupted.

While she was trying to figure out what to say, Sean poured 7-Up into one of Crystal's martini glasses. "You and I will do it together, okay, Charlie Brown?"

"Okay."

"Do you want an olive or a twist with that?" he asked.

"An olive? Eeuw."

"Straight up, then," he said, and handed her the glass.

Lily discreetly set down her cracker. Really, using the good bar glasses was no crime. Judging by the state of the house, those might be the only clean ones left. The place seemed more cluttered and chaotic each time she visited. At one end of the room was an indoor putting green. The stand by the door was stacked with old magazines and books. Cameron came downstairs, looking sullen and disheveled. "Hey, Lily," he said. He squirted cheese onto a cracker and ate it in one bite. Speaking with a full mouth, he said, "Anyone seen a compass? I need it to do homework."

"What's a compass?" asked Charlie.

He rolled his eyes. "Never mind, moron."

"Uncle Sean! He called me a moron."

Sean was preoccupied with wiping a smear of cheese off the baby's chin. "Don't call your sister names."

Charlie stuck her tongue out at Cameron. "You're just all mad because Uncle Sean put parental control filters on the computer."

"Big deal, moron."

"Uncle Sean! Lily!"

A timer sounded somewhere in the house, like the bell at the end of a boxing round. "That's the dryer," Sean said. "Cam, go get the stuff out and fold it."

"But—"

"Now." They locked gazes. Cameron's eyes narrowed, then he stalked out of the room.

Charlie gave an injured sniff.

"You go help him fold," Sean said.

"But—"

"Do it, Charlie."

She looked to Lily as though for support. Lily said nothing. Charlie's chin trembled, and she turned and marched away like a prisoner to an execution.

Sean held the 7-Up can so Ashley could drink from it. Lily bit her tongue again, and their eyes met over the baby's head. "My world and welcome to it," he said.

"You got through another day," she told him, determined to be supportive. "You got through the whole week."

"Good for me."

Ashley climbed into his lap and laid her cheek on his chest.

His hand, big enough to cover her back, came up and cradled her with surprising tenderness. There was a smear of processed cheese on the baby's temple, but a smile on her lips as she blinked a few times, then closed her eyes. Lily was fairly certain that it was too late in the day for a nap. The baby would have trouble getting to sleep tonight.

Stop it, she told herself. "I'll take these things to the kitchen," she told Sean.

He didn't respond, so she gathered up the crackers, cheese, soda cans and glasses, making two trips to get everything into the kitchen. She took great satisfaction in dropping the can of squirt cheese into the trash. She spent a few minutes loading the dishwasher and straightening the kitchen. Other people's casserole dishes, pie plates and Tupperware containers littered the counter. The Holloways' friends had been generous with their offerings of food. After such an immense tragedy, the gifts seemed both inadequate and completely in earnest.

She finished with the dishes, then decided to sort through the mail. She'd promised Sean she would take care of Crystal's business, closing her various accounts, canceling subscriptions, submitting bills to escrow. There was something particularly awful about going through Crystal's bills, seeing her charged purchases for cosmetics and children's clothing, gifts and gallons of gas for the car. Crystal had not been the most practical person, but she was generous to a fault.

Lily made stacks of bills and junk mail. An invoice from Riverside Medical Laboratories showed Ashley had had a blood test the Monday before the accident. Lily frowned, wondering if the baby was coming down with something. All the personal items seemed to be addressed to the kids, or to Sean and the kids. Most had the oversize shape and weight of sympathy cards. At the bottom of the stack, she found a few large, padded envelopes addressed to Sean Maguire, each in different, loopy, feminine handwriting. They'd been opened already. One was from Kalamazoo, Michigan, another from Long Beach, California, and still another from San Diego. Friends in faraway places? she wondered, studying the return addresses. Kat, Nikki, Angelina.

Quit being so nosy, Lily told herself, even as she threw a look over her shoulder. The largest of the envelopes slipped through her fingers and dropped on the floor, its contents spilling out. Pink stationery, loopy handwriting: *Dear Sean, We've never met, but I saw in the paper about your terrible tragedy, and I just want you to know I'll be there for you....* Paper-clipped to the letter was a photograph of a young woman with huge breasts.

Shaken, Lily put it back. Then she peeked into another envelope to find a different letter, different photos. *Now that you have all those kids, you'll be needing a wife....* The picture of Kat made Lily gasp aloud.

"He gets stuff like that in the mail every day," said Cameron. "Pretty rank, huh?"

Lily spun around, her cheeks flaming. "What?"

"Women sending him letters and pictures. They're like, all hot for him because he's been in the papers."

"Oh." Lily swallowed. "I...see."

"It's totally weird. Who knew this would make him bachelor of the year?"

Lily busied herself with putting the bills in her bag. "I should go," she said, her stomach churning. This was Crystal's house, and it was being turned into something else altogether. Yet Lily had no authority to change things, even if she knew what to do.

"See you later," Cameron said, bending down to explore inside the refrigerator.

As she walked to the door, she tried to figure out what to

say to Sean. He sat very still on the sofa, the baby snuggled against him. Holding a balled-up blue nightgown, Charlie leaned against his other side. Late afternoon light fell over them, and she realized all three were fast asleep. Grief was exhausting business; they were discovering that.

She stood for a moment, watching them sleep. Watching *him*, studying the fine shape of his jaw, the muscles of his arms. She felt an unexpected wave of yearning and melancholy. No wonder perfect strangers were proposing to him.

Lily came home tired and troubled, but on this particular day, an unexpected distraction awaited her. She found her sister's thirty-seven-foot Winnebago parked alongside her house. As Lily got out of her car, the door of the RV opened and out jumped Violet, her face pinched by strain. Behind her came Megan and Ryan, her children, who were nine and ten respectively. They were a rambunctious pair who always seemed to be either fighting or being best friends. At the moment they were having a shoving contest, and Violet looked too exhausted to discipline them. Before her sister even spoke, Lily knew the news was bad.

"Okay, before you say anything," Violet began, "it's only temporary, I swear."

"I was going to say hello to my niece and nephew, actually," Lily told her. "Hello, niece and nephew." She doled out the hugs, and they returned them with firm enthusiasm. Vi's children were usually slightly disheveled and grubby, but they were a happy pair, as affectionate and easygoing as their mother.

"Why don't you two go around back and play," Lily suggested. "I've got a tetherball set up."

"How come you got a tetherball but you have no kids?" Megan asked.

"Maybe I play with it all by myself," Lily said with a wink. Honestly, she didn't want to go into it as she felt a now-familiar twinge. She and Crystal had put the ball up together only a few weeks ago when the first signs of spring appeared, so Charlie could play with it when she visited with her mother. The reminders of Crystal sneaked up on Lily and seized her heart, and the sense of loss took her breath away. When did it end? she wondered. Did it ever?

Megan and Ryan resumed their shoving contest as they made their way to the backyard.

Lily gave her sister a hug. "I barely got a chance to talk to you at the funeral, but thanks for coming. So how are you?" she asked.

"Fat, that's how." She ran a hand around the cinched-in waistband of her jeans.

"Oh, come on. You look great."

"I look fat. You know I always overeat when I get stressed out."

"What's stressing you out?" Lily asked, though she could probably guess. Violet's life seemed to have been designed for stress. She had married straight out of high school and had the kids soon after. Her husband, Rick, rarely held a steady job. He had a habit of starting oddball businesses that were marked for doom from the start, and when they failed, no one was surprised except Rick himself. Plant day care, professional clowning, ice delivery, fly-tying lessons and extreme topiary were just a few of the enterprises that were supposed to earn him his first million.

"So what's up?" she asked Violet as she unlocked the door and led the way into the house.

"We had to move," Violet said, sinking down on the couch. "Our lease was up and the landlord raised the rent ridiculously high. We're living in an apartment in Troutdale now."

Lily got two bottles of organic juice from the fridge and handed one to Violet. "I take it the, ah, voice-acting business didn't work out?"

Violet shook her head. "Disaster. He dubbed one Japanese commercial and they sent him packing. He said he had to talk so fast, he sounded like he was on helium. I feel so bad for Rick." She met Lily's gaze. "What?"

"Nothing."

"Bull, nothing. You're giving me a look. What's that look mean?"

Lily offered a smile to cover her frustration. "You're amazing."

"I am? In what way?"

"Your devotion to Rick. Does he know how lucky he is to have you?"

Violet sipped her juice. "I'm the lucky one."

Lily bit her tongue. Lucky. The man had all but ruined them financially several times in a row. Still, she conceded, he never stopped trying, and his wife adored him. Love was such a strange business. No wonder she didn't understand it.

Violet took her silence for disapproval. "All right, so he's not exactly Donald Trump. But I didn't marry him for his ability to make a buck. I married him because I love him, and here we are eleven years later and I love him more than ever." Violet's eyes shone, and Lily had no doubt she believed her own words.

"That's wonderful for you," she said. Was it? she wondered. Was it wonderful to adore someone in spite of his flaws, or was it madness?

"Don't do too many backflips for me, big sister." Violet laughed. "I'm not a brain like you. I don't have a college degree, but I do know what love is."

Lily regarded her thoughtfully. "Meaning I don't."

"Meaning it's different for everyone. For me, it's the way I feel when Rick walks into the room and my heart speeds up. It's how safe I feel in his arms and how sweet he is with the kids, not what our bank balance is or isn't. Sometimes you just need someone to fall back on, someone to put his arms around you and tell you things are going to be all right. Everything else is just details, Lily. They don't matter. That's what love does. It makes the small stuff…small."

Violet's passion shone through; she truly believed that having someone to love without judgment made anything bearable—financial ruin, loss, hard times. Was that why everyone insisted you needed love in your life? Lily wondered, her thoughts drifting to the Holloways. Losing Crystal brought home the fact that life was hard and enduring hardship alone was a humbling ordeal.

"Listen to me," Violet said, "going on about myself."

Lily smiled. "It's fine. I think you're really something."

"Not sure what, though, huh?" Violet looked around the neat, well-organized kitchen. "We're so different. How did we turn out so different?"

It was a good question. Only a year apart in age, they'd each branched off in wildly different directions. One became a true believer in love and the other an utter heathen when it came to matters of the heart. Raised by bitter, embattled parents, Violet had rebelled, determined to have her own happy family. She'd rushed headlong into an impractical love and a chaotic family life. Lily, on the other hand, built a wall around herself and refused to take risks with her emotions.

"I bet a psychiatrist would have a field day with us, eh?"

"No, because you never talk about the past," Violet pointed out. "Then again, I suppose you don't have to. You live your life in a way that screams out what you won't say aloud."

Lily felt as though the air had been sucked out of her lungs.

She recovered quickly and smiled as though Violet had made a joke. "How are dear old Mom and Dad, anyway?" she asked.

"Old. But not dear." Violet shook her head. "Maybe all the fighting is good for them. They are in excellent health, as always."

"Mom came to see me right after the accident. Surprised the heck out of me. I was surprised to see them at the funeral, too," Lily admitted.

"They're not the enemy, you know."

"No," Lily conceded. "There are no enemies in this, just like there weren't any when we lost Evan." Her family had been forged by tragedy and its aftermath. And now it was happening all over again to Crystal's family.

"I hope they do a better job than we did," Violet said.

They were quiet for a while, listening to the children at play in the backyard.

"I'm glad you're here," Lily said. "How long can you stay?"

"Only until Rick picks us up in a little while. I'm hoping we won't have to leave the Winnebago here for long. Just until we get a house with a place to park it. Actually, we're going to need to sell it."

"So why not just sell it?"

"You know Rick. He hasn't come around to my way of thinking yet. So in the meantime, we'll keep it parked." She eyed Lily uncertainly. "That is, if it's okay with you."

Okay? Having a land yacht parked amid her prize-winning rhododendrons?

She took a deep breath. This was a family affair, she reminded herself. Blood was thicker than…plant matter. "It's fine," she said.

"Thanks, Lil. We'll be forever in your debt. Oh, wait. We *are* forever in your debt. We'll never get out."

"Don't be silly. I wish I could help you more."

Violet beamed at her. "You're a saint, I swear. And hey, you can take it out anytime you want. I mean it. The thing is a lot of fun. It sleeps six. Rick wanted a big one in case we have more kids."

Good plan, thought Lily, but she held her tongue.

"You could take Crystal's kids camping, maybe."

"I doubt I'll be taking your Winnebago anywhere," Lily said.

"You never know."

"That's the story of my life these days," Lily confessed. "I never know what's happening next."

Violet sobered. "How are you doing?"

"Not great." Lily felt a now-familiar prickle in her throat. "I miss her so much, Vi. She meant the world to me, and now that she's gone, I hardly know what to do with myself."

Violet gave her a hug. "Ah, Lily. I wish you weren't so alone." She pulled back and looked Lily in the eye. "Listen, I know what you're probably thinking. Just because someone you love died doesn't mean you should never love again."

How well her sister knew her, Lily thought. "It means I never should have loved in the first place."

"You don't get to choose, Lil. Why not let yourself be crazy about Crystal's kids? Lord knows, they need it. Who's raising them?"

"Sean, the uncle on Derek's side. You met him at the funeral."

"The hunk? How could I forget? So he's single, right?"

Lily flashed on an image of Maura, all long legs and intelligent eyes. "For the time being, I suppose. He's seeing someone, not that it's any of my business."

"Lily Raines Robinson, I swear you are blushing." Violet leaned forward, intrigued. "What's up with you and this guy?"

"Nothing." Lily was annoyed. "We both want what's best for the kids, that's what's up with us, but we don't always agree on the way to approach this."

"Since he's the uncle—"

"Half uncle, if you want to get technical. A guy who barely knows them. Still, he's the children's only blood relative besides Dorothy, and according to social services, that trumps my claim to them. It's so frustrating, Vi. Crystal wanted me to take care of them, but she never got around to discussing it with Derek. I'm sure she thought they had all the time in the world."

"Wow. So are you going to try to get them placed with you?"

"Honestly, that was my knee-jerk reaction when this all came to light, but I backed off. The children need stability right now more than ever. If I initiated a legal action, it could disrupt their lives even worse. Even Crystal's attorney said my chances of winning are slim to none, since the will isn't valid and I'm not a blood relation. Still, sometimes it's all I can do to keep from rushing in and taking over."

"The guy might like it if you did. Ever think of that?"

"All the time," Lily admitted, picturing Sean asleep on the sofa. *More than I should.*

"Wow. Rick and I have never even made wills."

"You're kidding. Vi, you've got two minor children. You really ought to put something in writing."

She nodded, watching Megan and Ryan out the window. "Hey, Lily?"

"Yes?"

"When I do make a will, I'm appointing you guardian of the kids. Is that all right?"

"You really need to discuss this with Rick," Lily said.

"He'll go along with whatever I say. His parents are getting on in years and his sisters' lives are too chaotic to take over raising kids. You're the perfect choice, Lily. Please say you'll agree."

She reached across the table and touched her sister's hand. "I'm honored."

"Good."

"You have to promise me I won't ever have to serve."

"Of course. I promise."

Lily tried to remember if she'd made Crystal promise the same thing. She didn't think she had, and deep down she knew it wouldn't make any difference in the way she'd lived her life, anyway. Crystal was who she was—a woman who found herself in a car with her ex-husband on a stormy afternoon. A woman whose heart ruled her head, every time.

A while later, Rick arrived to pick up Violet and the kids. At the sound of his clanking Astro van pulling into the driveway, Violet's face lit up. "He's here," she said, jumping up and running outside.

Lily stood and watched them from the window—a smiling man in an ill-fitting suit, embracing his exuberant, slightly overweight wife, while the kids swarmed around, welcoming him.

Lily wished she had a camera handy. In that moment, you couldn't see that they were broke and living in a dump, that Rick was going to have to pick himself up, dust himself off and find a way to support them. In that moment, they made perfect sense, a complete world unto themselves.

Feeling intrusive, she went outside to say goodbye. After they were gone, she stood in the driveway. The days were getting longer, she thought. Ordinarily, she loved the springtime. The accelerated glide toward the end of the school year was filled with fresh energy as everyone prepared for summer. This year was different, of course. This year, Crystal was gone, the kids were in the care of Sean Maguire and she worried about them constantly.

Because of what had happened, her life was not her own. She'd had her summer all planned out. Now she had all these people in her life and things were no longer in her control.

Never before had she changed her plans to accommodate other people.

She stood lost in her own living room. Had her house always been this quiet or did it just seem that way now? It had a curious sterility about it, too. Her sister described it as a freakish neatness. To fill the silence, she turned on the stereo. Bocelli singing "Mille Lune, Mille Onde" from a CD she'd bought to get her in the mood for Italy.

Now the silky tenor voice kept her company as she went to her desk and put away all her maps and guidebooks, her language tapes and itineraries. Then she called and left a message for her travel agent: *Cancel everything.*

Finally, with the music radiating out to the corners of the room, Lily poured herself a glass of wine. Chianti, of course. Letting go of a dream should have been devastating. Instead, it felt exactly right.

chapter 26

Sean Maguire heard an insistent knocking at the front door. He had been circling around Ashley, trying to psych himself up to change her. No matter how many times he did this, he couldn't get used to it. Last night's pinto beans and scrambled eggs had been transformed into toxic waste in her diaper. According to one of the library books on child development, he had another six months of this before potty training, possibly more.

"Someone's at the door," he said. "Maybe it's the hazardous waste removal team."

"Okay." She waddled into the front room.

Damn. The kid could talk but couldn't use the toilet. What was up with that?

As he headed for the door, he glanced around the house. It looked as though a bomb had exploded, cluttering the place with toys, schoolbooks, clean laundry he'd been in the midst of folding, a stray cup, a plate of someone's half-eaten breakfast. How had it gotten this way? Only yesterday, Mrs. Foster had everything straightened up while she was here babysitting. He himself had swept the floors.

Too bad, he thought, glancing at the clock. Anyone who showed up at this hour deserved what they saw. With a less-than-welcoming expression on his face, he pulled the door open.

"We need to go on a family excursion today," said Lily Robinson, walking into the house before he'd even decided whether or not to extend an invitation.

He was surprised to see her. She always visited in the late afternoon. Ordinarily, he was glad—even relieved—to see her. She brought order and calmness to the house, and the kids were bonkers for her. But this morning... She wore jeans and red sneakers, and for some crazy reason, the outfit made her look wildly sexy to him. As did the look she gave him, as though she'd never seen a guy who'd just rolled out of bed before. Maybe she hadn't. He reeled in his thoughts. He had no business thinking about stuff like this. "You might have called first," he said.

"It was too early to call."

"I like a logical girl," he said.

"Whose car is that parked outside?" Lily spotted Ashley and her face lit up. "Hello, Miss Adorable." Squatting down, she opened her arms and the baby tumbled into them.

Your funeral, thought Sean, pretending he hadn't heard the question.

"Whew," said Lily. "Someone's been busy."

"We just got up," he said, rubbing his unshaven jaw. "She hasn't had a change yet."

Lily stepped away from the baby. "Don't let me stop you."

He grumbled and muttered under his breath as he did the honors. Sometimes he woke up in the morning and thought, I can't do this. I'm not even supposed to be doing it. This is not my life.

Then somehow he slogged through, making mistakes along the way, like buying the wrong-size diaper or putting it on backward, or putting Twinkies but no sandwich in Charlie's lunch bag.

Ashley seemed to find him vastly amusing, and by the time he got her cleaned up and dressed, they were both in a better mood. That was the thing about a little kid, living moment to moment. The bad ones were over fast and there was always a smile on the horizon. No wonder you had three of them, Derek, he thought.

Mrs. Foster helped out with the baby, but she was expensive. Sean's allowance from the court-mandated insurance trust was meager at best. The perception that he'd come into a fortune along with Derek's kids was wrong, but that didn't stop nosy sports reporters from asking about it. Constantly. And assuming the worst about Sean's motives.

Lily was restlessly moving about the living room, straightening up. Let her, he thought. Don't make excuses. He was not going to become the sort of person who got defensive over a messy house.

"We need to take the children to see their grandmother," Lily said.

He looked at her blankly.

"Dorothy Baird. Crystal's mother."

The stroke patient, he recalled. He'd never met Derek's mother-in-law, and her health had deteriorated to the point where she hadn't even been able to attend her daughter's funeral. He looked at Lily's eager, insistent face and said, "I don't have a problem with that. We'll do it one of these days."

"I was thinking today. Family is so important for these children, especially now. If we leave soon, we can be in Portland for the morning visiting hours."

"Suppose I have other plans?" he asked, annoyed.

She folded her arms in front of her. The stance accentuated her breasts. She had surprisingly big breasts for a school-marm, not that he knew for sure whether or not there was a standard breast-size for marms.

"Do you?" she asked.

He was planning to get in a round of golf with his nephew. Something was happening with Sean's game these days, an unexpected new power, and he wanted to explore the change. Both he and Cameron had noticed it, and they played several times a week, sometimes even bringing the girls along in the cart. Now he found himself contemplating a drive to the city and a visit to a bedridden woman who didn't know these kids anymore.

Lily waited, watching him.

"All right," he said. "We'll go."

"Go where?" Stifling a yawn, Maura walked out of the bed-room, wearing only the top of her oversize surgical scrubs.

As awkward moments went, Sean decided, this one defi-nitely ranked right up there with Asmida's father walking in on them in the Johor Bahru Hilton.

"Hello, Maura," Lily said politely. As she spoke, she reached for the baby's hand, as though needing to anchor herself.

"Hi, Lily." Maura glanced at the clock, then at Sean. "Is there coffee?"

"I haven't made any yet." Sean suppressed a beat of irritation. This woman was his girlfriend, he reminded himself. So what if they hadn't had a great night last night? He'd been exhausted and morose, missing Derek, and had found himself questioning what he was doing—with her, with the kids, with his life.

She shrugged. "That's all right. I'll get some on the way to the hospital." She sent Lily a quick smile. "I've got to work today. It's the start of the thirty-six-hour shift."

"That's a long shift," said Lily.

"Standard for fourth year." Maura bent down to peer at Ashley. *"Bonjour, jolie mademoiselle,"* she said, and Ashley giggled as she usually did when Maura spoke French. Then she straightened up. "So are you taking the kids on an outing?" she asked Lily.

"That's the plan. We're taking them to see their grandmother in Portland."

Maura shot Sean a look. "I see. Well, have a good time." She headed for the shower, and Sean could tell from her posture that she was ticked off. She probably thought he'd planned this excursion with Lily and hadn't bothered to tell her.

Well, hell, he thought, heading upstairs to rouse Cameron and Charlie. Lily could be anywhere she liked this morning, and she'd chosen to spend it with the kids. He respected that about her. He just wished she had called first.

chapter 27

Lily kept trying to shake off the sight of Maura Riley, looking like Medical Student Barbie, coming out of the bedroom she'd so obviously shared with Sean the night before. But Lily couldn't forget. Nor could she keep silent the minute she got him alone in the kitchen.

"I think it's a bad idea to have your girlfriend living in the house with you," she said. Crystal's house, she thought, her resentment firing up.

"She doesn't live here."

"She shouldn't even be spending the night." God, she sounded so sour and judgmental. "What I mean is, it's bad for the kids."

"Get off it, Lily. Not that it's any of your business, but last night is the first time she's stayed. The kids don't care. They like Maura."

"What about Maura?" asked Charlie as she came into the kitchen. "She stayed over last night, didn't she?"

Lily pursed her lips. Sean acted as though he hadn't heard.

"She's boring and she doesn't have time for kids," Charlie said, sending a sidelong glance at her uncle.

"It's the truth. I asked her. She said she wasn't ready to have kids, but when she was, then she would like them."

"She didn't mean you," said Sean. "So you watch your mouth."

Charlie gave an offended sniff, then shrugged and went trolling for breakfast. She gravitated toward a box of Pop-Tarts, and Lily was too preoccupied to object.

If this had been Lily's problem to solve, she would have launched into a detailed explanation of how inappropriate it was for Charlie to talk like that about an adult, and how hard Maura worked at becoming a doctor, and how important it was for Charlie to respect her. Lily discovered that Sean's curt imperative worked just as well.

"You look pretty today," she told Charlie, admiring the creative combination of red sneakers, pink sweater and purple clam diggers. Her hair was braided and adorned with a sparkling array of tiny barrettes.

Charlie held out her hands. "Uncle Sean did my nails. *And* my hair."

Lily nodded in approval. "I see." Over Charlie's head, she caught Sean's eye, but he was acting busy as he organized the baby's diaper bag. A bit of self-conscious color touched his cheeks.

Uncle Sean, it seemed, was developing an unexpected talent for doing hair. It had started with Charlie's return to school. Lily never knew what the child would look like on any given morning. Over the past few weeks, she'd arrived in the classroom sporting any number of looks—B-52s, Princess Leia, Pippi Longstocking and Alicia Keys were favorites.

"We should get going," Sean said.

Cameron was the last to join them, sliding into the car just as Sean was about to lose his patience.

"Hey," Charlie squawked, "get your muddy feet off me."

"They're not on you," Cameron muttered. "Move over."

"On the way home," Sean said, "maybe you'll do some of the driving."

Cameron opened a can of Coke and took a slug. "I forgot my learner's permit."

Sean held up a small leather sleeve with a plastic window. "You're in luck. I found this on top of the refrigerator."

Sean had told Lily that Cameron was avoiding driving. Most boys his age couldn't wait to get behind the wheel. But of course, most boys hadn't lost their parents in a horrific accident.

"I don't feel like it," said Cameron, and he turned to glare out the window.

Lily shifted sideways in her seat so she could talk to the kids. The social services supervisor had given Sean permission to appropriate Crystal's car. Since his truck only had three seat belts, they couldn't go anywhere as a family in it.

She told herself not to resent him for moving into her best friend's home, looking after her kids and taking over her life. It seemed to be the most compassionate arrangement for the children at this time, maybe for good. But being pushed out of the picture didn't feel right at all. She didn't know where she stood—teacher, family friend, fifth wheel? After encountering Maura this morning, she was more confused than ever and more bothered by the fact that she had no authority here, no control.

"How's school going?" she inquired, trying to engage Cameron's interest.

"Okay," he said, predictably.

"I deserved that," Lily admitted. "All right, let's try this again. How's your state-history project coming?"

"It's coming."

"He hasn't even started," Charlie said.

"Shut up." Cameron elbowed her.

"Don't talk like an ass," Sean warned him. "I mean, a jerk."

"Do you need help with it?" Lily asked.

"I don't need anything." He took a slug of Coke.

She wanted to ask Cameron about all sorts of things. She wondered if he felt like talking about his worries when it came to driving, but that conversation was not for here or now. That was something she was learning about the dynamics of this patchwork family. You had to pick your moment.

As they passed Echo Ridge, Sean slowed the car. "What the hell?"

Lily was going to chide him for his language, but when she looked at the golf course, she forgot to speak. A police squad car was parked on the side of the road and an officer made notes on a pad. Someone had trenched the putting green closest to the road. The green had been charred, too, by lighter fluid splashed on the grass and then set aflame. In the water hazard adjacent to the fairway, a golf cart lay half submerged. Workers and members from the course stood around, probably trying to decide where to begin fixing things.

Sean pulled over and got out.

"What do you make of that?" Lily asked Cameron.

He shrugged. "Maybe someone had too much time on their hands last night."

She felt a strange flutter in her stomach. "How do you know it was last night?"

He rolled his eyes. "I doubt something like this would happen in broad daylight," he said.

"I don't understand. Why would anyone do such a thing?"

He shrugged again. "I guess some people trash things for no reason."

Sean returned to the car. "Vandalism," he said. "They're assessing the damage at five thousand dollars for now. Ten times that if they have to replace the whole green."

"Do you need to stay?" asked Lily. By asking, she was giving him an out. An escape hatch. A perfect excuse to let her take the kids by herself.

"I told them I was busy," he said, clipping his seat belt in place. "They've got my cell phone number."

The rest of the way to the city, they speculated about what could've happened. They concluded that the crime was almost certainly caused by kids. The cart belonged to a member who, according to Sean, had a bad habit of leaving his cart shed unlocked. He wouldn't be doing that anymore.

"The greens are so manicured," Lily commented. "How will they get it back to the condition it was before?"

"They'll never get it back to its original state," said Sean.

"I think it's terrible," she said. "What were those kids thinking?"

"I'm sure they weren't thinking at all. It can be fixed. New grass always comes in greener after burning, anyway."

The Golden Hills care facility was beautifully landscaped, with a view of the Columbia River and the snow-clad cone of Mount Hood floating in the distance. Crystal and her mother had chosen this place together a long time ago, after the first series of strokes, from which she made only a partial recovery. In March, a massive stroke had nearly been fatal. "Sometimes," Crystal had told Lily, "I think it would have been a mercy if it had taken her. It's taken everything else, all her memories, everything that makes her *her*."

To Lily, it seemed a singularly cruel existence. Her condition had stolen all the years of a rich, full life, and left Dorothy bedridden and unaware that she had a daughter who had died and grandchildren who loved her.

"Grandma stays in bed all the time now," Charlie told Sean as they headed for the covered walkway leading to the entrance. "She can't even go out in a wheelchair anymore."

He took her hand. "What was she like before she got sick?"

"Only the best grandma in the whole wide world." There was a bounce in Charlie's step as she walked.

"I'll bet she was." He lifted his arm and Charlie twirled under it.

"Now me," said Ashley, straining to get down. "Me!"

Outside the doors of the nursing home, he twirled both girls, their images reflected in the glass of the foyer windows.

All right, so the house is a mess and he lets his girlfriend spend the night, thought Lily. At least he dances with his nieces. She glanced over at Cameron to see him watching, too, with a very slight and cryptic smile that disappeared the moment he felt her watching him. He was so angry, she thought. So unsure of himself. "When was the last time you saw her?" she asked him.

"Last month," he said. "We brought some pictures to hang in her room. She's not doing so hot." He stepped in front of the automatic doors and they swished open. "She'll probably die pretty soon." He hurried inside.

Regardless of the pristine beauty of the gardens and the luxurious, upscale decor of the facility itself, there was no disguising the fact that this was a place where people came to endure the most difficult phase of their lives. A peculiar hush pervaded the lobby and the long hallways lined by doors wide enough to provide wheelchair access. The scent of air freshener didn't quite mask the ever-present odor of urine and disinfectant.

The staff didn't wear standard nursing uniforms, but rather color-coordinated sweaters and skirts or slacks. Lily thought they looked a bit like flight attendants or casino workers. Yet everyone here seemed to treat people with compassion and dignity, a trait Dorothy used to be quick to notice back when she was capable of noticing such things.

Crystal had admitted the cost of the care facility was wiping her out, but she didn't care about that.

Lily glanced at Cameron as they headed toward Dorothy's room. "That was a pretty rotten thing to say. I hope your sisters didn't hear."

He surprised her by saying, "I wouldn't have said it if I thought they could hear."

Lily touched his sleeve. He was being painfully honest, and he probably had the facts down better than anyone. What she really wanted to do was hug him, but she doubted he'd tolerate that. He was pushing her and everyone else to treat him normally, to dare people to get mad at him. And in Cameron's anger and isolation, she recognized a little of herself, and that worried her. "Cameron—"

Charlie rushed past them, breaking the moment of connection. "Come on, Uncle Sean. I'll show you where Grandma lives. She knit me this sweater. It used to be extra big because she wanted me to wear it as long as possible." She showed off her pink cardigan, holding out her arms. "It's getting really small on me."

"Then you'd better quit growing," said Sean. He gave one of her pigtails a gentle tug. "Be sure to thank her again for making it."

"She won't understand."

"Thank her, anyway."

The door to Dorothy's sunlit room, which she shared with another patient named Mrs. Withers, was plastered with cards and notes of sympathy, a storm of silver, gold and white fluttering as they walked past it. Ashley chortled with delight.

An orderly had wheeled Mrs. Withers out for a walk. Someone else had readied Dorothy for company. The mattress was raised nearly to a sitting position, and Dorothy wore a pretty pink robe tied with a satin bow below the cervical collar that supported her neck. Her hair had been combed, her nails done and the blankets folded precisely across her lap.

Lily's heart tightened. All her life Dorothy had been beautiful and was proud of that beauty. It was a curious, unsought blessing that she was no longer aware of her circumstances. She would hate to be here, institutionalized, looked after by others, no longer capable of dealing with her own most basic needs. She would hate to know that she had outlived her daughter.

"Hello, Dorothy," Lily said, trying to sound natural. "It's me, Lily. I've brought your grandchildren to see you. And this is their uncle Sean."

"Ma'am," he said, "pleasure to meet you."

Dorothy blinked but offered no sign of recognition. Her face had a stiff, almost claylike aspect, as though it was a mask. With a thoughtful expression, Sean perused the family pictures that covered the wall at the end of the bed.

Lily took hold of one of Dorothy's hands. It was cool to the touch, the skin dry and fragile, like onion skin. "I think about you a lot these days, Dorothy. I suppose after my own family, you and Crystal have known me longer than anyone else." She smiled, remembering how calming it used to be to go to Crystal's house, where everything was placid and pleasant, where tempers were quiet and no ghosts lurked. "You're very special to me. I have to think that in some way, you know that."

When Lily looked up and saw the others staring at her, she felt a little flustered. She had revealed too much of herself.

The baby giggled and talked nonsense as she explored the

room. Sean kept an eye on her while Lily motioned Cameron and Charlie over to the bed.

"I never know what to say," Cameron muttered. "Since she's been…like this, it's just weird."

"I know," Lily said. "Be yourself. Tell her something you remember about her. Before she was sick, she adored you. She still does, but she can't show it the way she used to."

Cameron stared at her for a moment.

"What?" asked Lily.

"Nothing." He bent down to place an awkward kiss on Dorothy's cheek.. "Hi, Grandma," he said. He jammed his hands in his back pockets and glanced up at Lily. "I still don't know what to say."

"Any little memory," she suggested.

He bent down again and said something in her ear. Dorothy looked startled at first, and then her face softened and her eyes drifted shut. A low sound came from her throat and she opened her eyes again. Lily could have sworn the old lady looked directly at her grandson, but that might have been wishful thinking. Then again, maybe Cameron really had connected.

Charlie came up next to him, the squabbling in the car forgotten. "Hello, Grandma," she said, her expression solemn. "My name's Charlie and you used to know that. I'm wearing the sweater you made me. I miss you lots, Grandma. I really do." She touched Dorothy's hand and then drew Ashley forward. The baby chortled and touched the ring on Dorothy's finger, smiling up at her.

Lily was so proud of them in that moment. They treated their grandmother with love and dignity, showing none of the apprehension people often feel for someone so ill. They broke through the discomfort and made her glad she'd spearheaded this field trip.

"I'll put up the new picture we brought," she said. There was a display on the wall opposite the foot of the bed. Crystal always hung bright, enlarged images of her and the children there, changing them frequently so her mother wouldn't get bored. The new photo showed Crystal accepting a plaque of appreciation from the Rotary Club last month. Unlike most pictures in the "grip-and-grin" genre, this one was attractive. Crystal was dressed to the nines, carrying a perfect onyx-beaded bag and flashing her trademark winning smile, filled with pride and gratitude.

Lily felt Sean's gaze as she replaced an older shot of Crystal with the new one. And then she sensed another pair of eyes on her and realized Dorothy's stare was fixed directly on the new photo.

"Good girl," she said in a rusty voice. "Good…daughter."

According to Dorothy's physicians and all the reading Lily had done, such clarity was nearly impossible.

"She is good, isn't she," Lily said, smiling through tears. "The best there is. She loved her life and all the people in it."

Dorothy was looking at her, not at the photo of Crystal. Lily approached the bed and patted the older woman's hand.

"Her husband's gone?" Sean asked quietly, studying the array of pictures.

"He died when I was eleven," Cameron said, indicating a photo of a handsome silver-haired man holding up a golf trophy. "Grandpa Frank."

"Pretty good golfer?"

"He was all right. A twelve handicap."

"What's yours these days?" Sean asked him.

"About a three," Charlie answered for her brother. "I keep track."

"Not too shabby," Sean said.

Cameron shuffled his feet in modesty, shedding bits of

dried mud. The five of them lingered a few more minutes, until Dorothy drifted off to sleep.

Charlie stood in front of the wall of photographs, her face averted, her narrow shoulders drawn in. Cameron scowled at her. "Come on, don't start sniveling."

"I can't help it," she said in a broken voice.

"Yes, you can. Just don't do it."

"How?" she snapped, whipping her head around, her pigtails flying out. "How do I just stop?"

"Like that, moron," Cameron said, giving her braid a gentle tug. "Get mad."

chapter 28

"So that's your Grandma Dot," Sean said as they drove away from the nursing home. He felt a curious sense of relief. The visit had been long overdue, and he'd been putting it off until Lily prodded him into going. Now that it was over and had gone reasonably well, he wondered why he'd waited.

"She used to be a lot different," said Charlie. "She used to be tons of fun."

"I'll bet she was." He checked the rearview mirror and saw that she was back to being her funny little self. Breakdowns and sad spells, like the one she'd had just now, were common, said Dr. Sachs. They were part of the healing process. Sean wasn't sure being called "moron" by your brother was particularly healing, but he tended to ignore their squabbles because they always subsided on their own. Sometimes, like just now, Cameron gave himself away. Beneath the surface, he was all heart.

The thought gave Sean a rare flash of hope. Maybe, just maybe, this broken family would survive.

"She was always nuts about her grandkids," Lily reminded

them, turning in her seat. "Remember the cedar chest in her basement? It had the most amazing things in it."

"A fur collar with little fox heads and tails on it," Charlie said. "Eew."

"She used to wear it to church," Lily said. "Did you know that, when I was your age, I sometimes went to church with your mom and her parents?"

"Nope. Why didn't you go to church with your own family?"

Lily turned back to face front. "They quit going. They…didn't go."

From the corner of his eye, Sean could see her throat work painfully as she swallowed. He decided it was time to change the subject. "I had a grandmother who went to church twice a week," he said.

"Twice?" Charlie asked. "Was she kind of naughty?"

"She was Irish, me father's mother, and she talked with a fair brogue like this." He demonstrated as he spoke, grinning as he thought of old Bridget Callahan Maguire for the first time in years. "Every Sunday after church, she used to whack the head off the chicken and serve it for Sunday dinner."

"Eew. Did you ever see her do the whacking?"

"Every chance I got. I was a ghoulish little kid." He saw Lily wince. Too bad, he thought.

"What else did you do for fun?" she asked.

"Played golf. Your dad and I learned at church, you know."

"He never told us that," said Cameron.

Sean checked the rearview mirror again, glad to see a spark of interest. At the same time, he felt a now-familiar jab of pain. He wondered when that would stop or if it ever would. Grief, he had discovered, was a palpable thing, but that didn't mean you could understand or control it. It was a sneaky enemy that strangled you in broad daylight sometimes.

"Sure," he said. "Father Campbell at St. Mary's was a

scratch golfer and we were altar boys. He was the first coach we ever had."

"That sounds like fun," Charlie said.

"It was fun—the golf, not being an altar boy."

"We never have fun anymore," she added.

He heard a now-familiar quaver in her voice, one that portended another crying jag. When Charlie cried, Ashley usually started up, then Cameron got mad and things unraveled.

Not today, Sean thought, gripping the steering wheel. They had planned to run errands on the way home, but he decided to make a detour. "I know something we can do that's fun."

"What?" she demanded.

"We'll do it right now."

"I thought we were going grocery shopping," Lily pointed out, always one to get rattled by a change of plans.

"Groceries can wait. I have a better idea," Sean said.

"What?"

"I can't tell you. It's too much fun. You'll get so excited you'll wet your pants."

"Uncle Sean! Lily, make him tell me," Charlie said, squirming against her seat belt.

"How would I do that?"

"You're a teacher. Just make him."

"Whoa, a teacher," Sean said. "I'm shaking." He trembled until Charlie started to giggle.

"Let's just be surprised," Lily said, pruning her lips with disapproval.

Too bad, thought Sean. With three kids, you had to learn to be spontaneous. He teased them along for the next ten minutes as they headed west. Then he pulled into a gravel parking lot and Cameron gave a groan. "I don't believe this."

"What, are you scared I'm going to beat you?" Sean asked.

"I'm scared someone is going to see me here," Cameron said.

"Twenty bucks says I whip you like a redheaded stepchild."

Lily's eyes flared behind her glasses. "Sean, I don't think—"

"You're on," said Cameron, and got out of the car. Predictably, he couldn't resist a challenge, especially when money was involved.

Charlie was beside herself. "Uncle Sean, this is so cool."

He grinned at Lily. "See? I'm cool."

She tipped back her head and read the sign arching over the entrance, painted in garish Day-Glo green: Welcome to Jurassic Golf Park. A Millennium of Fun.

"What are we waiting for?" Sean took the baby out of the car seat and they went to the ticket kiosk.

"Two adults, two kids, the baby's free," said the attendant. "That'll be $18.50."

"Oh, I won't be playing," said Lily.

"Yes, she will," Sean contradicted her, and slid a twenty-dollar bill across the counter.

They were given putters and balls that had seen better days, and Ashley received a hollow plastic mallet. "Right through there, folks," the attendant said.

They stepped through an archway so low Sean and Cameron had to duck under it.

"Bugga bugga," yelled a caveman, jumping out at them.

"Bugga bugga," yelled Ashley, clapping her hands. Even Cameron laughed at that.

"Smile!" The caveman snapped a photo of them. "What a great-looking family," he said, showing them the photo on the screen of his digital camera.

Lily looked flustered. "Oh, we're not—"

"This photo will be available for purchase before you leave," the caveman said.

Family or not, it was a great shot. Against a backdrop designed to resemble a primeval rain forest, they all looked as though something funny had startled them, which it had.

"How much?" asked Sean.

"Ten dollars for an eight-by-ten print. I'll have one waiting for you at the exit when you leave."

Sean handed a ten-dollar bill to the caveman.

"You're going to keep score, Charlie Brown," he said, handing her the scorecard and pencil.

"I don't know how."

"Sure you do, honey. Keep track of everyone's strokes and compare them to par for each hole." Weird, he thought. Derek Holloway's kid didn't know how to keep score. What was up with that? These kids were so easy to get close to, especially when golf was involved.

"But—"

"No buts. I need to whup some big brother ass, so I need for you to be in charge. Make sure nobody cheats."

"Okay, I guess. I don't think you're supposed to say *ass.*"

"He's definitely not," Lily said.

Sean ignored her. The woman had a strange way of simultaneously getting on his nerves and under his skin. He sent Charlie and Cameron to the first hole, and Ashley toddled after them. "I don't know what it is about you, Miss Lily. You make me want to misbehave."

"How can I make you stop?" she asked.

"You could try spanking me."

She made a sound that was sort of half gasp, half hiccup, and walked on ahead of him, fists pumping and cheeks red. Good old Lily Robinson, he thought. What a girl.

He liked to needle her. He didn't know why. Maybe because she was so incredibly…needle-able.

The eighteen holes of Jurassic Park were designed around no known principles of putting. There were uphill shots, downhill shots, holes that roared when the ball went in, a volcano spewing fake lava and smoke, sound effects that excited Ashley to shrieks of delight.

Cameron gave Sean a run for his money. It was golf after all, and there was money at stake. The two of them traded the lead back and forth.

Charlie was a natural. Sean stood behind her, wrapping his arms around her slight form, and demonstrated a good stance and grip. She caught on immediately and was just as quick to grasp how to keep score, absorbing the terminology like a sponge.

Lily was a terrible golfer, as it turned out. Her stance was awkward and she had a ridiculous grip. By the fourth hole, Sean couldn't hold his tongue anymore.

"Care for a little advice?" he asked.

She looked up, clearly exasperated. "But what I've been doing has been working so well. What's my score, Charlie?"

The little girl frowned, pencil tapping the scorecard as she counted. "Well, it's kind of high."

"I can take it."

"You're twenty-three over par, actually." Charlie giggled and skipped away, following Cameron and Ashley to the next hole.

"Boy, do I ever stink at this," Lily muttered.

"You do," Sean agreed.

She leaned down to set her ball on the next tee box. "So about those pointers..."

He started with the basics, correcting her grip and stance. She actually did slightly better on the fifth hole, though she still took eight strokes to get there.

"You have no swing," Sean said.

"Very funny," said Lily. "I have no idea what you mean."

Treating her like one of his students, Sean demonstrated. He made par on the hole. Cameron birdied it, and Charlie made two over par. "That's called a double bogey," she said importantly.

"The swing," Sean reiterated. "It's a rhythm. Hips, shoulders, arms. Very subtle when you're putting."

She addressed the ball, and he could already see things going wrong.

"Wait," he said, stepping up behind her. "Be still and I'll show you."

He put his arms around her from behind. At the club, he did this ten times a week giving lessons. With Lily, it was different. He found himself distracted by the way she felt—surprisingly soft. And the way her hair smelled—clean and fresh. And the heat of her body, tucked up against his. In light of the fact that he'd spent the previous night with Maura, he knew these were completely inappropriate thoughts. He forced himself to concentrate on helping her as if she were any other golf student.

"Okay, feel this."

"Feel, um, what? What am I supposed to be feeling?"

Good question. "Relax your arms and I'll show you the movement. This is a putt. The movement is very delicate." He helped her hit a solid straight shot that left her just one or two strokes from the hole. "Feel the difference?" he said.

"I'm not sure."

"Want me to show you again?"

"Absolutely not." She spoke quickly, clipping off her words as she moved away from him.

Clearly she hadn't noticed the feeling between them when he had his arms around her. It was just as well, he thought. Things were complicated enough for him.

By the end of the round, she showed a slight improvement. Sean and Cameron went into the last hole with a gap between their scores. Sean was ahead by three strokes, a comfortable lead by any standard.

"It's not looking good for the twenty big ones, Cam," Charlie said.

"Yeah, real helpful of you to point that out."

"You could still win," she said. "There's a hazard on this hole, see? So if Sean gets in the hazard, he'll have a tough time recovering."

Lily grinned at her. "Where did you learn to talk like that?"

Charlie shrugged. "Watching my dad on TV."

"Well, you sound like a golf commentator," Sean said.

"I could get into the water hazard, too," said Cameron.

"You won't," Charlie assured him.

"How do you know I won't?"

She rolled her eyes with an excess of patience. "On account of the twenty bucks."

"That little boy's birthday party is catching up," Lily warned, looking over her shoulder at the group behind them. "I think they're just two holes back."

Sean gestured to Cameron. "You won the last hole, so you have honors."

Cameron stepped up and hit a safe but admirable shot that got him where he needed to be—two strokes from the hole. Sean followed, putting his ball on the tee. As he drew back to putt, his stomach growled with hunger. And against his will, he thought again about having his arms around Lily.

The ball rolled straight toward the water hazard and fell in with a plop.

"That's a two-stroke penalty," Charlie piped up.

"Hot dog," said Ashley.

Sean was ticked off. Concentration was everything. He of all people should know that. If his thoughts strayed a hairsbreadth, it was all over.

Cameron took his next shot and it was a good one, setting him up to hole out with one more stroke. Sean's lead had been shaved to one, but he still felt confident that the last hole was his, and he would wind up keeping his twenty dollars.

"Uh-oh," said Charlie, and Ashley mimicked her.

He'd somehow made another terrible putt, overshooting the hole. Now his ball lay a seriously long putt away.

Cameron hit in easily. He was too experienced a golfer to gloat, but his posture as he walked off the green clearly said, "I win."

Not yet, you don't, thought Sean. This would be a long and difficult putt, but if he could sink it, they would be tied and they'd have to play another hole. As he lined up for the putt, he heard Lily whisper to Cameron, "It's only twenty dollars."

Cameron whispered back, "It's not about the twenty dollars."

Then everyone got quiet. Even the baby was quiet, as though she had an innate respect for the proceedings.

Somehow, Sean's thoughts strayed again. He found himself wondering what Lily looked like without her glasses, and why she was making him question what he had with Maura.

And he missed the putt.

"Oh, no!" Charlie jumped up and down. "Cameron wins by a stroke!"

Putting on his game face, Sean took out his wallet and handed Cameron a twenty-dollar bill. They left the Jurassic forest and turned in their equipment.

"I'm sorry, Uncle Sean," said Charlie. "I was silently rooting for you."

"Never be sorry. Cameron kept his game together and I let mine fall apart."

"Why?"

"I blew my concentration."

"Why?"

"I kept thinking about things that distracted me."

"Like what?"

He caught the gleam of amusement in her eye. "Like nieces who ask too many questions and have to be tickled." With an animal roar, he snatched her up.

She gave a squeal of fearful delight, then laughed helplessly as he attacked her most vulnerable spot—the hapless armpit. Ashley joined in with the laughter on principle and kept giggling even after the tickling stopped. Cameron swung her up on his shoulders as they headed for the exit.

Sean sensed Lily's presence beside him and smiled. "All in all," he said, "not a bad day."

"I had no idea I was such a terrible golfer. I'm ashamed."

"Don't be."

"How can something so simple be so hard?"

"Because it's golf, that's how," he explained. "It wasn't the real game, anyway. I need to teach you to play real golf." He wasn't sure why he said it. He wasn't sure why he could still feel her in his arms.

"As bad as I am, I'm starting to understand why golf is so delicious to so many people."

It was the last thing he expected her to say. Maybe that was why he was so intrigued. Just when he thought he had her figured out, she surprised him.

"Camcron! Hey, Cameron!" a feminine voice called out, then a tall girl in an oversize Jurassic Park T-shirt came running toward them.

Sean and Lily exchanged a glance. He grabbed Charlie's hand to keep her from interfering. They watched as the girl, long-limbed and coltish, approached Cameron near the exit. She was about his age, with brown hair in a ponytail, silver braces and glasses.

Cameron did not look thrilled to see her. "Hey, Becky," he said, lifting the toddler off his shoulders.

"Here's the photograph you ordered," said Becky, handing

him the eight-by-ten in a cellophane bag. She flat-out worshiped him, that was clear enough. "I was so surprised to see you here. I wanted to deliver this personally."

"Thanks." Cameron took the picture from her. "We just stopped in as a treat for my little sister. We're on our way home now."

"Oh." She bounced on the balls of her feet, smiling at the baby and then at Sean, Lily and Charlie as they approached. "So is this your family?"

"No," Cameron said. "I mean, well, this is Ashley, and that's my other sister Charlie, my uncle Sean and Lily."

"I'm Becky Pilchuk." Her face lit up with unabashed delight.

"Do you work here?" Charlie asked.

"Yep. In the restaurant, every weekend."

"Boy, are you ever lucky," said Charlie.

"I think so," Becky agreed.

"We should get going," Cameron said, clearly chafing under her adoration. "See you around."

She darted her gaze nervously at the main building of the complex. "The snack bar just opened for lunch," she suggested. "It's not too bad, that is, if you're hungry."

"I'm starved," Charlie said dramatically. "Starved."

"Me, too," said Ashley.

"That settles it, then," Sean said. "We'll eat at the snack bar. My treat. I won't even make you spend the twenty bucks you won off me."

"Great," muttered Cameron.

"I'll go get a table ready," Becky said. "See you inside, Cam." She hurried across to the food-service area, a covered awning shingled with phony palm fronds.

When she was out of earshot, Charlie said, "Ooh, Cam. I'm so in love with you, Cam." She batted her eyes at him.

"Cut it out, twerp," he said as he took hold of Ashley's hand.

"Ooh! I love it when you talk to me like that," Charlie cooed. "You are just so…so…manly."

Sean and Lily stared straight ahead, not daring to look at each other.

Becky was waiting for them at the snack bar. Now she wore a Jurassic Park service apron with pterodactyls on the pockets. "Table for five?" she asked.

Sean glanced at Lily and the kids, and was bowled over by the idea that the five of them were functioning as a single unit, redefining themselves as something bigger than each of them—a family, he thought. They were a family.

"Yes, please," Lily said, taking a seat and studying the menu. "We should make sure everyone eats so we don't go to the grocery store hungry."

"What's wrong with going to the grocery store hungry? That's the only time I feel like it," Sean said.

"That's when you impulse shop and wind up buying things you don't need, things that aren't good for you. If you shop on a full stomach, then you make better choices."

Great, he thought. Shopping with Miss Making-Better-Choices was going to be a barrel of laughs.

chapter 29

In the grocery store, Lily tried to seize control. After her humiliation at miniature golf, she felt the need to show she was good at something. And of course, the real reason she was stewing was something she'd only admit to herself—she was still smarting from encountering Maura this morning.

She quickly lost out there as well. Cameron headed off to the books and magazine aisle to find the latest issue of *Rolling Stone*. Charlie insisted on standing at a music display with the headphones on, listening to samples of music from the "Soothing Sounds of Nature" CD collection.

That left Sean and Lily to put Ashley in the cart and do the grocery shopping. As soon as Lily saw him reach for a box of s'mores-flavored Pop-Tarts, she knew she had to intervene. "Nutrition is the single most neglected health issue among children today," she informed him.

"You don't say."

"Look at the ingredients in this," she said, tapping the box. "It's stuffed with carbs which turn instantly to fat."

"These are skinny kids. They can use some fattening up."

"With this? Type-B gelatin—you don't want to know where that comes from. And seldane syrup—that's actually a toxin. In concentrated amounts, it's been shown to cause brain damage in laboratory mice."

"Then they should quit giving it to laboratory mice. Where do you learn this stuff?" he asked.

"Anywhere I can. The big food companies would like for us to stay ignorant, but we can't afford to do that." Pointedly, she returned the Pop-Tarts to the shelf. Then she couldn't help herself and said, "Today's medical professionals do virtually nothing to raise awareness of the issue."

Either it went right by him, or he didn't care about a dig at Maura. "So what's Charlie going to eat for breakfast?" He spotted something and his face lit up. "Devil Dogs! I've never seen them on the West Coast before. I love these things."

Lily stared, aghast, at the strangely shaped, cream-filled cakes. "You're kidding."

"Have you ever actually eaten a Devil Dog?" He grinned. "Dumb question, sorry."

Lily selected an organically grown oat crunch. "Would Charlie go for this?"

"She'd gag on that."

After some debate, they compromised on a cereal with no additives and some raw organic honey to sweeten it. They started arguing again in the snacks aisle.

"A handful of Fritos isn't going to kill a kid," Sean said.

"True. It's the trans-fatty acids that do it. Don't keep this stuff in the house and they won't even be tempted," she said.

"Yes, ma'am. Now, tell me, what are your views on dairy products?"

So it went, each item debated over, each purchase negotiated, until Ashley fell asleep in the cart. Lily took the opportunity to give Sean the rundown on nutrition for growing kids.

To his credit, he didn't argue with her. He even seemed to be listening.

As they waited in the checkout line, she plucked a *Parents* magazine from the rack. "Maybe we should get this," she said. "There's an article on what to expect from the toddler years."

"Who reads these things? People who have no kids. They're the only ones who have time." He glanced at Ashley, who was still sleeping, her limbs spilling from the seat in the grocery cart. "She tells me everything I need to know."

"It makes more sense in the context of expert commentary."

He shook his head and selected a copy of *Golf Digest.* "Reading that is not going to make me a better parent any more than reading this would make me a better golfer."

Her first instinct, as always, was to argue with him, but she forced herself to put both magazines away. She pursed her lips and, when the checker called for a price check on the order in front of them, drummed her fingers on the handlebar of the cart. "Maybe we should pick another line," she suggested.

"This one's fine."

Another urge to argue prodded at her. "That one over there is actually moving."

"So will this one. They always do, eventually."

She picked up a pack of gum, read the ingredients, put it back. "I have to say, I admire your patience."

"Thank you. I suppose I learned it from living overseas, waiting around in foreign airports and taxi lines."

It was a rare reminder that he had a past, a whole lifetime of experiences in exotic cities. She wondered if he missed that life, yearned for the adventure of it. "Why did you move back to the States?" she asked. She knew what Crystal had thought. She wanted to hear his version.

The line shuffled forward a few paces. "I was banned from the tour for cheating."

His bluntness surprised her. That was exactly what Crystal had said. "Why would you cheat?"

"There are plenty of reasons for a guy to cheat. The stakes are high in this game, especially for a player with something to prove. I didn't do it, though. Didn't cheat."

"Why would they say you did?"

"A major sponsor wanted me off the tour."

"Why?"

He started unloading the produce onto the conveyer belt. "You don't want to know."

She resisted the urge to rearrange the groceries on the belt, even though it meant the canned goods would probably bruise the produce. "Yes. I really want to know."

"I was bonking the sponsor's daughter, and he had promised her hand in marriage to some guy from the Malaysian royal family. Ever heard of the yakuza?"

"Isn't that the Japanese mafia?"

"Pretty much. Turns out daddy was a yakuza boss with high hopes for his daughter." He laughed at Lily's expression. "Well, you asked."

"You're kidding."

"I'm not making this up."

"Didn't you try to defend yourself? Deny that you cheated?"

"There was no point in wasting my time. Things are done differently by the mob, and I made the colossal mistake of forgetting that."

"So how did this work?"

He finished unloading the groceries and the line moved again. "I was set up. At the end of a major tournament, I was handed an erroneous scorecard, and like an idiot, I signed off on it."

"What do you mean, signed off?"

"I certified that my score was true and accurate. I was in a rush and didn't check the numbers."

"So even though you were set up, you're just going to surrender? That's absurd. You're a golfer, Sean. It's what you do. Why would you let someone take that away from you?"

"Now you sound like Red."

"How so?"

"He thinks I should stick with the plan to get back on the tour. Get my PGA card. The trouble is, Q School only comes around once a year."

"Q School?"

"It's an annual event, 108 holes, and the top thirty-five scorers get their PGA cards. Prior to that, I'd have to clear preliminary stages. It's a long process, and there's no way I can juggle that along with the kids."

So he was sacrificing more than Lily thought. She needed to think about this, about the fact that he'd gone for his dream and had blown it, and he was yearning for another shot. The more she got to know this man, the more he surprised her. A new respect for him rose in her. "Is that the only way to get your PGA card and start playing in tournaments?"

"Red's looking into some other options, but he's wasting his time. I've got other priorities now."

She could hear a peculiar note of taut frustration in his voice. "Why not think about doing both?"

"I can do all the thinking I want. There's too much travel to actually do anything about it. I have a different life now." He reached down and buttoned Ashley's sweater.

"But you don't have a different dream," she reminded him. The look he gave her felt intimate, like a touch. It must be her imagination, she thought. "What?"

He offered a slightly enigmatic smile. "I like the way you think, Miss Robinson."

* * *

By the time they got home, Lily was surprised to realize she didn't want the day to end, and she lingered over helping put away the groceries. She came across a few contraband items that had sneaked into the cart—most notably, a jumbo pack of Devil Dogs—but didn't make an issue of it. Sean Maguire already thought she was hopelessly regimented.

Ashley stayed asleep in her car seat, so Sean brought the whole apparatus inside.

"Are you going to put her in her crib?" Lily asked.

"She's happy just like that." He hit Play on the CD player. "She sleeps better with music playing, too."

The clear, strong voice of Stephanie Davis singing "Talking to the Moon" drifted from the speakers.

"This was Mom's favorite," Charlie said, getting a big box of crayons from a drawer.

"I know." Lily set a grocery sack on the counter and busied herself putting things away. The last time she'd heard this song, she'd been with Crystal, relaxing over a cup of tea.

"Want me to change it?" Sean asked.

She shook her head, liking and hating the bittersweet feelings. There was a funny ebb and flow of the tension between her and Sean. One moment she had the urge to argue with him. The next, she simply wanted to get along.

Cameron grabbed the cordless phone and wandered into another room. Charlie went to the dining room table to labor over a detailed drawing of the miniature golf course. To Lily, it always felt strange, perhaps vaguely forbidden, to be with Sean in Crystal's house. The reminders of her friend were still so palpable, and often appeared without warning—an earring wedged between sofa cushions, magazines and mail addressed to her, phone solicitors asking for Crystal by name.

Lily picked up a thick recipe book, noticing a bookmark

on which Crystal had scrawled, "cake for Ashley's b-day." She opened the book, passed her finger over the writing.

"You okay?" Sean asked.

She nodded. "Sometimes I get the weirdest feeling that she just stepped out and she'll be back any minute, that maybe she just ran out to pick up a box of frozen strawberries for this cake."

"I think she already did that." He reached in the freezer and took out the strawberries. "I've been wondering what these could be used for."

Lily glanced at Ashley, still buckled in her seat and sound asleep. "Crystal had a nice party planned for her." Instead of celebrating Ashley turning two, they'd had the meeting with the lawyers.

"We should have it now," he said. "Today."

Lily fell instantly in love with the idea. "That's brilliant. We'll make the cake Crystal wanted."

He lifted one eyebrow in that intriguing way that made her want to emulate him. "Birthday cake, Miss Robinson? Tsk, tsk, all that sugar."

"We'll give them really small pieces."

"Speak for yourself. I think Charlie should help make the cake."

Now Lily found herself grinning like an idiot. It seemed so silly, but somehow this was making her feel better. "Cameron, too. I'll go get them."

"In a minute," Sean said, motioning her toward the walk-in pantry. "I need to show you something."

She stepped into the darkened interior, where the air was musty with the scent of spices, and she could feel the warmth of his body close to hers. "What is it?"

"She already bought things for the party." He turned on the overhead light and showed her a boxy shopping bag filled with rainbow-colored napkins and party hats, matching horns and balloons.

At the bottom of the bag was a doll, soft as a marshmallow, with bright button eyes. It was exactly the sort of thing Crystal would have picked. Lily also found a card in an unsealed envelope. Her heart sped up as she opened it. She felt Crystal's presence next to her as she angled the card toward the light to reveal a sentimental picture of a mother pushing a small child on a swing and the saying, "Spread your wings and fly away…" On the inside, it continued, "…home to me."

In neat printing, Crystal had added a message of her own. "I'm so very proud of my big girl! I'll love you forever, Mommy."

Lily carefully closed the card and put it back in the envelope. "I'm glad she wrote something," she said. Only when Sean handed her a tissue did she realize she was crying, and that his arm had slipped around her shoulders.

"How do we do this?" she whispered, overwhelmed. "How do we bear the unbearable?"

"Sometimes we don't," he said simply. "Sometimes we just breathe."

"I'm not staying home to make a cake," Cameron said, nearly stepping on Miss Buzzy Bee on his way to the refrigerator. He resisted the urge to send the pull-toy out the door with a soccer kick.

"It's Ashley's birthday," Lily said, tying on one of his mom's aprons. It was the one with the picture of Glinda and the caption, "Are you a good witch or a bad witch?" Cameron could perfectly picture his mom wearing it, and the sight of it pissed him off.

"It's not her birthday. Let's pick another day." Cameron felt the air pressing in on him. It wasn't enough that he'd been dragged out of bed to visit Grandma Dot, that he'd played miniature golf. Now they wanted him to have dinner and a birthday party?

"We picked today," Sean said, coming into the kitchen with Ashley held like a football under one arm. "Kid's got to turn two one of these days."

"She's already two, and it doesn't matter when she gets her stupid party."

"It matters," Sean said simply.

Cameron felt a slow burn of anger. Everything pissed him off—the sound of the radio clicking on in the morning, reminding him that he had to face another day without his parents. The sight of his mom's handwriting on the kitchen chalkboard. The smell of her hairspray on the headrest of her favorite chair. And then there was Sean, with his dumb simple statements—*It matters*—that were supposed to make sense. "I wish you'd quit acting like we're a regular family," he said.

"Is that what I'm doing?" Sean said. "What the hell's a regular family, anyway? Maybe you can explain it to me."

"Sean—" Lily cast a worried look at the baby, but she had discovered Miss Buzzy Bee and was in another world. Elsewhere in the house, a TV blared—Charlie, watching cartoons.

"I mean it," he said. "I want Cam to enlighten me. What's a regular family? Mom, Dad, two-point-five kids? Who has that anymore? Does anyone?"

"You know what I mean," Cameron snapped back. "A regular family doesn't have two dead parents and a 'Remembering Derek Holloway' special on ESPN."

"Here, Cam." Ashley waddled over and handed him a package of balloons. "Do it."

He ripped open the plastic package and blew up a red balloon, filling it in about three big huffs. Ashley's eyes shone with admiration as she watched him. He tied a knot in the balloon and let it float to her. "Ah," she said, delighted. "'Nother one."

She was the one person in the world he couldn't say no to. She had him blowing up balloon after balloon until she was swimming in a sea of them. While Cameron made himself dizzy blowing up balloons, he wished he could push the dead-weight of fear out of his lungs. Now that he'd lost his parents, he was scared that those left behind might have to become a new kind of family. And even more scared that they might not.

Lily reached over, switched on the radio and found an oldies station playing "Ain't No Mountain High Enough." She and Sean worked together, their movements slightly rhythmic as they followed his mom's recipe. "A few weeks ago, you could only do Pop-Tarts," she said to Sean. "You're a quick study."

"In all things," he assured her. "My goal is to make Charlie red, white and blue pancakes for the Fourth of July."

"Ambitious," she said.

There was a kind of rhythm in their conversation, too. They weren't exactly flirting, but they had a peculiar ease and flow going on between them.

"Yeah?" Sean lifted a bowl of pink batter and poured it into a cake pan. "Maybe you'll think of me when you're spending the summer in Italy."

"Who told you I was doing that?" Her spine stiffened.

"Charlie, I guess. Is it some big secret?"

"No, of course not. It's just…I canceled the trip."

"Why?"

She shot a glance over her shoulder. Cameron kept blowing up balloons, acting totally preoccupied with the baby. "I should think that would be obvious," Lily said. "I wouldn't feel right going away now, or even six weeks from now."

While he held the bowl, she scraped it down with a spatula. "Because you think I'm doing a bad job," Sean said.

Whoa, thought Cameron. The rhythm had changed. At the same time, he took a perverse satisfaction in the idea that they were arguing in front of him. In a way, it showed a measure of trust.

Lily opened the oven and he slipped the cake in. She said, "Don't make this into something it's not. I'm not criticizing you for stepping up to the plate. I sacrificed a summer trip. You're sacrificing a lot more than that."

"'Nother one," Ashley said, and Cameron picked a yellow balloon.

Charlie came in and her face lit up brighter than he'd seen it in weeks. "Cool," she said. "Can I lick the bowl?"

"Me, too!" Ashley tossed a balloon in the air. A new song came on the radio—"Nah Nah Hey Hey"—and Lily and Charlie sang along, swaying their hips. And Cameron had a peculiar thought. This—the way they were now—was how holidays and celebrations were going to be. It was hard to believe, but they had to figure out how to laugh and have fun and tease and fight, even though his parents were gone.

"Well, you managed to blow up a roomful of balloons instead of helping with the cake," Lily said to him.

"Yep," he said. "So?"

"So nothing. I was going to thank you. It's better than lollygagging around."

"Nobody says 'lollygagging' anymore," Cameron said.

"I say it all the time." Lily tossed him a roll of pink crepe paper. "So quit lollygagging."

chapter 30

"**Y**ou know what's weird?" Sean asked Lily after the birthday celebration.

"Pretty much everything these days," she answered.

"I used to wonder what it was like to live here."

They sat on the back porch of Crystal's house. Under a blooming apple tree, Ashley and Charlie were playing an elaborate private game in the sandbox, involving all of the furniture from Barbie's dream house, a collection of troll dolls and Ashley's birthday doll. The sun was going down, its amber rays slanting across the lawn, and a light breeze stirred a shower of apple blossom petals through the deepening light, giving the scene a dreamlike quality.

"Where, here?" she asked. "In Comfort?"

"In this house." He picked up a stray golf tee and rolled it between the palms of his hands. "Derek and I used to pass it every day on our way to school, and we always used to claim we'd live here one day. We envisioned a sort of colony populated by boys and dogs."

She smiled, trying to picture him as a little boy. Blue eyes, of course, and lighter hair. Probably a mischievous expression. "It's funny where life takes you."

He nodded. "Derek never gave up this house, but I went looking for something else."

"And what was that?"

"Someplace a little more exotic. The French Riviera or maybe Buenos Aires. Or hell, Monterey. Everywhere is more exotic than good old Comfort, Oregon."

"And here you are."

"Here I am." He raked his open hand through his hair. "Christ, I miss him. Everything's just wrong. I shouldn't be here, living this life. I'm not the one to fill his shoes."

"That's not what you're supposed to do."

"Then what the hell *am* I supposed to do?"

She thought about the way Charlie and Cameron had been today—wounded but healing. "I think you're doing it."

He rested his wrists on his knees and looked out at the yard with its garden of rhododendrons and fruit trees, old hostas spreading their huge leaves in the shade. "I sure as hell wasn't expecting this."

"No one was," she pointed out. "Listen, about Maura…I didn't mean to seem so judgmental this morning."

"You were thinking of the kids."

Was I? Lily wondered. I was, I had to be. If I was thinking of anything other than the kids, I'm in trouble. "She seems like a fine person. I admire her for working so hard on her medical degree." She sounded so phony. He probably knew it, too.

"I'm going out, okay?" asked Cameron from the back door.

Sean stood and turned to face him. "Out where?"

"Just around."

"You're going to have to be more specific."

"Why?"

"So if I decide to cruise by later, there won't be any surprises. Remember, we talked about this. I can't stand surprises."

Cameron stepped outside. He had his skateboard under his arm. "If you checked up on me, I'd shoot myself." There was a note of barely suppressed annoyance in his voice.

Lily bit her tongue to keep from protesting his choice of words. Sean waited.

"I'm just going to hang with some friends."

"Which ones?"

"Jeez, Uncle Sean—"

"Jeez nothing." Sean waited, his stare locked to Cameron's.

Lily was intrigued. She could feel the tension between them like a vibration in the air. Sean's parenting style, if you could call it that, fascinated her. He operated solely by instinct, not experience, but his confidence never wavered. Maybe that was the key, she thought. Never let them see how scared you really are.

Cameron broke the staredown first. He surrendered first with his posture, then verbally, clearly not considering this an issue to lock horns over. "I'm headed to my friend Jason's house. He lives over on Meadowmeer."

"Call me if you go anywhere else."

"I will."

"And be home by eleven."

"It's a Saturday night."

"That's why I didn't say ten o'clock. Be home by eleven or don't bother going out at all," Sean said.

Cameron gave a graceless farewell and stalked off.

Lily said, "You're good with him."

"Yeah, thanks. He's a real happy camper."

"I'm not kidding. He's pushing and you're not giving in."

"I have no idea why there's conflict at all. Hell, we're on the same side."

They sat together watching the sun sink away. Peepers raised a song from hidden places in the dark, and Lily finished her glass of iced tea. It was on the edge of her lips to say goodbye, I've had a nice day, see you later, but instead she just sat there, enjoying the breeze and the last colors of the day, the sounds of twilight settling around them.

"Did you mean what you said?" Sean asked suddenly. "About the good job?"

"Yes." She didn't hesitate. "Considering all that these kids are going through, they'd be a handful for anyone. This is a horrible thing to have to adjust to, but all things considered, they're getting by."

"So I get an A+ from the teacher." There was a smile in his voice.

She looked over at him, watching the light play across his face. This mattered so much to him, she could tell. "When it comes to relating to the kids, I'd say so."

His eyes narrowed. "Why do I sense a 'however' in that?"

"I didn't say 'however.'"

"You didn't have to." He chuckled softly. "All right, Miss Lily. Let me have it. I can take it."

It was strange, how he seemed to see through her. "I question the value of *American Chopper.*"

"You're kidding."

"I don't kid."

"That's right, I forgot for a minute. So you're objecting to the best show on television?"

"Charlie can quote from it chapter and verse."

"And this is a bad thing?"

"It's a show about motorcycles. It has no redeeming value."

He threw back his head and laughed aloud then. She found herself staring at his throat and having unsettling feelings. "You slay me, Lily, you really do. Watching a show about motorcycles is not going to warp the kid's mind. It's something we do together. We like it." He sobered, his gaze piercing through the gathering darkness. "Maybe, just for a minute, she…forgets, feels normal. She deserves to do that every once in a while."

The truth of it struck Lily and she nodded. "At least it's not *South Park.*"

"Nope, that comes on a half hour later," he said, then laughed at her horrified expression. "Kidding," he said. "I know you don't kid, but I sure as hell do."

"Very funny." She offered a smile of relief.

"You sure are a fussy little thing, Miss Lily," he commented. "Food, TV, loading the dishwasher… How'd you get that way?"

Being raised in a house full of hate will do that to a person, she thought, but couldn't bring herself to tell him. "I guess I'm just a creature of habit."

He nodded, and they sat together in curiously companionable silence, listening to the peepers and to the girls playing together. Finally, Sean stood up. "I need to put these little grubs to bed."

As he walked toward the sandbox, Charlie put up a hand in a defensive gesture. "Five more minutes."

"Sorry, kid. Time's up. You both need a bath."

"No bath," Ashley protested.

He picked her up and tucked her under his arm. "You like taking a bath."

"Lily, will you stay?" asked Charlie, dragging her feet as she headed inside.

"I can't," she said automatically.

"Please."

"But—"

"The kid said please," Sean pointed out.

"All right."

"Yay!" Charlie and Ashley gave each other high fives.

Lily wished she had a hot Saturday-night date. She wished she was headed out for an evening of drinking and dancing, but the fact was, she had no plans at all. The prospect of sticking around here was disconcertingly pleasant to her.

Sean and his nieces stampeded upstairs. In the kitchen, Lily heard the swish of running water and random giggles from the girls. Today, for the first time, Lily began to believe that Crystal's children would survive their terrible loss. Until now, doubts had been all twisted up inside her, knotting into hard despair. Finally, she was able to relax. A little, at least.

Something else had happened today, a connection to the children and Sean that troubled Lily. She knew she had to keep her distance from this family, because they didn't belong to her. He might decide to move to Phoenix next week, and just like that, they'd be gone. Lily didn't know if she could survive a loss like that.

The dishwasher light indicated that the cycle was over, so she decided to unload it. Sean and Charlie had insisted on doing the dishes, and they were haphazardly piled in the racks. Lily pursed her lips, vowed not to let the disorganization ruffle her. Despite the way the dishes were loaded, they all came out clean. She was finishing up when Sean came downstairs alone.

"That was quick," she said.

"They're still in the tub. I just came down to get some towels out of the dryer."

Her blood froze momentarily, then rushed boiling hot through her. A plastic cereal dish tumbled from her fingers. "My God, you can't leave them alone." She raced upstairs and burst through the open door of the bathroom. She felt Sean's presence behind her but ignored him.

The girls were facing each other, up to their armpits in bubbles.

"Lily," said Ashley, squishing a sponge in her hands.

She didn't answer but turned and grabbed a towel from Sean, who stood in the doorway. The towel was still warm from the dryer. She got Ashley out of the tub, dried her off and got her ready for bed. "You, too, Charlene Louise," she said to Charlie. "Unplug the drain."

"Are you mad at us?" Charlie asked, clutching a towel around her. Bubbles still clung to her skinny legs.

Lily tried to will her heart to stop its panicked leaping. "Of course not."

"Are you mad at Uncle Sean?"

Lily said, "It's bedtime. Let's see how quick you can get your jammies on."

"That's what grown-ups always say when they want a kid to shut up and go to bed."

"That's because it's more polite than saying 'shut up and go to bed.'"

Apparently satisfied with that answer, Charlie put on an oversize satin peignoir that dragged along the floor behind her. Noticing Lily's look, she spread her arms like pale wings. "It was Mom's," she explained. "I sleep better when I wear it. Come and say good-night, Uncle Sean," she called as Lily tucked her in bed.

He came into the room the girls shared. "Good-night, Uncle Sean," he called back, clearly a running joke with them. He kissed the baby and handed her a toy to hide in the crib. Then he kissed Charlie on the head. "Good night, Zippy," he said.

"'Night, Duke."

As they went downstairs together, Lily felt disoriented by his sweetness with the girls. She wondered if he understood the power of that moment, and if he realized, as she did, that this arrangement was actually working. Then she remembered that, sweet or not, he had just done something extremely frightening. "What were you thinking, leaving them in the bath unattended?"

"They like taking their bath together. I ducked out for maybe thirty seconds to get some towels."

"They can't be left alone in the bath ever again, do you hear me? Ashley is too little to take a bath unsupervised. And Charlie is too young to watch her even for thirty seconds. You need to promise it won't happen again."

He waved off her concern. "They were fine."

"If you think that, you're fooling yourself."

"Hey, I'm doing the best I can. It's awkward as hell with Charlie. I'm not her father and I don't want to cross the line, if you know what I mean."

She pushed down the panic climbing up in her throat. "All right. I get it. Charlie will have to take a bath on her own, but keep the door open and make sure you can hear her. You're going to have to monitor the baby every single second, do you understand? You cannot even *blink* when she's in the bath."

He looked surprised by her vehemence. "Got it. No blinking."

"I'm not fussing about this, Sean. You can't dismiss this like you do my ideas about nutrition and TV and the right way to load the dishwasher." She felt a fury of tears stinging her eyes and turned away to hide it. "This is life and death. Things can happen—everything can change—in the blink of an eye."

"You think I don't know that?"

"Think of what it would do to Charlie if something happened, just think." Her words came out in a passionate rush and when she stopped, she felt exhausted.

She looked up to find him staring at her, his expression cryptic. If he dared to argue with her, if he offered so much as a breath of contradiction, she would lose it, she just knew she would.

He inhaled a breath and then let it halfway out. "You're right," he said. "I was being stupid."

Lord, thought Lily, his honesty was amazing. *He* was amazing. A few weeks ago he was some playboy golfer with nothing but his own selfish interests at heart. Now he had put all that aside and was willing to admit a mistake. She'd never really seen a man do that before.

He was trying to learn how this worked, to knit these wounded children into a family, and he was so sincere that it broke her heart.

"Thank you," she said softly. Then it was on the tip of her tongue to tell him the truth—the truth about what happened to Evan and the way it still haunted her. She had never said a word to anyone, not to her parents or even to Violet. Now she astounded herself by saying, "I know you think I overreacted, but there's a reason for that. I lost someone close to me a long time ago. It was an accidental drowning."

"Jesus, Lily. I'm sorry to hear that."

She took his arm and pulled him out to the screened porch to make sure they were out of earshot of Charlie. And out of the light. For some reason, she knew she wouldn't be able to talk about this in the light. "There used to be three children in our family, but my brother Evan...well, he didn't survive being a Robinson." She paused, weighing the burden crushing down on her, wondering if it could possibly be shifted. "If you ask my parents, he didn't survive me."

"You just said he drowned."

She nodded. "I was right next to him in the bathtub when it happened."

"Jesus," he said again. "So you were a kid, right?"

"Three years old."

"And your brother...?"

"He never saw his first birthday." All her life, Lily had

tried to recapture that night. She could still feel herself deep in the fluffy softness of Mr. Bubble, but she had never been able to remember Evan beside her. She sometimes wondered if, without her mother's reminders, she would recall the incident at all.

She scarcely remembered Evan, either. Occasional flashes and flickers of memory, nothing more. A glint of light upon a smooth baby cheek, that was all. The sound of a soft cry in the night. When she looked at old family photos, she saw them together, and judging by those photos, she adored her brother.

Lily sometimes wondered what Evan would be like if he'd survived. She found herself studying men his age, trying to imagine her brother all grown up. Would he be tall and substantial like Violet, or small and slight like Lily? Would he be gregarious, successful, emotional, reserved? She couldn't even begin to imagine how different her own life would be, had he survived. Maybe then she wouldn't be so cautious and reserved. She might trust herself to fall in love, make a family, be a mother.

The gathering darkness had the closed-in feel of a confessional. She'd been raised Catholic but had never gained absolution no matter how many times she recited the Act of Contrition. "I always thought I should remember such a huge disaster," she told Sean. "How can I not remember it? How is it that my brother, my own flesh and blood, slipped underwater and drowned with me right next to him? How did I fail to notice?" A thousand times, she had asked herself why she hadn't reached out and grabbed his wet, slippery arm to pull him to safety.

"You were three years old, that's how," Sean stated. "A baby. The question I have is, where were your parents?"

"There was some emergency with Violet, and my mother stepped out for one minute," Lily said. "Three, tops." She braided her fingers together. "Sometimes I think what came after was even worse. My mother was investigated for neglect, and Violet and I were sent to a foster home for a time, though I have no memory of that, either. When we came home, everything was different. We were a family who forgot how to be happy." She shivered, although the night was balmy with the promise of summer. "So that's it. To this day I have no idea exactly what happened, but my mother was right about one thing. I was old enough to have saved him."

Lily knew her loss governed everything. The fact that a life had slipped away in her presence had defined her and affected every choice she made. She had never forgiven herself. How could she? Because of the past, she forbade herself to get attached to people. She remained childless, translating her yearning for a child into teaching.

"With all due respect to your mother, she fed you a line of crap, I suppose to relieve her own sense of guilt," Sean said. "I'm sorry, Lily. For your whole family, but especially for you."

They were quiet together, and for no particular reason, she felt oddly comforted. In grief counseling, they spoke of good days and bad ones. Lily didn't really have those. She had good moments and bad ones, around the clock. This particular moment was a good one. She felt curiously light and warm.

"Would you like to have a glass of wine?" she asked him.

"No," he said, then grinned at her thoroughly discomfited expression. "I'd like to have a beer. However, I do have a Fetzer merlot—all organic—you might like."

"Yes," she said, ducking her head. "I might."

He went and fixed the drinks, handing her the glass of wine. They went outside to sit on the back steps and watch the moon rise. Lily tasted the wine, watching him over the rim of the glass. He ought to be in a beer commercial, she thought. A beer commercial aimed at women. No woman in America could resist a man who did the dishes, put the kids to bed and then sat down to crack open a cold one.

"Want a sip?" he asked, tipping the can toward her.

Yes. "No," she said. "No, thanks. The wine's fine."

"You looked as though you wanted some of mine."

"I've never been a beer drinker."

"I'll remember that. So," he said, "what do you usually do on a Saturday night?"

"Well, not this. Not baring my soul to an unsuspecting man. Sorry about that, by the way."

"I didn't mind. Maybe next week you'll bare something else."

The man had a girlfriend and he was flirting with her. What a jerk, she thought. But deep down, she knew he wasn't a jerk. "Anyway, Friday's generally movie night and Saturday is—" Date night. She didn't say it aloud. "I tend to go out with friends, people from school, mostly. Crystal and I have—had—season tickets to the Portland Opera." She took a hurried drink of her wine. "I told her lawyer to give them away."

"I don't blame you one bit."

"Yes, the memories would be too painful."

"I was thinking the opera would be too painful."

"So you're not an opera fan," she mused. "There's a surprise."

He stifled a yawn, but she noticed.

"I should go," she said, looking for a place to set her wineglass.

"Don't." He put a hand on her arm, gentle but insistent. "Stay. Please."

His touch made her feel strange, tingly all over, and languid. She was grateful for the darkness that hid her blush.

He took his hand away and grinned at her. "These days I need all the adult conversation I can get."

And he couldn't find that with Maura? Maybe he just had sex with Maura, no conversation.

The thought sparked her temper. "There's something you should know."

"What's that?"

"I think we can get along," she said, "but when I'm here, I'm here for the kids. Because their mother was my best friend and she wanted me to care for them."

He leaned back against the stair rail and finished his beer. "Okay. I get it. Didn't mean to assume you have any other reason to give me the time of day."

She gave a dry laugh of disbelief. "Oh, forgive me for not falling down at your feet."

"For that, I thank you. I can't stand it when women fall at my feet. Makes it hard to get around."

"Very funny."

"Which reminds me, I have a serious question to ask you."

She caught her breath, flirting with a brief fantasy before reminding herself of what she'd just told him—she was here for the kids. "What's the serious question?"

"I'm having a will drawn up." He smiled. "My first. For the first time, it actually matters if I die."

"That's a very strange thing to say."

"But truthful. Before this, before the kids, I had nothing. Now I'm all they've got, and if something happens to me, they should be provided for. So I'm asking you, Lily. Can I designate you as guardian in my will?"

"Absolutely." She spoke without hesitation. She didn't allow herself to ask him why he'd pick her and not Maura; she wasn't sure she wanted to hear that Maura was too busy preparing to serve all humanity as a physician. "When it rains, it pours," she said. "My sister asked me the same thing. So you have to make the same promise she made."

"Anything."

"Don't let anything happen to you."

"Deal," he said, clinking his can to her glass. "So you have what, nieces? Nephews?"

"One of each. I could find myself with five kids if you and Violet check out on me."

"You'd make a fine guardian, being a teacher and all."

Lily shook her head. "I never planned to have kids."

"Because you lost your brother?"

She nearly choked with outrage. "I can't believe you said that."

"It's pretty obvious, Lil. You love kids. I can see that in you. But you're scared to be a mother and I bet it's because you never got over a loss you don't even remember." He paused, and she could think of no reply. Then he asked, "Are you mad?"

Still she said nothing.

"Hey," he said. "I never planned to have kids, either. And look at me now—Mr. Mom."

She noticed that the wine was imparting a pleasant buzz. It occurred to her to ask for a refill, but she had to drive home. "You're the one who makes a fine guardian," she said.

He looked at her, startled. "You're really something, you know?"

No, she didn't know. "That's not the sort of thing people say to me."

He brushed the back of his hand against her arm briefly, yet she felt that touch all the way to the middle of her heart. No, she thought, this was wrong. "Sean—"

A car's headlamps swung across the backyard, illuminating the garden. Sean frowned. "I wasn't expecting anyone."

They stepped out onto the driveway just as a man got out of the driver's side. Small and wiry, he looked both vaguely familiar and hopping mad.

"Something the matter, Duffy?" asked Sean.

It was Charles McDuff, the greenskeeper from the golf course.

"A little something, I'd say," the older man replied with a hint of a Scottish brogue.

The passenger door opened, and Lily's heart dropped to her stomach. She felt it land like a lead weight. She heard Sean catch his breath.

"What's going on?" he asked.

"We need to talk about your nephew." Duffy glared at Cameron.

The boy tossed his head and glared right back.

chapter 31

"So did your uncle just completely freak on you?" asked Jason Schaefer. He kept his voice down to a low murmur so Duffy, the greenskeeper who was overseeing their punishment, couldn't hear them.

Cameron was snapping on oversize coveralls in preparation for his enforced community service. Because they'd trashed the golf course, he and his two friends would be spending a long time with the greenskeeper. A very long time.

"So did he freak out or what?" Jason prodded.

Cameron sat down to put on the waders Duffy had provided. "Yeah, I guess."

It was worse than that, actually. His mother, had she been alive, would have gone into freak mode, crying and wringing her hands and wondering what people would say. His father would have bust a cap, too, thundering warnings about how Cameron was jeopardizing his future.

His uncle and Lily, who for some reason had stayed late the night Duffy had gone to the Schaefers' and threatened to bring in the cops, had reacted with an almost eerie quiet. Sean had thanked Duffy for bringing Cameron home and promised a call to the police wouldn't be necessary—this time.

Then he and Lily had taken him inside. Cameron had expected anger or at least a frustrated "What were you thinking?"

His uncle hadn't freaked. Neither had Lily. They hadn't said much at all and Cameron had the uncanny feeling they both knew exactly what he was thinking, probably better than he did.

"Well, shit," said Andrew Meyer, their other accomplice. "I wish you'd listened to me. We had a story and we should have stuck with it."

"*You* had the story," Cameron muttered. "You told it to anyone at school who'd listen."

"I only told one person, just one," Andy said. "She promised she wouldn't say a word."

"Idiot," Jason said.

"You're the one who sang like a bird when the coach questioned you," Andy said.

"Only after you told them to question me," Jason snapped.

"All right, that's enough chatter," Duffy said. "You gentlemen have some work to do."

"Yes, sir, right away, sir." Andrew snapped him a salute.

The sarcasm seemed to be lost on Duffy, an old guy from Scotland, and Cameron was just as glad. The three of them filed out of the greenskeeper's building and Duffy gave them their marching orders. Today they were to clear the pond near the Number Ten fairway. The marshy pond was choked with duckweed that had to be piled in a cart and taken away.

And that, of course, was only the beginning of their punishment. Suspended from the golf team, they were to spend every day after school at the course, virtual slaves performing acts of contrition.

Andy and Jason treated the punishment like a big joke,

singing an off-key rendition of "Back on the Chain Gang" as they worked amid the weedy fringes of the pond. Cameron tried to joke around, too, but it felt forced and he soon lapsed into sullen silence. The brown mud sucked at his feet and he could feel the chill of the water through his rubber boots.

This sucked, literally and figuratively. Everything sucked lately.

He worked like a robot, bending, uprooting a handful of weeds, flinging them onto the bank. The mud felt like cement, closing around his feet, holding him captive.

"And to think we could be at the driving range with the team," said Jason. "Look at all the fun we'd be missing."

Although Cameron wouldn't admit it, he did miss practicing with the team. He liked hitting drives, dozens of them in a row. He liked matching up his skills against a tough course like Echo Ridge.

It was stupid, the way he used to argue with his dad so much about golf. He wished he hadn't done that. He wished he had simply told his dad the truth, that he loved the game and wanted to make it his life, just like his father and uncle. Cameron had blown it, though. He'd been given one chance to caddie for his father in an important tournament and he'd been a disaster. After that, he had to pretend he didn't care, about caddying, about his father's game or his own.

At least he'd managed to get himself suspended from the team. Mission accomplished. He should have done this a long time ago, except it wouldn't have happened. No way would he have been suspended from golf when his father was alive. God, how many times had Cameron been tempted to tell his dad exactly why he wanted to quit the team? Of course, Cameron always chickened out or told himself it was pointless because as far as his father was concerned, you never quit for any reason.

"Hey, take it easy, Cameron," said Jason, dodging a flung weed, its roots trailing mud. "You don't need to throw stuff so far."

"Sorry, wasn't watching." Cameron wondered why messing up the golf course had been so unsatisfying. He had taken intense physical pleasure in the act of destruction, but as soon as he was finished, he felt empty. His friends had been triumphant, declaring it a good night's work. Cameron hadn't shared their satisfaction. No matter what he did, he still felt empty. It was like eating cotton candy. It never filled you up, but eventually you made yourself sick on it, anyway.

As he slogged toward the next section of the bank, something caught his eye. "Hey, check this out," he called in a stage whisper, gesturing to his friends. "It's some kind of nest."

"Ducks, probably," said Andy. "Look at the size of the eggs. Hand me one, will you?"

"Me, too," Jason said. "I bet I can hit that cart trail with one. Splat!"

"No way." Cameron planted himself in front of the nest. "We're not disturbing this. I'm not even going to pull the weeds around it."

"Come on, we're bored. It's just a bunch of eggs. They're probably all over the golf course."

"Forget it," he said. "We're leaving these alone."

"Guess what else we're leaving alone?" said Jason, dropping his rake and gloves. Andy quickly caught on and followed suit. "If Duffy asks where we went, tell him we flew north for the summer."

"Right." Cameron was just as glad when they left. Sure, they were his friends, but sometimes he wished they meant something more to him than the occasional good time. He especially wished he hadn't listened to them the other night when they came up with the plan to mess up the golf course.

He worked alone, relieved that Duffy didn't come to check on him. He didn't want to have to lie for his friends, but he didn't want to get them in even more trouble, either.

He left a thick fringe of vegetation around the nest and finished just before dusk fell.

His coveralls stank of brackish water and he was covered in mud. His shoulders and back ached, but he felt curiously light. Maybe he shouldn't have skipped lunch, he thought. Then he admitted to himself that it wasn't hunger making him feel this way. It was the fact that he had been caught. Finally. The weight had been lifted off his chest.

Duffy had said he could go home at sundown. Cameron wasn't sure how to accomplish that. He was supposed to get a ride with Jason, who had his license.

It was a long walk home.

Most of his friends had their licenses by now, but not Cameron. He was too scared to get behind the wheel of a car and completely humiliated by his failure. Not humiliated enough to drive, though. He'd tried a few times, but it didn't work. He broke into a sweat, couldn't see straight, started shaking like a leaf in the wind. Dr. Sachs was "working" on the issue with him. They were "working" on a lot of issues, but Cameron thought it was all a waste of time. How did talking about something you can't change fix it?

He eyed the gas-powered cart Duffy had given them to use. He was fine with driving a golf cart, but Duffy would have a fit if he drove it off the premises. He wasn't about to call his uncle, though. He'd already screwed up enough for the time being.

He puzzled over the matter while he loaded clippings and debris into the cart. He stopped when he saw someone walking toward him. In the low light, he couldn't make out her features, but he recognized the lanky figure and swinging ponytail instantly.

Great.

"Hey," he said, barely slowing down his work. He felt kind of embarrassed, dressed like a jailbird, filthy from the day's work.

"I heard about what happened," Becky Pilchuk said.

"The whole school heard about it."

"Pretty much."

While he worked, she just stood there. He could feel her watching him.

"Is there something I can do for you?" he asked, loading the last bundle of debris into the cart.

"No. I just came to see—oh!" She was startled when a pair of mallard ducks landed in the water, throwing up a tail of spray in their wake. It was a male and female, gliding in tandem toward the reeds.

"Don't go too close," Cameron said. "There's a nest."

"Really?" Pushing her glasses up her nose, she craned her neck to see. "Where?"

He pointed. "In those reeds. Right in the middle."

"I see it now." Excitement lightened her voice. "Look at all those eggs! Cameron, that is so cool."

It wasn't *that* cool, he thought.

"I'm glad you left the nest alone. I bet they'll hatch any day. It'll be fun to watch. We should check on them every day, shouldn't we?"

Oh, like he was going to agree to that. It was practically a…a date. A date with a dork. "I'm about finished here. I have to cart this stuff away." He felt her studying him as he worked. Her intensity was disconcerting. "So go ahead and say it," he blurted out.

"Say what?"

"All the stuff you're thinking, like why I did it and how stupid and pointless it was."

"I know why you did it. And I'm pretty sure you know that it was stupid and pointless." Without being invited, she hopped into the cart.

He loaded up the tools and got behind the wheel. "All right, Dr. Freud, why did I do it?" he asked as he took off toward the decant and composting area of the golf course.

"Because your parents died and you're going a little crazy," she said simply.

That did it. He slammed on the brakes of the golf cart, so hard that she put out her hands to brace herself. Her vulnerability made him even madder. "How the hell do you think you know that? You don't know anything about me. What makes you think you know why I'm such a screwup?"

She winced as though stung by his temper, but she didn't stop looking him in the eye. With deliberate, unhurried movements, she got out of the cart. "Because," she said, "I felt the same way when my own mother died."

Ah, shit, he thought. Shit, shit, shit. That was the last thing he'd expected from her. "Get back in the cart," he said.

She walked away at an unhurried pace, her head down.

He pulled the cart next to her. "Please. Please, Becky."

That stopped her—either the *please* or the fact that he'd called her by name for the first time. She looked up at him, and the evening light streaked across her face, burnishing it with deep gold. She wasn't so homely, he thought, remembering the stupid scores he and his friends kept on the chalkboard in the locker room. Becky Pilchuk always came in dead last. Now he knew that was because no one ever really saw her. You just had to look past the dopey clothes and eyeglasses.

She sat down next to him and stared straight ahead. "I know you think I'm a dork, but there are some things I understand better than anyone else."

"I don't think—" He stopped. Why lie to this girl? She'd

never done anything to him but try to be his friend, and he just went along with disliking her because everyone else seemed to. "All right, maybe I used to think you were a dork. I bet you used to think I was a— I don't know. A tool or a poser."

"Or a dumb jock."

"Yeah, maybe that. Anyway, I'm sorry. I didn't bother getting to know you and I should have."

She glanced over at him, the sunlight slipping through her hair, making it shine. "It's not too late," she said.

"Tell me about your mom."

She folded her hands very carefully in her lap. "It wasn't a shock or anything, like yours was. She was sick for about a year when I was in middle school. She's just as gone, though, and sometimes I miss her so much my whole body aches. And the worst thing is, I can't make it go away. I loved my mom so much, even when I was in seventh grade and being rotten to her. I loved her like—I don't know, in a way I can barely describe, you know?"

He nodded. He did know. Every night he lay awake and prayed his parents knew that, too. "There's something else," he said, tentative but yearning to get this out. "The very last thing I ever said to my father is 'screw you.'" There. It was out. He hadn't even told this to Dr. Sachs.

"Bummer," she said.

"Bummer? I tell you something like that and all you say is 'bummer'?"

"Everybody says 'screw you' to their parents. It's not like you invented the phrase. I was horrible to my mom sometimes, even when I understood how sick she was. But I never stopped loving her and she knew that, same as your dad."

Did he? Cameron wondered. He conjured up a picture of his dad and himself, and surprisingly, in every memory, the two of them were happy.

"And now that she's gone," Becky said, "where does all that love go? Where do I put it? Who do I love like I loved my mom? It's still in me like it was when she was alive, but now it doesn't have anywhere to go." She took off her glasses and looked at him. "This isn't very helpful, is it?"

"Actually, it makes more sense than anything else people have said to me."

chapter 32

"Five more minutes," Sean begged. "Just give me five more minutes."

"No." Standing next to the bed, Ashley peered at him over the edge of the mattress. "Up."

"Who let you out of your crib, anyway?"

"Up."

Next to him, Maura sighed and stretched, but didn't fully awaken. Sean glanced at the clock—7:00 a.m. A school day. "All right," he grumbled. "I'm up." He wore pajama bottoms but no shirt. Having little kids around had quickly cured him of his habit of sleeping in the buff. "I bet you're soaking wet, aren't you?"

She smiled coyly.

He glanced back at Maura. She might be faking sleep. Diaper changing was not her favorite chore. "All right, you." He picked her up and carried her away to change her. It was like this every morning. The baby first. It didn't matter if he needed to take a piss or wanted to brush his teeth. Only afterward, when she was watching cartoons and eating dry

Cheerios under Charlie's desultory supervision, could Sean see to his own needs. He took the stairs two at a time, in a hurry to duck into the bathroom and then maybe get lucky with Maura. As he was brushing his teeth, he heard a burst of crying. Down the stairs again, two at a time. He could distinguish between Ashley's cranky cry and her pain cry. This was a pain cry. He found them both in the kitchen.

"What happened?" he asked Charlie as he scooped Ashley up.

"She fell. She tried to climb up on the counter for more Cheerios and she fell right on her bottom."

"Weren't you watching her?" As soon as he spoke, Sean regretted his words. "I'm sorry, honey," he said, jiggling the baby in his arms. "I shouldn't have left her with you."

"She made a ladder out of the drawers, see?" Charlie pointed out, indicating the counter drawers. "Mom always said Ashley's too smart for her own good."

Dogged by guilt, he trudged upstairs again. After what Lily had told him about her own experience, Sean should have known better. "Can't even take a piss when I need to anymore," he muttered under his breath.

Ashley was still whimpering when he set her on the bed next to Maura. She stirred and offered a sleepy smile. "What's up, buttercup?" she asked the baby.

"She fell," Sean said. "I don't think she's hurt, but could you check her out?"

Maura pushed herself up on her hands. "Sure. Wait here a minute. I need to pee and brush my teeth."

When she was gone, Sean looked at Ashley, who had stopped crying. "Where does it hurt? Head? Elbow? Bottom?"

She shook her head but waited patiently for Maura. Sean glanced at the clock. Seven twenty-five. T minus thirty-five minutes and counting. Maura seemed to be taking her time in the bathroom; it was all he could do to keep from yelling at her to hurry up. When she finally came out, he said, "I need to go make sure the other kids are ready for school." Pulling on a T-shirt over his head, he walked down the hall, hammering at Cameron's door. "You up?"

"I am now" came a grumpy voice.

Sean went downstairs and made sure Charlie ate something. She was looking down in dismay at her Brownie jumper. "This needs to be ironed."

At that, he laughed aloud. "You're barking up the wrong tree, kid."

She looked wounded. "Will Maura do it?"

"Doubt it. You look fine, Charlie, I swear. Come over here and I'll fix your hair." It was their morning ritual, and Sean was getting pretty damned good at braids. This morning, however, with her yellow braids and weird uniform, she looked like a member of the Hitler youth. He said nothing, though. Charlie was as fragile and volatile as a vial of nitro.

Cameron came thumping down the stairs, as surly as he dared to be without Sean calling him on it. Since the golf course incident, he'd been reasonably well behaved. Nothing like a sentence of hard physical labor to keep a kid out of trouble.

"Where's my backpack?" he asked.

"Wherever you left it," Charlie said before Sean could.

"Yeah, that's real cute." He found it on his own under the kitchen table, exactly where he'd left it.

Sean didn't nag him about breakfast. The kid was old enough to know he was supposed to eat. There was a chaotic flurry of last-minute paperwork—a permission slip for Charlie, a surprisingly adequate grade report for Cameron—and then they both rushed out to catch the bus. For a moment, the kitchen was utterly silent. Sean looked at the digital clock on the stove. The glorious silence lasted approximately one minute. Then Maura came in with Ashley who looked happier but still wasn't dressed. He had the urge to ask, *Do you think you could have dressed her?* But he resisted. Maura hadn't signed up for this, any of this. She tried to be a good sport about it.

"Is there coffee?" she asked, her usual morning greeting.

He dumped some into a filter, filled the reservoir of the coffeemaker and flipped it on. "In about five minutes."

Maura took out her Blackberry to check messages before heading to the hospital. Sean put Ashley in her high chair and opened a can of diced peaches for her. The phone rang, and he reached for it with one hand while the other dumped the peaches into a bowl. It was Mrs. Foster, saying she wouldn't be able to babysit today. "I understand," Sean said, because there was nothing else to say. "Call me when you're better."

He hung up and checked the coffeepot. Maura had already taken the first cup. "Mrs. Foster can't come today. She's sick."

"That's too bad." She finished her coffee. "Listen, I need to run." She gave Ashley a quick kiss on the head and Sean a longer one on the mouth. "See you."

"So it's just you and me, kid," Sean said to Ashley, who was placidly eating her peaches. "I was going to get in a round before work today." Nerves and frustration made him hyper, and he cleaned up the kitchen while he talked to his niece. "Instead, I've got you," he said. "Not such a bad deal. What do you want to do today? Watch *Teletubbies?* Discuss toilet training? We could answer fan mail from all the wackos who keep writing to us," he suggested.

She offered him some of her peaches.

"No, thanks," he told Ashley. "I ought to be going nuts. I've got so much on my plate I'm about to drop something. My career's in the shithole, I have this confusing pseudo-relationship thing going on with Maura and I'm having a hell of a time making ends meet." He picked up Maura's coffee cup and rinsed it in the sink. "She's great in the sack, but…not exactly mother material, so we're in commitment limbo. And Lily." He shook his head. "What's up with her, huh? No idea where I stand with her, or if I even care." He watched Ashley slurp down the last of her peaches, then wiped her face. "Who knew I'd actually like this?"

Mrs. Foster's illness turned out to be the best thing that ever happened to Sean's golf game. Initially, he thought the temporary absence of the babysitter would be a fiasco. Without her to look after Ashley during the day, he'd be on round-the-clock duty.

He sent Charlie and Cameron off to their respective schools as usual. Cameron was still in turmoil. After the stunt he'd pulled, he seemed as angry as ever, but also more introspective. The grief counselor said this was normal, but Sean wasn't buying that. What was normal was for a kid to laugh and cut up with his friends, to become obsessed with girls and golf. What was normal was for a kid to yearn to drive a car, not avoid it.

Give him time, counseled Dr. Sachs.

"Nobody seems to know how much time this takes," he explained to Ashley as he drove to the golf course.

"Nope," she said, rattling an individual-serving-size box of Cheerios.

"So what do you say we go nine holes?" he said.

"Okay."

Outside of tournaments, nongolfers weren't supposed to be on the course. Toddlers in particular, even those strapped into a car seat in a closed cart.

He didn't care. He was the club pro, it was an overcast weekday morning and there was no one around. He and Cameron had taken the girls out several times before, and they'd behaved themselves. Ashley seemed to think it was funny to be loaded into her car seat in the golf cart.

"You're going to love this," he promised her. "I bet you'll grow up to be the next Annika Sorenstam."

"Yep," she agreed.

The natural hush of the golf course seemed to work its magic on her. Low-lying mist insulated sound and softened the edges of the world. The moment his driver smacked the ball with a resounding *thwok,* he knew he'd hit an excellent drive.

"Wow," said Ashley approvingly.

"Wow is right," he said, getting into the cart. "That was a 360-yard drive."

He birdied the hole, and it only got better from there. Each time he hit, his assurance grew. He even beat his own performance on the morning of Derek's funeral. This was, quite possibly, the best round of his life. And unlike the funeral round, this one was no fluke. He felt his game coming together; the judgment, the drives, the putts.

Rather than distract him, Ashley somehow enhanced his focus. Never had he concentrated so well or to such good effect. He achieved a peculiar rhythm that he recognized from his very early days as a tournament golf player. It was something he thought he'd lost long ago, and now, stroke by stroke, yard by yard, he rediscovered it.

He was taut with excitement as he filled out his scorecard. "How about that, sugar?" he said. "You must be my good-luck charm."

"Yep," said Ashley.

He got into the habit of bringing her to the course every day, and rarely went a single stroke over par. The two of them became a familiar sight at Echo Ridge, a golf cart with a child's safety seat and a few toys, a set of clubs and a cooler filled with bottled water and Gerber pear juice.

There was not a doubt in his mind that his game had changed. Some golfers rebuilt a flawed swing; Sean rebuilt his attitude. Having a tiny child wholly dependent on you put things in perspective. He used to sweat his score, treating each stroke like a matter of life or death. Now that he was in charge of three kids, he had a different perspective and a new way of listening to himself. Somehow, understanding the things that really mattered eased the pressure to perform, and the game he played was wholly his own, not influenced by expectations or advice from outside.

Sean worried about the kids, about money, about the future, all the time. But when he was on the golf course with his niece, everything fell away, everything but a little girl and the game.

On Friday afternoon, he saw Cameron dressed like a convict and hard at work on the pond. All three boys were supposed to be working off the expense of fixing the green, but the others were nowhere to be seen. Sean still hadn't figured out what demons had possessed Cameron and made him vandalize the golf course that had meant so much to his father. Or perhaps, he reflected, that was precisely the point.

At any rate, rebuilding the things he'd ruined seemed a reasonable occupation for him. Since the vandalism episode, the kid had kept his nose clean. Or so it seemed. If he was still screwing around, it didn't show.

"Cam," Ashley called out, waving both hands at him.

He wasn't alone. That girl was with him…Becca? No, Becky—in muddy gloves and gardening clogs, her ponytail pulled through the back of a baseball cap. They were putting in a large bed of impatiens.

She hadn't been involved in the vandalism, but she didn't seem to mind helping Cameron with his community service.

"Hi, Ashley," she said, smiling broadly. "Hi, Mr. Maguire."

"Hey, Becky." Sean could tell they were both surprised he remembered her name.

"Be really quiet," Cameron instructed them in a whisper. "I need to show you something."

He took Ashley out of her seat and carried her down the bank to the edge of the pond. "We've been watching them all afternoon," he said. "They just hatched."

A female mallard glided out of the reeds, followed by a line of eight tiny brown-and-yellow ducklings.

Cameron set his sister down at the edge of the pond and she chuckled with delight. "Want ducks."

"We have to leave them alone," Cameron told her, "so they'll feel safe."

"Want ducks."

He kept hold of her hand and they stood together on the bank, just watching while the breeze tossed their hair. The image struck at Sean. They looked so vulnerable, just the two of them linked by her hand in his. Sean was seized by a now-familiar feeling. How will I do this? How will I protect them? He was all that stood between these kids and disaster. Unlike most families, there were no spare parents or stepparents or blood relatives to fall back on. He was it. He hoped like hell that was enough.

He felt Becky watching him and they shared a strange moment. They didn't exchange a word, but he had the impression she knew exactly what was on his mind.

Eventually, Sean lured Ashley back to the cart with the promise of a cracker. He wondered if Cameron was really doing better or if he was just getting better at acting normal. Since the vandalism incident, he seemed less angry and troubled. Or maybe that was just wishful thinking on Sean's part.

He decided not to argue with fate when things were going all right.

"Come on, caddie," he said. "Let's go post this score. I think it might be a club record."

Actually, he knew it was. If he brought in a superb score like this in tournament play, he would be the recordholder. And the score he'd just beat was his brother's.

He wouldn't turn in the card, because he'd played alone. Because of what had happened in Asia, his scorecards were suspect. And honestly, it didn't matter. He'd spent the day with one of his favorite people—his niece—and had played a great round.

Finally, he trusted the new development enough to talk about it. That evening, he found Maura on the living room sofa with bound printouts and textbooks surrounding her like a fortress. With one look, he could tell she'd had a rough week. She had that too-much-indoors pallor, the droopy posture, the distracted air about her.

"What do you mean, you turned a corner in your game?" she asked after he explained how his week had gone.

"He means he's reaching the next level," said Charlie, looking up from the puzzle she was putting together. If golf were schoolwork, she'd be a straight-A student. She had applied herself to learning the game like the most dedicated scholar. Then she turned her attention back to SpongeBob on the TV. She and Cameron had spent the past twenty minutes fighting for control over the remote, and Charlie had prevailed.

"Let's play," Ashley said to Maura, trying to breach the barricade of books and papers surrounding her.

"Not possible, you cute thing," Maura said distractedly, tucking a stray lock of hair behind her ear. "I've got a grant application and a case study due tomorrow."

Ashley pushed at a thick black binder. A handful of papers wafted to the floor.

Maura folded her arms across her middle and took a deep

breath. Then she said, "Tell you what. I'll play for ten minutes and then I have to get back to work."

She took the baby's hand and they went upstairs where the toys were kept. Charlie went along, too, and suddenly the room was very quiet. Sean and Cameron looked at each other, then bolted for the remote control at the same time. Sean beat him to it.

"Friday night fights," he said, switching to ESPN.

"I like *American Chopper* better."

"Not tonight, you don't," Sean said, settling into his chair as Vladimir Klischko pummeled his opponent.

·The flurry of punches caught Cameron's attention and he offered no further argument. At the commercial break, he got two root beers from the kitchen and settled down to watch.

In precisely ten minutes, Maura came down in time to see a close-up of the contender's eye bleeding, his nose stuffed with white absorbent pads.

"That's disgusting," she said.

"That's entertainment," Sean told her. He offered her a sip of his root beer, which she ignored.

"Right. Listen," she added, gathering all her books and her laptop into a giant tote bag, "I really do have two major projects I need to work on. I've decided to do it over at my place."

"You can work here," Sean said. "Take over the whole dining room table. We never eat in there." He elbowed Cameron. "What's the story on dining rooms, anyway? Did you ever have dinner in there?"

"Thanksgiving, I think."

"So you can have it until Thanksgiving."

"Thanks." She bent down and kissed his cheek. "I need to concentrate. I should also water my houseplants while I'm there...."

She left a few minutes later and a commercial came on. "I can't taste my beer!" screamed the actors.

Sean felt Cameron staring at him. "What?" he asked.

"So did she just ditch you? Or did she actually dump you?"

"I don't know what the hell you're talking about." Oh, but he did. Deep in his gut, he did.

"Ditching and dumping. There's a difference."

"I don't think she—"

"See, when someone ditches you, it's a one-time deal. It means she got a better offer."

"Like watering her houseplants?" Sean asked.

"Well, that's pretty lame. She must've really been bored with you."

"That's shit." Sean's neck prickled with unspoken awareness.

"Maybe it was an actual dumping," Cameron suggested. "Now, if it was, you've got some work to do, because a dumping is permanent. Got it?"

"I've got nothing," Sean snapped. "She's not ditching or dumping anybody. She's going to her apartment to get some work done."

"I'll bet she waters her plants and watches reruns of *ER* all night."

"How did you know she likes *ER?*"

"*Duh.* I can put two and two together." He got up and went to the kitchen. "I'm making popcorn in the microwave," he added. "You want some?"

The conversation with Cameron nagged at Sean. He called Maura the next day but got her voice mail, so he left a message telling her where to find him. Then he dropped off his nephew to work at the golf course and took his nieces to Derek's condo, where he'd arranged to meet Jane Coombs to finish clearing the place out for a new tenant. Though it was a prefurnished rental Derek had lived in since his divorce, all his personal effects were still there. Cameron had declined to help with the removal. Sean didn't blame him.

Charlie and Ashley clutched each other's hands as he unlocked the door and let them in. The air was chilly and still with disuse, though everything lay untouched since that day in April, waiting as though Derek had just stepped out and would return at any moment.

Sean glanced at the girls, who walked into the living room with the sort of breath-held hush of churchgoers. He could see Charlie trying to stay calm, pressing her lips tightly together.

"You sure you want to stay?" he asked her. "I can take you over to Lily's if you—"

"We'll stay," Charlie said stoutly. "Won't we, Ashley?"

"Suit yourself." In fact, he hadn't cleared anything with Lily. Maybe she had plans. Maybe those plans didn't include looking after two kids. He had to quit assuming she'd drop everything anytime he needed her, even though that was exactly what she did. She wasn't just a schoolteacher and grieving friend, he reminded himself. Maybe she slept in on a Saturday morning or went to the beach. Hell, maybe she was seeing someone, not that it was any of his business.

He found the TV remote right where Derek would have left it, on a table to the right of the lounge chair, and when he turned it on, the Golf Channel came up.

Sean handed the remote over to Charlie, who quickly switched to cartoons. Because she wanted to help, he gave her a box and two bags and told her to empty the TV console in the living room.

"Everything?" she asked.

"Everything. If you think we should keep it, put it in the box. If not, in the trash bag or the Salvation Army bag. You decide."

"What if I can't decide?"

He kissed her head. "Then keep it, honey, just in case."

He turned away then, because the anguish hit him hard. Here in this house, with its beige walls and furniture, he could still sense his brother's presence, could imagine him here, never knowing it was his last day alive.

He hoped it had been a good day. He hoped Derek had hugged his kids, had a laugh, found joy in something that day.

"I'm going to get to work," he said to the girls. "You tell me if you need anything." He brought a stack of empty moving boxes into the bedroom. Jane was late, but that didn't surprise him. She had weathered the tragedy poorly, vacillating between rage and uncontrollable tears. What Sean sensed from her most of all was bitterness, that she hadn't held Derek's heart longer or shared enough of his life. Sean had invited her to visit the kids anytime she wanted, but she claimed it made her too sad to be around them. Whenever she saw them, she cried so hard that the baby cried, too. She'd managed to compose herself enough to do an interview for some cheesy entertainment magazine, though.

"She's a real prize," he muttered to the open door of the walk-in closet. The air smelled of shoe leather and expensive after-shave, as real as if Derek were standing right behind him. Damn it, thought Sean. You're not supposed to be dead. He tried to remember their last conversation. Golf, women, small talk. He tried to remember the last time he'd told his brother he loved him. "That would be never," he muttered. "I sure as hell hope you knew."

Jane had evidently already stopped by to remove her own things soon after the funeral. There was an empty space on the rack and adjacent shelves. That pissed him off, and when he heard her arrive, he was ready to unload on her.

But it wasn't Jane standing in the bedroom doorway, and the bitter words dissolved on his tongue. "Hey," he said.

"Hey." Wrapping her arms around her middle, Maura walked toward him. She looked tired, he noticed, tired and sad. "I got your message."

He jerked a shirt off a hanger, folded it awkwardly, put it in one of the boxes for the Salvation Army. Some of Derek's fans had suggested holding an eBay auction with his memorabilia, but Sean couldn't stomach the idea of his brother's things being picked over like meat from a carcass. He'd rather see some homeless guy in Derek's still-new Tommy Bahama golf shirts.

"Jane was supposed to meet me here to get rid of this stuff," he said to Maura. "She's a no-show."

"I'd offer to help, but I need to turn in a project this morning," she said. "And Sean…"

Her voice trailed off, but he knew what was coming next. It was the we-need-to-talk part of the conversation. The one he'd seen coming ever since the accident.

From the moment it became clear he was in charge of three kids, he and Maura had been heading in different directions. Sean understood that. Still, it hurt to look at her, to imagine the way they used to be together, unencumbered, living from day to day. He yanked another shirt from the closet, folded it.

"I'm twenty-five years old, Sean," Maura said in a breaking voice. "I get my MD this summer and I have no idea where I'll wind up for an internship. I'm sorry, I…"

"Don't apologize for that," he said. "The world needs doctors." He pulled out a pair of FootJoy soft spikes, added them to the box. He'd miss the sex, he decided. Yeah, he'd miss that.

He stopped working for a moment and studied Maura. Her eyes looked as lonely as they had the day he'd met her. Back then, they had seemed like a great match. He'd been footloose and flexible, living on the surface, looking out for number one. He was a different person now. He had a different life. The personal cost of Derek's death belonged to Sean. This was something he'd discussed with the social worker in charge of the kids. He did have a choice, she assured him. No one could force him to take over Derek's responsibilities.

There was no force involved, he'd discovered. His heart belonged to his inherited family, a fact he found both painful and joyous. "This is my life now," he told Maura simply. "It's who I am."

She nodded, and he saw her swallow hard. "I really do love you," she said, and the tears started to fall. "And I could learn to love this family, but I can't take on three kids right now, maybe never."

You didn't learn to love these kids, he thought. You just did. Sean saw no point in trying to explain that to her.

Maura's shoulders shook as she cried. Maybe she really did care about him, but since moving in with Derek's kids, he'd learned a lot about the meaning of caring and commitment.

Maura was just following the usual pattern. Women loved him and they left him. That was the way it worked.

chapter 33

"You got some lipstick in your purse, Miss Robinson?" asked Charlie, hovering around her desk at dismissal time. "Or maybe in the drawer here?"

Lily frowned slightly. "Do you need to borrow some?"

"No way. I mean, no thank you." Charlie looked disheveled at the end of the day, but in a good way. Her uncle had given her hair the Heidi look today, braids crisscrossed over the top of her head. Now stray tendrils had sprung loose around her face. "So have you got a comb somewhere?"

"Why would you ask that?"

"I figured you might want to freshen up, is all. You know, on account of my uncle Sean's coming this afternoon for the conference."

"He's…why, yes, he is, isn't he?" Lily felt a funny little spike of panic. She'd completely forgotten.

She checked her planning book, which lay open on her desk. Sure enough, it was this afternoon. Memorial Day was practically upon them, and the class was doing a major project at the veterans' cemetery in Tigard.

She helped Charlie with her backpack. "Isn't your Brownie troop meeting in the cafeteria this afternoon?"

"Yes. I did a crappy job with my badges, though, see?" She showed Lily the brown sash, its badges fastened haphazardly with safety pins.

"Maybe I could help you with it over the weekend, but you have to promise you won't say that crude word anymore."

"What, *crappy?*"

"Let's make that the last time, Charlene Louise."

"Yes, ma'am. Uncle Sean used to say the s-word all the time, but he switched to cr…the other one when Ashley started saying 'shit,' too."

At least he was trying, Lily acknowledged.

"That's a nice pin," Charlie said, clearly stalling as she indicated the small silver brooch Lily wore on her collar. "What is it?"

"A student gave it to me one year," Lily said, touching the brooch. "It's the owl and the pussycat and the runcible spoon. Remember the poem by Edward Lear—we learned it last Valentine's Day. 'They dined on mince, and slices of quince…'"

"'Which they ate with a runcible spoon,'" Charlie filled in.

"You have a good memory."

"It's just Uncle Sean who's coming."

Lily paused in straightening the papers on her desk. "Yes. It's right here on my agenda."

"I mean, he's coming alone," Charlie said with a meaningful look. "Without Maura."

"I see." She didn't, of course. She straightened the already neat pile of papers.

Charlie pushed her thumb thoughtfully at her lower lip. "Cameron said she either ditched him or dumped him, I can't remember which."

"What are you talking about?"

"She went back to her apartment to water the plants and never came to see us again. I didn't do anything bad, did I?" Charlie's eyes widened with sudden fear.

Lily could have smacked Maura Riley just then. Didn't she know better than to flit in and out of a child's life with no consistency whatsoever? Didn't she realize what that would do to a child like Charlie?

Masking a stab of anger, Lily touched Charlie's cheek with the back of her hand. The girl's skin was so smooth and tender, so fragile. "Not at all. You're even good citizen of the week." She indicated the star chart.

Charlie traced her finger around the big gold star. "I wish my mom knew that."

Lily put her arms around the little girl. "She does. I promise you, she knows, and your dad does, too." Oh, God, she thought. How do I do this? In her mind, Charlie had connected her own misbehavior with her parents' deaths. She had to leave that notion behind. "What happened is not your fault," she whispered in Charlie's ear. "It's so important for you to understand that."

Charlie nodded. "I'm trying," she said, her voice muffled against Lily's shoulder. "I hate how different everything is."

"I think we all do," Lily admitted. "Tell me one specific thing you hate."

"Mom used to cut the crust off the sandwich in my lunch, and Uncle Sean never does."

"Boy, I hate that, too. I never eat the crust," Lily said. "What else?"

"I used to get to stay up until nine-thirty, but Uncle Sean says that's too late. He wants us in bed a whole hour earlier."

Good for you, thought Lily. "I can see why you don't like that," she said. "Maybe after school's out, you can stay up a little later. Tell me something else you don't like."

"Summer, even though it's not here yet," Charlie stated. "Mom promised us a cruise and Dad promised us Hawaii."

"Did your uncle promise you anything?"

She raised and lowered her shoulders in an elaborate shrug. "You could ask him, I guess. He's got news, too. Kind of."

"What news?"

"Well, Red's coming to see him this week. He keeps calling him, wanting him to play in tournaments and stuff."

"So why doesn't he? Isn't he any good?"

"He's great. He's going to the next level. Red says he could be even better than my dad, but Uncle Sean says he's too busy with us to do any tournaments."

Lily tried to imagine what that might be like, turning down a second chance at your dream. "And what do you think?"

"Same as Red," said Charlie. "A racehorse has to run." She sent Lily a meaningful look.

Lily walked her to the door, straightening the badge sash on her shoulder. "The conference is about you, not about golf. Tell you what. Give me one specific thing to tell your uncle that you don't think I've thought of."

Charlie paused. "I feel better," she said, a tentative smile playing about her lips. "I quit crying a zillion times a day. Sometimes I only cry once, and some days, not at all."

Lily felt a rush of affection. You idiot, Maura, she thought. Look at what you walked away from. Lily immediately curbed her thoughts. Who was she to judge? Just a short time ago, she had believed herself perfectly content to live alone forever. It had taken a life-altering tragedy to shake her awake. Perhaps Maura would learn her own heart without suffering such a loss.

"That's good," she told Charlie. "And I'm giving you a special badge today." She took off the runcible-spoon brooch and pinned it to Charlie's Brownie sash. "You earned this, and it's for keeps. It's the feel-better badge. Now, scoot."

A twinkle flashed in Charlie's eyes and she headed for the Brownie meeting with a spring in her step. Lily carefully waited until she was gone. Then she darted a look at the clock. Sean Maguire would be here any minute. She dove for her purse, hoping she'd find a lipstick there.

chapter 34

Sean cleared his throat and straightened his sports jacket. He had no idea how to dress for a parent-teacher conference, so he'd dressed up a little. He wanted to make sure Lily knew he took this seriously. Then he pushed open the main door of the school and followed the signs to the office. Emptied of students, the place looked completely different.

A woman with long silver hair and a flowing dress greeted him with a smile of Zen-like serenity. "Mr. Maguire," she said. "Edna Klein. I was at the funeral."

"I remember," he said, shaking her hand. "Thank you."

She wrote down his name and the time he checked in, then sent him to Lily's classroom. Peering through the door, he saw that it looked like Munchkin Land, all bright, primary colors and undersize furniture. He knocked at the half-open door. "Hello?"

"Sean, hi, please come in." She looked slightly flustered as she greeted him, a gleam of fresh lipstick on her mouth. She had a truly gorgeous mouth, he thought, and then decided that was an inappropriate observation. Or maybe not. With Maura gone, he was a free agent once again, sort of. A free agent with three kids.

As he took a seat at a low, round table, he noticed that all the desks, with chairs upended, were aligned in four rows of six. Every bulletin board display had a hand-lettered sign: Our Changing World. Fractions Are Fun. Manners Matter. Today's lesson was still up on the board: "Things We Remember on Memorial Day."

Everything here was excruciatingly neat, earnest and sincere, just like Lily. This classroom explained more about who Lily Robinson was than an FBI profile.

Then, when she opened a closet behind her desk and started rummaging around, he realized she'd managed to surprise him again. Behind the door was utter chaos, an almost kidlike disorder of brightly colored art supplies, Post-it notes stuck all over the place, a set of Mickey Mouse ears and what looked like a kimono on a hook behind the door. She caught him inspecting the closet and gave a nervous laugh. "My creative outlet," she said. "Keeping these children engaged takes some creativity. This is a toga I wear when I teach them Roman numerals."

"What's the pig nose for?"

"Literature, of course."

So he still hadn't figured her out. There were layers of complexity to this woman, and against his will, he found himself wanting to explore them.

She opened a file folder and turned it toward him. "I have a bit of good news. She's doing better in math," she said. "This is a unit test we took on Wednesday."

"Eighty-three percent," he said, looking over the pages. "Not too shabby."

"She seems to like fractions and money." She tapped a pencil idly.

"I like money, too. Fractions I can do without."

"Yes, well, a strong conceptual understanding of fractions is essential—"

"Lily." He stopped the tapping pencil.

She looked up at him, her eyes startled behind the eyeglasses. "Yes?"

"I was kidding."

"Oh." She looked more flustered than ever. "Now, I want to go over this reading inventory with you."

He thought about telling her he could already read just fine, but she never seemed to get his humor. "All right, shoot."

"Well, I'm somewhat encouraged. A month ago she was struggling with sound-letter combinations and her comprehension was very low. She's still below grade level in most areas, but she's showing genuine improvement. Charlie says you've been reading aloud to her every night."

"Yes, that's true. She's a big fan of *Golf in the Kingdom*."

"I'd venture to say she's a big fan of you. I'll bet you could read her the phone book and she'd pay attention. She told me that she's feeling better about the situation." Clearly pleased, she went through the rest of the work in the folder. Across the board, Charlie was trailing behind, but doing better. "I think you're doing a good job."

Sean felt a cold tightness inside him. "I'm not."

"Not what?"

"Not doing a good job."

"I just showed you the inventory—"

"Screw the inventory."

She flinched.

"Look," he said, "you can check off all the lists you want, but it doesn't change the fact that Charlie's still way behind, Cameron's into vandalism and the baby can't figure out what to call me. So I'd hardly call that a good job." Agitated, he got up and paced. "It's all screwed up. Their parents died and there's no damned inventory for that. I'm trying to do this right, but I can't fill that empty space." He felt as though he was on a knife's edge, trying to balance the immense loss with some sense of hope.

She looked startled, maybe a little scared. "Sean…I appreciate your honesty. Have you talked to Dr. Sachs about this?"

"Hell, yes, I've talked to her. I've talked until I'm blue in the face. She claims I'll see improvement over time, but these kids are living their lives now, they're suffering now. She wants to send me to a support group, like Parents Without Partners, but how the hell do I find the time to go to a support group?"

"I don't know what to tell you, what more I can do. I can't wave a wand and suddenly make everything better. No one can. But we can work on fixing this. Charlie, for example. The signs of improvement are encouraging."

"She ought to be spiraling downhill, but you say she's doing better."

"It's a positive sign no one expected. A welcome sign," she added. "The main reason I wanted to talk to you today is to discuss plans for the summer. It's my opinion that Charlie needs intensive remediation throughout the summer in order to prepare for fourth grade."

"Explain intensive remediation."

"Tutoring. Initially, I recommended the Chall Reading Institute in Portland for Charlie, but obviously things have changed. There's been so much upheaval in her life that I think it's best she stay home during the summer and work with a tutor. Two hours a day should do it."

"What do you charge?"

She started tapping the pencil eraser. "I don't think I should be her tutor."

"Why not?"

"It's difficult to keep the relationship on a professional level when I have such close personal ties with Charlie."

"I don't see the problem here. You don't need to be professional with Charlie. It *is* personal."

"I understand what you're saying, but…I have a policy of treating all my students the same. It wouldn't be fair otherwise."

"Screw fairness," he snapped, getting up to pace the room.

The pencil stopped tapping. "I beg your pardon."

"I said, screw fairness. It's not *fair* that Charlie's parents died and she wound up with me. It's not *fair* that there isn't a goddamn thing I can do about it. So don't tell me about fair."

"Sean, why don't you have a seat."

"Because I don't want to have a goddamned seat."

"Then what do you want?"

"For you to admit just once that these kids are special. That they deserve special treatment." He could see she was fine-tuned to this moment. At last she'd quit hiding behind the teacher persona and he could see the real Lily, the one whose heart ached for Charlie the same way his did. It probably wasn't right to take comfort in her pain, but at least he didn't feel so alone.

Tears glimmered in her eyes. She swallowed and blinked, and the tears were gone. Maybe it had been a trick of the light.

"So you'll do it," he said.

"I can't," she said. "I know how special these kids are. I adore them and yes, I could give them my heart, but then what? Then you move away, or get married, or something changes. Suddenly I don't have them anymore, and they don't have me. And there's not a blessed thing I can do about it."

"Wait a minute, so you're saying you can't be a part of their lives because we might move or things might change?"

"They need stability. Having people flit in and out of their lives can cause problems." Although she'd dodged his question, she regarded him pointedly.

Somehow, he knew what she was saying with that look. *Maura.* One day she was there, then she was gone. The kids acted like her departure was no big deal, but maybe he wasn't looking closely enough.

He paced some more. "I don't get you at all. You're so damned worried about the future that you're forgetting right now. Yeah, that's right. Life is what's happening to you right now, not what might happen in a month or a year. So if you're afraid now, then you're spending your life being afraid."

"I'm thinking of the children," she said quietly. "It's not that I'm afraid—"

Right, he thought, studying her terrified eyes. "What is it, then?"

"I have no discretion over them because I'm not the one raising them, so I can't play that role."

"What gives you that idea?"

"The terms of Derek's will, for starters."

"Ask me."

"What?"

"Ask me. Their legal guardian. The one who's giving the kids to you in *my* will. Ask me if you get to be a part of their lives, if you have a say in their future."

"I don't doubt you, Sean. But suppose you work things out with Maura. Suppose you meet someone new, someone you want to spend your life with. I doubt she's going to want me hanging around like some maiden aunt."

Sean was incredulous. "So you're afraid to love these kids because they might not always be available to you?"

"Because it would be cruel to give them the impression that I belong in their lives when I don't."

"That's shit, Lily, and you know it. The kids are nuts about you. Charlie needs *you* to be her tutor, not some stranger."

As he drove home, Sean tried to figure out if he'd managed to settle anything at all at the conference with Lily. Not really, he decided. Well, that wasn't quite true. There was something he was now sure about. It was possible for pulled-back hair, eyeglasses and sensible shoes to be sexy. He wasn't supposed to regard her as anything but Crystal's slightly annoying, judgmental friend, but lately, he kept catching himself thinking of her in other ways.

He wondered what she wore under that crisp, buttoned-up Peter Pan collar. A sexy bra or plain white cotton? What would that scraped-back hair feel like falling between his fingers? And those lips, what did they taste like, what would they feel like against his?

He made himself quit with the schoolteacher fantasies. Maybe it was because of his situation, maybe he wanted a woman in his life because of the kids. Except that wasn't true. He didn't want a woman in his life. He wanted Lily Robinson.

You're in trouble, buddy, he told himself. You're in big trouble. He emptied his mind and drove in stolid, mindless focus, frowning when he spotted a rental car parked in front of the house. Inside, Red Corliss sat in the living room.

"Hey," Sean said, "where are the kids?"

"Cameron's got them upstairs."

Puzzled, Sean shook hands with him. "What's up?"

Red grinned and his eyes sparkled. "I've got news," he said. "Big news." He held out a familiar-looking legal-length set of papers, stapled together.

Sean frowned as he took them. "You're setting me up with a sponsor? I'm not even playing."

Red grinned. "You will be. Am I good or what?"

Just for a moment, Sean's hopes soared. This was what he was truly about, playing a game that had given his life its shape and meaning. A sponsor meant somebody believed in you.

"Wonder Bread?" he asked, his hopes heading back toward earth. Not Nike or Chevrolet, but Wonder Bread. "Is this a joke?" he asked.

"Hey, don't knock it. I stuck my neck out to get this. They're prepared to back you in a major tournament. You won't need your PGA card because they bought you an exemption, Sean."

His stomach flip-flopped. It was a huge gesture. When a player didn't qualify for a tournament through the usual channels, a sponsor had the power to buy him a spot in the game. It often meant a vanity entry for someone who could never qualify on his own. But sometimes, every once in a while, it was a way to give a long shot a chance.

"What tournament?"

"The Colonial Championship in Pinehurst, North Carolina. There's a million dollars at stake."

Sean felt a lurch of excitement. Then he ground it out and lay the contract on the coffee table. "I have to turn this down, Red."

The agent laughed loudly. "I'm sorry," he said. "I just heard something hilarious. I heard you turn down a lucrative sponsorship and a shot at the majors."

"You heard right."

"I heard bullshit. I put my damned reputation on the line to get you this deal. What am I supposed to do now, tell the sponsor their dog won't hunt?" He took out a cigar and a lighter.

"You can't smoke in the house, Red," Sean told him.

"Well, excuse me, Sister Mary Maguire."

"Hey, I'm looking out for the kids. That's what this is about,

Red. The kids. I can't take off for a tournament now that I'm in charge of three kids." Something struck him as he said it. He wouldn't want to take off. He'd miss them too much.

"Don't do this, Sean. You need this deal. Derek made a ton of money, and they spent a ton and a half. After probate, you get nothing but a mortgage on this house."

Sean felt an acid discomfort in his gut, the one that had been keeping him awake at night. "I'll deal with that when the time comes."

"Well, fiddle-dee-dee, Miz Scarlett. You need to make a living. I'm offering you a way to do that. You'd better think twice before turning this deal down."

"I'm thinking," he said.

"Sit down, Sean," Red said. "Read the damned contract."

"I've seen contracts before." He probably still had a couple of them as keepsakes. A six-figure deal with Bausch & Lomb, a Banc One contract with bonus escalators based on his performance. He kept them around to remind himself that he used to be somebody in this game, somebody other than a disgrace. "Red, thanks for trying, but my life is complicated now. It's the wrong time to start playing golf again. I've got Derek's kids to think of."

"You think I didn't consider Derek's kids? What the hell do you take me for, anyway?"

Sean didn't think he wanted an answer so he waited for him to go on.

"I saw your face when you saw it was Wonder Bread. They're sponsoring all of you, Sean. It's a package deal. You and all three kids, get it? You're the new family-man icon in golf."

Sean looked around the cluttered room. Kids' toys and schoolbooks, dishes someone forgot to carry into the kitchen, mail and newspapers lying around. Suzy Homemaker he was not. "You're shitting me."

Red spread a magazine article on the coffee table in front of him. "This is last month's *Sports Illustrated.* My PR manager got it in."

Sean's stomach twisted. There was a boxed feature on Derek's funeral, with a shot of Sean standing with Ashley in his arms, Charlie and Cameron flanking him. They had that slicked-down, chastened look of lost children, and the photo was a heartbreaker. He'd seen the article when it first came out, then stuffed the magazine away somewhere. "Gee, Red. I could have gone all day without seeing that."

"Shut up, Sean. You've captured the imagination of sports fans, and it's crossing over. People are in love with your story. The bachelor uncle and three orphans."

Sean was all too well aware of that. Since the funeral, offers from scary, desperate women had flooded in. He'd had to change his e-mail account, get a post office box. He never knew if a package from a stranger might contain a proposal couched in Bible verses or a pair of split-crotch panties.

"It gives people something," Red went on. "Hope, belief that families matter. This is powerful stuff and it's opening a door for you, Sean."

He had the urge to jump around with excitement, but at the same time, reason prevailed. "I'm not doing it, Red. Going on the road like the frigging Partridge Family? No, thanks. I can't exploit my brother's death and these kids' lives in order to sell more Wonder Bread."

"Then you're an idiot. You're pissing away an opportunity that won't knock twice."

chapter 35

"I was hoping you wouldn't pick up," Lily's mother said on the phone.

Lily tightened her grip on the receiver, tensing up as she always did around her mother. "Then why did you call?"

"To see if you were sitting at home and stewing even though it's a Friday night. Apparently, you are." Sharon didn't speak unkindly, but matter-of-factly.

"What does it matter to you, Mom?" Lily asked.

"What a question," she said. "Summer will be here before you know it and you'll be off to Italy."

Lily stayed silent. Eventually, she'd tell her mother she'd canceled the trip, but she didn't like talking about it. The fact that she'd changed her plans naturally brought up questions about her motivation, questions she didn't want to answer.

"I think it's time you got back to your own life," her mother said. "You should do something you'd normally do on a Friday night."

"It's funny, I can scarcely remember what that is."

"Nonsense," her mother said. "You went out with friends

from work. Sometimes you had a date. I always liked that gym coach…."

"Everyone likes Greg," Lily said. "He's the world's biggest flirt."

"So call him up. Flirt a little. I mean it, Lily. You can't keep hiding away, worrying about Crystal's family. You have your own life to lead."

Lily looked around her simple, tastefully decorated and orderly house. Her mother had a point. She *did* have a life of her own, except lately she had trouble remembering what that felt like. She spent so much time with Crystal's kids— after school, Saturday mornings, Sunday afternoons—that being with them was starting to feel more like her life than…whatever it was she'd had before.

She made herself take an inventory of that, to remind herself of the things she valued. Solitude and order. Excellence in her job, intellectual curiosity, the occasional company of friends. Since Crystal's death, all of that had fallen by the wayside.

"I can't," she admitted to her mother. "My life is completely different now. I'm in this weird limbo where I'm not in charge of Crystal's kids but I don't feel right leaving, either."

"Nonsense," her mother said again. Then a sigh slipped through the receiver. "You've done such a beautiful job with your life, Lily. Don't mess it up now over someone else's family."

"God, Mom—"

"I'm speaking out of compassion for those children. It's cruel to make them dependent on you when they can never really belong to you."

Lily winced. Did her mother know how much this hurt or did she think she was being helpful?

"Their uncle could decide to move and then what will you

do? Follow them around the country as what? Their unpaid nanny?"

"What do you do, lie awake at night and think up things to worry about?" Lily asked with a humorless, incredulous laugh. It struck her that at the conference with Sean, those very same concerns had come out. Which meant Lily was more like her mother than she cared to admit.

"You were always the one I didn't have to worry about," her mother said. "You were the reliable, levelheaded one. You of all people should know that when a tragedy happens, it's best to move on as quickly as possible."

Lily wondered if her mother was speaking ironically. In twenty-six years, she had never moved on from losing Evan. "You know what, Mom," she said with false brightness. "You're right. I should call someone and go out tonight."

She sat there with the phone in her hand for a long time. Then, finally, she stabbed in the number before she chickened out.

"It's Lily Robinson," she said. "Would you like to go to a movie tonight?"

Fulfilling the terms of Crystal's will was a bittersweet exercise. In accordance with her friend's wishes, Lily had helped herself to some of the beautiful clothes Crystal had left behind. Wearing an outfit that made her feel quite dashing, she drove to the Echo Ridge Pavilion in her Volkswagen Beetle. He was already there, waiting for her. She felt him checking out her red cap-sleeved dress and shoes, a red-and-white polka-dot scarf tied to the strap of her red purse.

"Wow," said Greg Duncan. "Am I ever glad you called."

"Me, too," she said, feeling both self-conscious and sexy in the outfit. She wanted to tell him how it felt to wear something that used to belong to Crystal. She wanted to tell him how much she missed her best friend, but that wasn't the sort of conversation to have with a guy like Greg.

"What's playing at the Pavilion?" he asked, holding the door for her.

She stopped to consult the marquee overhead. The choices were action-adventure, romantic comedy, an art film and a children's flick. Naturally, he chose the action-adventure flick, which featured Vin Diesel and a lot of car wrecks. At least she got to look at Vin for ninety-six minutes, so that was something.

Afterward, they went to a crowded café adjacent to the multiplex. Lily toyed with the polka-dot scarf. "So do you have plans for the summer?" she asked him.

"You bet," he said. "I've decided to qualify for Paradise Ridge. There are spots for local amateurs in the tournament. It's going to mean training all summer until the tournament over Labor Day. There's a place in British Columbia where I can work with the best in the game. It's pretty pie-in-the-sky, but I want to go for it. It's time. I've got no family ties, nothing holding me back."

She flashed on a thought of his phantom kids, but said nothing.

"If I do all right at Paradise Ridge, I'm going to Q School," he said.

"That's wonderful, Greg. I bet you'll get your PGA card the first try." She saluted him with her cup of mimosa iced tea.

"I'm impressed that you've even heard of Q School."

"Don't sectionals take place in the fall? How are you going to juggle it with teaching?" she asked.

"Between you and me," he said, "I'll be requesting a sabbatical."

Lily reflected that she and Greg used to have a lot in common—they were both young and single, free of all obligations. Now he seemed like a stranger to her, a sort of pleasant stranger. Lily recalled that Crystal had never agreed with that. Back in February, when Lily had mentioned she'd gone on a date with Greg, Crystal had told her to steer clear of him. "He's a player," she'd said. "He has no sense of loyalty. I've known him for years, as Cameron's coach, and I know he's not a sincere guy."

When Lily had pointed out that she wasn't looking for sincerity, but just someone to go out with now and then, Crystal had thrown up her hands. "You make me crazy, Lily. One of these days you're going to fall flat on your face for some guy. Just make sure it's not Greg."

In the parking lot, they stood between her Beetle and his Trans-Am, and he slid his arm around her waist. Lily was startled; he'd never come on to her before. He bent down and kissed her. She tried to kiss him back, but all she could think about was how awkward this seemed, how inappropriate. Pushing against him, she said, "Greg—"

He pulled back and looked down at her. "Don't say it. You're not into this. You're a thousand miles away."

That's where I need to be, she thought. *Away.*

Lily returned home in defeat. The date was supposed to re-affirm her belief that the single life was tailor-made for her, that she could enjoy a man's company without worrying about a Relationship with a capital *R*.

She parked her Volkswagen and walked dejectedly toward the door. As she passed the dark, ugly Winnebago, she had dark, ugly thoughts about her sister. "A few days" was turning into a few weeks. Finally, Violet admitted that they were going to have to sell the RV and promised to see to it right away, but nothing had happened yet. Lily suspected the market was crowded with used RVs.

As she found her house key, a shadow moved on the back steps. Lily gasped, too startled to scream.

"It's me. I didn't mean to scare you, I swear." Cameron stepped into the pale glow cast by the porch light. He wore jeans and a hooded sweatshirt, a backpack with reflective tape on the back. His bicycle leaned against the house.

"What are you doing here?" she asked. "Is something wrong? Does your uncle know you're here?"

"Nothing is wrong and he doesn't know. I sneaked out."

"You know better than that," she said, pushing open the door and turning on the kitchen light. "I'm calling him immediately."

"Don't." Cameron's voice was sharp with urgency. "At least listen to what I came to say. Please."

She studied him, this boy she had known all his life. He was, and always had been, amazing to look at. The girls were adorable, of course, yet Cameron had the truly classic beauty of his mother and the graceful athleticism of his father. He had Crystal's fine features and vivid coloring, and Derek's intensity. His appearance seemed to set him apart from the rest of humanity, as though he was a storybook prince about to leave on a quest.

He took off the backpack. "We need your help," he said.

"We, as in…?"

"Me and Charlie and Ashley. See, it's about Uncle Sean."

Oh, God. Lily braced herself. She'd thought he was doing a good job, but now terrible possibilities flipped through her mind.

"Don't look so worried," Cameron said. "It's nothing bad."

"Sorry." She motioned him inside. "I didn't realize I was so transparent. So what's up?"

"Red Corliss got Uncle Sean a sponsorship for a tournament. It's a big deal, Lily. Huge. It means good money and the chance to get his career back. It's a good deal for all of us."

She nodded. She and Sean had not whitewashed the truth

about the family finances. Cameron understood that there were complications.

"So this is good news, right?"

"The best," Cameron agreed. "Except that Uncle Sean turned the deal down."

"Why would he do that?"

Cameron looked annoyed. "It's idiotic. He's all worried because the sponsor wants us in the picture."

"You and your sisters?"

"Yep. It's Wonder Bread."

"The sponsor?"

"Sure. I mean, it's not Chevrolet, but it's a sponsor. And anyway, they're marketing to people who want to believe Uncle Sean is the New Male, a family man."

Lily felt a tickle of inappropriate humor in the back of her throat. "New Male."

"Did you know he's been approached by a bachelor TV show?"

"You're kidding."

He shuddered. "Nope. Luckily he turned that down. But he needs to take this offer because it's all about golf."

"What's stopping him?"

"He thinks it's exploiting us kids."

"Is it?"

"We wear the hats and shirts to the games, we eat the sandwiches. Big deal."

"Tell me about this tournament."

"That's the other thing. It's not just the one tournament. He'll need to play all summer."

"How far out of town?"

"The big one, with the big payoff, is in Pinehurst. That's in North Carolina."

"That's pretty far."

"My dad used to fly all over the place for tournaments."

"And your mom looked after you and the girls. Your uncle doesn't have that."

"No," Cameron agreed. "But he has you."

Lily let out a startled laughed. "Cameron, you know I love you and the girls, but I can't stay behind and babysit—"

"I didn't mean you'd stay behind. You could come along, you know, so he wouldn't worry about us when he's supposed to be thinking about his game."

"Oh, Cameron. Do you hear what you're saying? This summer is supposed to be a time for you and your sisters to build a life in a new situation. It's the work you're supposed to be doing. And now suddenly this is all about Sean and his game."

"But—"

"No wonder he's rejecting the offer."

"You're wrong. It's about all of us," Cameron said fiercely. "Me and Sean and the girls and maybe even you. This is not just a game. It's a chance to change everything."

"By focusing on Sean."

"By focusing on something besides my dead parents for a change," Cameron snapped. "What about that, Lily?"

"I can't disagree with that," she said tentatively.

"I'm sick of being sad about my mom and dad," he said. "Sick of worrying about what's going to happen to us. The girls are, too. They're just too little to say so."

Lily's throat heated with tears. His anguish touched her, and so did this new maturity she saw in him.

He unzipped the backpack and took out a photograph of Sean wearing a green sports coat with a crest insignia on the pocket. "Do you know what this is?"

"An egregious fashion mistake."

"He's as wardrobe-challenged as I am," said Lily.

"You don't know what this is," Cameron said.

"My guess would be a donation to the Goodwill bin."

"It's the green jacket given to a golfer when he wins the Masters."

She felt a tickle of recognition. "That's a golf tournament, isn't it?"

"It's *the* golf tournament," he told her. "The Masters. The most important one in the sport. Only the best in the world can win it—Arnold Palmer, Jack Nicklaus, Tiger Woods. And one year a long time ago, Sean Maguire."

He took out an old, yellowed issue of *Sports Illustrated*. The cover showed a shot of Sean Maguire modeling the jacket and laughing into the camera. The lead article was pitched as "Jolly Green Giant: Golf's New Great."

Lily felt a strange sense of discovery. This was a Sean Maguire she'd never known. Maybe she'd sensed the presence of a champion in him, but he certainly hadn't given her any hint. "How is it that I've never heard this? Your mom would have told me."

"I don't know. It was a long time ago. Most people don't remember the winners from one year to the next."

Lily had been just starting college. Crystal was a new mother. It was possible they hadn't talked about it.

"Dad said he went into a slump right after that and ended up going overseas," said Cameron. "That's not the point. The point is this is a second chance." He hesitated, then added, "For all of us."

She stared at the photograph for a long time, then looked at Cameron's hopeful face. "That's a really ugly jacket," she said.

chapter 36

"You're kidding me, right?" Cameron asked Becky when he visited her after work one night. "You're *moving?*"

"My dad's company is sending him to work on a project in Sonora, California, and it starts Monday," she said, thumping her bare heels idly against the floor of the front porch. The swing creaked and its chains clanked into the quiet night. "I have to finish the school year there."

"That's stupid. Why can't you at least finish the last few weeks here?"

She shook her head. "Not an option. In the first place, I wouldn't have anywhere to live—"

"With us," Cameron said. "My uncle would understand."

She laughed. "Oh, I'm so sure. I'd be like, Dad, I'm going to live with a boy for a month, is that okay with you?"

"So stay with some other friend, a girl—"

"There's one problem with that," she said, her heels thumping again as she sent him a quick, bashful glance. "You're the only friend I have. And besides, my dad...he can't really handle being apart from me, you know, ever since my mom died."

"Does that mean you're never going to leave home?"

"Not this year. Listen, it's all right, Cam. I've already got a job lined up at a church day camp. The pay's decent and I'll be working with kids, which I love. The job is twelve weeks, so I'll be back at the end of summer."

Twelve weeks. That was forever. What the hell was he going to do without her for twelve weeks? He still didn't know if he'd managed to convince Lily to embrace their summer project. He hoped he'd made her understand how important it was to get on the road, to see the kind of life his father had led but had never really shared with his family. Cameron knew he had to get away for the summer, especially now that Becky wouldn't be around. It was making him crazy, being here in this town, missing his parents, trying to pretend he didn't know what he knew.

Lily hadn't agreed that the plan had any merit at all—but she hadn't disagreed, either. That was the thing with Lily. You never really knew what she was thinking.

"Becky," called her father's voice from inside the house. "It's late. You need to finish packing."

"In a minute, Dad," she said, then walked with Cameron to the curb, where his bike leaned against a lamppost. "I'm keeping the same cell phone number and e-mail address," she said. "Call me."

"I will," he promised. "Every day."

"Be careful going home, Cameron." Then she just stood there, like she was waiting for something.

His heart drumrolled in his chest. The palms of his hands felt sweaty. Kiss her, he told himself. Do it. Just do it. But the moment passed and she was already turning away, and he'd missed his chance. Dweeb, he called himself. What kind of dweeb was he that he couldn't even kiss a girl goodbye?

* * *

Lily couldn't stop thinking about Cameron's proposal. It seemed like a huge mistake to plan the whole summer around Sean and his golf career. The focus needed to stay on the children, though according to Cameron, they would all benefit. She worried the problem in her mind as she went through the usual end-of-school rituals. Ordinarily it was a special, bittersweet time for Lily, a time to step back and look at what she'd done, to sever the ties with the children she'd taught all year.

The last day for the children had been a day-long party, a time for ripping the covers off textbooks and carefully shelving them, for cleaning out tote trays, taking down artwork and going through the lost-and-found. As she doled out hugs and report cards and told each child she was proud of him, there was a sense of accomplishment, and one of sadness, as well. She couldn't help but wonder where life would take these children.

"Goodbye, Miss Robinson!" The farewell went up like a cheer in the wake of the final bell.

Lily didn't even try to keep order in the mad scramble to the door. The children looked at her, clearly expecting her to order them to form a straight line. This once, she didn't. Why try to suppress all that exuberance? Russell Clark, the cheekiest boy in the class, naturally took the lead as they surged in a pack to the buses. Before heading to his bus, he offered her a smile of unexpected sweetness. "Have a nice summer, Miss Robinson."

"I will," she said. And she had no idea if she was lying.

"Where you going?" he asked her.

"On a big adventure," she said with a grin, not knowing if that was the truth or not.

"Cool." He led the class on a race to the bus circle.

Charlie brought up the rear. She caught hold of Lily's hand

and beamed at her. "No more Miss Robinson," she said. "After today, I can call you Lily, right?"

"Absolutely right. So how are you celebrating the last day of school?"

Charlie made a face. "Uncle Sean's working. He told Mrs. Foster we could stay up late and watch videos, though. Bye, Lily. I'll see you soon, okay?"

Lily promised and held her smile in place, though she felt a special agony for Charlie. All around the parking lot, children were running into their mothers' arms while Charlie walked briskly to her bus.

In her classroom, Lily lingered over the clearing off of her desk. There was the snow globe Charlie had taken from her desk, precipitating that last disastrous conference with Crystal and Derek. Lily gave the globe a shake and held it up to the light, watching the swirling flecks of glitter dancing and spinning around the tiny figure of the angel. *I'm so sorry,* she thought, aching with regrets, wishing things could be different.

She shoved the snow globe into a drawer and got up, giving the room a cursory glance as she prepared to leave. She had to make a decision. She had to figure out what was right for this family. The hell of it was, she couldn't figure this out on her own. Though the idea was galling, she had to consult with Sean Maguire.

There was no reason in the world that such a prospect should make her heart race, but it did. She tried not to think about it as she locked up her classroom for the last time and headed to the teachers' lounge to say goodbye to her colleagues. She didn't stay long, though. Everyone was talking about their plans, asking about hers. And for the first time in her adult life, she had no answer. She didn't have every moment preplanned and mapped out. As soon as she was able, she ducked out and drove home. There, she fretted some more and came to an inevitable conclusion. She had to go see Sean.

Her mind made up, she showered, washing off the chalk dust, fussing uncharacteristically over her hair and then agonizing over what to wear. He was working tonight, tending bar at the country club, and Mrs. Foster was watching the girls. Cameron, finally released from servitude at the golf course, was out with his friends. She could only hope he wasn't joyriding along the back roads at the edge of town. Unlikely, she thought. Not after his loss.

"Come on, Lily. Just pick something," she muttered, glaring into the depths of her closet. It was the closet of a conservative, boring person, redeemed only by the splashes of color and style added by Crystal. She fingered the red dress she'd worn to the movies with Greg, then dismissed it. This wasn't a date but a discussion and she should dress accordingly. Slacks, then. No, not slacks. Jeans. With a lime green shirt and clogs that made her taller. She forbade herself to fuss over hair and makeup, reminding herself even as she drove to the country club that this was not a date.

It was so much more important than any date.

Get a grip, Lily, she told herself, crossing the parking lot toward the clubhouse bar. She paused in the front to reel in her nerves. She'd never noticed how pleasant a golf course was, how peaceful. The sun was just setting over the shoulders of the distant mountains, and deep shadows stretched across the fairways. The cry of a bird and the murmur of a car's engine were muted. And the cool air tasted sweet as she took a deep breath and squared her shoulders. All right, she coached herself. Just go talk to him.

She reminded herself that she had gotten to know Sean in ways she'd never known anyone else, not even a boyfriend or lover. Sharing what they did, it couldn't possibly be otherwise.

Their love for the children had created a unique, inevitable bond between two strangers who ordinarily wouldn't even give one another the time of day. She wondered if he realized that; if, like her, he marveled at the impact these three orphaned children had on their lives.

When she stepped into the bar and her eyes adjusted to the dim light, her first glimpse of him swept away those misty illusions. He stood behind the carved oak bar, surrounded by three women. Three attractive women. Three attractive women who were coming on to him. Even from a distance she could see that at least two of them wore wedding bands.

Resentment boiled up in Lily, unexpected and bitter. You're a family man now, she wanted to scream. You can't hang around, flirting with married women.

She stood there unnoticed, breathing the yeasty smelling air of the bar and watching a Sean she had never seen before. Without a break in style, he drew draft beer and mixed drinks, refilled snack trays, wiped down the counter and treated the three women as though they were the last ones on earth. He fixed a fresh cosmopolitan for one of them, and she leaned over to thank him, her breasts pressing forward as she slipped a bill into the tip jar.

Forcing herself to overcome her discomfiture, Lily went to the bar and slid onto a leather-covered stool, as far from the three women as possible. He turned to her with that beguiling smile. She saw the instant he recognized her. The smile froze, the eyes turned wary. He excused himself and approached her with a wary air.

"Hey, Lily. Is everything all right?"

"Why would you assume anything is wrong just because I came here?"

"To see me? In a bar? I'm thinking dire emergency here."

She ground her teeth. Here she was, intending to discuss

his future and his career, and he was teasing her. "Maybe I came to celebrate the last day of school," she said.

"I'd celebrate with you, but Charlie and Cameron brought home their report cards today," he remarked.

She knew what Charlie's grades were—definitely room for improvement. But Cameron… "He's always been an A student."

"Streaks are made to be broken."

One of the trio at the other end of the bar signaled. "Seanie, I'm ready for another Kir royale, hon."

Lily sniffed. "Seanie?"

He winked at her and turned away, easing back into his banter with the customers as he fixed the champagne and Chambord and served it with a flourish. By the time he returned to Lily, she was having second thoughts about bringing up the topic at all. This wasn't exactly the best place to discuss the children. She cut a glance at the three women. "Your fan club?"

"My best tippers. Don't look at me like that. We can't all do something noble for a living." He braced his hands on the bar and leaned forward. "Now, what can I get you?" he asked in an intimate whisper.

Somehow he managed to make her feel silly and small. Lily bristled. "What's the house special?"

"Prune juice." He offered an angelic smile.

"You're not funny," she said.

"And you're no fun."

She glared at him. "We'll just see about that."

Memorial Day was the one day Sean could sleep in, so the honking of a horn outside at eight in the morning was particularly annoying. Who the hell was up at eight in the morning on Memorial Day?

He'd gone to a lot of trouble to get off work so he could be around the kids today. And God knew, he could use the sleep. Wearing paisley pajama bottoms and a deep scowl, he shuffled downstairs and yanked opened the door.

Belching a cloud of diesel smoke, a huge Winnebago idled in the driveway. Except that it wasn't exactly in the driveway. The wheels on the right-hand half were in the flower bed that bordered the asphalt. And it wasn't exactly a Winnebago, either. The sides had been painted to resemble an enormous loaf of Wonder Bread.

The engine coughed and died. Lily Robinson got out, leaving the flimsy aluminum door open behind her. "Good morning," she sang cheerily. She wore jeans and sneakers and had a bounce in her step. She reminded him of a kid, and he wondered what had gotten her all excited.

He managed a grumpy nod, trying not to gag on diesel exhaust.

She walked around the RV, noting that she'd missed the driveway. "Oops," she said. "I'm not too good at parking yet."

"Maybe you should go practice in a place where people aren't trying to sleep."

"I'm sure I'll get plenty of practice where we're going." Her gaze kept drifting to his bare chest.

Instead of feeling self-conscious, he stood a little straighter. "I need coffee. And I think you have some explaining to do." In the kitchen, he flipped on the coffeemaker and yawned while it started to drip. "Don't say a word," he said, robbing the pot of its first cup. "I know your opinion of coffee."

"Then you should know it's a leading cause of the yips." She marched outside and turned, motioning him to follow.

He blinked at her. "What?"

"You know, the yips." She climbed in through the narrow doorway and stepped back to make room for him. "It's an involuntary muscle spasm that occurs while stroking a putt, caused by dystonia or severe performance anxiety. Ben Hogan suffered from it, did you know that?"

"I know. I'm just surprised you do."

"I've decided to educate myself." She showed him a small library of golf books on a built-in shelf. "There's so much to learn about the game of golf. I had no idea it was so complex and fascinating."

"Yeah, well, it's not rocket science."

"No, it's an ancient art begun in the fifteenth century in the Kingdom of Fife. That's in Scotland."

Maybe she'd had something stronger than caffeine for breakfast. "Lily," he said, "what the hell are you doing here?"

"Helping you relaunch your career."

"What?"

"Cameron told me about it."

"Did he tell you I turned it down?"

She ignored him. "Your sponsor is really behind you, did you see?"

"How could I miss it?" He wondered what the genteel residents of the neighborhood thought.

"My sister needed money, so the sponsor leased it and had their logo painted on the sides. They're really wonderful people to work with."

Her intention finally penetrated through the fog. He held himself very still, but the effort was too much. He burst out laughing, the amusement coming from deep in his gut.

When he finally stopped, he saw her looking at him.

"Are you finished?"

"Yes, for now. But thank you. That was refreshing. Now, if you'll excuse me, I'm late for a nap."

She planted herself in his way, easy enough to do in the narrow confines of the RV. "Oh, no, you don't. You have a contract to sign, and we've got plans to make." Like a gadfly, she darted around the camper, giving him the guided tour. "The girls can sleep together here," she said, indicating a bunk over the cab. "I'll take the bed in the rear. You and Cameron will bunk right here." She showed him a tiny side room with a compartment like a train. Now, there's only one bathroom but I made out a schedule and posted it on the door, designating—"

"Lily." He grabbed her by the shoulders. He didn't mean to touch her but it was the only way he could think of to get her attention.

She regarded him with wide, startled eyes. "You don't like the schedule? Because I can change it—"

"The schedule isn't the problem. It's the whole plan that won't work." ·

"Of course it'll work. I've figured it all out, down to the last detail."

He didn't doubt that. She micromanaged everything. "It won't work because we're not going." He dropped his hands, letting her go. "I'm not taking the deal."

She held very still and watched him. Her gaze never wavered as she said, "Chicken."

"Give me a break."

"No, this is fascinating. I've finally figured out what you're afraid of. It's not taking care of the kids and being a family man. Lord knows that scares most men but not you. The thing you're afraid of is the thing you love most—golf."

"That's shit."

"Ah, now you're getting hostile. Further proof that you're chicken."

"I'm thinking of the kids, okay, about doing what's best for them."

"What's best for them might just be this trip, Sean. They

need to get away from this house, this town for a while. It's too sad here, too haunted. You want me to be Charlie's tutor. If I come along, I can do just that."

"You were dead set against it."

"I'm willing to compromise. I adore Charlie, and the change of scenery will be good for everyone. Cameron thinks so, anyway, and in case you haven't noticed, Cameron is one smart boy. He showed me the green jacket, by the way."

"You're kidding." Sean always kept the thing buried in a piece of luggage but could never quite bring himself to get rid of it.

"He wanted me to see for myself what you're capable of. The night he told me about this opportunity was the first time since the accident that he's shown me anything but rage and defeat. He was hopeful, looking forward to the future. He believes in you, Sean."

Sean's stomach tightened. *He believes in you.*

"He says he'll be your caddie," she added. "Apparently he's quite good at it."

"I'm not turning this family into a Wonder Bread commercial," he said.

"No. That's the sponsor's job as I understand it. Yours is to show up and play golf and look wholesome."

He glanced around the RV. Its tacky laminated walls seemed to close in on him, squeezing tighter and tighter. "I'm not doing it," he said. "I'm not dragging this family across the country in a damned Winnebago."

part five

Grief can take care of itself, but to get the full value of a joy
you must have somebody to divide it with.

—Mark Twain

"**W**here the hell is the turn signal on this thing?" asked Sean, searching the console of the Winnebago as he drove east toward the interstate.

"Don't cuss," said Ashley, whose car seat was buckled to one of the bench seats.

"I'm not cussing," he said, finding the turn signal and heading up the on-ramp.

"You said hell," Charlie informed him. "You said, 'Where the hell—'"

"All right." He briefly put up his hand in surrender. "Sorry."

"That's okay," Charlie said agreeably.

By checking in the rearview mirror, he could see her seated at the table, her legs tucked underneath her, drawing vigorously with a green crayon. Across from her, Cameron lounged with his nose in Ben Hogan's *Five Lessons.*

Finally, Sean cut a glance sideways at the co-pilot's seat. Lily was busy with her computer-generated maps that had the route highlighted and all the distances measured to the last tenth of a mile.

Last night when they'd had their final predeparture meeting, he had looked at her printouts and brochures in bewilderment.

"I'm pretty sure we could make it just by following the signs on the interstates."

"Pretty sure isn't good enough. My way, we'll be absolutely sure we don't miss any important landmarks."

"Do you always plan ahead like this?"

"Absolutely."

Grinning at the memory, he said, "How you doing, Miss Lily?"

"Fine, so far."

Seven miles from home and she was fine. "Reason I ask," he said, "is you're kind of quiet. My driving make you nervous?"

"No." She checked her watch.

"Do I make you nervous?"

"No," she said again, but the sudden pink blush in her cheeks contradicted her. She shifted in the high-backed seat, looking monumentally uncomfortable.

And then, for no reason he could put his finger on, the smile stayed in place. They had left a place where every minute of the day was saturated with reminders of grief and loss, and as the miles rolled past, the air felt lighter, clearer, as though they'd driven out of a fog. He wondered if the others felt it. Cameron was quiet, eagerly watching the screen of his cell phone to see if there was a signal so he could call Becky. He never said she was his girlfriend, but Sean recognized the funny, faraway look on that young face as Cameron watched the miles go by out the window.

By midmorning, the landscape had shifted to the harsh drama of the Columbia gorge, and the highway was nearly empty. Bald mountains reared up on either side of the river, and yellow grasslands rolled away to the east, into eternity. They found a driving range near Gadsden, and that was where

Sean decided to stop for lunch. There were only two other vehicles in the parking lot, but he still felt self-conscious about the bread-wrapper design on the RV.

"Nobody eats until each of us hits a bucket of balls," he stated. Charlie had her own set of cut-down clubs, and Cameron had his dad's. Sean had brought along Crystal's clubs for Lily, though when he handed her the pink designer bag, her brow knit in a frown.

"What?" he asked.

"This stop wasn't on the schedule."

"It's on *my* schedule. Loosen up, Lily. Come on, I'll show you how to hit a drive."

She protested, of course, right up until he stationed her with a bucket of balls and a driver and teed one up for her. She hacked away, missing or topping the ball, hitting a grounder once or twice.

"Try this grip," Cameron said, showing her. "No, not so tight. Easy."

Sean felt a welling of pride for his nephew. The kid had problems, sure, but he had a heart, too. Sean and Red had argued long and hard about choosing a caddie, Red wanting someone with experience and a record of success. Sean wouldn't hear of it. Cameron would caddie for him or the deal was off.

"Like this, Cam?" asked Charlie. "Like this?" She and Ashley had a plastic Wiffle ball they were chasing around.

Watching the kids with Lily, Sean felt something else, a funny warmth in his gut. Two months ago, the idea of spending the summer with a schoolmarm and three kids would have sounded like a joke to him—or a nightmare. Now he couldn't think of anywhere he'd rather be.

They fixed sandwiches for lunch, though he noticed Lily couldn't quite bring herself to try the smooth white bread his sponsor had provided in such generous quantities. Once they hit the road again, Lily kept her word about being Charlie's tutor. She launched into teacher mode, and the afternoon was spent studying landmarks along the trail of Lewis and Clark. Amazingly, she had managed to find the historical significance in practically every bend in the road—the signal fire Meriwether Lewis had used when he lost some of his party at Dry Canyon, the rock formation around the rapids where they'd spent six weeks in one springtime. Glancing in the rearview mirror, he saw Ashley unhappily sucking her thumb and Charlie yawning with boredom. Cameron looked too bored even to yawn.

Sean turned off the highway, following signs to a Taste-T-Freeze drive-in.

"This wasn't on the schedule, either," Lily said.

"Oh, yes, it was," he said. "According to local lore, Lewis and Clark stopped here for onion rings in the winter of 1811." He pulled up in front of a menu board covered with illustrations of dancing chocolate-dipped ice-cream cones. "This was where Sacajawea befriended them for bringing soft-serve to the savages."

"Very funny," Lily muttered.

"I love you, Uncle Sean," Charlie shouted from the back of the RV.

"Lubyou," yelled Ashley.

Sean clutched at his heart. "God, you girls slay me. Take the wheel, Lily. I'm dying here."

Munchkin-like giggles erupted from the rear.

After they placed their order, Charlie decided to teach Ashley "The Rainbow Connection," and the two of them sang the first line loudly, over and over again. Cameron put in the earpieces of his iPod. Sean laughed at the expression on Lily's face.

"And to think," he said, "you gave up Italy for this."

chapter 38

Late at night, Lily stood at the edge of the gorge that reared up around the Snake River. A perfect moon at the height of fullness spilled pale light down into the canyon, turning the fast-moving water into a stream of silver. In front of her, the darkness was pierced by stars. She couldn't tell how deep the gorge was, but judging by the silence, the river was a good distance down. She lifted her gaze to the moon. The clarity of the air out here in the middle of nowhere made it stand out like a crisp white communion host. She discovered that if she stared long enough, the pattern of shadows and light definitely did resemble a face. Crystal's face, maybe.

How am I doing? she asked her friend. Is this what you would have wanted?

A vast silence was her only reply. About fifty yards behind her lay the Take It Easy Campground, a collection of tents and RVs filled with wayfarers.

She stuck her hands in the rear pockets of her jeans and shook back her hair. It was late and she should be dead tired, but instead she felt keyed up. Some feeling that was quite new buzzed through her veins.

The beam of a flashlight flickered over her. Turning, she put up a hand to keep it out of her eyes.

"Who's there?" An edge sharpened her voice. She was suddenly very aware of the deep isolation of her position, the sheer danger of standing at the lip of the gorge.

"It's me," Sean's voice called reassuringly across the darkness.

The new, buzzing feeling sped up. "How did you find me?"

"It's that spiffy Wonder Bread jacket," he said. "The letters on the back are reflective."

"You're kidding." She took it off and looked at the back. It was a satiny white baseball-style jacket, complete with the trademark colored dots, provided by Sean's sponsor. Sure enough, the name "Maguire" glowed and flickered when the moonlight hit the letters. "Jackets, hats, umbrellas, ponchos, shirts, tote bags… they've got everything."

"And enough actual Wonder Bread to feed an army."

She shuddered. "Don't remind me."

"Hey, most of us grew up on that stuff. Builds strong bodies eight ways, remember the ads?"

If only he knew. She remembered because when she was a kid, TV had been her life. It was her escape from the darkness of her family, the accusing looks of her mother. It was her glossy, artificial window into the hyperrealistic world of the Bradys, the Waltons, the Jeffersons. Even the smart-alecky griping of the Bunker family seemed a sweet and desirable family dynamic. Twenty-five minutes of quarreling and then all troubles were resolved.

"I don't believe I've eaten white flour or refined sugar since I moved out of the dorm in college," she said.

"Maybe this will be the summer you throw caution to the

wind. Maybe you'll find more happiness on this trip than you would have in Italy."

His lighthearted voice teased her and she was grateful that the darkness masked her reaction.

"You're blushing, aren't you?"

"I beg your pardon?"

He took the jacket from her, draped it over her shoulders and held it in place. His hands were incredibly gentle, imparting warmth through the satiny fabric. "I can tell when you're blushing," he said, his voice dropping to a low, intimate whisper.

"That's impossible." Her own voice was a not-very-intimate hiss.

"No, I can tell. I can feel it."

Lily felt compelled to resist him. "We shouldn't be doing this. You can't just start up all of a sudden—"

"It's not sudden at all. This has been building for a long time," he assured her, his hand gently tipping her face up toward his. "Tell me I'm wrong."

"You're out of your mind."

"Yeah," he said, bending his head, tilting it a little to the side. "I reckon I am." His lips brushed against hers as if by accident.

She lost it then, grabbing him before he got away. Her arms went around his neck and she pressed herself against him. He felt wonderful, his lips just firm enough, his body strong and protective against hers. Then the kiss went deep, deeper than she thought possible, deeper than reason, deeper than loneliness. She strained against him, standing so high on her tiptoes that she trembled. His arms slid down, cupping her hips, bringing her closer, tighter. She forgot to think. She *couldn't* think. His warm, pliant lips coaxed her into surrender, and she stopped even trying. This was wholly strange and wonderful and impossible, and she felt swept in an updraft, flying high to a place she'd never been.

By the time the kiss ended and she settled back to earth, she was dizzy. In the night sky behind him, the stars spun like a kaleidoscope of cut glass.

"Oh, boy," she said, breathless and flustered, a girl at a junior high dance.

"Oh, boy, is right," he said, sounding neither breathless nor flustered as he reached for her again. "Why, Miss Lily, I had no idea."

"No idea of what?"

"No idea you had a kiss like that in you."

She jumped backward to escape him. "I don't know what I was thinking."

"I sure as hell know what I was thinking."

Lord, that voice. Even in darkness, when he was nothing more than a shadow, that voice reverberated through her like the plucked string of a fine instrument, its subtle, compelling vibrations radiating outward to nearly forgotten places inside her.

She took another step backward. "This isn't like me. I can't think why I…maybe the moon made me insane. I've heard it can have that effect on people in the wilderness."

"Lily."

"Yes?"

"This isn't exactly the wilderness. It's a campground." He advanced on her; she edged away.

"It's certainly a wilderness to me," she said. "When I travel, I stay in hotels with swimming pools and coin laundries."

"Ah, a first-class traveler. But Lily—"

"What?" She pulled her hands into fists to keep from grabbing him again.

"I need to tell you something."

"Yes?" She swayed, stifled a moan, edged away. She had

to get out of his force field, that was all there was to it. He was a magnet, an irresistible energy, and she was nothing but a helpless piece of scrap metal.

"If you keep heading in that direction," he said, "you're in for a nasty fall."

"What? I don't—"

The air left her in a whoosh as he grabbed her and pulled her swiftly against him, back into his arms, that hard, lean body pressing against her. Then, ever so gently, he turned her and shone the flashlight beam on the ground. The light outlined the edge of the cliff.

"See what I mean?" he said. "Call me crazy, but I'm thinking you don't want to get away from me that bad."

She put on her jacket. "I'm the crazy one."

He chuckled. "Yeah? Maybe we're crazy together. I like you like this," he added. "Want to make out?"

"Last time I heard you say that was at Crystal's wedding," she said. "You were obnoxious."

"And did you say yes?"

"You didn't say it to me."

"Whoa. I *was* obnoxious. I'm saying it now. Come on, Lily. It's only a kiss."

"Right. Only a kiss. Got it." Suddenly, humiliatingly, her throat filled with tears. God. Could he feel her crying the way he could feel her blushing? She turned and stumbled away from the cliff, toward safety.

"Now what?" he asked, pursuing her.

"To you it was only a kiss," she blurted out. "To me it was—" She stopped, forced herself to fight for control.

"It was what, Lily? I'm no mind reader. You're going to have to tell me."

"All right, listen. Just because kisses like that are a common occurrence in your life doesn't mean they are in mine."

"Then you're in luck. We can do something about that."

"We already did and now it's done and we don't have to do it anymore."

"I don't get you, Lily. I don't get you at all."

"I simply wanted to see what it was like to kiss someone like you," she said. "That's all."

"Someone like me," he repeated. "You'll have to explain that."

She stopped walking to face him. The moon had risen higher in the sky, and the light washed over the empty trail in the gaping chasm of the river. All right, she thought. Maybe honesty was the way to go. The way to scare him off for good.

"Someone who's so good-looking he doesn't even seem real to me," she confessed in a broken whisper. "Someone whose picture is on whiskey posters in Taiwan."

"Japan," he said. "I did that poster in Japan."

"Whatever," she said impatiently. "You understand what I'm saying. You're not the sort of man I usually find myself with, so I was curious."

"What sort of man do you usually find yourself with?"

The kind I can walk away from anytime I want. She cleared her throat. "The last guy I dated was a gym teacher."

"I'm an athlete," he said, clearly baffled.

The difference between a gym teacher and Sean Maguire was the difference between a lightning bug and a lightning bolt.

"The guy before that collected model trains as a hobby. You get the idea. They're all…ordinary. Like me."

That silky laugh again. "You, ordinary? Give me a break."

"My point is, you're not my type."

"Because your type is ordinary guys who teach gym and collect trains."

"Exactly." Finally he was grasping the concept.

"I know why that is."

"Oh, so now you're psychoanalyzing me."

"Hey, after all the hours I've spent with Dr. Sachs, I'm qualified. See, those guys are safe," he said. "Now, me, I'm the guy you could actually fall in love with, so you're resisting me."

Now it was her turn to laugh. "If your performance in this tournament matches up to your ego, you've got nothing to worry about." She headed toward the RV park. The few lighted windows and glowing tent domes pierced the darkness, and a couple of campfires still burned.

"You're walking away from me?" He sounded incredulous.

"That depends," she said.

"On what?"

"On whether or not you follow." She didn't look back. She had to get control of herself. He probably wasn't used to women walking away from him. Well, she sure as heck wasn't used to men talking about falling in love, so they were even.

chapter 39

"Seventy-six bottles of beer on the wall," sang Charlie and Ashley as they sped along a sunbaked highway, the RV sweeping past a shaded rest area.

Lily thought she would need seventy-six bottles of beer very soon. Charlie had been recalcitrant during tutorials today, and Lily's patience was wearing thin.

Abruptly, Charlie stopped singing.

Only Ashley kept going. "Seben-sibe bobbles of beer on the wall…"

"Uncle Sean, stop!" Charlie yelled. "Right now, you have to stop!"

Lily turned around, alarmed by the note of panic in her voice.

Sean reacted instantly, pulling off to the side of the road. "What's the matter?"

"You have to go back to that rest area. You have to do it right this very minute." She was nearly hysterical.

"Honey, there's a bathroom on board."

"Please go back," she begged. "Please. I saw something."

Lily felt Sean's skeptical look. Her instincts told her to respect Charlie in this, and her instincts were getting pretty sharp. When Lily told her sister why she wanted to use the Winnebago, Violet had said, "Just remember, when it comes to being a parent, you know more than you think you know."

She jerked her thumb behind them, signaling for him to go back. "We're making good time today," she said. "We can stop for a few minutes."

Lily just hoped it wasn't more roadkill. The inevitable sight of dead animals lying at the side of the road made Charlie cry. When she cried, so did Ashley, and it made the miles creep by with excruciating slowness.

Because the road was completely empty as far as the eye could see, Sean made a U-turn, cutting across the weed-infested median. The moment he turned into the rest area, Charlie raced for the door. Both Lily and Sean yelled at her, but she shoved the door open at the exact moment the RV stopped moving.

Cameron leaped out after her, as protective as any adult. Sean grabbed the baby and they all filed out to find Charlie in the grassy picnic area, pointing excitedly to a hand-lettered sign swinging from a table.

"See?" she said. "See? I knew this was what I saw. It says Free to a Good Home, and that means we get to keep him."

"Keep what?" Cameron said.

"For a kid who can't read, she sure read that sign quickly enough," Sean murmured.

At the base of the picnic table was an aluminum roasting pan filled with dirty water and a twenty-five-pound sack of Ol' Roy dog food, half spilled in the grass and crawling with red ants.

"Perhaps someone else picked him up," Lily suggested, relieved to find no sign of life. The last thing they needed was a lost animal.

"No, someone's here, I saw when we drove past," Charlie insisted. She walked around the area. "Hello!" she called. "Is anybody there?"

A half-grown boy with lanky limbs and a mournful expression appeared beyond the boundary of the rest area, at the top of a bank sloping down to a stream. He was joined by an equally lanky brother who was perhaps a year younger. Finally, a streak of black-and-white flashed by—a dog, scampering up the bank.

"See?" said Charlie. "See? Here, doggy," she called, clapping and making smooching sounds with her mouth. "Here, doggy."

The animal darted back and forth, a bundle of energy. Ashley laughed with delight and babbled at the dog. Cameron hung back, though Lily could tell he was intrigued.

"Are you giving that dog away?" Charlie asked, wide-eyed.

"Have to," said the older boy. "Our dog had puppies, and Dad said we can't keep them."

Lily cleared her throat. "Charlie, we really should go."

"Hang on," murmured Sean, putting his free hand on her arm and offering that easy grin, which made Lily think about that wild night of kisses. No matter how hard she tried, she couldn't stop thinking about that night.

"Is he friendly?" Charlie asked. "Can I pet him?"

"Her," the younger boy corrected. "She's six months old and real smart. Housebroken, too, and crate-trained, but our dad said not to bring her home tonight."

His brother whistled and patted his thigh. "Here, Babe."

The dog stopped, its silky ears like flags at half mast. It turned, belly low to the ground, tail wagging as it approached the boys.

"You can pet her if you want," the younger boy said. "We call her Babe, on account of she was the smallest one in the litter. She's the only one left."

"Babe like Babe Didrikson," said Charlie, her voice low with portent.

"My God, do something," Lily said to Sean. "It could be dangerous."

"Nice dog, nice Babe," said Charlie, her voice as soft and sweet as a song. The dog rolled over, chest and paws in the air and submitted to her. "Look," she said as it licked her hand, "we're best friends already."

Lily shook her head. "No way," she said. "We can't keep a dog. We'll take it to the next town and drop it off at the local animal shelter. That way she'll go to a family that needs her and can care for her."

The four of them stared at Lily. So did the two brothers.

"No dog," she reiterated. "You have no idea what you're taking on when you get a dog. Especially a strange one. It's probably got worms."

"She's been wormed," the older brother said.

Lily crossed her arms. "A dog will break your heart, you know that, right? A dog never outlives its owner."

"Aw, Lily," Charlie said, scratching its feathery chest.

"No dog," Lily said, "and that's final."

"Hold still, Babe." Lily glared at the newest member of the family. She'd joined them two days and five hundred miles ago. Lily's plan to drop the dog off at a shelter in Elko, Nevada, had been shot down by four adamant protests.

"You don't just ditch an animal because it's inconvenient," Sean had said.

"Yeah," agreed Charlie.

Even Cameron spoke up. "Yeah."

Lily had looked at Ashley. "Your turn," she said.

"Yeah," the baby said.

And now, of course, the adored mongrel had become Lily's

project. Sean had gone to the campground showers and Cameron had taken the girls to the playground, leaving her with the dog. Babe was filthy, and the only way to get her clean was in the shower. The campground bathrooms were clearly marked No Pets Allowed, so Lily had no choice. The two of them were crammed into the tiny closetlike space, wrestling for a good twenty-five minutes with the shower sprayer before the water ran clear. Then they both emerged wet and bedraggled and ill-tempered. Babe had sprayed the entire inside of the RV, rushing up and down the aisle, shaking and sneezing.

"Hold still," Lily said again, advancing with the towel. It was a designer towel from Nordstrom's, the kind usually reserved for company. Crystal would hate the idea of her good towels being used on a dog. Lily filled the fluffy white Egyptian cotton with wet dog and started rubbing vigorously. This immediately stopped her from racing around, because Babe's favorite thing in the world was being rubbed. They had found that out about her instantly. The vet they'd taken her to in Tooele, Utah, had laughed and patted her belly while giving her a checkup and shots.

"She's less than a year old," he said, confirming what the boys had told them, "and in fine health."

Lily scrubbed away with the towel, determined to have Babe clean and dry by the time they rolled into the next stop on their itinerary, a golf match in Park City. The dog collapsed in ecstasy, purring like a cat and moaning every now and then.

Sean came inside, looking infuriatingly fresh and relaxed from a shower at the campground. "Whoa," he said, "smells like wet dog in here."

Lily glared at him. "I wonder why."

He bent down and scratched Babe under the chin. "Aren't you just the prettiest thing," he said.

"She is now," Lily agreed. "All it took was a spa treatment."

"I think you have a new best friend."

Lily sat back on her heels. "I still say it's a mistake to keep her."

"The kids are nuts about her and vice versa. How can that be a bad thing?"

"Being nuts about one another is no reason to stay together." She found her fallen glasses and put them on. The lenses fogged, but she stubbornly left them in place.

He laughed. "Your logic slays me, Lily. It really does."

"I'm just thinking of the kids," she said. "They've already lost so much. If something happens to the dog—"

"Here's what will happen to the dog," he said with exaggerated patience. "She'll be our pet for however long she's meant to be our pet. Nobody knows how long that's going to be. We're going to do our best to make it last forever."

"Nothing lasts forever," she whispered, her face suddenly very close to his.

"That doesn't mean we won't try for it," he said, ending the pronouncement with a kiss.

She nearly melted but then pulled away. "You have to stop doing that."

He laughed and slipped Babe's new collar on her. "Oh, yeah, I'll stop," he said. "When hell freezes over."

chapter 40

Lily had never needed a best friend more. A best friend was the person you called up when someone kissed you and made you forget the whole world. A best friend was the one you told when you were falling in love. A best friend talked you out of making a complete fool of yourself over a man who could only mean trouble.

Crystal was gone and Lily had no one else to discuss her heart with. Violet would only egg her on and tell her to go for it. Edna would find some deep spiritual reason for the unexpected chemistry that burned between Lily and Sean. Calling her mother was out of the question. Lily decided she was better served trying to fend off the feelings on her own.

One thing she discovered—her sleep pattern was shot. She found herself lying awake at night, unable to stop thinking about Sean Maguire. She tried everything—listening to the sound of the girls' breathing, reading with a tiny flashlight clipped to the pages of her book, tallying up the miles they traveled. And once she did fall asleep, she woke up too early, ears tuned to the first birds of morning. And of course, even before the rest of her woke up completely, her mind was already hard at work, thinking of Sean Maguire.

The smell of coffee told her he was already up. Why did coffee have to smell so good? And why did he make it every day? To remind her that she was depriving herself?

She forced herself to lie still until she heard him leave, probably to take the dog on morning rounds. Then she lay awhile longer, hoping to fall back asleep. Finally she gave up and was driven from her bed by restless, impossible thoughts and the insidious smell of coffee. She slipped past Charlie and Ashley, who lay in a sweet tangle under the comforter. She went to the bathroom, grimacing at the person in the mirror— heather-gray jersey pajamas, puffy face, rumpled hair.

"You even look boring when you sleep," she muttered, then sawed away with the toothbrush.

She came out and glared at the coffeemaker, its red on button glowing. She switched it off and fixed a cup of ginseng tea, wishing it was coffee. An organic sesame bar sufficed as breakfast, which she ate while glaring resentfully at the box of Froot Loops on the table. After a brief but red-hot fantasy involving coffee, Froot Loops and Sean himself, she finished her tea and told herself to get a grip.

Then she put on shorts, a Wonder Bread T-shirt and running shoes, and looped her hair in a ponytail. Each new place they visited, she explored by going for a jog. She was no athlete, but she stayed in shape with a faithful adherence to her regime. During the cross-country drive, she had jogged past the rats, cactus and mesquite of a Nevada desert. She'd run among stunning snow-capped peaks of Utah and Colorado, past endless prairie grasslands of the Midwest, along tree-lined riverbanks and hilly country roads. She thought she'd regret having given up an adventure in Italy, but her inner child was having the time of her life.

When she returned to the RV, she often found Sean and the kids eating Krispy Kremes and engaging in inappropriate behavior like armpit-farting or burp-singing. Who needed Italy when you had that?

This morning, when she got out of the RV and softly closed the door, she knew she was in a special place. A hush hovered in the air, as light and translucent as the morning mist, insulating the calls of mockingbirds and whippoorwills.

We're here, she thought. This is our destination. Pinehurst, North Carolina. They had arrived the night before and this was her first time to see it in the daylight. Home of world famous golf courses and a number of sectional and national tournaments, including the Colonial Classic. The five of them had driven across the country just so Sean could play.

She'd read about the area in her guidebooks, of course. It was a quiet community surrounded by towering loblolly pines and white-fenced, emerald pastures where hunting horses grazed. A network of unpaved bridle paths wound through pristine forests. Each white-painted house sat like a jewel on a green cushion of lawn, idealized as a movie set. This was a place where famous families settled—Firestones and Beauregards, Banfields and Whitneys.

None of the guidebooks had prepared her for the splendor of a Southern morning the moment the sun came up, the way the light fell through the long-needled pines, the grassy smell riding the breeze. She jogged through a neighborhood with the self-important name of Royal Oaks, although she had to admit there was something majestic about the open-armed live oaks lining the main street. Tara, Tara, Tara, she thought in rhythm with her breathing, and listened to the muffled sound of her feet hitting the soft trail.

She didn't have to go far to find the golf course where the tournament would take place. At this hour, the parking lot was deserted except for two eighteen-wheelers, one painted with a flying American flag and the other an intense green. One contained a huge generator, the other a lot of high-tech equipment, perhaps for keeping score. At the moment they were completely silent, two sleeping giants.

She slowed to a walk and stepped between the trucks to an apron of perfect grass fringed by magenta azaleas and a whitewashed fence. A sign in the shape of a pointed finger indicated the way to the driving range.

As she walked along the pinestraw-covered path, she felt as though she had entered a magical emerald forest. It was so quiet she could hear the beating of a bird's wings overhead and the sound of her own heartbeat. There was not one lick of wind, though the morning mist cooled her bare arms and legs.

She heard the now-familiar sound of a swinging club. Sean had practiced or played every day during the crosscountry drive, and she'd grown accustomed to hearing the rush of a shaft through the air, the *thwok* of the club head meeting the dimpled ball. Then a long, impossibly long silence ensued, followed by the faint thud of the ball dropping many yards away.

It was interesting, how she knew it was the sound of Sean hitting a golf ball and no one else. She was learning the sound and rhythm of his game.

At the driving range, she expected to see a number of players lined up and practicing. Instead, there was just one. Sean looked so alone, there in the morning mist, the sun filtering over him. He had a certain intensity of concentration that seemed to possess him like a magic spell. He worked with such total absorption that Lily felt certain he hadn't noticed her.

The dog was tethered to a bench next to him, her breath making little puffs in the air. Each time he hit a ball, her ears would prick forward and she'd quiver with anticipation, but she never went after the ball. Sean had taught her to retrieve range balls, but only on command.

Sean maintained his fierce concentration as he hit ball after ball, far beyond the yardage markers.

She stood still on the path, loath to interrupt him until he finished the entire bucket of balls on the ground behind him. It was fitting that he was the first one out, she thought. For the sake of the children depending on him, he needed to do well. But he was driven by something more than that powerful need. He wanted this more than any of his opponents possibly could.

"Good morning," she said when he paused.

Babe wriggled and sneezed in greeting, then bowed and whined a little. Lily was still opposed on principle to keeping a dog, but she had to admit, it was fun having someone go into paroxysms of ecstasy every time she saw you.

"Good morning, Miss Robinson." Sean smiled and wiped off his club head.

"Isn't your caddie supposed to do that?" she asked.

"Last I checked, my caddie was facedown in a wad of blankets."

"He was still that way when I left, too."

"I'm too easy on him."

"Probably."

He finished polishing the clubs he'd used. As he worked, his attention stayed on her. She felt a sudden wave of self-consciousness. As usual, she was at a disadvantage in her jersey shorts and T-shirt, a frumpy contrast to his golf shirt, fresh out of the package, and creased, dun-colored trousers.

"I thought I'd see more players out here," she said. "Why are you so early?"

He rolled his shoulders. "I need more practice than everyone else. I need to make up for lost time."

"According to Red, you've got more innate talent than anyone in the field."

"Talent's only part of it. You've got to practice as though you're not going to get any help whatsoever from Mother Nature. Because you're not. A player who has been practicing nine hours a day will beat a player with natural ability every time. Got it?"

"Why do I get the feeling that's not the right attitude to take?" she asked.

"Now you sound like my agent." He gestured at a bench where he'd parked his street shoes, a thermos and a box of Drake's Devil Dogs. "I'd offer you coffee," he said, "but I already know you'd turn me down."

"I might surprise you one of these days. I might just help myself to coffee and Devil Dogs."

He grinned. "I'd like to see that," he said. "I'd like to see you do a lot of things."

She knew the conversation was headed into dangerous territory, but more and more, she edged closer, even though she knew better. "Like what?"

"I don't know. All sorts of things." He sat down and bent to change his shoes. "Get drunk and take your shirt off. I'd like to see that."

"You and all the seventh-grade boys in America. Grow up, Maguire."

"Why?"

"Because you're a grown-up. You should act your age."

"I like my inner seventh-grade boy."

"Apparently, so does *American Golfer*." Red Corliss ar-

rived from the direction of the parking lot. He held the tab-
loid-style paper out to Sean. "Front page, my friend. You
caught their attention at the match in Park City."

Sean jumped up, grinning with delight. "Red. I wasn't expecting you."

Babe was battling with the impulse to leap at the new-
comer and check him out, Lily could tell. Sean seemed to control her with a subtle motion of his hand, which Lily found
fascinating.

As she stood up to greet Red, she understood that this was
a big deal. Red Corliss was a busy agent who didn't have time
to come to every client's event.

"Red, you remember Lily."

"You bet." They shook hands. "It's good to meet you under
happier circumstances," he said kindly enough. "How are
the kids?"

"We're taking this summer one day at a time," Sean said.

His inclusive statement gave Lily a sense of solidarity with
him. There was a peculiar intimacy that came from their shared
devotion to the children. Maybe that was it, she thought. Maybe
that accounted for the chemistry between them. If so, then she
was wise to avoid getting tangled up with him. Falling for a man
because he was in charge of three children she happened to love
was a bad idea.

"Let's go see if the kids are up yet," she said.

"This is our newest addition," Sean told Red, clipping the
leash to the dog's new collar. "Her name's Babe. Charlie spotted her at the side of the road and we adopted her."

"Nice," Red said. "Maybe she'll get signed by Purina."

"You old softie," Sean said.

They walked back to the RV park together. Lily watched
Red with some amusement. He was clearly accustomed to a
different standard of travel. Crystal would have recognized

the brand of his suit and shoes. Lily knew only that they were expensive.

"So what does the sporting press have to say?" asked Lily.

He handed it to her. There was a close-up of Sean after he'd just hit a shot, when his eyes were tracking the flight of the ball. The camera loves this man, she thought, illustrating to best advantage the classic features and crystal-blue eyes, the tension and concentration in his face.

The headline above the fold read, "From Playboy to Family Man."

She read it aloud and laughed.

"Go ahead and make fun of it," Red said. "The press is eating it up." He took the paper and rattled it at Sean. "Just remember, you're today's feel-good human-interest story. You screw up the next round and you'll be tomorrow's—"

"He's been playing wonderful practice rounds," Lily cut in. She was new to the world of professional golf, but she knew instinctively that focusing on the positive was the surest way to a good outcome. "He and Cameron work together like a well-oiled machine."

"So I hear. I wanted you to have a more experienced caddie, but it's probably just as well you stick with the kid. Helps with PR, too."

"That's not why I'm using him," Sean said. "I'm using him because he's good for me."

chapter 41

Cameron sat in the driver's seat of the Winnebago, pretending to drive. He had to caddie in the biggest match of the summer and he was sick of being afraid—afraid to caddie, afraid to kiss a girl, afraid to drive. He sat high in the bucket seat, feeling the easy spring of the pedals under his feet and the big steering wheel solid in his hands. He was the only one home. The others were at the pretournament barbecue at the golf course. Cameron had taken the opportunity to slip away and try to call Becky, but got no answer. She was still at work.

A three-hour time difference sure was a pain in the neck. He missed her so much it hurt to breathe sometimes. She was so incredible to talk to, funny and smart and not at all concerned with what people thought of her. Until they'd become friends, he hadn't realized how liberating that was. A few of his regular friends had ditched him after the accident and Becky had told him to quit fretting about it.

"Dr. Phil always says you wouldn't care so much what people think of you if you knew how seldom they actually did."

He wished he could drive all the way to Sonora, California, and see her. Hell, he wished he could drive, period.

He knew how to drive. He'd been the best one in his traffic-safety class at school. Knowing what he was doing was not the problem. Having some kind of weird freak-out the minute he got behind the wheel of a car, now, that was the problem.

Yet at the moment, he felt remarkably calm, sitting in the Winnebago. The RV park was practically deserted. Most of the pros were staying at the nearby resorts with room service and pools. Other than a bullet-shaped Airstream at the far end of the park, Cameron had a long, straight section of the park all to himself.

The windshield framed a view of Dogleg Creek and the woods beyond. Cameron turned it into a picture of the highway rolling out in front of him in all its asphalt glory, leading him straight toward the horizon. He discovered that even though he hadn't done it for years, he still remembered how to make the revving sound with his mouth. It sounded the same as it did when he was six years old and part of a happy family. Before long he was halfway to Memphis.

Outside of Phoenix, he pulled over and made the shushing sound of brakes. This was idiotic. He ought to be driving for real.

He dug in the pocket of his shorts for the keys. He had no idea if the key to the door worked in the ignition, like a car.

It didn't. He felt simultaneously relieved and disappointed.

He looked at the keys in his hand. They were strung on a key tag that read, "Rex Slug Bait." Maybe it was one of those other keys. Maybe it was the one labeled Ignition.

All right, so he was out of excuses now. He had an empty parking lot with all the room in the world. He had the whole Winnebago to himself. It was time. They would be heading west again, back to Comfort and to the complications and dilemmas that would still be waiting there.

A hint of the panicky freak-out feeling knocked at his chest. He took a deep breath and ignored the sick sensation as he got out to undo the RV's hookups. Then he climbed back into the driver's seat.

Now, he thought.

Seat belt on. Key in the ignition. Gear in Park.

The engine flared to life, its power reverberating through the undercarriage, then up into Cameron's gut. He felt his grip on the wheel tighten and forced himself to relax.

"Easy now," he said under his breath. "Take it easy."

Step by step. He released the parking brake and put the gear in Drive. It was easy. He had done this a thousand times in his mind. And then, smooth as a fish swimming downstream, he was off. Driving. He went little-old-lady slow, but it didn't matter. This was a barge of a vehicle and it took some getting used to.

As far as Cameron was concerned, he was flying. He drove through the park, passing the empty herringbone-patterned slots. He took each corner like a pro, quickly sensing when to turn and how sharp the angle. He went around three times and felt relaxed enough to switch on the radio. Aerosmith, perfect. A few more times around and he had the window down, his elbow propped on the edge like a long-haul trucker.

Finally he took her right out the exit. The family might be tired after all of the day's activities. He figured they would appreciate a ride home even though it was just a few blocks to the golf course.

He went under the speed limit along residential streets leading to Royal Oaks, but it didn't matter. No one was behind him.

When he turned into the golf course parking lot, he stuck to the periphery, not wanting to get into a jam. The barbecue was still going strong. He could smell the meat cooking and could hear the country swing music playing over the loudspeakers.

A catering truck was backed up to the main building, white-coated workers scurrying back and forth. A girl who looked a little like Becky wheeled a huge trash can toward the Dumpsters.

Cameron watched her for a split second too long. By the time he turned his attention back to where he was going, a second cartload of trash cans emerged from behind the caterer's van.

Even though he was driving at a snail's pace, there appeared to be an explosion on impact. Everything in the container erupted—used foam plates and cups, corncobs and gobs of barbecue sauce, wadded up napkins, half-eaten hot dogs, ashes and ketchup. A glob of something—coleslaw, maybe—landed on the windshield with a splat.

Cameron somehow managed to slam the RV into Park and shut off the engine. He leaped out and hit the ground running. "Is anyone hurt?" he asked, the panic back and clawing at him.

A catering worker, whose white coat was embroidered with the name Roy and spattered with red sauce, glowered at him. Roy weighed about two hundred fifty pounds. He had a shaved eight-ball head and, now, a wide streak of mustard on his pants.

"No, fool," Roy said, "but you got some cleaning up to do."

"Of course," Cameron said. "God, I'm sorry. I didn't see you." He cast about, trying to figure out what to do first. A small crowd had gathered. People pointed and talked among themselves.

Great.

A reporter and photographer came forward, the reporter yelling questions. "Anyone hurt? Whose Winnebago is that?" He turned to Roy. "Sir, did you see what happened?"

Roy jerked his head at Cameron. "Fool wasn't looking where he was driving that thing."

The camera lens and the reporter both turned to Cameron.

He had the thought that he didn't actually want to die, but if lightning did happen to strike him right now, it would be a mercy.

There was no mercy for him, he realized as he saw his uncle weaving through the crowd toward him.

Here it comes, thought Cameron. He and his uncle had been getting along great, better than he and his dad ever did. Apparently that was about to come to an end. He'd just be the worthless screwup his dad thought he was; now Sean would think so, too.

"Slow news day, Donny?" Sean growled at the reporter.

Donny was unfazed. "You know this young man?"

"Give me a break," Sean said, approaching Cameron.

"Hey," he said.

Uh-oh. Cameron shuffled his feet, waiting for the storm to gather and break. "Hey."

"So you, ah, you were driving this thing?"

Every excuse in the book crowded up inside his throat, but all that came out was "Yes."

"Think you can back her up out of the way so you can get this cleaned up?"

Jeez, thought Cameron, with everyone staring at him? "Yes," he said. He hoped he wasn't lying.

Sean cast a glance at the windshield with the chunks of coleslaw still sliding down. His face looked all hard, his lips taut and his eyes bright. Cameron had never seen him look so furious before.

"And do you know how to turn on the windshield wipers?" he asked, his voice as taut as the rest of him.

"I think so." Cameron's mouth was dry, as though shame had sucked all the moisture out of him. Then he noticed something about his uncle. It wasn't fury that was keeping him so stiff and taut. It was laughter. He was dying with it, sweating from it.

And finally, he couldn't keep it in any longer. It came out in long guffaws as he said, "Then I guess you'd better turn the wipers on before you drive that thing again," he said.

Lily was pleased to see that Red Corliss took charge. Dealing with a garbage can-versus-RV situation wasn't in his job description, but he didn't miss a beat as he had Cameron drive him to the nearest car wash. Afterward, they all met at Red's hotel, because he had promised Charlie she could swim in the pool there.

Adjacent to the golf course, the Colonial was a grand and elegant resort that housed most of the top players in the tournament. Two doormen in red top hats and tails held the doors open to the brass-and-marble lobby. There was a rotunda with a stained-glass ceiling, a replica of the veiled Christ by Sammartino as its centerpiece. Lily stopped in her tracks to look at it. This was one of the chief works of art she had planned to study in Italy this summer, a sculpture so perfectly wrought that it was said to move people to tears.

She nearly wept over the replica, which was displayed on a huge, polished marble pedestal. The unflinching portrait of suffering touched a nerve, and she quickly looked at Charlie, Cameron and Sean to see if they were similarly moved. Cameron was busy checking out a pair of smooth-haired teenage girls in tiny skirts and halter tops, while Charlie was showing Ashley how to hopscotch on the black-and-white marble floor. Sean and Red had kept walking, deep in conversation. And Lily felt herself missing Crystal with a painful intensity that left her breathless. She had no idea what sort of job she was doing with this fractured family. Some moments she thought it was going well. Cameron had gotten behind a wheel finally, regardless of the results. Yet other times, Lily felt utterly lost, as lost as Charlie looked when she first woke up in the morning and discovered all over again that the mother she'd been dreaming about was just that, only a dream.

"Lily," Charlie said, grabbing her hand. "Look at the pool!"

They could see it through the glass doors at the end of the colonnaded hallway. It was a gleaming turquoise octagon with a model Trevi Fountain and even a grand twisted staircase leading down to the shallow end. It was the perfect picture of gaudy ostentation.

Lily took the girls to the ladies' dressing room and helped them into their swimsuits. "Where's yours?" asked Charlie.

"I was just going to watch."

Charlie screwed up her whole face in confusion. "Watch? Did you see that pool? How can you only want to watch?"

"It's fine," Lily said, keeping her voice light. No point in confessing to this child that she'd harbored a lifelong fear of water. The only reason she knew how to swim at all was that she'd had to pass water safety in college in order to get a summer teaching certificate.

"Come on, Lily. It won't be the same if you don't get in the water," Charlie said. She and Ashley looked adorable in their yellow swimsuits. Ashley's even had a rumba ruffle across the bottom.

"I didn't bring a suit." She had one in the RV but had managed to make it all the way across the country without having to put it on.

"We'll go get you one," Charlie said, sounding both loving and bossy—exactly, eerily, like her mother. "There's a shop right across the hall."

"Hotel shops are too expensive."

"Uncle Sean's going to win a million dollars tomorrow," Charlie said stoutly. "He'll give you the money for it."

"Your uncle isn't going to give me a dime," Lily said quickly, defensively. "I have my own money."

"Then you'll use that. Charge it and forget about it." It was exactly the sort of thing Crystal would say. Then Charlie grew downcast. "I really want you to swim with us."

"Please," said Ashley softly, as though she'd understood the whole conversation.

Lily heaved a sigh. "You two." She took the baby out to the pool deck and handed her over to Sean. For a few seconds, her mouth went dry and she was speechless at the sight of him shirtless and muscular, already wet from diving in. Then she explained to him that she'd forgotten her suit and had to buy one at the hotel boutique.

"Charge it to my room," Red said, lounging in Hawaiian-print shorts, an unlit cigar clamped between his teeth.

"I'll pass."

"Say you'll do it or I'm coming shopping with you."

"This is a conspiracy," Lily said, hurrying toward the shop.

Charlie insisted on coming, and she shopped with her mother's keen eye for color and style. She dismissed the black and navy tank suits Lily picked out. "Try this one," she said, pushing a suit on a hanger under the door. "And no whining."

It was an almost-scandalous cherry-colored bikini, and against her better judgment, Lily had to admit that Charlie was right. It looked...hot. Before she could change her mind, she asked a salesgirl to cut off the tags and made the purchase. Drowning in self-consciousness, she stepped out onto the pool deck with Charlie.

Any hope that she could simply sit discreetly on the side was dashed by Charlie. "Uncle Sean, look at Lily," she yelled. "She let me pick it out."

With Ashley in his arms, he turned to look at them. The stare he fixed on Lily swept over her like a sunburn. "Good job, Charlie," he said. "Jump in."

Lily crept to the edge of the water and sat down, putting

her feet in the shallow end. The water felt delicious after the oppressive Southern heat of the day. She imagined sinking all the way under, letting the water close over her face, her head, and the thought made her recoil. She hoped no one noticed that she didn't get in the water, because she didn't want to have to explain that she was afraid. It seemed so silly, but the old sense of terror was so real.

While Red watched the girls in the shallow end, Sean swam across the pool underwater and surfaced in front of Lily. "You're not getting in the water," he said.

"I'm getting my feet wet."

"I want to see all of you wet."

"You're a pervert, you know that?"

He paddled backward, his arms spread wide. "I'm golf's Family Man. Don't you read the sports pages?"

"Then you'd better behave like a family man, not a pervert."

"But, honey, when I'm around you, I can't help myself."

$$chapter\ 42$$

Lily had, in fact, become an avid reader of the sports pages. The next morning, she turned to the sports section of the *Raleigh Durham Gazette* and almost choked on her tea. There was a picture of Sean with his hand on Cameron's shoulder, his head thrown back with laughter. Cameron's look was one of cautious relief. The headline read, "Tournament Underdog and Rookie Caddie." The reporter, Donny Burns, had written a tongue-in-cheek piece about "the Dumpster incident," as he dubbed it.

"Let's hope the collision of Sean Maguire's Winnebago and a wheeled garbage receptacle from Carolina Catering is not a harbinger of things to come in Saturday's tournament. And let's further hope the caddie-caterer affair doesn't affect young Cameron Holloway's judgment. Although his pedigree in golf is impeccable—he's the son of the late PGA champion Derek Holloway, nephew of one-time Masters winner Maguire—Cameron Holloway is untested in tournament play. His performance as Maguire's bagman could be the key to the longshot's success—or to his failure…"

"Lily, what's the matter?" Charlie asked, picking at her granola.

Lily was about to fold the paper shut but stopped herself. There was no reason to hide this. She turned the photo toward Charlie. "The paper printed this really tacky article about your brother and your uncle."

Charlie studied the paper intently while Lily gave the baby another banana. It was just the three of them at breakfast. Sean and Cameron had left at dawn to warm up for the first round of the tournament.

"That's a good picture of Uncle Sean," Charlie remarked.

There was no such thing as a bad picture of him, Lily thought.

"I think this paper's wrong, though," Charlie said. "Cameron's not untested in tournament play."

Lily's head snapped up. "What did you say?"

"The paper is wrong. One time, he caddied for our dad—"

"Charlene Louise Holloway." Lily smiled. "You read that article all by yourself."

She scooped granola into her mouth, took her time chewing and then said, "We should go. It's a shotgun start."

Lily pulled her hair back in a ponytail and put on the sponsor's sun visor, which matched the tote bag and water bottle she carried—bright white with primary-colored dots. Crystal would be appalled. Her sense of style would have been hugely violated.

"Just a little bit of fashion sense could change your life," she'd say.

Lily smiled at the memory. Crystal truly did think that way—change your look, change your life.

"You look good in that hat," Charlie said. "You going to put some lipstick on?"

"I'm wearing lipstick."

"I meant colored lipstick."

"For daytime?"

"Of course."

Lily showed her three options and went with the one Charlie picked, something called Wild Watermelon.

"And you should wear the foot socks, not the ankle socks," Charlie advised.

"You're wearing ankle socks."

"Yeah, but I'm a kid."

"I'm getting fashion advice from an eight-year-old." She patted Charlie's head. "You are your mother's daughter."

"Am I?"

"Absolutely. That's one reason I love you so much."

Lily felt Charlie's steady gaze. "What?" she asked.

"You never told me that before," Charlie said.

"Nonsense. I tell you that all the time," Lily replied.

"No, you don't. You say 'love-you' all the time, but this is different," Charlie insisted.

Inside, Lily felt a strange upheaval. Day by day, it grew more impossible to hold herself back from this family, to keep her independence intact. It was too late, she acknowledged, to protect herself from hurt. She'd given up that option long ago. Now all she could do was brace herself for the fall. She let all her feelings for Charlie shine out as she said, "You're right. What's the matter with me?"

"Nothing. That's why I love *you* so much."

They took Babe for one last walk before putting her in her crate in the RV. Even with an air conditioner running and the radio left on, Babe was not going to be a happy camper. As Lily coaxed the dog into the crate with a Milk-Bone, she flashed on the thought—Look at what my life has become.

From complete independence and autonomy, she had been transformed into someone in charge of three kids and a dog.

She shut the cage and went outside, Babe's mournful howl coming from the back of the Winnebago.

Putting on a bright smile for the girls, she said, "Ready?"

"Ready," Ashley declared.

Lily had her usual wrestling match with the folding stroller, which never seemed to want to unfold. She sorted it out and buckled Ashley in. She put some extra sunscreen on her chubby knees, even though she and the girls were already slathered with it.

As she pushed the stroller onto the grounds of the Royal Oak Country Club, she immediately sensed that everything had changed. The atmosphere here was completely different—the parking lot was as busy as an airport, the whole area bustled with spectators, technicians, marshals and well-dressed people Lily couldn't quite identify. The air itself hummed with a different sort of energy.

A ripple of excitement went up as a huge gleaming vehicle parted the crowd like the Red Sea and came to a stop in front of the clubhouse.

"What's that?" Charlie asked.

"It looks like a Hummer limo," Lily said. "Who knew?"

Red Corliss joined them, mopping his brow as he crossed the parking lot. "If it isn't the Wonder Girls," he said, beaming.

"Who's that?" Lily indicated the limo. She caught a glimpse of a black shirt with a Nike swoosh before the tall, good-looking man was swallowed up by the crowd.

"That's Beau Murdoch. Last year's player of the year."

"Who are all those people around him?" she asked.

"His entourage. Let's see. He's got his caddie, his swing coach, his putting adviser, publicist, probably a lawyer and therapist—the list goes on."

"That's amazing."

"It's big business." At the gate, they showed their badges. A stern-faced official glared at Lily. "And you are?"

She drew herself up. "Sean Maguire's entourage," she said loudly.

An older woman in pink golf togs in line behind them smiled at Charlie and Ashley. "What a beautiful family," she said. "He's a lucky man."

Lily's face heated as she fumbled through thanking the woman for the compliment and pushing the stroller through the gallery.

"That happens all the time," Charlie said to Red. "People always think we're a family."

"You got a problem with that?" he asked.

"Naw."

"Can I be in your family, too?"

"Sure, Red." She took hold of his hand and balanced on the balls of her feet. "You can be the grandpa."

"Very funny," he grumbled.

Lily felt a surge of gratification, though she kept her head lowered and her eyes averted from Red. He was way too good at reading people and she was way too bad at hiding her feelings. This summer was turning out like nothing she could have anticipated. Being with Sean and the kids brought her face-to-face with matters she ordinarily hid from herself, like how lonely her life really was and how much she cherished the connection she found with Crystal's children. And yes, with Sean Maguire.

She watched Beau Murdoch take leave of his wife. Their adoring looks at each other seemed genuine, although Lily wondered how they could stand having camera flashes popping off while trying to kiss. The Murdochs had twin babies in twin strollers, each looked after by its own private nanny.

"The wife's a Firestone," Red murmured to Lily. "Like the tires."

"I thought she was Mrs. Murdoch."

The couple looked like the former king and queen of a high school prom, poised and smiling for the camera. Another flash went off, and then it was Lily's turn with the girls. Standing in front of the screen printed with sponsors' logos, Lily was amazed at Charlie and Ashley. The girls both possessed their mother's beauty-queen DNA in abundance. They looked absolutely delighted to be photographed.

Lily couldn't tell whether or not her apprehension would show in the photographs. Even as the flashes went off, her mind was somewhere else. She knew that today's tournament wasn't a make-or-break moment in Sean's career. Golf didn't have that. There were too many chances to succeed—or fail. But today was huge, his reentry into the highest ranks of the PGA.

After the photo shoot, they spotted him and Cameron in the distance, warming up. Lily sensed that all eyes were on him, some to watch him fail, others hoping for a triumph. It was a bloodless sport but one that brought crowds of an amazing size and density.

Take it easy, Lily told herself. This was what this summer was supposed to be about. It was the goal of the whole cross-country odyssey they had endured.

"They look good," Charlie said, practically bouncing up and down with excitement. "I feel proud of them."

"Me, too." Lily picked up the baby and had her wave from behind the gallery ropes. Sean and Cameron both spotted them, and Sean responded with a blown kiss. Lily wanted to close the moment into her heart, because it was one of those rare times that made her believe this family was going to be all right. Over the summer, she'd watched the broken pieces turn into a flawed-and-fractured whole. It wasn't the same sort of family they'd had when Crystal and Derek were alive, but it was unmistakably a family. And even though she hadn't planned it, Lily was a part of them. It wasn't what she had set out to find this summer, it had found her.

Each day she woke up thinking of them and made choices with them in mind. She didn't put herself first. But what scared her the most was that this family didn't belong to her. Depending on the outcome of the match, Sean could be called to move away from Comfort, to take the children lord-knew-where as he battled his way through the ranks of the PGA. It almost made more sense for her to hope for his defeat, but she didn't, of course. This family was an immensely bigger concern.

$$chapter\ 43$$

Hours later, Lily stood at the eighteenth hole, her heart in her throat as she watched Sean finish the round. Charlie stood in front of her, chest against the gallery rope. Beside her was Red, chomping on his third piece of nicotine gum. They had left Ashley at the clubhouse with sitters provided by the country club. Golfers, it turned out, were a prolific lot and there were plenty of other toddlers for her to play with.

When Lily saw Sean and Cameron coming up the fairway, it was all she could do to keep from letting her hands turn into claws, clutching at Charlie's shoulders. Sean was only two strokes off the score of the leader, Wyatt Allen. Red assured her that on a course of this degree of difficulty, anything could happen. The leader could stumble. A contender could catch up. An unknown could come out of the blue and dominate the field.

Lily found being a spectator rather enjoyable. Relaxing, even. There was a sort of old-fashioned grace about a golf match. She liked the mannered way people moved en masse along the course, the polite applause, the instant hush, like an indrawn breath, that went out when the marshals lifted their Quiet signs.

She wasn't relaxed now. Neither was Charlie. Lily could feel the little girl quivering with excitement. School problems notwithstanding, Charlie was gifted when it came to understanding tournament play.

She caught Red looking at her. "What?"

"Take it easy. Our boy is doing great."

Charlie turned to gaze up at him. "This is a really important hole, Red. Uncle Sean is lying one or two strokes away, depending how he plays it. If he birdies it, he could push into second position going into tomorrow's round."

"Who's that, young lady?" asked a man who had overheard her.

"My uncle Sean, Sean Maguire, that's who," Charlie said.

The Quiet signs went up. Her braids whipped like chopper blades as she spun back to watch.

The second-place challenger was Murdoch himself, who seemed not the least bit worried about his ability to capture the lead from Allen. It was just a matter of time. He hit the perfect shot, a layup that landed him next to the water. His next shot would take him onto the green and then he would putt for birdie, claiming the championship. Unless Sean did the impossible and caught up.

In the middle of the fairway, Sean and Cameron had a murmured conversation. Even from behind the ropes, Lily could feel the tension emanating from them.

Based on the position of his ball, he had a critical decision to make. The hole was nearly three hundred yards distant, protected by a water hazard next to a big sand trap gouged out of the earth under the brow of the green. Wyatt Allen had made par on the difficult hole, not a brilliant finish but one that was good enough to keep his lead.

Just making par would keep Sean in contention. A birdie would give him a shot at second position. An impossible-to-achieve eagle—two under par—meant a true shot at winning.

The safe move would be for him to hit the ball to the edge of the water, an easy enough shot. Then all he had to do was hit over it and the sand trap, landing on the green for a possible birdie putt.

So what were he and Cameron arguing about?

Cameron was trying to get him to hit a certain iron, one that would get Sean just to the edge of the water but not in it.

Sean shook his head, refusing the iron. Instead, he reached for a fairway wood.

A collective gasp went up from the spectators. He wasn't going to go the safe route. He wanted to try smacking the ball up and over the lake, over the bunker and onto the green in one go, giving himself a shot at an eagle.

Red cursed under his breath. "I don't know why I bother."

"He hasn't even hit it yet," Lily said, thinking positively. "I've seen him hit this shot a hundred times this summer."

"There's a difference between a Donald Ross course and a driving range."

"Hush," she said. "Give him a chance."

"I did," Red growled. "He's blowing it right now."

"Hush," she said again.

"Yeah," whispered Charlie. "Hush."

Cameron's demeanor changed from contention to encouragement. It was, Lily knew now, the sign of an excellent caddie. Even when the player made a bad move, once he committed to a course of action, it was the caddie's job to be supportive whether or not he agreed with the strategy.

Good for you, Cameron, she thought.

Lily held her breath. She felt an odd ripple of warmth, watching Sean. As he stepped up to address the ball, she felt all the tension ease into a strange calm. He could do this. Surely the universe would not be so cruel as to take it away from him.

Sean swung at the ball, a graceful stroke with intense power behind it—his trademark swing. Then there was nothing to do but wait. The flight of the golf ball seemed to slow in proportion to the tension of the people watching it. The tiny white orb arced upward as though rocketing toward heaven.

Some people talked to it: "Go, go, go," or "Get up there…"

It wasn't that Sean had so many fans. It was that true fans of the sport always wanted a brave shot to make it. And this was more than a brave shot. This was a Hail Mary. Which Lily caught herself praying as the ball reached the peak of its arc and started its descent toward earth. Or, in the case of this particular shot, toward water.

No, please, she thought, please don't go into the lake.

"My God," someone nearby said, "it's…it's going on the green."

Lily couldn't believe her eyes. The ball found the smooth slope of the putting green. It had cleared the lake, where so many balls had gone to rest. It had cleared the trap and landed on the putting green only a few feet from the hole.

She caught a glimpse on the monitor of Sean's face—pure elation, a joy so powerful his eyes glowed.

"It hit too hard," Red muttered, speaking over the applause and yells of encouragement.

"So what if it did?" Lily said.

Then a collective groan flowed through the crowd. The ball came down so hard that it rolled downward off the green. It went into the frog hairs, the slightly taller, coarser grass at the edge.

Stop there, Lily urged. Stop right there and he can still make a birdie.

The ball didn't stop. It spun downhill, gathering speed, and then dropped, like a bird shot from the sky, into the sand trap.

The groans of disappointment became *tsks* and I-told-you-sos.

Lily knew the sports commentators would have a field day with this. This was why Maguire was a contender, not a champion, they'd say. He thought too much of himself. He refused to be humbled by a game that rewarded humility.

She noticed that Wyatt Allen didn't look particularly happy with this development, and she gained a new respect for the man. He took no joy in winning simply because his opponent made a bad move.

Murdoch wore a game face, but the spring in his step betrayed him. He was happy to see his opponent in trouble.

His gloating, however cleverly masked, was apparent to Lily. When he settled himself into position to take an easy shot up onto the green, she thought, Come on, you weasel. Miss.

And, unbelievably, he did.

The champion missed his easy shot to the green. His ball struck the sandtrap, plowing a furrow deep into the soft earth before coming to a stop a few yards from Sean's.

There were no groans from the spectators now; there were gasps of disbelief, even outrage.

As Lily grabbed Charlie's hand and surged with the crowd to the final green, they passed a commentator who was speaking in a low-toned, excited voice.

"Ladies and gentlemen, this is an incredible turn of events. Just incredible. It seems that, by wildly different techniques, the two contenders have found themselves in the exact same position. Now there's a horse race to see who finishes second today."

Murdoch's turn. He circled the sandy bunker like a lion around its prey. He bent down to study the position of his ball.

He conferred with his caddie who, incidentally, was even younger and more beautiful than his wife. A moment later, Murdoch signaled for an official.

"What's he doing, Red?" Charlie asked.

"Son of a bitch is going to try for a free drop," Red growled.

"That son of a bitch," Charlie said.

Lily was too tense to correct her. After an excruciating delay during which frazzled nerves frayed to the breaking point, it was ruled that an anthill next to the champion's ball constituted an abnormal ground condition. Red confirmed that whether a groundhog or an ant, the rules were clear. A "burrowing animal" is an animal that makes a hole for habitation or shelter, such as a rabbit, mole, gopher, salamander—or even the lowly ant.

Sure enough, the ploy worked. It was declared that Murdoch's ball had encountered an obstruction. He was allowed to drop it.

"He can drop that thing where the sun doesn't shine," Lily muttered, feeling decidedly vicious.

"Yeah," said Charlie. "Right in his ear."

"Golf is an unforgiving game," the commentator murmured into his headset. "A player has to use every advantage he can find."

"Why doesn't Sean take a free drop?" Lily demanded.

"Too far from the anthill." Red's voice was taut with sarcasm.

As Murdoch set himself up to hit the newly positioned ball, Lily tried her weasel curse on him again. This time, it didn't seem to work. He chipped his ball neatly onto the green within striking distance of the hole.

"He should just get it into the hole right now," Charlie declared. "Right this very minute, in one stroke."

The nearby spectators sent Charlie fond, indulgent looks.

Lily had never been able to tolerate it when people patronized children.

"She's right," Lily agreed. "He's got to hole out with this next stroke."

"Yeah, and I've got to win the lottery," said a man in a jaded voice.

Interestingly, Cameron appeared supremely confident as he handed Sean a club.

Sean settled his stance as best he could in the situation. His ball lay on a slope, having driven itself into the sand. It was under a lip of earth, screening the pin from Sean so that he was hitting blind.

Sean hit the ball. A flurry of sand obscured everything. Then the ball broke free, sailing up and over the brow of the bunker. The ball didn't even touch the putting green but dropped right in with a hollow *thunk,* rattling around before settling home.

There was a heartbeat of disbelieving silence. Then pandemonium started. Cheers and applause thundered from the gallery. This was what people came to see.

Sean's hand went straight up in the air, a gesture of supreme satisfaction.

Lily remembered to breathe again as she watched Sean walk to the hole, lean down, pluck the ball from the cup and hold it aloft in his fist. Then he hugged Cameron and gave him a resounding kiss on the head. Cameron seemed too overjoyed to mind.

Charlie screamed and jumped up and down, pigtails flying.

Lily, on the other hand, didn't make a sound. She stared at Sean in wonder, feeling absurdly happy for him. His posture was taut with triumph, his face lit by joy. Then he looked directly at her. When their gazes met, the world fell away, the crowd's noise turning to an indistinct hum. She heard nothing but the rush of blood in her ears, saw nothing but his smile.

She touched her hand to her heart. Although she knew he

couldn't hear her, she said, "I am so proud of you," moving her lips distinctly as she spoke from the heart.

He seemed to understand. His grin widened and his gaze held hers as he brought the golf ball to his lips and kissed it, just as Beau Murdoch missed his putt.

chapter 44

"Some say it was a love match," said the ESPN commentator during that night's national broadcast wrap-up. "A contender came out of nowhere to capture the hearts and minds of golf fans everywhere...."

The TV in the clubhouse bar suddenly commanded everyone's attention. Lily sat with Sean as the clips showed his progress, hole by hole. After all the post-game hoopla, Red had taken charge of the kids while Sean and Lily went to the bar for a drink—and for more hoopla, of course. Lily didn't mind. She felt as though she was among friends tonight. So did Sean, laughing at the good-natured ribbing of the other players. He looked relaxed and natural, a man in his element. "This was a big win for Maguire," one of the commentators said. "He played so well, it makes you wonder why he stayed away so long."

"Well, Chad," the female commentator said with phony sincerity, "as you know, Sean Maguire has endured a major upheaval in his personal life. The sudden death of his brother, top-rated champion Derek Holloway, has dovetailed with Maguire's comeback."

Lily touched Sean's arm. "Let's go."

He shook his head and focused on the TV. People nearby shifted uncomfortably in their seats.

"Jan, I'm sure there'll be a lot of speculation about Maguire's performance in the wake of a tragedy," said the commentator called Chad. "There was so much riding on his performance and he dealt with enormous pressure. Some will wonder if this is a fluke, or if he's really back in the game."

"And just why it is he didn't show up on the radar until after his brother was out of the picture." Jan gave her colleague a smarmily knowing look.

"I've heard enough," Lily said, imagining steam coming out her ears.

"Take it easy," Sean advised her. "You have to treat this stuff like a fart in church. Hold your breath for a few minutes and the stink goes away."

Sure enough, the recap shifted back to more replays of the action, and she felt Sean let out his breath. There was an endearing close-up of Cameron's face as he and Sean conferred about a shot. It felt slightly surreal, seeing them on the screen.

"You look wonderful together," she said.

"You're not so bad yourself," he replied, directing her attention back to the wide-screen TV.

"Oh, God," she whispered. "Please, no."

Red and the sponsor's media coach had warned them all to assume they were in the camera's eye every moment. At the very end of the round, she had completely forgotten the warning.

The camera focused tightly on her so that she looked larger than life. Every gesture and nuance seemed impossibly dramatic. The hand coming up to her heart. The words meant only for Sean: *I am so proud of you.*

Then the picture cut to Sean, looking at her and then kissing the ball.

"...with that kind of devotion, can love be far behind?" the commentator concluded with a sly inflection and a completely straight face.

"All right," Lily said, her cheeks flaming as she pushed back from the bar. "I have to go now."

"Where?" asked Sean.

"I have to go hide under a rock, okay?"

She felt every eye in the bar on her as she stumbled, blind with humiliation, for the exit. She was horrified. The camera hadn't lied. It had told the truth she'd been running from ever since they had left Comfort, Oregon, in her sister's Winnebago.

Any fool could see that she was completely and ill-advisedly in love with this man. It was too embarrassing. How could she face the world now?

"Lily, wait." Sean caught up with her on the patio of the clubhouse. "Where are you going?"

She offered a slightly bitter laugh. "I don't have a lot of options here." It was painfully true. She couldn't drive off by herself, couldn't hide out at home with a pint of Cherry Garcia, couldn't escape a situation that terrified her even though her instincts screamed at her to run.

"Let's take a walk," he said. "Let's go somewhere private." He took her hand in an easy gesture. "That's something we've never had in this relationship—privacy."

Lily's mouth went dry. The R-word. He'd just said the R-word.

"But the kids—"

"Red's in charge of the kids tonight." He paused, then offered his trademark aw-shucks grin, the one that melted her bones. "I asked him to do it. I asked him to keep them until late. Until really, really late."

"Sean, I—"

"Hey, Mr. Underdog," called an overly hearty voice. Beau Murdoch and his wife strolled arm in arm across the parking lot.

"It's the big dog himself," Sean said. He shook hands with Beau's wife, Barbara, and introduced her to Lily.

"Nice job today," Murdoch said. "I would've told you sooner but you got mobbed."

And you had to go sulk, Lily recalled, but she didn't say so. She watched them go. "I can tell the two of you are going to be great friends."

"Right."

The Murdochs put their arms around each other like high school sweethearts, and for some reason, that made her self-conscious. "You're sure the kids are all right with Red?" she asked.

"Absolutely. I heard something about another swim in his hotel pool, and he'll probably teach them to play blackjack."

"Oh, dear—"

"Oh, nothing. Blackjack is a life skill."

"It's not in my curriculum."

"Believe me, I use blackjack a lot more than I do long division."

"You know what?" she said. "I'm not going to let you annoy me tonight. Today was an incredible day and I don't feel like being annoyed."

"I never annoy you," he protested.

"Right. Never. Got it." She stuck her hands in the pockets of her Wonder Bread hooded sweatshirt. "You should ask me what was so incredible about today."

"My round."

It's all about you, she thought, desperate to find fault with him. "Besides that."

"All right, what else?"

"Charlie read an article in the paper this morning," she told him, eager to avoid the topic of the R-word. "I'd have to give her a score of a hundred percent for comprehension."

A grin broke over his face. "Yeah?"

"She's really improving. At this rate, she'll be ready for fourth grade by the end of summer."

"You're really something, Miss Lily Robinson."

"Charlie is really something." She paused, thinking about the little girl's unforced comprehension. "I think she's been holding out on us. She's been capable of reading the whole time and simply refused or let herself be blocked."

"Why would she do that? For the attention?"

Lily frowned, puzzling that. The stealing last April—that had been a classic bid for attention. Willfully avoiding reading, now, that was more complex. "I'm not sure," she admitted. "I need to work on this. I should have volunteered to help her ages ago. If I had—" She bit her lip, unable to finish.

"Now, honey." His hand found the small of her back, a perfectly natural gesture that nearly unraveled her. "Don't go thinking that way or you'll make yourself nuts."

"It's not so nuts. If I'd helped Charlie sooner, maybe I never would have asked Crystal and Derek to come to the conference that day last April. And then they never would have—"

"Damn it, Lily, stop," Sean said. "You're blaming yourself for them, same as you've spent your whole life blaming yourself for your brother. It doesn't work that way. You're not that important. It rains on the just and the unjust, don't you know that?"

"That's from the Bible."

"Don't look so surprised. I'm a dumb jock, but I know my catechism. Listen, you've worn the hair shirt about Crystal and Derek long enough. Get over yourself. Quit thinking you're responsible for the state of the universe."

She stared at him, stunned. He had never spoken to her with such cutting anger.

The anger appeared to startle him, as well. He seemed to conquer it right away, though, a grin easing across his face. "I guess what I'm saying is, it's time to take off your shirt."

She tried not to let his humor or the gleam in his eye affect her. "I'd freeze to death." She moved away from him, sticking her hands in her pockets and walking along the dimly lit trail. "And how about Cameron today? He was amazing."

"Oh, I get it, change of subject."

"Well, he was amazing." She refused to swerve. "Red got a call about him from *Teen People* magazine. I can see the headline now, 'From Vandal to Victor.'" She gave an exaggerated shudder. "One media star in the family is enough."

"So you think I'm a media star?"

"The media thinks so."

"I hope they report that my round today belonged to him. He's the best caddie I've ever had."

"I think you made him sweat a little on that last hole."

"Hey, I made *me* sweat."

"You're the one who decided to shoot for the green. Cameron wanted you to take two strokes to get there."

"Sometimes you just have to give yourself a kick in the ass."

"Cameron definitely figured that out. He had total confidence in you." She felt like touching him but didn't let herself. "He's different since the Winnebago incident, don't you think?" She slipped into the familiar routine of discussing the kids with him. This was their relationship and she meant to keep it that way. "I meant to tell you, I think you handled it well. Initially, I didn't believe humor was the way to deal with it, but now I see that was the perfect response."

"Good, because I couldn't help myself. I look at Cameron and I see Derek and me as boys. We were idiots sometimes, just like he is."

"That's the key, then, treating him like the kid he is." She sighed. "That's what I want for all three of them, Sean. I want them to remember their parents without being frozen or stuck in grief or guilt."

"Ever notice how we always talk about the kids?" he asked suddenly.

Notice? She did it on purpose. "Is that a problem?"

"We should talk about us."

"The only reason there's an *us* is that we've got these three kids—"

"Bullshit, Lily." He grabbed her then, giving her no chance to get away or make excuses, and he kissed her, hard and long, openmouthed, his tongue doing things that made her forget what they were arguing about or if they were even arguing at all.

That was the thing about Sean. He made her forget. He made her forget all of the things she trained herself to remember—that going to bed early and getting up early made a person productive. That a proper diet and exercise regimen were crucial to good health. That love was always a precursor to hurt. He was making her forget that, and suddenly she was kissing him back with a hunger and intensity she'd never felt before.

By the time he ended the kiss and gently lifted his mouth from hers, she could barely remember her own name.

"We should get drunk and celebrate," he said.

Feeling reckless, she said, "I know something I want more than to get drunk."

"Miss Robinson," he whispered, his thumb outlining the shape of her jaw, "you are full of surprises."

She slipped her hand into his, lacing their fingers together. She felt reckless and bold, not like herself at all. "You'd be even more surprised if you knew what I'd like to do right now."

He laughed, the sound as soft and smooth as a caress. "Then I'm not letting you go until you tell me."

chapter 45

Back in the RV, Sean couldn't take his eyes off Lily. Her hands shook as she moistened her lips and then parted them, artlessly tantalizing as she lifted the fresh, dark Devil Dog to her mouth. He watched her teeth sink into the tender flesh of it, watched her lips close around the soft inner filling. She shut her eyes and gave the sort of moan he usually only heard from a woman when she was flat on her back.

She chewed slowly, ecstatically, and swallowed. Under the table, Babe thumped her tail. Then at last Lily's eyes drifted open. "That…was…incredible," she said breathlessly. "My teeth are singing."

He pushed a steaming cup across the table to her. "Coffee?"

She sipped the freshly brewed coffee he'd made to go with the Devil Dogs. "I missed my calling," she confessed. "I should get a job with Drake's."

"The caffeine might keep you up all night."

"Fine with me. We've got all these Devil Dogs to eat."

He helped himself to one and she to another. "You're really something, Lily Robinson."

She licked a bit of white cream from the corner of her mouth. "Really? Why?"

"I don't know. Something."

"A puzzle wrapped in an enigma?"

"Took the words right out of my mouth. You're just not like most women I've known."

"What, boobs too small? Brain too big?"

"You really think a lot of me, don't you?" This was the way it always was with him and women. If Lily was like the others, she'd leave him eventually. That's what women did. They left him. He didn't seem to know how to make them stay or how to make himself want them to.

"All right," Lily said, "you tell me. How am I different?"

He shoved away the troubling thoughts. "Usually before I sleep with a girl, we drink champagne or do tequila shots. Not coffee and Devil Dogs."

She licked the cream from her fingers, one by one, taking her time as though she knew what it was doing to him. "What makes you think I'm going to sleep with you?"

"Well." He reached across the table and very gently removed her glasses, setting them aside. "It's actually just a manner of speaking." He reached again, this time taking apart her ponytail, watching her hair spring free. Goodbye, Marian the Librarian, he thought.

"What I mean is, I don't think we'll be doing any sleeping at all." He stood slowly and came around the side of the table, drawing her up and pulling her close. "That is, if that's okay with you."

She kissed him. It was the first time she'd made the first move and she was ravenous. And breathless when she finally pulled back. "You taste like Devil Dogs," she said.

chapter 46

When Lily awakened, she had a smile on her lips. A warm, slightly bruised and tender feeling reminded her of the night before, the secret hours in Sean's arms before Red had brought the children back. Though their time was limited, she had been well and thoroughly loved, and memories pulsed through her, touching off signal fires in hidden places. Last night had been a revelation. A dream. An ecstasy that was softer and sweeter than a dozen Devil Dogs.

Sean Maguire, she thought, letting his name drift through her mind like an unforgettable song. Sean Maguire. I'm in love with Sean Maguire.

It was outrageous and wonderful. She was more afraid than she'd ever been in her life, but for the first time, she wasn't going to let fear hold her back. This was the burden she hadn't realized she was carrying. Over time, her heart had grown heavier and heavier, dragging her down until she couldn't even remember to keep her head up. Now that she'd finally given her heart away, something unexpected was happening. Her burden had disappeared. She was light as air, content to drift inside a moment rather than planning ahead. She didn't feel like herself at all, like super-organized, goal-driven Lily Robinson. She felt like Carmen, like Delilah, like... Cleopatra.

All right, she thought, so maybe she didn't know what to do next. Today, Sean would have a round of interviews and appearances, with everything arranged by Red. Lily wanted to make herself scarce, to savor her feelings in private. She lay very still, alone in her bed, listening, wondering what it would be like to sleep all night in Sean's arms. No one else seemed to be up. She reached for her cell phone and slipped outside, letting the dog out with her. Hugging her sweatshirt around her, she called her sister. Even though it was five in the morning on the West Coast, she needed to hear her sister's voice. She felt a sweet sense of revelation. She had a sister who was wise in ways Lily was only now coming to appreciate.

Violet answered on the second ring. At first, Lily could do nothing but sob into the phone. She somehow managed to convey to her sister that for once they were tears of joy, not grief. When she finally gained control, she said, "Oh, Violet. I've never been in love before. I don't know how it's done."

"You don't have to do anything. Just be."

"It sounds very Zen."

"I don't know about that," Violet admitted. "I only know that if it's the real thing, you don't have to push it or question it. Just let love do the work."

"That's pretty much what we did last night."

Violet laughed. "Way to go, Lil."

"It's so...so ill-advised."

"Will you listen to yourself? Ill-advised, like this is a bad investment or something." She paused. "The heart doesn't work that way," she added, sounding older and wiser than her years. "Just be happy with him."

"I think looking for happiness with another person is like looking for the rainbow's end. The minute you think you've found it, it fades away."

"You're crazy, Lily, you know that?"

"I'm already worrying about the impact of this on the kids."

"The kids are going to love this. Seeing two people falling for each other—how can that be a bad thing? They took a direct hit, losing their parents like that. They need to believe in something again. Like you and Sean."

"Me and Sean," Lily whispered, looking out at the misty day. There was still a part of her that didn't dare trust what was happening, but she didn't tell her sister that. The feelings were too new and raw to describe. "I have to go," she said. "But…thanks, Vi. You know where your priorities are."

When she returned to the RV, Sean was fixing the girls' hair, mincing around and speaking with an accent in a poor imitation of a hair stylist. "You just need a little loft here, darling," he said, fluffing Ashley's wispy brown hair while she giggled. Charlie had Heidi braids this morning, crisscrossed over her head. With the headphones on, Cameron was fiddling with the radio. The dog burst in, tracking dirt all over the place.

Lily paused in the doorway for a moment. They all looked so dear to her just then, in this little contained world that felt cozily insulated against the outside.

Sean spotted her and sent her a grin that she felt like a physical touch. "Good morning, madam," he said. "Do you have an appointment?"

"I'm afraid not."

"I'll see if I can work you in. Devil Dog?" he offered, holding out the box.

She met his gaze. "Maybe later."

"I want to go swimming at Red's hotel again," Charlie said. "Can we, please?"

"Your uncle Sean has some meetings today."

"Not until this afternoon," Charlie said. "Please, Lily."

"Fine with me," Sean said.

A few minutes later, they were headed to the Colonial. Red had ordered breakfast poolside and he greeted them like a benevolent uncle. "Welcome to your new life," he said to Sean. "The fun's about to begin."

Lily's heart pounded as she walked to the edge of the pool. She was about to put one foot in the shallow end when she changed her mind. She walked the length of the pool and stepped up on the diving board. The clear, placid water looked very far below, very deep. Her heart sped up faster and she saw Sean watching her. She was afraid, but for once she was going to ignore the fear. Then, before she could change her mind, she stepped off the end and plunged in. She didn't resist the water, didn't struggle to the surface. She sank deep, felt her foot brush the bottom, then slowly rose. Her swimming was clumsy, but she managed to glide to the edge. That wasn't so bad, she thought. That wasn't bad at all.

She propped her arms on the edge and gazed up at the sunny sky. She could hear the girls laughing and splashing with Sean. Red and Cameron were deep in conversation at the breakfast table. There was a lull in the unrelenting grief that had been their constant companion all summer.

She watched a small wisp of a cloud drift, then shut her eyes. This was not the real world. Out here on the road, they were a family. But summer was coming to an end, and the real world awaited.

chapter 47

Summer's end brought a return to Comfort and changes no one talked about, although everyone except for Ashley thought constantly about what the future held.

For Sean, it was a career he approached with a new maturity. He didn't have to live out of a suitcase or worry about a world ranking, just about staying in the game.

Cameron got his driver's license and, along with that, a certain easing of the anger inside him and perhaps even a sense that life could be fun again. He still caddied for Sean in tournaments and counted the days until Becky Pilchuk returned from her summer job.

Charlie was reading. Perhaps her scores would show her performing below grade level in some areas, but she could read and understand, and she didn't dread the start of school as Lily had feared she might.

Ashley blossomed like a late-summer rose. She grew more beautiful and learned more words every day. Sometimes Lily would sit with her in the evening and they would go through photo albums together.

"Mama," Ashley would dutifully say.

"Never forget that," Lily whispered. "Please don't ever forget."

"Okay." She patted a page with her hand. "Da?"

"Right there." Lily indicated a snapshot of Derek. The fact that he'd made Crystal so unhappy was not something these children should have to deal with. And truly, looking at the family photos, she sensed they'd once brought each other joy. At least she hoped so.

Now that they'd returned to Comfort, she refused to spend the night with Sean, though this didn't mean an end to the insane lust that possessed her. She was worried, though; in some moments, terrified at what lay beneath the lust. This was not some summer romance, some vacation flirtation that would end on Labor Day. She very much feared that this was the love of her life. She'd spent all her adult years avoiding precisely this situation, protecting herself from uncertainty and anguish. She was well aware that with a man like Sean, the potential for disaster was enormous. They were together, but what did that mean?

Labor Day and the start of school loomed, and she dared to hope the rhythm of the new academic year might make this feel more like her own life once again. Then she caught herself trying to remember what was so great about her own life.

It was normal, she told herself. Settled and predictable, relaxing. Life with Sean and the kids was just the opposite, and it couldn't be good for her.

On the Thursday before Labor Day weekend, they met with Susie Shea, the social worker who had been there for them at the start of the whole ordeal. "My hat's off to you," she told Lily and Sean. "The children are adjusting well." She paused, looked from one to the other. "What about the two of you?"

Lily panicked. Sean cleared his throat. "We're adjusting, too," he said awkwardly.

"Yes," she agreed. "We're adjusting."

Susie closed her casebook and checked her watch. "I'll be back next month."

The moment she was gone, Sean wiped his brow in an exaggerated gesture. "I feel like I just brought home a good report card."

"You did," Lily said. "We all did."

Later that day, Violet and her family came to Comfort to finally reclaim the Winnebago and attend the annual golf tournament at Paradise Ridge. It was early morning, but everyone was up when they arrived.

Sean's house, Lily thought. When had she stopped thinking of it as Crystal's house?

They were waiting in the driveway, which was lined with buckets and rags and a vacuum. The RV sparkled, inside and out. By contract, the Wonder Bread logo had been removed. Lily made the introductions and the younger kids fell into an easy camaraderie, inventing some game in the backyard with rules even Ashley seemed to understand.

"Congratulations on your season," Rick said, enthusiastically pumping Sean's hand. "Really impressive, really. I snared a vendor's contract for this weekend's tournament, so we'll be pulling for you."

"Hey, thanks. That means a lot." It was a big match with a big purse. Held at the legendary course at Paradise Ridge, the tournament was high profile and high stakes. Lily knew he was ready. She also knew he was nervous.

"My lord," murmured Violet, standing back and watching them, "he's even better than I remembered."

You have no idea, thought Lily.

"Have you told Mom and Dad yet?" Violet asked.

"Why would I do that?"

"Well, they're family, for starters. People generally want

their family to know—never mind." Violet waved her hand impatiently. "You figure it out, Lily."

Rick, Violet and their kids would be staying in the RV at the golf course. Violet invited Charlie and Ashley to spend the day with her and the children. Within minutes, everyone had left, including Cameron, who was driving to Portland to pick up Becky at the Amtrak station.

Lily looked at Sean. She ducked her head, trying to hide the delicious sense of anticipation she felt, but it was no use. He saw straight through her, every time.

Sean didn't say a word to Lily, but walked into the house with long, hurried strides. He seemed almost angry. A bit wary, she followed him, startled as he snared her wrist the minute she stepped inside. He reeled her against him and kissed her hard, his mouth lingering, tasting until she felt light-headed.

"I've missed you," he said, pressing her back to the wall in the hallway. His hands undid her—hair, glasses, blouse, shorts—while his mouth set her on fire.

Very, very fleetingly, it occurred to her to protest. But to protest what? She wanted this as badly as he did, had missed him as much as he'd missed her, and they both knew it. There was a recklessness in the way they came together, a rough hunger that should have shocked but instead turned her on. She wanted this, wanted *him* with a terrible need, and she loved his palpable sense of urgency, the way he seemed to want to engulf her. It felt both thrilling and dangerous to be stripped bare by him, their clothes in a heap, his arms engulfing her in an embrace of possession. She collapsed against his bare, sweaty shoulder, a little amazed at herself, at the abandon and passion she felt.

They were both breathing hard, Sean laughing a little as

they put themselves together again. "Miss Robinson, I need to make an honest woman out of you. I could have thrown my back out just then, and I've got a tournament coming up."

"I'll keep that in mind." She finished buttoning her blouse. "Don't you have some sort of PR appearance today?" In conjunction with the tournament, Red's publicity department had lined up a number of press interviews.

He nodded. "More than one. They're sending a car around."

Sending a car. It sounded surreal to Lily, almost as surreal as seeing him interviewed on ESPN.

He walked her to the door, caught her against him for another kiss. "Don't think I'm going to forget what I said earlier, about making an honest woman of you," he said.

I am an honest woman, she wanted to tell him. I honestly love you.

Still warm from Sean's lovemaking and feeling oddly fragile, Lily stepped into Room 105 at Laurelhurst Country Day School and tried to proceed as if this was any other school year. She wanted to pretend she was plain old Miss Robinson again, with nothing more pressing in her life than getting her classroom ready for the first day of school. Yet as she stapled fresh butcher paper on the bulletin boards, as she labeled tote trays and sketched out a lesson plan for next Wednesday, she felt distracted and unsettled.

She wasn't the same, not even close. And she sure as heck wasn't comfortable in her new skin.

It wasn't about being comfortable, her sister would say.

The rhythmic thump of a basketball sounded. She looked out the window to see a tall boy dribbling a basketball in the playground court. It was Russell Clark, one of her favorites from the previous year. How he'd grown over the summer, she

thought. She hoped he was still the same irrepressible opti-
mist. She hoped he'd never lose that.

Turning from the window, she made a place card for each
child, writing each name in print and then in script: *Loretta
S., Deanna K., Pete M.*... Third grade marked the transition
from stick-figure printing to cursive writing.

The flip chart was ready for the first lesson. "What I Did
on My Summer Vacation" was the topic, as always. Without thinking, she found herself writing a list in orange
marker:

> went camping in a Winnebago
> stayed up all night
> hit a golf ball two hundred yards
> learned line dancing
> ate Drake's Devil Dogs
> fell in love

"Well, well," said Edna, who appeared in the doorway.
She was her usual serene self in a batiked dress and beaded
sandals. "You've been busy. Do they have Winnebagos and
Devil Dogs in Italy?"

Lily's face heated as she ripped the sheet off the flip chart
and crumpled it with both hands. "I didn't go." She quickly
explained that she'd spent the summer driving cross-country
in a Winnebago with the Holloway children and their uncle.
It sounded crazy, saying it aloud, crazy and wonderful.

"How are they?" asked Edna.

"Light-years ahead of where they were at the beginning of
the summer. They still have a ways to go." She offered a fleeting smile. "There are whole moments, sometimes hours or even
days, when they're just like any other kids. Then something
happens—a piece of mail comes addressed to Crystal, or one of

the kids finds an old scorecard of Derek's—and I realize they'll never really get over it."

"It's not about getting over it. It's about healing and going on." She flipped back her silvery hair. "So you've been in love with him all summer and you haven't told him yet?"

So much for hoping Edna hadn't noticed. "Well, not in words."

"Words matter, Lily. You know that."

She thought of her parents and the idea that words could wound. They could also heal; she knew that now. But she didn't reply to Edna's suggestion. She felt like a stranger here in her own classroom, the place that used to feel so safe and familiar to her. This had been her world, her garden, the children her flowers. Now she felt distracted by thoughts of Sean and the children, and the idea of home had a different meaning.

"I feel torn," she confessed to Edna. "For the first time, I can finally understand what a working mother faces every day."

"Most of us do just fine," Edna assured her. "However, the Holloways are dealing with extraordinary circumstances. I've been thinking…perhaps you should take some time off to be a family."

The words stole Lily's breath. "They're not my family."

"Oh, no?" She gestured at the page crumpled in Lily's hand. "Look at your list. I'm not making this suggestion lightly. You're one of my best teachers and I'm an idiot for saying this, but if you want a sabbatical or professional leave, I'd approve it without question. The new crop of third-graders will muddle through without you. The Holloways might not."

"I can't believe what you're saying."

"So what's she saying?" Coach Greg Duncan stepped into the room, carrying his clipboard and grinning broadly.

"None of your business," Edna said, but her voice was teasing. "How are you, Greg? Have a nice summer?"

"Summer was fine," he said. "Hey, Lily."

"Hey yourself."

"Ask me what I'm doing this weekend," he said, his grin widening. "Just ask."

"All right, what are you doing?"

"Playing in the Paradise Ridge tournament. There was a spot for a local amateur and I made the cut."

Lily beamed at him. Over the summer, she'd come to appreciate the hard work, talent and concentration that went into winning a golf match. "Greg, that's fantastic."

"Congratulations," Edna said. "Lily will be there watching, won't you, Lily?"

"I'll be in the gallery with the Holloway girls. Their brother is going to be caddying for his uncle."

"Excellent," he said. "Wish me luck, ladies."

chapter 48

Cameron paced up and down the platform at the train station. He'd felt totally weird all day, ever since getting up super-early and telling his uncle, "I'm going to the city to pick up my girlfriend at the Amtrak station." Not so long ago, he couldn't imagine getting in his mother's car and driving to Portland by himself. He couldn't imagine declaring to anyone that Becky Pilchuk was his girlfriend. Yet he'd done both and the world hadn't come to an end, so that was something.

Sean had seemed distracted when he agreed to let Cameron have the car. Cameron was pretty sure his uncle and Lily Robinson were getting it on. He'd had his suspicions ever since the Colonial tournament. That night, Red had treated him and his sisters to a feast of prime rib, baked potatoes and hot fudge sundaes in the hotel's fancy restaurant. They had been surrounded by the best golfers in the country and Cameron had acted like a total gawk, but he couldn't help himself. When Phil Mickelson complimented him on the job he'd done caddying for Sean, Cameron had felt ten feet tall. He

asked each player for the same greeting with his autograph—
To Becky.

When they got back to the RV that night, Lily and Sean were seated at the table, not talking but just looking at each other, a half-empty box of Devil Dogs between them. Lily's hair was loose and her glasses lay on the table in front of her. There was a different energy around them, and Cameron knew. He wasn't sure how, but it was perfectly clear to him that they were together now. A couple.

It made Cameron feel funny, but in a good way, a way he had not felt since he was little and his parents were still kind to each other. Seeing his uncle and Lily like that made the earth feel solid under his feet. After they returned home, he expected them to open up about it, but so far they hadn't. Cameron couldn't understand that. After what had happened to his parents, he didn't see any reason to hold off on something you wanted.

Still, he felt awkward and unaccountably nervous as he waited for Becky to get off the train. At the same time, he felt curiously adult, knowing Becky's father had approved of his plan to pick her up at the station. And there was, as always, that undercurrent of sadness that rode with him every moment like a low-grade fever. His own mom and dad were missing this. They'd never meet Becky, never see him dressed up for a formal dance or win the state golf championship. They'd never see him make something of his life, never be there to help him decide on a college, or to celebrate with him or criticize him. He missed them so much that sometimes he felt like putting his fist through a wall.

There were all these warning notices about security and passengers-only all over the station, but he ignored them and everybody seemed to ignore him as he went down a set of stairs and up another, emerging on the platform. The macadam surface of the platform was marked off in diamond-shaped segments with ridges to prevent people from slipping. He stood on one segment and thought about his father. Dr. Sachs said he should do this often, should think about his parents in a concrete and deliberate fashion. In his mind, he should wrap up each thought and store it away in a special place.

Even the bad ones? Cameron had asked.

Even the bad ones.

Cameron looked down at his shoes. He thought about the fight he'd had with his father that last day. *I hate you, you son of a bitch. I hope I never see you again.*

Go ahead and hate me, you little shit. Just make sure you don't screw up in the tournament this weekend.

It's not like you'll even be there to see me screw up.

And this was supposed to help? he wondered, and moved to another square. When other kids' dads were teaching them to ride a two-wheeler, Cameron's father taught him to drive an electric golf cart. He'd been so little he couldn't reach the pedals while sitting, so he stood like a streetcar conductor. His first time out, he ran right over a ball washer, leaving the nylon bristles like roadkill in his wake. Dad hadn't gotten mad, though. He'd laughed and showed Cameron how to putt that day, and ever since, Cameron had sunk his putts with incredible accuracy.

You're a natural, Dad used to say. Don't let it fool you. Knowing you have talent only makes you lazy. The truth is, you have to work twice as hard.

Cameron's father had lived his life that way, working hard, focusing, never falling back on talent alone. Now, Uncle Sean, there was an example of talent alone. It was erratic, winning him the Masters one year and losing him his PGA card the next. He'd changed, though. He was a different sort of golfer now, in control of his game.

Cameron didn't know which brother he resembled more. A little of both, probably. But mostly, he was himself. He stepped to another square.

A woman pushing a kid in a stroller came out of the elevator. The kid was about Ashley's age, with a grubby face and a smile that told the world he was happy for no particular reason. Dad used to sit on the floor with Ashley, stacking up blocks so she could knock them down, pretending to throw a tantrum when she did. That used to make her giggle uncontrollably, and Dad just loved that.

Had he known? Cameron had asked himself the question over and over again.

If Dad knew, it hadn't mattered in the way he'd loved her, that was for sure. And somehow, Cameron knew in his heart that his father's love for the baby wouldn't change even if he knew the truth.

It meant the end of his parents' love for each other, though admittedly that was probably gone well before Ashley came along. His father had fooled around before his mother did—with Jane. He didn't even bother to hide it. Cameron's mother took things a step further and had another man's baby. By then, of course, the whole family was in pieces. Sometimes you go with the wrong person and do the wrong thing because you're not thinking. Maybe that was what his mom had done.

It seemed like a lousy thing to do, but now they had Ashley. And Ashley was…simply a gift. An undeserved gift to this whole screwed-up family.

Stepping into another square, he saw the toddler in the stroller looking at him and he winked. He started a game of peekaboo behind his hands, but the mother didn't see, and she wheeled the stroller away. Cameron tried to get his mind off his family, but reminders were everywhere—a magazine rack with a headline about a celebrity custody battle. A flyer advertising divorce for $99. His stomach churned with the fear that Ashley was at risk. If she was taken away, the whole family would collapse, he just knew it. They had survived losing his parents, just barely. But losing the baby...

He wondered how to get advice from a lawyer without letting on that there was a problem. Could he just go to some guy's office and say, "This is a purely hypothetical situation, but if a kid is being raised by her uncle because her parents are deceased, and then it turns out he's not her biological uncle after all, will that change who gets to raise the kid?"

If that was the law, then the law was wrong, he thought. As soon as he turned eighteen, he'd vote out the fools who had legislated it.

Cameron stood up very straight. The noise and bustle of the station seemed to fade into the background as one clear, perfect thought took hold. In less than two years, he would be a legal adult.

And he was Ashley's blood relative. He would be her guardian. No one would take her away from him, ever. *Ever.*

For the first time in weeks, a peculiar calm spread through him. Ashley was going to stay where she belonged.

The train hissed and groaned its way into the station, and Cameron's nerves thrummed with anticipation. He was amazed at how many people seemed to be on the train and how long it took them to get off. This was worse than on an airplane, when everybody in front of you took forever to get their stuff out of the overhead compartment. There was a family of six from Mexico, looking bewildered but cautiously pleased, emerging from a silver passenger car and blinking at the light. A man alone in a suit that looked clean and pressed even though he had probably spent hours sitting on board stepped down, his perfectly shined shoes gleaming. There was a woman in a tie-dyed dress carrying a birdcage, and a pair of backpackers who were maybe college-age. For the first time since the accident, Cameron could picture himself like that someday, striking out toward a future.

Last April, he hadn't thought much about the future at all. He'd drifted from day to day, goofing off with people he called friends. Now he knew what a true friend was—someone who cared enough about you to make you want to be a better person, and these days he actually cared about that. Being better. Doing his best in school, because it mattered. He grudgingly conceded that school was important. He wanted to go to college, see the world, be with someone special, look after his sisters.

The moment he spotted Becky squeezing through the train-car door with an overstuffed duffel bag, the churning eased. He could tell by the way she was scanning the platform that she hadn't spotted him yet. He was about to run toward her, but he hesitated a moment. She looked…different. Way different. Something had happened to her over the summer, something indefinable but very real. He felt a little intimidated by the tall girl walking toward the exit like a supermodel, her hair a silky flutter behind her. Then she spotted him and smiled, her teeth a dazzling flash of white in her tanned face. That was the Becky he knew, shining through.

He hurried toward her, weaving in and out of the milling crowd. Now what? He wondered if he should grab her and give her a hug, maybe even kiss her. Instead, he just stood there like an idiot.

"Hey," he said.

"Hey, yourself." She was blushing beneath the tan. "Thanks for meeting me."

"That's okay. Can I give you a hand with that?" He grabbed her duffel bag and headed for the exit. Stupid, he thought. Stupid, stupid, stupid.

He kept sneaking glances at her and noticed her doing the same. There was more blushing on both sides. His ears were so hot, he was sure the flames were visible.

He noticed that her hair was almost white-blond from the sun. Neither of them seemed to know what to say, where to put their hands or their feet or their thoughts or their yearning.

"My car's over here," he said, leading the way. *My car.* Not my mom's car, but mine. It finally felt like a good fit. He opened the hatchback and put her bags in. And at some point, for some reason, he stopped thinking about what to do or what to say next. He turned to face her and put his hands on her shoulders. She felt just right. Perfect.

"I've missed you," he said, and leaned down and kissed her, simple as that. She tasted sweet and her lips were warm, and he felt a wave of happiness as pure and clean as anything he'd felt since the accident.

She pulled back and looked up at him with shining eyes. "I've missed you, too."

He took both her hands in his. "I didn't kiss you goodbye," he said. "I thought about that all summer. I should have done that. I wish I had."

"You kissed me hello. That's better, anyway."

A fresh wind through his bedroom window awakened Cameron. He knew it would rain soon. He had a powerful sense of the weather, feeling the damp in the atmosphere and the wind like a phantom breath on the back of his neck.

He slipped out of bed and went downstairs, shushing the dog as she greeted him with ecstatic whining and thumps of her tail. He opened the door to the damp morning, letting the dog scamper out in front of him. Dark-bellied clouds hung low over the neighborhood and a breeze kicked up, turning over the leaves to show their pale undersides.

It was weird to be the first one up. He was usually the late sleeper in the family, especially after staying out so late the night before. With Becky.

He couldn't stop a smile from unfurling, didn't even try to stop it. He shivered in the morning air and watched Babe sniffing the periphery of the backyard. He automatically checked his cell phone. Too early to call her. He was desperate to hear her voice even though he knew what she'd say. She'd ask him if he'd had a talk with his uncle yet. That was Becky, straightforward and matter-of-fact. When he'd told her his dilemma about Ashley, and the solution he envisioned, she said the longer he put it off, the harder it would be.

He noticed a movement out of the corner of his eye and turned to see Charlie coming toward him. She had on their mother's long blue nightgown, which she'd worn to bed every single night since last April. The thing was getting ratty from overuse and it was way too long, but no one would ever tell Charlie that. She held the hem up with both hands while she walked and just for a second, a weird, dreamy moment, Cameron blurred his eyes and turned the figure coming toward him into his mother. *There you are, honey. I've been looking all over for you.*

Then the vision was gone and it was just Charlie again, looking small and maybe a little lost. "What are you doing up so early?" he asked her.

Babe came bounding up to snuffle and greet her, then took off again, skimming across the dew-wet grass with her nose low to the ground.

Charlie shrugged. "My eyes just popped open."

The dog circled back, bowing playfully. Cameron found a fuzzy green tennis ball nestled in the grass. Picking it up with two fingers, he shook off the dew and lobbed the ball to the far end of the yard. Babe streaked off after it and brought it back, dropping it at his feet and looking up with eyes full of hope.

"Yuck, it's all slimy," Charlie observed.

"Washes right off," he said, throwing the ball again and wiping his hand on his shorts.

"Why're you up so early?" she asked.

"Thinking about things."

"What things?"

"Ashley," he said simply. He and Charlie rarely mentioned the matter. Now, seeing her worried frown, he thought that might be a mistake. Thunder growled in the distance. She moved closer to Cameron. Her tiny flip-flops slapped against her heels. She seemed really little to him, little and scared. He took her hand in his.

"It's Coach Duncan, isn't it?" Charlie said in a quiet but distinct voice.

Cameron froze. It was on the tip of his tongue to say he didn't know what she was talking about, but he was done lying. Why did people lie to little kids, anyway? They always found out eventually, or they were never fooled in the first place. Besides, Cameron had carried this around long enough. He loved golf but hated playing for Duncan. He couldn't figure out how to get out of it, though. What was he supposed to say to Sean? "I don't want to play for Duncan because Mom slept with him." Oh, that would be a wonderful thing to say to your father's brother.

His throat felt dry and scratchy all of a sudden. "You don't need to worry about that," he said.

She looked up at him and then out at the wind-stirred yard. The first fat raindrops fell, spattering the pavement of the driveway. Babe returned with the ball again, and Cameron hurled it, all the fury inside him finding a way out. He threw it so far that it went into the next yard where the dog couldn't locate it. They could see the vertical feather of her tail tracking back and forth in the distant tall grass as she searched.

"I knew I was right," Charlie said.

"How, um, when did you find out?"

"Mom said. Back in April."

Cameron remembered the blood-test results he'd found in the car, dated the first Monday in April. He figured his mother had been checking out a hunch. Had she been shocked, or were the results exactly what she expected?

"You mean she told you?" he asked Charlie, incredulous.

"I don't think she meant to, but she was all sad and she told me."

Cameron felt a dart of rage at his mother, but the anger had nowhere to go.

"I'm afraid Coach Duncan will take Ashley away," Charlie said.

"That's not going to happen. She's our sister, and I'll be the one to take care of her, whatever it takes."

Babe came roaring back and dropped the ball at his feet.

"That's not the same ball you threw," Charlie said.

"You're right," he said, stooping to pick up the shiny blue racquet ball the dog had yielded up. "Doesn't matter. A ball's a ball." He didn't throw it but held it gingerly in one hand and grabbed Charlie with the other. With Babe loping along, they went back inside just as marble-size hailstones began striking the roof. Almost the moment they got inside, the storm passed. As Cameron fixed his sister a bowl of cereal, he felt curiously relaxed. At peace. It wasn't his job to spend each moment of his life worrying about this family. He wasn't worried anymore. He had a plan.

chapter 49

Lily had never invited Sean over to her house. Given the events of the summer, that seemed strange. She had let this man get closer than anyone into her life, perhaps even Crystal. There were things he knew about Lily's heart that no one else had discovered, perhaps not even Lily herself.

It was time. Violet had insisted on keeping Charlie and Ashley for the evening and the girls were delighted to be back in the RV, this time with children to play with. Cameron was out with Becky; she was officially his girlfriend now. So when Sean called and asked to see her, she had invited him over —into her home, into her heart.

And she was a wreck. She'd straightened and cleaned all afternoon. She'd tried on and discarded four different outfits. What did you wear to tell a man you were in love with him?

She settled on a pink sundress and matching sandals and resisted the urge to pull her hair back into a ponytail, because he seemed to like it hanging loose. She put a six-pack of beer in the fridge. Then she paced and wrung her hands. She was setting herself up for all kinds of hurt, maybe even a rejection. He'd never actually told her he loved her. Maybe their connection was based on their mutual concern for the children. And sex, of course. Like a hormonal teenager, she couldn't stop thinking about that. True love had to be more than that, she thought. Didn't it?

This was absurd. She shouldn't be doing this. A few months ago, her life was going completely according to plan. Since Crystal had died, and Sean and the children had come along, she'd lost control of the reins. And now this? Now she wanted to bare her heart to him? Was she out of her mind?

In the midst of pacing the floor, she came up short in front of the framed photo of herself and Crystal at Haystack Rock. Those shining eyes and laughing faces seemed so terribly young to her, as though they belonged to two strangers. In that moment, the grief struck her like a fist in the dark, as intense as it had been the morning Sean told her about the accident. Lily wrapped her arms across her middle and sat down as the waves swept through her. It happened like this sometimes; just when she began to think she'd adjusted to her loss, the grief came smashing through again like a destructive storm, a natural disaster.

There was a knock at the door and she shot to her feet. As she hurried to answer it, she wiped at her eyes. She was an idiot. She had no business telling this man she loved him. It would only complicate the situation.

He seemed distracted when she greeted him; his kiss was perfunctory and his mind was clearly on something other than her. She studied his face and realized it was more than distraction. "We need to talk," he said, striding into her living room. He seemed to fill the whole place with his presence.

Well, thought Lily. So much for romantic declarations. "All right," she said, determined not to let him rattle her. "Sit down and we'll talk."

He sat on the sofa but didn't relax. Instead he leaned forward like a coach in a team dugout, wrists balanced on his knees, fingertips touching, a scowl on his face.

"Is everything all right?" Lily asked. Dumb question. She already knew it wasn't. He was probably dumping her, that was it. Dumping her for twin tire models or a Hooters waitress. She reeled in the loopy thought and waited.

"Cameron told me something that I think you should hear."

Lily's mind ran through the possibilities. There were so many of them. "And?"

"He said…I mean, he's known for a while now that Derek isn't—wasn't—Ashley's father."

It was the last thing she'd expected, and the sound that came out of her expressed wordless disbelief. She felt a terrible shift in the world. Here was the man she loved, telling her something that could change everything. No, she thought. *No.*

"Did you know anything about this?" Sean asked her, his eyes narrowing as he looked at her in a way that was not altogether pleasant. In fact, it was singularly discomfiting to be regarded with suspicion and mistrust.

"Anything besides the fact that it's patently untrue? No."

He shoved his hands in his pockets and looked around the room, his gaze lighting on the photo of her and Crystal laughing, their arms around each other. "I was surprised, too," he admitted. "Regardless of my opinion of Crystal, I never dreamed Ashley belonged to anyone but Derek. Neither did he. I know that for a fact."

"There's a reason for that," Lily said. "She *is* Derek's child. I have no idea why Cameron would say she's not. He must be mistaken, must have misunderstood something—"

"Cameron's not stupid. He didn't make a mistake and he wouldn't dream this up out of thin air."

"It's simply not true," she said. "He's not a liar, but he's laboring under some misinformation—"

"I didn't come here to debate this with you, damn it."

"Then why did you come here?" Her temper rose right along with his. That was the crazy thing about love. It could turn in the space of a heartbeat. She should have respected her instinct not to trust it.

"To tell you something important about a family you supposedly care about," he said.

"Supposedly? Oh, you mean the family I spent the summer with, in an RV with a dog? Gee, whatever gave you the idea that I care?"

He set his jaw, took a breath. "All right, so there's no question about your commitment to this family. That's the reason I'm here. You have a right to know. And I wouldn't have told you if I didn't have proof."

Lily sat down. "Proof?"

He stayed standing as he handed her the envelope. "This is a copy of a blood test Crystal had done the Monday before the accident. I picked up a copy from her doctor as soon as Cameron told me. The test removes any doubt. Derek's blood type is AB, and Crystal's is B. The baby's is O, which any high school biology student will tell you means she can't be Derek's."

Lily's hand shook as she thrust the lab report away. Unfortunately, she remembered high school biology all too well, and she knew these test results were no lie. She nearly gagged on the next question. "Then who...?"

"The father's Greg Duncan, the golf coach," Sean concluded, "and he doesn't know."

Lily discovered that she'd stopped breathing. She started up again in panicky little gasps. Greg Duncan. She had worked with him, dated him. One time, she'd even kissed him. How could she have missed this? Crystal used to try to warn her away from him. He's a player, she'd said. A user. You can do better. Lily assumed Crystal wanted her to find someone to get serious with. Now she wondered if Crystal warned her off because she herself had been with Greg.

Somehow, Lily found her voice. "That's completely absurd." Even as she spoke, she was comparing Ashley to Greg in her mind. Brown hair, brown eyes, big deal. Ashley looked like she could have been fathered by Keanu Reeves, too, but that didn't mean he was her father. Yet Sean had cracked open a door and she couldn't resist peeking in. In her mind's eye, she caught a glimpse of Crystal, who had been team mother three years in a row. Lily remembered this because she'd urged Crystal to give it up when her marriage fell apart, since she had enough to deal with, but Crystal had refused. Maybe, just maybe... She kept picturing Crystal's shell-shocked expression when she had come over to Lily's house one night and said, "Derek has someone else. And I'm pregnant."

"She would have told me," Lily said. "She told me everything."

"Apparently not."

"Even if it did happen like that, she would have told Greg."

"Not Crystal. She needed to be the injured party in the divorce. Winning child support for three kids meant more money for her, and she knew she'd get more from a golf pro than a high school coach."

"That's a horrible, bitter thing to say."

"Not nearly as bad as having one man's child and attributing it to another."

Lily felt queasy. "Crystal wouldn't do that. She simply wouldn't." Lily stared at the dated test results and remembered that day with brittle clarity. It was a Monday, the same day Charlie had started stealing. Good God, she thought. Could Charlie have known? It was bad enough that Cameron was in on this. His mother and his coach. No wonder he vandalized the golf course.

"What's your point, Lily?" Sean asked.

"Obviously, from the timing of the test, she wasn't sure herself until just before she died. Maybe she didn't want to know. Up until the blood test, she probably thought Ashley was Derek's."

"She might not have known whose DNA the baby has, but she sure as hell knew who she was sleeping with."

"My God, you really did hate her, didn't you?"

He shook his head. "This conversation is going nowhere," he said. "Maybe we shouldn't have had it in the first place." He headed for the door.

"Wait," Lily said, her voice very low. Too low, perhaps, for him to hear. If he didn't hear and kept going, she wouldn't call him back.

He did hear. He stopped and turned around.

She squeezed her hands together until they hurt. "We have to tell him." She startled herself with her own words, because by saying them, she acknowledged the truth. Queasiness swelled inside her, tangling with questions that would never be answered. The trouble with being angry with a dead person, she reflected, was that you could never sit down with her, talk things out, get an explanation, make amends.

"That's not what I want to hear from you," he said.

"It's not my job to tell you what you want to hear. That will never be my job, do you understand?" Her eyes burned with tears of fury. What did he expect, coming here and telling her this about her best friend, a woman she had loved and trusted and respected all her life?

"Cameron and I have already discussed this. We're not telling him."

She winced at the thought of Cameron discussing his mother's infidelity. How could you, Crystal? Lily wanted to scream. How could you, with your son's coach? "Sean, you can't fix this with a lie or another deception. Greg deserves to know, and so will Ashley when she's old enough to understand."

"You're not thinking this through, Lily," Sean said. "The baby is with me because I'm the kids' blood relative. If Duncan's the father and not my brother, then I'm not related at all to Ashley. He is. So don't you tell him."

"Don't threaten me."

"It's not a threat. You have no right. You were Crystal's friend. Big deal. I'm the guardian of this family and the decision's mine to make."

She wondered what it was she saw in his eyes besides anger. Fear, perhaps? Then she told herself she didn't have to worry about what he was thinking or feeling. It was a far different conversation from the one she thought they'd have this evening. And this angry, autocratic man was a far different person than the one she thought she knew. Clearly, she was only a part of this family so long as she agreed with Sean. She got to her feet, crossed the room and held the door open. "I think you should go."

"Fine." He strode out the door, then hesitated and turned back. "Was there something you wanted to tell me?"

Only a few minutes ago, she'd wanted to tell him she was in love with him. They should be having dinner together, sharing a glass of wine, making love deep into the night. She swallowed a knot of bitterness that had lodged in her throat.

Thank goodness she hadn't told him yet. At least she hadn't given him the hammer to crush her with. Then she realized she felt crushed all the same. "Not really. Nothing important, anyway."

After he was gone, Lily sat very still. Darkness crept in, but she didn't bother getting up to turn on a light. She wondered how long she would sit here, just like this, before someone noticed her absence. Would she be like one of those forgotten, friendless people you sometimes read about in the paper? She used to savor her independence and solitude. Now that she'd had a taste of family life, she wanted something else. And it had been so close, within her grasp. Sean had wanted just one thing from her, just her cooperation in dealing with Greg Duncan. Why hadn't she given him that? Love was supposed to be about compromise. Surely they could have found a solution that worked for everyone.

A dozen times she reached for the phone, then changed her mind. She was terrible at this. She didn't know how to be a woman in love, and she certainly didn't know how to deal with the aftermath of a quarrel.

The thirteenth time she picked up the phone, the doorbell rang. Lily nearly jumped out of her skin. Then she laughed aloud. He'd come back.

With a broad smile on her face, she flipped on the porch light and opened the door. "Oh," she said, her heart plummeting. "Hi, Mom and Dad." She offered them dutiful hugs and invited them in.

"We decided to drive down for the tournament," her father said. "Violet told us it was a big deal."

"Vi told you to come?"

Her mother made a sound of impatience. "No, your father said she told us it was a big deal—for you. So we decided to come."

"We have a room at the Hampton," her father added. "Have you had dinner yet?"

Dinner. She had fixed dinner for Sean but they hadn't gotten that far tonight. "Tell you what," she said with false brightness. "Let's see what we can scrounge up here."

The three of them went to the kitchen. When Lily put out the dinner she'd prepared—caprese salad, pasta with a lobster and cream sauce—Sharon raised her eyebrows. "This doesn't look like scrounging to me."

Lily's father nodded. "You're overdressed for scrounging, too."

She gave a short laugh. "I can't believe you're criticizing me for that." Two years ago, when she'd declared to the world that she would never marry, Lily had started a collection of colorful Italian dishes from Scala. She served her parents in the dining room, treating them like honored guests. She herself had no appetite whatsoever, and it didn't take her mother long to notice.

"What's going on?" she asked.

"Nothing." Lily struggled to put up the old wall, the one that used to protect her, but she'd lost the knack.

"You've always said that, all your life," her father pointed out.

"Because you've never wanted to know the truth," Lily blurted out, surprising all three of them with her candor.

"Why on earth would you think that?" her mother asked.

"You want to think I'm fine, and Violet's fine, that everything is peachy and always has been in this family."

Her parents exchanged a mystified look. "That's not so," her father said, and her mother added, "We've always dealt realistically with whatever problems come our way."

"Then why did we never deal with Evan?" Lily asked. There. She'd said it. She'd dared to mention the elephant in the corner of the room, the one they all knew was there but no one talked about. This time, she wasn't going to let them change the subject.

"There's no 'dealing' to be done," her mother said. "You never get over a loss like that."

"And you let it ruin your marriage and make a mess of your kids," Lily pointed out.

"I can't imagine why you'd think that," her father said.

"We've been married thirty-five years, and you and your sister are doing fine."

Lily pressed her sweaty palms on the table, as though to brace herself. "I can't speak for you and Mom and I can't speak for Vi. But I'm not fine. I'm not. I can't even tell the man I love that I love him."

"How is this our fault?" Her father took a handkerchief from his pocket and polished his glasses.

"It's not, but I've always felt responsible for Evan's death." Lily heard herself whisper the words, yet she couldn't believe her own ears. "Why do you suppose that is?"

The room became a vacuum of shocked silence. Her father started to speak, but her mother reached across the table and touched his hand to stop him. "Terence, let me tell her. She's right, you know. We were never happy after Evan died. We just…were. But Lily, I never blamed you. How can you think that? I blamed myself. You, I could forgive. Myself, never. And there's no one meaner than a mother who can't forgive herself." As she spoke, she kept hold of her husband's hand. Then Lily, with tears in her eyes, put her own over both of theirs.

chapter 50

"Lily? I'm afraid I'm going to forget my mom." Charlie stood in her underwear, holding the peignoir she had slept in every night since the accident. With a tragic expression on her face, she lifted the garment, and Lily could see that it was unraveling at the seams, the lace insets full of gaping holes.

Lily took it from her and set it aside, then sat down on the bed and gathered Charlie into her lap.

"Me, too," said Ashley, clambering aboard.

Lily breathed in their scent and felt their warm bodies relax against hers. How did I live so long without this? she wondered. How will I go on without it? She took a deep breath and pushed aside the thought. Whatever her differences with Sean, they would not change her devotion to Crystal's children. She had arrived this morning to find that he and Cameron had already left for the tournament. Mrs. Foster was watching the girls.

Charlie rubbed the worn, satiny fabric between her thumb and first finger. "It's all coming apart, and when it falls apart, I'll forget her."

Lily took a .Barbie hand mirror from the nightstand. "Sweetie, that's impossible. Look here. What do you see?"

"My face."

"And whose face does it remind you of?"

"It's just my face."

"And your mother's face." Lily was startled that she saw it, too, an echo of her best friend in Charlie. "You have her eyes and her smile, and every day you'll grow more like her. Most of all, you have her in your heart. All the love she and your dad gave you is there, and it's only going to grow. It's yours to keep forever and ever."

Ashley babbled something and grasped the mirror with both hands.

Charlie slumped against Lily. "I'd rather have my mom. And my dad."

"I know, honey. We all would." Lily rested her chin on her head.

Charlie stood up and, with a curiously adult solemnity, folded the nightgown carefully and put it in a bottom drawer. Her movements had the gravity of ritual, and she shut the drawer with a decisive push. "Maybe I'll sleep in something else," she said. "Uncle Sean gave me an *American Chopper* T-shirt."

"I have a great idea," Lily said. "How about I take you to the golf tournament."

"Uncle Sean said we have to stay with Mrs. Foster."

After last night, he'd assumed Lily wouldn't show up to watch him play. Which only meant he still didn't know her. Sure, she'd sent him packing and he'd willingly walked away, but the visit from her parents had convinced her that love was worth any fight.

"Finish getting dressed," she told Charlie. "I'll tell Mrs. Foster she can go home for the day."

* * *

Playing the game was different without Lily and the girls watching. Sean noticed that the moment he hit his first drive, though he tried not to let their absence affect his performance. The fact was, they were everything to him—his audience, his purpose. Knowing they were watching, he was able to see each shot as clear and clean as the morning sky.

Without them, it was just a game. One he happened to be good at, but still just a way to spend the day and see how things turned out.

Cameron studied his lie in the fairway. It was a perfectly good lie, just inside the crook of a dog leg, giving him a decent shot at the green. "What's wrong?" he asked.

"Nothing's wrong," Sean said. "Why would you think something's wrong?"

"*Duh.* I just watched you hit."

"And I landed where I need to be."

"Because you're good and so is your luck, but you'd better start playing your game."

Sean stared at him as they walked together toward the ball. "You sound just like your father."

Cameron grinned a little and straightened his shoulders. "Yeah?" When they reached the ball, he dug in his pocket and took out the Indian head penny, Sean's old good-luck charm. "I was thinking you might need this. Just in case."

Sean nodded and accepted the token. Lord knew, Cameron wanted him to succeed, so he would try to forget his troubles with Lily. He felt terrible about the way they'd left things. Maybe he shouldn't have lashed out at her. It was fear, not anger, that had driven him—fear of losing Ashley. If he wasn't her blood relative, he had no claim on her at all.

That made Greg Duncan even harder to forget. They were

cordial and professional, but their conversation the night before ratcheted up the tension between them.

After leaving Lily's house, Sean had driven around for a long time, thinking about what she'd said. *You can't fix this with a lie or another deception.* Fighting every instinct, he'd gone to Greg Duncan's and the two of them had a long and difficult talk.

This morning, Sean had told Cameron about the deal he'd worked out with Duncan. That was what kept him going through the game today, Sean realized—the look on Cameron's face when the weight of knowing about Ashley passed into someone else's hands.

"All that's left is to finish the tournament, then," Cameron had said.

When Sean looked at Cameron now, he could see how much his nephew had matured over the summer. No longer a raging boy, he still carried a burden of grief that would always be a part of him, but now he bore it as a man.

"What?" Cameron asked.

"What do you mean, what?"

"You're looking at me funny. What's the matter?"

"Nothing," said Sean. Then he lowered his voice and told the truth. "I'm proud of you."

Cameron's reaction made Sean wonder why he hadn't said so sooner. "Yeah, same here," said his nephew.

Though Sean held the lead, Duncan had won the previous hole, giving him honors to hit first at number eighteen. It was a challenging, four-hundred-yard par four and the pressure was on Duncan, who needed an eagle—a nearly impossible two under par—to win.

Duncan's drive flew three hundred twenty yards and landed dead center in the fairway.

For the first time during this tournament, Sean's stomach

knotted. This was a bad time for an attack of nerves. He squinted at the hole, measuring it, remembering all the ways he'd played it successfully in the past. He wished Lily and the girls were here. Hell, he wished Derek was here. Derek was the champion, not Sean. It was stupid to pretend he could fill his brother's shoes.

He knew he was in trouble the minute the grooved iron face made contact with the ball. Within a heartbeat, he saw the shot go bad, a deadly snap hook that flew out of bounds and landed in the rough.

"An instant two-stroke penalty," the commentator murmured in a stage whisper.

Duncan pressed his advantage, his next shot sending the ball just inches from the cup. The spectators buzzed and shifted in a wave, their emotions vacillating from one player to the other.

In the rough, Sean addressed the ball. Cameron didn't say a word, but Sean could feel the tension emanating from him. Sean was seized by doubts. What in God's name was he doing, and who the hell did he think he was? Derek Holloway?

He lowered the club to the coarse grass next to the ball. He saw the rough grass bend, and the ball moved—slightly, imperceptibly—and nudged the tip of the iron. It was a tiny touch, like a fleeting kiss. But a touch nonetheless.

It was over, then. The rules were clear. He had to call a penalty on himself.

No one saw. Not even Cameron had noticed. If Sean said nothing, if he hit out of the rough and got back in the game, no one would be the wiser.

His hand began its determined assent to signal the marshals.

"Uncle Sean," whispered Cameron, *"please."*

Sean realized then that the boy had seen the ball move, too. That was always the case in golf, as in life, it seemed. No error went undetected. If this was Derek's call, he'd keep it to himself, because Derek always did what he had to do in order to win. But that was Derek's game, Sean reflected. Not his. He looked his nephew straight in the eye and raised his hand. Cameron looked as though he wanted to cry, but at the same time, a grudging admiration shone on his face.

The spectators erupted when he called the penalty on himself. Even Duncan looked stunned. Sean felt weirdly calm now. He stood to lose the tournament by one stroke.

Then he saw something in the gallery—a flash of white with giant colored polka dots. He stood stock-still and then laughed aloud. "Better late than never, girls," he said, even though he knew they couldn't hear him. Their jackets and hats stood out in the crowd. "Better late than never."

Cameron was grinning, too. "I knew they'd come."

"Sure you did," said Sean. "Now, step aside. I need to get this onto the green."

To his credit, Cameron didn't look dubious in the least. Sean felt a new surge of energy. Just knowing Lily had come, even after their bitter words the previous night, filled him with confidence. He stepped up to the ball again.

It was a miracle shot, one of those that would be replayed and talked about for years to come. His stroke launched the ball up out of the rough, over the water hazard and onto the high lip of the green before rolling down the slope…and into the cup.

Excitement roared through the crowd. Sean and Cameron headed to the green, veering toward the ropes to pass by Lily and the girls.

Lily kept her eyes on Sean. "You could still win," she said. "He hasn't hit in yet."

He looked at Cameron and then at his girls, felt their love lifting him up, and he wondered if life offered anything better than this. Somehow, he doubted it. "Doesn't matter," he told her, speaking over the noise of the crowd. "I've already won."

Over the summer, Lily had learned to like the taste of champagne nearly as much as she'd liked toasting the end of a tournament with Sean Maguire. She had learned that in golf, victories were few and fleeting, and there was no shame in finishing second. Today, though, she murmured "No, thank you" to the waiters in the clubhouse as she wove her way through the crowd, looking for him. At the post-tournament rush of press questions, he'd hurried through his responses to incredulous sports reporters, who simply could not understand why he'd given away a major tournament to a complete unknown.

"I didn't give him a thing," Sean assured everyone crowding around him. "He fought hard and got exactly what he deserves. Now, if you'll excuse me, ladies and gentlemen…"

Lily watched him abandon her. She had swallowed her pride to come here, but maybe that wasn't enough for him. With an effort, she kept a gracious smile on her face and greeted people in the reception room. There were her parents and Violet, uncertainly circling the caterer's table.

Her mother touched her shoulder. It wasn't quite a hug, but close. After the things she'd said last night, Lily understood her better. She glanced over her shoulder, but Sean had left the room. "Come and say hi to Crystal's kids," she added. Cameron had both his sisters with him, one holding each hand. Sometimes their adoration embarrassed their brother, but today he looked perfectly content. Lily could see the reason—Becky Pilchuk, who had undoubtedly watched his every move in the tournament. She looked wonderful, fit and blond from a summer of working outside. There was a sweetness in the way she and Cameron treated each other, though Lily recognized Becky's caution. It made her want to yell at the girl: *Don't hold back. You're only cheating yourself. Quit worrying about what might happen and go for it.*

She spotted Greg Duncan talking on a cell phone in the parking lot and hurried to his side. "Excuse me," she murmured, edging through the foyer of the clubhouse. She didn't know what she was going to say to him. He'd had an affair with her best friend, had unknowingly fathered a child with Crystal and still managed to date a variety of women—including Lily. "Greg," she called out.

He wore a victor's smile when he put the phone away, but his expression changed when he saw her. "Hey, Lily."

"Congratulations on your win." Now what? she wondered.

"Thanks," he said. "Listen, Lily, I—"

"Mr. Duncan," someone called, rushing over with a microphone. "Tell us how you feel about your win. What's next for you?" A number of others flocked around him.

Lily stepped back, knowing better than to try to compete with aggressive reporters. Yet a hundred questions burned inside her, questions that were nothing like those from the sports reporters. *Did you and Crystal love each other? Did you make her happy?*

When he replied, Greg seemed to be addressing her. "Looks like I'm leaving Comfort," he said.

Lily caught her breath. *Leaving?*

"...Corliss agreed to represent me, and I'll be competing in Q School through the fall and winter. If everything goes all right, you'll see me ranked in the PGA next year."

She fell back and let him bask in the attention. *Leaving.* More questions crowded into her mind. *How can you be leaving now? What about the child you made? Does that matter at all to you?* Now she knew for certain that Greg Duncan had to be told the truth.

When she turned to head back to the clubhouse, she nearly ran right into Cameron. "Where are the girls?" she asked him, not even attempting to hide her worry.

"With Becky," he said. "They're fine."

"And your uncle?"

Cameron gestured behind him. In the distance, workers were breaking down the bleachers and ropes, loading them into trucks. A lone figure, silhouetted against the sunset, stood at the edge of the last fairway.

As she stood there, torn by indecision, Cameron said, "Coach Duncan knows. My uncle told him last night."

She caught her breath, struggled to find her voice. Disbelief and then elation stole the words from her for a moment. So he had done it after all. Despite what they'd said last night—or perhaps because of it—Sean had told Greg the truth, and Greg had still elected to leave. She didn't know why Sean's wisdom about human nature always seemed to surprise her, but it did.

She took Cameron's hand, needing to touch him when she finally spoke. "Are you all right?"

With a curiously adult dignity, he gently removed his hand from hers. "So long as Ashley's with us, we'll all be fine."

When had this boy grown so tall? Lily wondered, looking up at him. "Your mother was the best friend I ever had and I loved her with all my heart," she said. "But I'm not going to make excuses for her. She made mistakes, just like everybody else. And this one was a doozy."

"Lily, no one says 'doozy' anymore."

She tried to smile. "What I'm trying to say is that being angry with your mother—and your father, for that matter—is a bad idea."

"I loved them, okay?" he said in a low voice. "That'll never change."

Lily's eyes blurred. "There was so much good in them, in your mother and father. So much love. They adored you from the first breath you took. You're the best part of both of them, Cam, you know that?"

He shuffled his feet. "Yeah. Whatever."

"All right. I won't embarrass you anymore." She looked at the ridge above the fairway. "I have to go," she said.

He smiled a little. "I know. We'll watch the girls."

Burnished by the colors of the sunset, Sean looked like a figure out of a dream, and for a moment, Lily was afraid to say anything, for fear that she'd wake up and he'd disappear, unremembered. Then he turned to her and she felt silly. Nothing in her life had ever been as real as this moment.

"You've been busy," she said.

He hooked his thumbs into his back pockets. "Yep."

"You might have told me." She tried to sound reproachful but couldn't keep the happiness from her voice.

"I intended to, but there was this small detail about a tournament…"

"Sean."

He opened his arms and she pressed herself against him, safe and sheltered, her heart so full she couldn't speak.

"It's going to be okay, Lily. There's nothing Duncan wants from this."

Because he already has what he wants, she thought. A hot sports agent, a dream career. "You gave it to him," she said, drawing back to study Sean's face. "You made sure he won today."

"You," he said, slowly lowering his mouth to hers, "have quite an imagination."

It was, she realized, as much of an admission as she'd ever get from him. A moment later it didn't matter, because his kiss sealed a promise he had made to her long ago.

The evening breeze held the subtle chill of autumn and she pressed even closer, hearing the steady thud of his heartbeat. Tell him, Lily, she urged herself, and it sounded like Crystal's voice. Tell him now.

She was afraid, but for once she was going to ignore it. She stepped back, keeping hold of his hands. The potential for giddy joy was, she discovered, even greater than fear. Loving Sean had changed the way she looked at the world. Some days she felt like Dorothy in Oz, seeing things in color for the first time, and she was finally ready to tell him. "This isn't the life I'd planned for myself," she said. "I'm always a planner. Sometimes I plan right down to the last moment, and being with you, with this family, well, all my careful planning goes out the window."

"I've never planned anything at all, and look. We both wound up in the same place. It's because we're supposed to, Lily. Believe it."

"We might be a disaster together."

"We probably are. So what? I love you, Lily. I love who I am when I'm with you, and I love that we're both crazy about the kids." He bent and gave her another lingering kiss. "In fact, we should make more."

She gasped. "You're getting ahead of me."

"You don't want more kids?"

Oh, my God, she thought. Oh, my God. "I love you so much, Sean." The moment she spoke those words, she realized she'd answered his question for both of them. The fear was gone. In its place, like a fire kindled under her heart, was a constant sense of yearning and anticipation for everything life offered. She knew that that might be hurt or happiness, but the difference was that now, she welcomed it all. She wasn't afraid to go where the heart might lead her.

"It's about damn time you said so."

"I didn't know how to tell you," she said. "It didn't seem…safe."

At that he laughed quietly and touched her cheek. "Ah, Lily. It never is, but don't ever let that stop you."

chapter 51

Something was up, Lily was sure of it. The invitation, hand-drawn by Charlie and hand-delivered by Cameron, gave only a hint: "Please have dinner with us at La Dolce Vita, Friday at 8:00. Dress: Semi-formal." Charlie had spelled everything correctly and illustrated the message with a picture of the four of them lined up by height. On the far side of the page was a portrait of Lily, a flattering one at that; Charlie had made her look a bit like Malibu Barbie wearing glasses.

Charlie's cursive writing was clear and bold, a contrast to the shaky, searching way she'd written in third grade. Her fourth-grade teacher reported that Charlie was working at grade level in most subjects. Occasionally, the little girl would seem to go away for a while, lost in sadness, but she always came back. Grief would forever be a part of Charlie's life, a facet of who she was, but she was no longer so haunted by pain that she couldn't grow and thrive. Her natural exuberance had returned over the summer, and Lily felt privileged to have been a witness to the process.

Cameron rejoined the golf team and had already won the

first tournament of the year. On the weekends, he caddied for his uncle, and Lily adored seeing them together, united in purpose, Sean treating Cameron as an equal and as the expert he was. Despite the fact that Sean had traded a major title for Ashley's security, he was rising through the ranks. He would never be the champion his brother had been, Lily knew. The difference was, now he no longer wanted Derek's career. He wanted his own.

Lily tucked the invitation into the frame of her vanity mirror and checked her hair and makeup—again. She felt a sense of gravitas about this evening. It was not just dinner. La Dolce Vita was a luxurious riverfront restaurant with a famous chef from Sorrento. With its formal gardens and air of luxury, it was the sort of place people went to celebrate their milestones—birthdays and anniversaries, bar mitzvahs and…engagements? After the tournament, after the things they'd said to one another, it was the next step. It had to be. Yet they'd gone their separate ways that night because Lily refused to stay over with him, not wanting to confuse the children. Then school started in a whirlwind of activity, and there never seemed to be enough time to explore what had begun between them that night.

The doorbell rang, startling her into smearing her lipstick. She quickly repaired the damage. Then, her nerves wound taut, she hurried to get the door. They all trooped in, filling her tiny house with their presence, and she gaped openmouthed at Sean. A tux. He was wearing a tux. Her knees went weak. Did he have any idea of how he devastated her? And the children looked glorious, Charlie with braids pinned on her head like a halo, Ashley all in pink and Cameron in a dinner jacket that made him look grown up and stunningly handsome. They stood waiting, polished and bright as new pennies, smiling at her.

"Wow," Sean said, his gaze coasting over her from head to toe, then back up again. "Look at you."

"I'm looking at everyone else."

"Let's just go. What're we waiting around for?" Charlie was bouncing up and down with excitement until Cameron put his hand on her shoulder.

"Take it easy, moron," he said. "It's just dinner."

"Is not. Uncle Sean's going to ask Lily—"

"Lily, up," Ashley said, tugging at her dress. "Please."

Lily didn't take her eyes off Sean as she picked up the baby. Ask Lily what? she wondered, aiming a look at him, but he was acting casual, whistling between his teeth. Oh please, she thought. *Please.*

"Pretty," said Ashley, plucking at the beads on Lily's dress. She'd bought it new for tonight, though the black patent leather shoes and onyx-beaded bag had once belonged to Crystal. She opened the evening bag to put in her keys and noticed a slip of paper curled against the satiny lining. Unable to resist, she took out the note. It was a fortune from a fortune cookie that read, "The tide carries away and brings in. Lucky numbers 44, 25, 61, 78, 99, 17." She wondered why Crystal had saved it. An image of her formed in Lily's mind. I miss you so much, she thought. I always will.

Discreetly, she put the fortune back into the bag. Then she shared a look with Sean and wondered if she looked as apprehensive and helpless with love as she felt.

"Hang in there, Miss Robinson," he said, lightly teasing. "This won't hurt a bit."

"Please can we go now?" Charlie asked in an agonized voice.

"I'll drive," Cameron said.

During the short drive to the restaurant, Charlie and Ashley chattered away. Lily kept trying to catch Sean's eye yet he gave her nothing but a secretive, flirty smile. She contented herself with watching the scenery out the window. The colors of autumn were creeping into the landscape—turning leaves, fields of yellow-eyed daisies along the water and mountains as crisp and white as sails against the topaz sky.

At the restaurant, a valet dressed like a gondolier took care of the car. "We're early," Lily said, checking her watch.

"Yep," Charlie agreed, grabbing her sweater. "We wanted to go have a look at the gardens. Uncle Sean planned it this way." Nearly bursting with excitement, she led the way beneath a laurel arch to the formal gardens. A plaque claimed that this was a replica of the Villa d'Este gardens in Italy. Lily was enchanted by the perfectly clipped box hedges, the symmetrical pebbled pathways and romantic arbors. Late-blooming verbena scented the air, and on the river below, barges and pleasure boats slipped past, gilded by the colors of sunset.

"Ducks," said Ashley, gesturing at the water's edge. "Want ducks."

Cameron took the baby from his uncle. "I'll take her to see the ducks. Let's go, Charlie."

"Put your sweater on," Sean said to her, and bent to help her button it. A glossy red, white and green folder slipped from his jacket pocket and hit the brick-paved walkway. Charlie stooped to pick it up.

"What's that?" Lily asked.

"It was supposed to be a surprise," Charlie said, bouncing again. "It's—"

"Tickets to Italy," Lily whispered, recognizing the Alitalia logo. She stared at Sean in wonder. "These are tickets to Italy," she said again. She counted them, five in all, and saw that the departure date was in late October, less than a month away.

He gave away nothing, though he blushed. *Blushed.* That was a first, for sure.

"What's going on?" Lily asked. She felt unsteady, her high

heels wobbling on the pathway. Sean held out his hand and drew her over to a curved stone bench. Holding the baby and catching Charlie by the wrist, Cameron took the girls closer toward the river, though Charlie kept looking at them over her shoulder.

Lily was having trouble breathing.

"Have a seat." Sean took the folder of tickets from her and set it aside.

"What's this about Italy?" she said.

"How does Christmas in Amalfi sound to you?" he asked, smiling down at her. "There's a tournament in Brescia. Red made all the arrangements, including the villa in Amalfi through to the New Year. The school agreed to let the kids do contract studies with you supervising. And Edna is behind your sabbatical a hundred percent. I checked."

She could barely process the information. She wasn't used to people making arrangements for her, including her in their plans. "We can't just take off for Italy—"

"True. I need to ask you something first."

This is it, thought Lily. Please let this be it.

She saw him sink down on one knee, and her heart took wing. She sensed the children watching them, and it seemed right, somehow, that they would bear witness to this. Lily felt a wave of gratitude for Crystal. It wasn't just for the memories or even the years of friendship; her legacy to Lily was something far more precious and unexpected. Family didn't have to be made of flesh and blood. This was the family she and Sean had created. They'd done everything backward, starting with the kids and then finding their way to each other. It wasn't perfect, but they had done their best. I'll take good care of them, Lily vowed to her friend. I'll give every inch of my heart and never hold back. I swear I will.

"Lily, I love you," Sean said. "I'm asking you to marry me."

Her voice was gone. She knew if she forced herself to say something now, she'd lose it, ruining the moment by weeping with joy.

When she didn't respond, he took her hand. She felt the cool smoothness of the ring he slipped on her finger, but she didn't dare glance down at it. She didn't want to look away from him for fear of breaking the spell.

"I'm the one saying the words," he went on, "but it's not just me that's asking. It's us. Me and the kids. We love you, Lily. We want to spend the rest of our lives with you."

Her chest squeezed with emotion as she stood, pulling him up with her. "*Yes* seems like such a small, inadequate word," she said.

"It's all I need to hear from you." He bent and kissed her, lingering just a little, then stepping back.

She saw him give the thumbs-up sign to the kids. She laughed aloud, feeling lighter than air as they headed toward the dining room. In the foyer, two doormen held open the doors. With endearing awkwardness, Sean put his hand on the small of her back and escorted her into the dim restaurant.

"Is it just the two of you?" the hostess asked.

"No." Sean turned and motioned for the children to join them. "We need a table for five."

Acknowledgments

Special thanks to Det. Scott Anderson of the Bainbridge Police Department, to Jay and the gang at Meadowmeer Golf and Country Club and to Lori Cross of the eagle eyes. As always, I'd like to acknowledge the Port Orchard Brain Trust and Test Kitchen: Rose Marie, Anjali, Kate, Lois, P.J., Susan, Krysteen and Sheila for their talent, generosity and literary judgment. I'm deeply grateful to my agent, friend and champion Meg Ruley, and to Martha Keenan and Dianne Moggy of MIRA Books. And finally, it should go without saying but I'll say it anyway—thanks to Jay, who knows that like a good round of golf, life is a process of exploration and change, and you have every chance to get it right.

ANOTHER SUSPENSEFUL PAGE-TURNER FROM

JAN COFFEY

A fast-attack nuclear submarine cuts silently through the waters of the North Atlantic, hijacked by two-dozen armed terrorists. The target: New York City.

Fighting for their lives aboard the hijacked submarine, ship superintendent Amy Russell and Commander Darius McCann have only one hope for survival. With the lives of millions at stake, they must play a dangerous game of cat and mouse, where capture would mean certain death.

SILENT WATERS

"…a swift, absorbing tale…certain to light a fire under readers."—*Publishers Weekly* on *Triple Threat*

*Available the first week of April 2006,
wherever paperbacks are sold!*

If you enjoyed what you just read,
then we've got an offer you can't resist!

Take 2 novels FREE!

Plus get a FREE surprise gift!

Clip this page and mail it to The Reader Service

IN U.S.A.	**IN CANADA**
3010 Walden Ave.	P.O. Box 609
P.O. Box 1867	Fort Erie, Ontario
Buffalo, N.Y. 14240-1867	L2A 5X3

YES! Please send me 2 free novels from the Romance/Suspense Collection and my free surprise gift. After receiving them, if I don't wish to receive any more, I can return the shipping statement marked "cancel". If I don't cancel, I will receive 4 brand-new novels every month, before they're available in stores! In the U.S.A., bill me at the bargain price of $5.24 plus 25¢ shipping and handling per book and applicable sales tax, if any*. In Canada, bill me at the bargain price of $5.74 plus 25¢ shipping and handling per book and applicable taxes**. That's the complete price and a savings of over 10% off the cover prices—what a great deal! I understand that accepting the 2 free books and gift places me under no obligation ever to buy any books. I can always return a shipment and cancel at any time. Even if I never buy another book, the 2 free books and gift are mine to keep forever.

185 MDN EFVD
385 MDN EFVP

Name	(PLEASE PRINT)	
Address	Apt.#	
City	State/Prov.	Zip/Postal Code

*Not valid to current subscribers of the Romance Collection,
the Suspense Collection or the Romance/Suspense Collection.*

Want to try two free books from another series?
Call 1-800-873-8635 or visit www.morefreebooks.com.

* Terms and prices subject to change without notice. Sales tax applicable in N.Y.
** Canadian residents will be charged applicable provincial taxes and GST.

All orders subject to approval. Offer limited to one per household. Credit or debit balances in a customer's account(s) may be offset by any other outstanding balance owed by or to the customer. Please allow 4 to 6 weeks for delivery.
® and ™ are trademarks owned and used by the trademark owner and/or its licensee.

BOB06R

© 2004 Harlequin Enterprises Limited

SUSAN WIGGS

		$ U.S.	$ CAN.
32019	HOME BEFORE DARK	___ $6.99 U.S.	___ $8.50 CAN.
32056	SUMMER BY THE SEA	___ $6.99 U.S.	___ $8.50 CAN.
32147	THE OCEAN BETWEEN US	___ $7.50 U.S.	___ $8.99 CAN.
32190	LAKESIDE COTTAGE	___ $7.50 U.S.	___ $8.99 CAN.
66689	THE DRIFTER	___ $6.50 U.S.	___ $7.99 CAN.
66710	A SUMMER AFFAIR	___ $6.99 U.S.	___ $8.50 CAN.
66755	THE HORSEMASTER'S DAUGHTER	___ $6.50 U.S.	___ $7.99 CAN.
66756	THE HOSTAGE	___ $6.50 U.S.	___ $7.99 CAN.
66757	THE MISTRESS	___ $6.50 U.S.	___ $7.99 CAN.
66758	THE FIREBRAND	___ $6.50 U.S.	___ $7.99 CAN.
66837	HALFWAY TO HEAVEN	___ $6.99 U.S.	___ $8.50 CAN.
66855	THE CHARM SCHOOL	___ $5.99 U.S.	___ $6.99 CAN.
66880	THE LIGHTKEEPER	___ $5.99 U.S.	___ $6.99 CAN.
66938	ENCHANTED AFTERNOON	___ $6.99 U.S.	___ $8.50 CAN.

(limited quantities available)

TOTAL AMOUNT	$ _____
POSTAGE & HANDLING	$ _____
($1.00 FOR 1 BOOK, 50¢ for each additional)	
APPLICABLE TAXES*	$ _____
TOTAL PAYABLE	$ _____

(check or money order—please do not send cash)

To order, complete this form and send it, along with a check or money order for the total above, payable to MIRA Books, to: **In the U.S.:** 3010 Walden Avenue, P.O. Box 9077, Buffalo, NY 14269-9077; **In Canada:** P.O. Box 636, Fort Erie, Ontario, L2A 5X3.

Name: _____

Address: _____ City: _____

State/Prov.: _____ Zip/Postal Code: _____

Account Number (if applicable): _____

075 CSAS

*New York residents remit applicable sales taxes.
*Canadian residents remit applicable GST and provincial taxes.

MIRA®

www.MIRABooks.com

MSW0406BL